"Not an aristocracy of power, based upon rank or influence, but an aristocracy of the sensitive, the considerate and the plucky. ... They are sensitive for others as well as themselves, they are considerate without being fussy, their pluck is not swankiness but the power to endure, and they can take a joke."

E.M Forster – *Two Cheers for Democracy*

Three Polish Sayings

"A guest sees more in an hour than a host in a year."

"When among crows, caw as the crows do."

"Don't go looking for holes in the whole."

OSCAR FOVARGE

POLES APART

To dearest friends
Janet and Vassilis
 *(aka Tony)*

Red Hawk

Red Hawk Books

London and Swansea

Red Hawk Books is an imprint of Red Hawk Media Ltd
whose addresses can be found at
www.redhawkmedia.co.uk

First published by Red Hawk Books in 2022

A catalogue record for this book is available from the British Library
978-1-9160843-7-7

Cover design and layout by Adam Evans

Poles Apart is a work of fiction. None of the characters or places de-
scribed in these pages bear any resemblance to any actual places or
people.

For Joanna
artist and inspiration

"Speculators may do no harm as bubbles
on a steady stream of enterprise.
But the position is serious when enterprise
becomes the bubble on a whirlpool of speculation."

John Maynard Keynes

CONTENTS

Part One

Summer

1/ The Inheritors

It is a truth universally avoided in the best society that the inheritor of a large estate needs a lot more cash than the previous generation. What were once considered luxuries are now viewed as necessities by the next in line.

So, the question becomes, how do inheritors leverage land to guarantee a sufficient flow of cash to support their lifestyles? The school and university fees are basic requirements, but the heated swimming pools, the sauna and jacuzzi suites, the tennis courts, biannual skiing holidays, perhaps a private jet, or at least a helipad – not to mention the warm-water marinas to over-winter the yacht – all demand more dosh, and oodles of it. Not just narrow streams of liquidity, but flash floods, underground reservoirs and broad, transcontinental rivers.

On this June morning in 2015, in the County of Ware and Tare, in a region of England known as West Hiding, there were two visitors to a local beauty spot who had every reason to understand these simple facts of British life.

The first was Peter Wilde, a college lecturer and Labour Councillor, who'd crested Briery Hill on a five-mile walk wondering if he'd ever manage the feat again without keeling over from fatigue or heart failure. His GP had recently issued a further warning about long hours spent in meetings – the shape of his body taking its cues from various chairs – and a diet selected mainly from pub menus. But this first attempt at a new regime did not encourage a daily repeat.

He squeezed through a "people's shortcut" in a boundary fence and was now standing in a layby surveying what locals called "the Forgotten Valley", urging himself to remember that he must consult a solicitor and draw up a will, if only for the sake of the daughter from his second marriage. In the event of apoplexy, the value of his house could be wiped out in care home fees – at a stroke, so to speak. There had to be ways of passing on some inheritance before he was dead or gaga, even if his offspring had been estranged since infancy.

He sucked at a bottle of water and hoped the panorama would calm his pounding heart. But though this corner of England was almost entirely undefined in the nation's consciousness, he knew far too much about it. Almost every angle of view brought to mind some cause of heightened blood pressure: an unneighbourly disagreement, a protracted court case or a battle of wills and won'ts. The only calming effect this view could have on him was a reminder that this was the place Wife Number One had called home. It was why he'd moved here thirty-five years before. Six happy months were spent renting a dilapidated farmhouse at the end of a narrow country lane, both long since swallowed up by suburban development and a business zone. Eventually, Wife Number One had left him and the area for good, citing some of the misgivings he'd suppressed for the sake of their relationship.

The Malvoir Valley was too far west to be part of the Cotswolds, too far east to lie in the shadow of the Malvern Hills. It was too far north to be part of genteel Cheltenham and too far south for assimilation into the great conurbations of Birmingham and the West Midlands. She seemed to be saying that it was somewhere but not quite anywhere; or anywhere but not quite somewhere.

Peter agreed, up to a point. Yet, for all that, the Valley had its own character. While constituencies all around returned Conservative Members of Parliament, a redrawing of electoral boundaries in the mid-1970s meant that the sprawling suburban estates of Manley Town guaranteed a Labour MP and a thumping Labour majority on Malvoir Council.

But even at the height of the New Labour supremacy, the Valley could not resist the effects of globalisation. Small-scale metal manufacturing held on grimly into the early nineties, the textile workshops a little longer. Furniture making took a hit in the early noughties, and several other mainstay businesses folded when they failed to outsource production to the Far East. The Valley's industrial estates became outlets for consumption instead of production, and many locals gradually maxed out their credit cards before discovering that booms had endings and bubbles still burst.

Even this sudden awakening did not convince voters in the Malvoir Valley to grudgingly give their votes to the Conservatives. More than half hated the Tories with a vengeance, believing that if New Labour had led the UK over a cliff and into the Great Recession of 2008, they had done so in ignorance but with the best of intentions. Had the Tories been in power, they'd have done the same with barely concealed glee. The rest of the country might reconsider their allegiances, but the voters of Malvoir Valley recalled that they were, and always would be, 'ignored' by those with money and power.

Peter was now an incomer of more than three decades' standing with much of it spent poring over the minute details of local planning applications. But he also had a panoramic grasp of how this landscape had come to be what it was.

The land to his left, where valley slopes subsided into the Malvoir Flats, had belonged to the Stourville family for over a thousand years. They were descendants of the Plantagenets and had managed to hold on to their possessions by means of astute marriages and political alliances, even though their Plantagenet overlord, Richard III, had been overthrown 800 years earlier.

Twenty-first century Stourvilles pursued careers in global banking, politics, academia and the media. Their only interest in their extensive landholdings lay in the steady flow of rental income that quietly underpinned their other endeavours.

For residents of the lower Malvoir Valley this meant a quarry here, a landfill there. They had intimate knowledge of which wind direction would swaddle them in the reek from an overburdened sewage treatment plant. If they were privileged with countryside views, they had sight of uniform, dark-green, fast-growing conifers on the valley slopes where ancient, mixed woodlands had once enlivened the hillsides with seasonal colours. If they lived close to the Valley's main road, they caught glimpses of the largest residential caravan site this side of Bristol, or they could view and hear the workings of the UK's biggest vehicle wrecking yard. Bordering this, an abandoned battery hen farm, partially camouflaged but not fully hidden by a long row of straggling leylandii. Higher still, a single file of electricity pylons belayed together like mountaineers as they skirted the newer ranks of turbines churning the winds along the ridge.

Peter swept his gaze a hundred and eighty degrees to the right, towards the gently undulating hills north of the valley. More pylons ran parallel to the motorway that joined the English Midlands and the Brittonic south-west. At this distance the pylons looked like miniature copies of the Eiffel Tower, their cables invisible to the naked eye.

At that end of the valley, Rollo Campbell-Stewart had just taken ownership of the Fontby Magna estate. Local gossip suggested he was keen to sell some land and to increase cash-flow from the remainder. His parents had lived comfortably on rents rising at the rate of inflation, but Rollo would soon need a boost to fund his young children through their private schooling and his aristocratic Danish wife through her expectations.

The hot gossip was that Rollo aimed to sell land to a developer for "prestige" housing. He and the builder had already approached Alex

Weaver, the leader of Malvoir Council.

This was no bad thing, in Peter's view, if enough of the new houses at Fontby Magna could be afforded by those on average incomes. But this was unlikely. Developers knew how to maximise their profits, assuming they'd bother to build at all. In Peter's experience, it was more likely that the builders would buy Campbell-Stewart's land, gain planning permission, break ground with a digger, then watch its value soar without so much as lifting a shovel for a decade to come. In the meantime, a shortage of housing would see property prices rise still further, rents increase and a generation of youngsters stand beholden to the banks of mum and dad or the tender mercies of the global variety.

But these developments at the northern and southern ends of the Valley were not Peter's main concern. The landed estate that lay straight ahead, between those owned by the Stourvilles and Campbell-Stewarts, had recently changed hands in surprising fashion. When Eleanor de Broche (pronounced 'Brook'), the dowager of Deverill Court, had died, it was assumed that her grandson, Hugh, would inherit. He had been managing the estate for the past few years, ever since he'd turned twenty-two. But news was now out that the ailing Eleanor had willed the estate to her niece instead.

For Peter, it meant that the summer camps he helped to run for the deprived children and youths of the Malvoir Valley were cancelled. The management of the estate was heading in "a different direction", or so the letter of cancellation from the new owner's solicitor had stated.

There was no time to arrange an alternative venue. No farmer in the Valley, with leases now in doubt, would commit a field or two to the enterprise. Besides, it was the manicured parkland of Deverill Court that had offered the prospect of adventure alongside comfort and security to the Council's outreach programmes. Any other venue would send insurance premiums through the roof.

Thus, within the space of a year, more than two-thirds of the Malvoir Valley found itself under new ownership. Few knew and fewer cared. Only someone with the knowledge and experience of Peter Wilde would hazard a guess at the effect these changes might have on the Valley and its residents.

Some might prove positive. When old Ralph de Broche decided thirty years earlier that dairy farming was more trouble than it was worth, commuters on a B-road, Peter included, no longer found themselves crawling their way home at the pace of a cow as the herd moved up the road to the milking sheds. That might have been replaced with a massive indoor poultry farm or a sprawling piggery, but Ralph's wife Eleanor had objected to the smell, whatever the profit.

Twenty-five years later, Alex Weaver, the Council Leader, and various business interests had tried to build the "South Midlands' most extensive haulage distribution hub" with various sources vying to raise and invest millions in the scheme. But Eleanor de Broche pointed out that the Malvoir Valley was not on a motorway, was not even in the Midlands and, in any case, the obvious place for such a hub was near Rugby, Coventry or Birmingham.

As an experienced Councillor, Peter had agreed, causing the Leader of the Council to throw a wobbly, accuse Peter of betrayal and claim that investment and jobs would pass the Valley by and end up in some less needy place. Peter's prospects of promotion to higher office disappeared along with the scheme, but he consoled himself that Manley Town and the Malvoir Valley had been spared several square miles of vacant lorry parks and empty distribution centres, both looming reminders of overreach and folly.

Now Hugh de Broche, with his touching preference for the more demotic surname of "Brooke", was gone from Deverill Court, somehow dispossessed, and who knew what schemes the new owners might visit upon the long-suffering folk of the Malvoir Valley. New brooms mean new piles of unintended consequences for somebody else to deal with.

Whatever these turned out to be, Peter Wilde was ready. He was one of those people who could read a single-paragraph news item, buried as it might be among the online ads and clickbait, and sense a battle in the making. It was the same with letters or phone calls from constituents. Present him with someone else's problem and he'd consider it a personal challenge.

In a desperate attempt to save his first marriage he had once offered to give up local politics. But Wife Number One was a shrewd cookie.

'It's in your blood, Pete. If you quit, you'll no longer be you. And you're good at it. You do a great job. It's just not for me. We should accept that we want and need different things.'

So, she allowed him to buy out her share of a semi-detached with garage that he'd never really liked or regarded as more than a temporary home.

Wife Number Two was initially impressed by his local standing but less forgiving after three years as a politician's spouse.

'You spend your whole life just pissing into the wind!'

He protested that this was harsh, but she took half the value of the house – by then much inflated – and the child, whom she skilfully turned against him in later years.

He gathered that she'd eventually moved to Italy, married an Italian from a wealthy family, had a second child, then divorced again. Rumour had it that she'd accepted a Tuscan farmhouse as compensation "on behalf of the children". Further reports suggested that while Peter's daughter should have been bilingual, a certain neglect had left her insufficient in both languages and therefore struggling at school.

That he was feisty and adept at fighting for the rights of others in the public realm, yet strangely deficient in securing his own in the private sphere, was an irony he contemplated on an almost nightly basis, usually at the same time as wondering who his daughter had become in the course of the twenty-nine years since she'd been strapped into a taxi's child-seat and driven out of his life.

When it came to his choice of spouses, he was reminded of Walter Donovan, the character in *Indiana Jones and The Last Crusade*. When faced with an array of candidates for the Holy Grail, Donovan "chose poorly" and achieved mortality in a spectacular meltdown of special effects.

Wife Number Two had persuaded Peter to watch that film, much against his inclination, and he credited her with the lingering after-effects of nightmare and regret. That he might "choose poorly" for a third time had removed the temptation to marry again.

Before turning on a blistered heel and setting off downhill with stiff knees and barking ankles, Peter hoped that Eleanor de Broche had known something that he didn't and had chosen her successor more wisely than Walter Donovan chose cups, or he chose wives.

The same vista held quite different associations for that morning's second visitor to the layby.

Lesley-Anne Dewum was the new owner of Deverill Court. She had spent the past thirty-one years abroad and returned to find herself, within months, the owner of almost all she surveyed from the crown of Briery Hill. This was the unforgettable valley of her youth, where she'd ridden ponies as a child, then horses as a teenager, until the day she left it all behind and set out for the great cities of the world. Viewed from here, the decades of her past seemed like panels that slid aside one by one to reveal this long-awaited scene. She felt that she had overcome numerous obstacles before finally entering into her rightful inheritance.

Directly ahead, about a mile away, were the towers and turrets of Deverill Court just visible above the crowns of beech and chestnut trees. Some three hundred acres of mixed farming rising to Cooper's Folly on the other side of the valley now belonged to her, most of it leased to farmers. In clear-sky sunlight it was a patchwork of bright golds and greens, its breeze-rippled rape and haylage grasses approaching time for harvest.

Away to her left, where the sides of the valley subsided into the Malvoir Flats and the River Bass meandered towards its meeting with the Severn, lay lands that belonged to the Stourville family. As a child, she'd been dimly aware that they were too rich to care much for this part of their holdings. As a teenager, she'd been snubbed by a young, metropolitan Stourville at a charity ball, and this confirmed for her their reputation for self-importance. In that respect, Lesley-Anne conformed to the template of the Malvoir Valley's more modest residents: they might be ignored, but they had long memories.

But this was no more than a fleeting recollection. Lesley-Anne had no reason for bitterness. She had travelled the world, had more adventures than most and returned to inherit a fortune. She had not climbed out of her Range Rover in a layby to consider past slights but to visualise exciting new ways to regenerate this not-so-tiny plot in this green and pleasant land.

This was a brief halt on her way to a meeting with Council Leader Alex Weaver, a pause to gather her wits, but made a touch light-headed by the prospect of change, the speed of events and a third coffee at breakfast. Despite her self-contained resolve, she was exhilarated by the sense that things were coming together. The Deverill Court estate was finally hers and saved from the modish plans of her misguided nephew. He had been safely sidelined and was no longer a threat.

She hadn't told her husband of her plans, but they were usually of one mind. He was unfamiliar with the conventions of English property development but had that characteristic American trait of driving forward once a goal was in view. She was confident he would climb aboard any wagon she set rolling and help her steer it home.

She knew that her neighbour Rollo Campbell-Stewart at Fontby Magna also had plans to sell land for housebuilding. He might have started his race earlier, but she sensed a clearer run for herself on the inside rail. Rollo's land straddled two Council areas, so he'd have to deal with two sets of officials, planning authorities and, most likely, campaigning objectors. Besides, he was away for long summer holidays in Denmark and Scotland while she intended to take full advantage of his absence.

Filling her lungs with the oxygen of possession, Lesley-Anne took a moment to register the faint smudge in the summer sky about half a mile beyond the turrets of the Court. It resembled smoke from a dampened fire, safely extinguished but still smouldering at ground zero. It caused her no alarm.

As she returned to her Range Rover, a hatchback drew into the layby and an extended family climbed out. From appearances, she guessed at parents, their two small children and a grandmother. The man led the way towards the fence bordering Lesley-Anne's property and pulled back the wire mesh to enlarge a "people's gateway" into the countryside.

'There's a public footpath down there.' Lesley-Anne pointed back down the road. 'With a proper gate.'

The man looked at her as if she were speaking a foreign language. 'That's half a mile away. Anyway, none of your business. I know Hugh Brooke, the owner.'

To Lesley-Anne, that was all very well as far as it went. She tapped at the screen on her phone, looking for the name of her estate manager.

'Adam? I need a fence repaired urgently. … On Briery Hill. At the layby. … Not just a repair. I need barbed wire along the top of the fence all the way back to the where the footpath begins. … Well, if you don't have time, I suppose I could ask Jim Piper. It is rather urgent, and I heard he was looking for work. It needs to be started in the next hour. … Oh, you could. … That's excellent. Thank you. … If you could start with the gap in the fence, then stretch the barbed wire. … Better make it two strands set at head height… I'll be passing again in an hour or so to see how you're getting on. See you then.'

She tapped her conversation to an end and took a last look at the turrets of Deverill Court. Those walkers probably did know her nephew and his laidback ways, but they hadn't heard about the change in ownership. For one thing, she always smiled inwardly at poor, misguided Hugh's attempts to grab some street cred by altering his surname to Brooke. If anyone bothered to check in Who's Who they would see him recorded, like herself, as a hereditary de Broche. When push came to shove, she knew the masses would be for the many, not the Hugh, regardless of what he called himself. She, by contrast, represented the security of tradition and continuity. That began and ended with the defence of property.

2/ A Steaming Pile

Beyond the turrets of Deverill Court and directly beneath the smoky haze noticed by Lesley-Anne lay the leaky roof of an ancient barn. Below that roof lay the sleeping figure of her nephew.

Bradley, his golden retriever, was at that moment licking his master awake with an affectionate slobber. It was well past his usual time to be let out for a first widdle of the morning, followed by sniff patrol and general foraging.

'Urghh!'

The shock to the contents of Hugh's twenty-seven-year-old skull as it rose from the pillow would have been familiar to a fence post being driven in by a rammer. The taste on his tongue suggested he'd spent the night sucking on a bag of rusty nails and his eyeballs felt like a pair of delicate lychees mistakenly pickled with onions.

'Erngh!'

Recognising his master's distress, Bradley jumped up to console, placing one of his leonine paws in Hugh's crotch.

'Ferchrissakesbradley!'

As a highly intelligent specimen of an intelligent breed, Bradley interpreted this as an invitation to desist. Which he did by using his master's tender bits as a launching pad to thrust off through the offending paw.

'Aayungh!'

He then sat and regarded Hugh with what looked like a combination of concern and anticipation. His tail brushed the floor, while the slowly moving figure before him contrived various stages of the vertical, before finally extending one leg in an exploratory manner, as if he were rediscovering human locomotion.

Each step see-sawed a mobile bruise from one side of Hugh's skull to the other. He was convinced that last night's excesses, whatever they were, had shrunk his normally buoyant, flexible and reasonably large amount of grey matter to a firm, minimalist solid, rather like a ball of mozzarella bouncing about in a saline solution. Left foot forward – unngh – right foot lift and forward – errghng – stub toe on a carelessly abandoned paving slab - ayeee.

Swinging the barn door outwards to release Bradley on his first foray of the morning brought painful dazzlement and a detailed reminder of his spectacular spiral downwards from the social and economic stratosphere to a place even lower than where most people experience the daily weather.

His trademark Land Rover, with its revolutionary, hydrogen fuelled engine and eye-catching moniker, 'Well-Sussed Land Management' – www.wellsussed.co.uk', was propped wheel-less on four neat piles of concrete blocks. There was an almost identical pebble-sized hole through each side window. Its windshield, rear window and roof panes were comprehensively demolished. All this suggested a criminal mind with a hankering for order and thoroughness.

On the far side of the circular drive lay his five-bedroomed country cottage - which the Architectural Monuments for West Hiding called a 'traditional fifteenth century fortified farmhouse'– the heat at its core still sending a mix of smoke and steam into the summer sunshine, the faintest of breezes carrying the aroma of charred thatch and beam to his nostrils like two hooks from a clumsily cast fishing rod. He winced, an action painful in itself, and decided more sleep would hardly make matters worse. Bradley was busy harassing squirrels. At least he was unaffected by their change in circumstances and was the only living creature who seemed, at that moment, unconditionally devoted to his master.

Not counting Mary, of course. But she now lived far away, having retired from her various roles as his 'Nanny', then 'Mrs Thompson the housekeeper', and finally 'Mary', Grandmother's indispensable home-help and general factotum.

If she were here, she would begin by making a pot of tea, then proceed to discuss Hugh's prospects over a single shortbread for her and half a dozen chocolate-coated digestives for him. Just as she'd done when he'd been a primary schoolboy picked on for his accent; or later as an independent school fifth-former, in trouble for taking two puffs on a suspiciously fat, hand-rolled and inelegant ciggie being passed from hand to hand; and yet again as an undergraduate who'd failed to identify his ambitious fiancée as the undoubted gold-digger that everyone else had detected.

On each occasion Mary had convinced him that the answer to his problems lay within. That, yes, he was an orphan, but his unique privileges trumped that deprivation. That a fundamentally charming boy, decent lad or idealistic young man would come through, if not with flying colours, then with a respectable show of courage, honesty, effort and integrity.

She'd performed her roles and functions more admirably than any adult he'd known, and she would certainly be prepared to stir her energetic seventy-five-year-old bones from her seaside retirement bungalow on the south coast to drive north and elicit some solutions to his present sea of bother.

But it was too much to ask. That disembowelled, smouldering remnant of his inheritance now misrepresented a large part of her life's work. The gutted cottage had been her grace-and-favour residence for a quarter of a century. The oak tree that now rose beside the ruins, one of the few unspoilt features left on the property, had been planted by her on Hugh's fifth birthday. She'd taken its vigorous and symmetrical growth as an auspicious sign of future success, not for herself, but for him. He reckoned that she deserved to keep her memories intact. She had more than earned her rest from putting others' needs before her own by always being on hand to tidy away everybody else's shambles.

As Hugh eased his way across the barn towards the scorched bed, rescued by firefighters from the recent blaze, he wondered where in the world he might find another Mary. Certainly not in Isabella, who had dumped him two nights earlier, shortly – or not so shortly - before he met that crowd of blurry young guys in a nightclub – or was it a pub? No, the pub came first – celebrating their team's victory in the something-or-other-finalish-sort-of-match earlier in the day. The more they talked about it the blurrier they became. But there was something Isabella had said before that, something important – he tried hard to recall her exact words – something along the lines of his being "awfully unlucky".

Whatever the detail, it faded to insignificance as renewed contact between head and pillow, a drawing of knees to chest in the recovery position, produced a welcome postponement of reality known as "the world out there".

3/ Movers And Shakers

Alex Weaver emerged from the hairdresser's feeling... contented. No... more than that... it was a feeling of fulfilment, of present goals achieved. Nearly, almost, soon. A feeling very few humans attain: that whatever happens now – natural disasters, some unforeseen cataclysm, personal tragedy – nobody can ever take away one's current status. It was on the record, entrenched in the annals, hard-wired into institutional memory. Weaver was here and had made a difference. Well, almost.

It wasn't just that feeling of well-being he always experienced during his fortnightly session in the hairdresser's chair, being shampooed by the young assistant and fussed over by the chief coiffeuse in person, while also receiving a complimentary manicure. It wasn't merely the beneficial after-effects of a two-week holiday in a luxury Costa del Sol apartment loaned by one of his oldest friends. Or the gift of tickets to the Malaga-Real Madrid football match arranged by his good friend Reg Barton, Chairman of Manley Town FC. To Weaver, these were now standard perks and indulgences that would only be noticed by their absence. No, it was the anticipation of something much more significant than personal contentment.

The mild autumn weather lent a glow to his tanned features and a gleam to his luxuriant, swept back, neatly coiffed, iron-grey hair. He'd represented the Manley Central ward for decades and exchanged friendly nods with a few constituents as he strolled across the square to the car park. He returned the tooting horn of a passing taxi driver with a wave and the customary working man's greeting: "Orright?" - two syllables representing a recognition and reaffirmation of his origins.

He was, in his own estimation, working class through and through. No amount of increasing affluence could weaken those roots. His early experiences were branded deep into memory: his grandparents' outdoor toilet; his father's struggle to get a mortgage from the la-di-da bank manager; himself as a teenager being snubbed by the same bank manager's granddaughter when he asked her for a date. More than any of this, he was a Manley man to his fingertips. Born and raised in the town. Spent every year of his life there, apart from his three years at university. (Manchester, History and Politics, worked like a navvy, scraped a second-class degree.)

The people who'd voted for him in the last thirty-four years knew all about it. As did his political opponents, who'd given up nominating candidates in his ward over twenty years earlier. They soon realised that he had the perfect profile for a Manley politician. Local, working class, university degree, always resident in the community, long and sterling service. Community Councillor, Malvoir Councillor, former Mayor, now Leader of the Council with a thirty-nine to six majority. Old Labour? New Labour? Forget it. Alex Weaver was an institution, very nearly a brand in his own right. He had a column in the Manley Observer. His views could make Ministers in Westminster sit up and take notice. His support was indispensable to the sitting Member of Parliament. He could make or break the careers of aspiring politicians. This in its totality was what made for his feeling of deep-seated satisfaction. After thirty-four years of constant endeavour, he was finally unassailable.

And yet...

As he climbed into his leather-upholstered Volvo – clean-lined, unpretentious, unimpeachably stylish yet down-to-earth, in his view – he thrilled to the thought of a crowning achievement, a project that would rivet his legacy into the consciousness of every living Manley resident for generations to come. All he had to do was impregnate every democratic and executive body with the seed of his idea and watch it grow into a mighty and very personal achievement.

Be that as it may – a phrase he'd been over-attached to as a young Councillor – he hadn't risen to the top of local politics by riding a wave of inspiring but woolly ideas. While driving the dozen miles or so to the headquarters of Rich and Quick Construction Ltd, he rehearsed the clinching arguments, their order of deployment and his responses to predictable objections. As part of his campaign he'd arranged to meet his old friend Gerald Quick, a man who knew an opportunity when he saw one and lived up to his name when it came to executive decisions. His partner, Steven Rich, was more circumspect, even timid, in the initial stages. But once a project was underway, he was tenacious in protecting his investment, a style of doing business that perfectly complemented his partner's opportunism.

'Alex! Good to see you.'

'Likewise, Gerry. Thanks for making the time.'

'Don't be daft. I've never known you waste a man's time. Park yer bum.'

Gerry Quick resembled his visitor in several ways. He, too, bore a suntan, in his case permanent and closer in colour to a fiery sunset, achieved by trips to various properties in Majorca, Miami, Bali and Cancun with such regularity that the weather of the English-Welsh borders never had time to refurbish the underlying white ground. His cream chinos and open-necked, light-blue shirt suggested the scion of a family so well-established that no one could remember the original source of their wealth. Even his hands, thickened and gnarled by work as a youthful labourer, then a scaffolder, could be passed off as the hands of a passionate yachtsman, which was, after all, his current ambition.

Now that Gerry had achieved such affluence, very few chose to recall the escapades of his youth. The most spectacular had occurred in his early twenties and involved a Chinese takeaway, a pair of chopsticks,

32

a roundabout and a four-car pile-up. There had also been a convenient loss of memory among his car's occupants, but not, thank goodness, of life.

Weaver's wife, Barbara, had never liked or trusted Gerry Quick, but her inclinations were known to be on the prissier side of prim. Weaver preferred to regard the man as a rough diamond. Criticise the flaws and rough edges, if you insist, but bury it in the ground or sink it in a cess pit, once you dig it out and hose it off, it's still a diamond. A politician had to get along with all sorts. Be finicky about who you work with and nothing worthwhile gets done.

'I've got an idea, Gerry.'

'Another one? Bloody hell! Wasn't last week's good enough?'

'This one is more than twice as good.'

Gerry's frown, designed to fend off daft ideas that would end up costing him money, dissolved into a grudging smile.

'Go on, then. I've never known you have a bad idea, Alex.'

They waited for the secretary to serve coffee and quit the room.

'It's quite simple. Manley Town FC are looking for a site to build a new stadium. It makes sense. Promotion to the Conference is in sight and Reg Barton has the money to invest bigtime in the team. They could go through the Conference in a season or two. The town's got the supporter base and it'll only get bigger with the new dual carriageway coming through.'

Gerry's eyes crinkled with pleasure while his forehead furrowed with suspended disbelief. He was nobody's fool. 'I can accept that Reg has got money to invest in players. But a new stadium's something else. Even the biggest boys in Europe sweat blood to pay for stadiums.'

'OK, I'm building a jigsaw. Those were the first pieces. Our football team needs to upgrade. But there are two top-flight rugby teams within a twenty-mile radius. Their grounds are rubbish. Newhampton has had to postpone two matches so far this season because of drainage problems…'

'I know. Visiting teams call their ground "The Sewage Farm", and all the players feel pooped after five minutes.' Gerry laughed like a jack hammer, and Weaver felt constrained to halt the intense forward drive of his reasoning to chuckle along.

'… and Rotherton Dragons had people standing in the rain when Coventry came visiting.'

'I get it. Multi-purpose stadium. Football, rugby. I like it. But where are the profit margins?'

Weaver played his first trump card without the slightest sign of a flourish. 'Much more than football and rugby. HyperMart are looking for sites in Manley.'

'Yeah, but supermarkets and stadiums don't mix. It's a traffic nightmare.'

His second and third trumps in quick succession. 'I've got a site close to the planned dual carriageway where you can separate the traffic flows. And it's a prime site. It'll attract a better brand of superstore.'

Gerry couldn't hide his surprise. 'HyperMart Plus?'

'That's right. I guessed the HyperMart Plus boys would kill for a prime, upmarket site in this area.'

'I know they would. There's a big gap they need to fill. Silvia has to drive to Bristol or Birmingham.'

Unyielding as his own wife was in the consumer stakes, Weaver swiftly established her credentials to shop with the best. 'Barbara, too. She was roaming as far as Cardiff yesterday, just for a decent pair of garden loungers.'

'There you go. A gap in the market. But let's face it, Alex, you're gonna need a very big site.'

His penultimate trump. 'I've got one.'

'Yeah?'

'Or rather I've got three sites linking up to make one.'

Gerry, he knew, was now intrigued. He was trying to conceal a smile with a show of scepticism. But his sparkling eyes gave him away. 'If you're talking brownfield, forget it. HyperMart Plus won't fall for that. It can cost a fortune to clean up sites like that.'

'I did say prime site, Gerry. And I mean it. I'm talking land across the river from Rokeby-on-Bass. Enough land for a stadium, upmarket stores and …,' pausing for effect wasn't usually his style. He liked to give it to people straight. Bang-bang-bang, go on, deal with that. But it seemed appropriate now. For all his achievements down the years he'd never been able to genuinely impress Gerry Quick. Small estates, roundabouts, multi-storey car parks… they were bread and butter to Gerry. But this was different. '… about eight hundred executive-style homes, I reckon. At least.'

When the smile faded from Gerry's features as he absorbed the implications, Weaver knew he'd achieved it. Another first. He'd finally managed to impress one half of Rich and Quick. It had taken a decade or three, but something this big was worth the daily political grind. He could almost smell The Big Time.

'Opposite Rokeby-on-Bass. That's de Broche territory. I don't get it, Alex. Since when is that family selling land for this sort of development?'

'Change of management, Gerry. The young de Broche – well, the one who calls himself Brooke – is out of the picture. The old lady left the estate to her niece, not her grandson. And the niece is a doer.'

'I hope so. The grandson turned us down as builders for his so-called eco-village. We weren't quality, apparently.' Gerry's resentment turned to schadenfreude. 'Who'd have thought it? Hugh the Broke, eh?'

They enjoyed the moment of pride restored, but Weaver was quickly back to specifics.

'So far, I've been offered two plots of Dewum land just across the river from Rokeby-on-Bass. But they're separated by twenty acres of land shaped like an upside-down mallet. The mallet head is the land along the riverbank.'

Gerry shrugged, his expression returning to dismissive. 'Then it's a problem. Joining the two parts... access... having a bit of river front. Lacks quality without those assets.'

This is where Weaver began to reveal his hand, playing an unbeatable Royal Flush one card at a time. 'But the land between is owned by Malvoir Council'.

'You mean, the old railway line? Where the station used to be?'

'Parallel to the river, then cutting inland, splitting what's now the Dewum estate,' said Weaver.

Gerry smiled. 'My grandad used to travel that line into Gloucester when he was a boy.'

Weaver refused to indulge in anecdotes, determined to make Gerry concentrate. 'That stretch could join the two tracts of Dewum land.'

'Go on.'

'One plot of Dewum's plus the Council land would provide land for the stadium, the HyperMart store and eight hundred new houses.'

'Sounds good.'

'But I reckon the Dewums are prepared to sell both plots. Which would give space for another six hundred houses.'

'What, you mean all the way from Rokeby village and down the river to Rokeby Castle?'

Weaver assented with a minimal gesture. Take that, my old friend.

'And the de Broches ... the Dewums... are prepared to sell that much?'

'Lesley-Anne Dewum met me this morning. Brought me the idea of selling land for building. But she's got *cojones*. The more I upgraded her basic idea, the more she went with it.'

'OK.' Gerry wasn't usually prepared to accept positive judgements about unseen folk offering deals, but he was prepared to give Alex the benefit of the doubt. 'But what about this connecting land? Can you persuade the Council to sell?'

'With my majority… our party's majority… it's pretty much nailed on.'

'What about cost? It's worth – what? – two, three mill?'

'The Council's been racking its brains for decades about what to do with that land. Whatever scheme they've come up with, the plot's either too big or not big enough. And it's a big cost to keep tidy. They'll be glad to get shot of it… for peanuts.'

'That low? What are we talking? Seven-fifty k?'

'Somewhere in that region,' Weaver speculated, then added with understated emphasis, 'if we're talking – y'know – all things considered.'

Gerry's eyes took his meaning then seemed to gaze inwards while a smile stretched almost reluctantly from the right side of his mouth, the left side desperately trying to hold on to reason, reality and common sense.

Weaver knew he was doing mental arithmetic. Fourteen hundred executive-style homes – with a few affordable ones thrown in for the sake of votes and appearances. That translated into more than half a billion, gross. Not to mention the stadium, shops, hotels…

At last, Gerry's barrel chest released a still-disbelieving sigh. 'Tell you what, Alex. If you can pull this off, you can call the place Weaversville as far as I'm concerned.'

'You can call the housing estates whatever you like. I'll settle for

Weaver Stadium.'

'Sounds fair enough,' laughed Gerry.

'But we've got to manage the timing.' Weaver was suddenly urgent. 'If we go public with a stadium and fourteen hundred houses, the opposition will kick off from day one. You know what those Rokeby toffs are like. They'll go on about land across the river being a "green wedge", and a lot of whataboutery on public amenities, and all the rest of it.'

'I know,' said Gerry. 'We'll have to manage the optics.'

'So, initially we should announce one tranche of Dewum land for the stadium and, say, four hundred houses. Once the building's underway we can up the numbers to eight hundred over time. Every Councillor likes to be known for encouraging housebuilding, so that won't be a problem. But we need to maintain radio silence about the Council land and the second tranche of Dewum land.'

'Makes sense. Don't worry, Alex. You know me and you know Stevie Rich. We've done enough deals to know how it goes. As far as I'm concerned, you look after the agenda and the timing. We'll follow your lead.'

Weaver relaxed, but Gerry was swiftly back to knotted-brow scepticism.

'What about this idea you had last week? About five hundred houses on Rollo Campbell-Stewart's land? Your Planning Committee's not gonna pass two big projects in the Valley.'

'They won't. But Campbell-Stewart still has to be talked out of putting the border of his estate right next to the pylons. He's in it for quick money, nothing else.'

'Well, put like that, sounds as if Rollo doesn't deserve the gig.'

They restrained their grins for all of two seconds.

'So, Rollo can roll on by!'

Once they'd stopped laughing, they continued to gaze upon each other with a large measure of self-satisfaction, but perhaps an even larger degree of wonder. How had they – the grammar school boy, of organised but modest talents, and the secondary modern school lad with a distinction in gang formation and medium-level menace – managed to end up so near the top of the pile like this? If the truth were known, they had very little idea. What they did know for sure was that they must have been very, *very* clever.

4/ Revelations

Hugh's dreams involved great shiftings of earth by enormous creatures equipped like JCBs. They begat dust clouds, razings, tree fellings, deluges, hailstorms and floods. Then the Almighty spoke with a surprisingly husky and feminine voice.

'I am Jacinta,' She announced, 'And I have come.'

He pondered his own and the world's astonishment at having mistaken not just the sex but also the name of the Supreme Being. Determined to catch a glimpse of Her work before his demise, Hugh encouraged his eyelashes to unpick one by one.

Lo! She stood before him – him of all people – repeating the words and offering a mug of steaming tea with milk, clearly the Deity's beverage of choice.

'I am Jacinta. I have come.'

Hugh eased himself into a half-sitting position against the pillow. He accepted the tea and took a sip.

'Is it good?' She enquired.

'Very good,' he murmured, not at all surprised that the Deity spoke English with a foreign accent.

'Are you sick?'

It occurred to Hugh that his condition felt and must therefore look like illness, but he wasn't quite sure about the Almighty's view of hangovers. 'Er... yes... very sick.'

'You poor boy.'

'Yes, that too.'

With eyes failing to focus, like a zoom lens unsure of its subject, and despite a thicket of intervening eyelashes and pools of ocular gunk, he began to sense changes in the general environment. It seemed a good deal brighter and less cluttered. There was a table with two chairs assembled at the far end of the barn. A garden bench had been dragged in from outside to serve as additional seating. Something was simmering in a large pot on what looked like a camp stove. The floor looked not only brushed but swabbed. Buckets dotted here and there were accepting drips through the roof with a regular and rather soothing plip-plop. On the other side of the bed some of his clothes had been suspended from hangers. Washing was pegged to a line across the far end of the barn.

And Bradley was barking indignantly outside the main doors.

'Why is he outside?' Hugh enquired.

'You like dogs inside?' The idea clearly gave offence, and this division of dogs and humans into separate spheres sowed the tiniest doubt in Hugh's mind about this Being's ultimate authority to speak either as, or even on behalf of, the Almighty. He decided to proceed more critically.

'Who the devil are you?'

'I told you two times. I am Jacinta. I have come from Mary.' She reached across to a shoulder bag and drew something from it. 'Here is the letter.' She dropped it on the duvet and went back to her improvised kitchen.

The envelope was inscribed in Mary's neat, no-nonsense handwriting. H.M.S. Brooke, The Grey House, Deverill Court, Malvoir Valley, West Hiding.

Dearest Hugh,

I understand from my usual informants in Rokeby-on-Bass that you have encountered a spot of bother regarding your inheritance.

I'd come myself to be of help, but a dear companion is ill and needs careful and constant attention. Instead I'm sending Jacinta. She hails

from Poland and has a reputation for industry and initiative, which may be just the sort of assistance you need at the moment.
No need to reply. Jacinta will keep me informed of your progress.
Yours as ever,
Mary

Hugh summoned Jacinta. 'Who is this sick companion of Mary's?'

'Her boyfriend.'

His eyebrows reared.

'It's the wrong word? He's old, like Mary. Maybe he's a man-friend. Is that the right word?'

'You mean they're living together?'

'Of course.'

'But… how long? Who is he? What's his name?'

Jacinta examined Hugh's features more closely, assessing them perhaps for signs of mental deficiency. She perched on the edge of the mattress and spoke slowly, as if to a child.

'His name is James. He was a lawyer. A top… how do you say… barista?'

'Er… barrister.'

'Yes, barrister. It's many years they lived together.'

'But Mary is… has only been in Budleigh a couple of years.'

'She met James here.'

'Where? In the town? In Manley.'

'No, here in Rokeby-on-What-you-call-it.'

Realisation dawned. 'Sir James Mansfield QC!'

'Yes, I see.'

'No, I mean… never mind.'

Was it possible? Mary surreptitiously having an affair with one of the country's leading lawyers? Right under his nose? Year after year?

But it made sense. The parts fitted. Sir James had moved from the village at about the same time as Mary. But how had she managed to be so discreet for so long?

Far from being scandalised that his former Nanny had been living on the margins of his late grandmother's code of morality, he was beginning to brim with admiration. Knowing Mary, there would have been no cunning involved, just watertight discretion and superb organisation. But now her cover was blown, never mind that she'd chosen to blow it herself. Timing is all. If Hugh's own circumstances hadn't nosedived well below ground level, he might have enjoyed their next conversation. Mary was well acquainted with pretty much all of his private foibles and failings. At long last he knew one of her secrets. And what mind-bogglingly sensational stuff it was. So much so that the mind boggled.

'You want painkillers, yes?'

'Please.'

'I'll get.'

While she got, Hugh examined her more closely. Late thirties or early forties, he guessed, nowhere near old enough to be his mother. Dark brown hair pulled back and tied in a functional ponytail. Plain top and blue jeans. A slender but strong physique. Her limbs seemed made of powerful springs attached to one central coil of prodigious power and flexibility. Correspondingly her movements were less elegant than determined, co-ordinated and snappy. The Armageddon he'd dreamt of must have been her doing a bout of highly-sprung cleaning.

'Here.' She presented him with a glass of water, two paracetamol and two ibuprofen. It was Mary's cocktail, guaranteed to knock any pain on the head, so to speak.

'So, Jacinta. What are you doing in the UK?'

'You mean, why'm I here?'

'Yes. Why'm you here... I mean....'

'My husband bastard left me. I have a daughter. I need jobs, plenty of money, so I came here.'

'I see. So, what do you do?'

'I do everything... except whore.'

'Well, quite, of course...'

'But enough of me. Now you. What happened?'

'Well, it's a long story...'

'Tell me the story short-style quick. I must report to Mary.'

'Of course. Well... my aunt came back from California, with her American husband some months before my grandmother died. Then we discovered that Grandmother had made another will and the estate would go to my aunt and not to me.'

'She is a beach, yes?'

'A what? Ah, yes, well, I'm biased, of course. Some people... as you say... call her... well, never mind. But maybe my grandmother wanted the estate to go to her niece and not to me.'

Jacinta regarded him closely. 'Mary is right. You are *ufny*.'

'What's that?'

'Nothing. It's a Polish word. Go on.'

'The thing is... and people say I'm a bit old-fashioned in that way... but I believe in judging people fairly...' Her look of total scepticism showed no sign of alteration. 'I mean, until you have evidence to the contrary.'

'In Poland we call this *frajer*. Not just kind but a bit stupid.'

'Ah, well...'

'What happened to the house and car?'

'Well, the house is the only thing I did inherit. But there was a fire. A bit of a mystery. The fire brigade haven't worked out why it burned so quickly. Thatched roofs burn much more slowly, if at all...'

'So, this aunt beach put fire.'

'No. We mustn't assume… There's no evidence for that.'

'And the car?'

'Somebody stole the wheels and trashed it.'

'The same bastards who burned the house.' There was no question mark in her intonation.

'Maybe. Maybe not.'

The dark eyes that locked on to his were filled with a doleful but unsentimental pity.

'It's worse than Mary thinks. We need a special team.'

'What do you mean, team?'

'I'll fix it. You have money? I must shop.'

Hugh ushered her towards the jacket he'd worn to London, even as he suspected the pockets would be empty. No cash, no bank cards, no keys. Just his return ticket. He'd known that ever since waking up on the first morning train out of Paddington. When? This morning? Yesterday? It seemed so long ago. Somewhere near Hanbury. Or was it Charlbury? Before falling back to sleep. Robbed on the train, he thought later. But, come to think of it now, there had been something suspicious about the blurry lads in London and their willingness to pay for everything, champagne and taxis included.

He'd gone on an uncharacteristic bender, thinking that he'd lost everything: inheritance, house, girlfriend. But give the opportunists a chance and you'll soon learn there's plenty more to lose: your wheels, wallet, mobile phone and self-esteem.

Jacinta seemed to see the position more quickly than he did. 'Don't worry. I have money.'

'Where are you going?'

'I told you. Shops.'

'But how will you get there? The nearest supermarket's about four miles away.'

'So? I have legs.'

And she used them, returning two and a half hours later with several bags bulging with provisions. She laid eyes on Bradley curled up on the bottom of the bed and promptly relegated him to the outdoors.

'Dogs will not dirty my clean... what do you call this?'

'Barn.'

'My clean barn.'

'You should have taken a taxi,' said Hugh, assuming her shortness of temper was caused by two long hikes along country lanes.

She was affronted. 'I don't waste my money. I help pay for my daughter's education.'

'I see. Where's she studying?'

'Delft University in Netherlands.' Jacinta replied, sitting down to peel potatoes. 'She studies architecture. My daughter will have ... how do you say? ... a real job.'

'Proper job.'

'Yes. Proper job. A good future. Not skinning potatoes.'

She said this without the slightest hint of doubt or misgiving. Hugh could well believe it too, if the daughter had half her mother's determination and energy, not to mention her springiness.

5/ A New Old Paradigm

'I've been thinking, Cal…' said Lesley-Anne.

Calvin scratched his stubble without raising his gaze from the copy of *Forbes Global*.

'Uhuh?'

'I'm sure we don't need some of these huge portraits hanging around the place.'

Calvin glanced up at Charles de Broche, Bishop of Inchester, occupying four times the space, in two dimensions, that he'd commanded in real life; and at James de Broche, his horse, dog, children and wife – in that order – monopolizing the landscape with languid ease.

'I wuz thinkin' the same thing, Lez.'

They exchanged smiles. Sometimes the serendipity of their thought processes was beyond coincidence. It was downright uncanny, and probably the reason why Lesley-Anne permitted her fourth husband to call her by a short form that she'd previously allowed to no one.

'They must be worth something,' he continued. 'Compared with some of the portraits I've seen in local museums.'

She loved the way he uttered 'mew' as 'moo' – *moozeems*. It seemed to underline his fundamentally can-do nature.

'We can get rid of that portrait of Eleanor and Hugh with the dog,' she said.

As it happened, Calvin was rather fond of that painting. It still hung over the fireplace in the bedroom where old Eleanor had died. There was something touching about the seated grandmother with a protective arm around the boy and his hand on the neck of a faithful Labrador. But he could see why a portrait like that would annoy the hell out of Lesley-Anne. Meemaw had spoiled the kid and created a brat.

'But I wouldn't like people to think we're looting the place,' Lesley-Anne havered.

Calvin changed his position on the settle, lifted one ankle onto his other knee in his "over the Pond" version of crossing one's legs, and considered the problem. 'I know what you mean. My first thought...'

She was often stimulated by the arrival of his first thoughts. They tended to be well crafted and firmly in the spirit of "expand ruthlessly or defend without mercy", summed up in his rather quaint American expression of 'OK, let's kick some butt around here'. To her mind this echoed and complemented the ancient de Broche family motto "In Chao Retineamus" – In   Chaos We Retain, which more than compensated for his poor seat in the saddle and bewildering waywardness with a shotgun.

'You could select the works, offer them to museums, galleries, dealers. Go for the highest bids, then commission reproductions to hang in their places. They can do that stuff with photographs and high-grade paper these days. Or get some Chinese artists to reproduce them. Guy I knew back in San Francisco did that and nobody could tell the difference. 'Cept he had over a million dollars in the bank after.'

'Well, we could certainly use the money. You know, I've been thinking...'

He loved it when she'd been thinking. Usually it was about spending money, and while he publicly disavowed any interest in consumption, preferring faded denim shirts, crumpled chinos and well-worn boots, he was keen on classy surroundings. These included high-class people, and he knew full well that more dollars bought a higher class of person.

'... this place needs a make-over.' As a girl she'd often fantasized about what she'd do with Deverill Court if she, instead of Hugh, had been first in line for the inheritance. 'It needs an orangery that would double up, of course, as a ballroom. Eleanor should never have allowed the old one to be dismantled.' She bridled. 'That was Hugh's influence, of course.'

'It also needs a heated indoor swimming pool, hon'. This English damp's jus' killin' me.'

'No question.' His Californian tan was fading fast, and for all the fashion statements of youth he was closer to sixty than fifty. 'But it also needs proper stables. I can't imagine what Hugh was thinking when he converted them into art and craft studios and business units.' She wrinkled her nose as if the last two words had released an offensive odour.

'Can't terminate the leases?'

'Not immediately. But I'm glad I decided to reinstate the shoot as a proper social occasion – no riff-raff. Can you believe I didn't see a single pheasant anywhere when we first arrived? People don't realise how the shoot maintains species. And we should definitely reinstate the hunt. Which means bringing back stables, kennels and gunrooms.'

'I thought hunting with dogs was illegal.'

'Drag hunting isn't. Even then, foxes do sometimes find themselves involved.'

He raised his eyebrows in mute but instant comprehension. That was another thing she liked about Cal. A nod was always as good as a wink.

'And I'm thinking, in the long run, of starting a training school for polo ponies.'

'Sure. But we definitely need a helipad. I'm not sitting in one of your traffic snarl-ups again. And it'll attract the right kind of guest.'

'And an indoor tennis court, of course. Or two.'

'And a pool room.'

'And a modern kitchen with a new Aga.'

'And a sound-proofed room where I can play guitar and let off some steam.'

Lesley-Anne had heard somewhere that one indicator of a superior gentleman is a man who can play the electric guitar but doesn't. A sound-proofed room was perhaps the next best thing.

'And we'll have to completely re-do the bathrooms.'

'And put in some hot tubs.'

'And a sauna.'

'And some power-showers, honey. I don't enjoy standing under a feeble spray to get clean.'

'And we must widen the drive and install a proper gate. Hugh should have done that years ago. The turning from the drive onto the lane is absolutely lethal.'

'Sure is. But you know, hon', there's a snag. All that's gonna need a lotta cash.'

'I know. But I've been thinking...'

'Uhuh.'

'The estate owns plenty of land. No one with any sense relies on farming for an income these days. And what's the point of owning fields with hedges that cost ridiculous amounts of money to keep tidy. At the same time there's a crying need for more homes. Especially in this area. People are trying to escape the high prices in London and the south east. The new dual carriageway will soon be finished and there'll be a rush to buy property around here.'

'Didn't Hugh have plans to build some houses?'

'As it happens, I popped into the Council buildings yesterday, after I'd met with my solicitors.'

'Uhuh?'

'And there was a very pleasant man there called Alex Weaver. He told me that Hugh had only really had talks about talks. His sustainable eco-village, so-called, was really just an idea. The Council were interested, of course. They can't attract businesses to the area if there's nowhere for employees to live. But they'd never committed themselves to Hugh's model.'

'Hugh's idea would likely take years to build.'

'Exactly what Mr Weaver was saying. He also said they need the houses two years from now, not five or ten.'

'Weaver sounds like a go-to man. So whaddyuh sayin, hon'? We sell the land and they build a suburb?'

'It would be the responsible thing. We shouldn't be holding on to land when the rest of society needs living space.'

'Sounds like the ethical deal. How much do you guess the Council would pay for the land?'

'The Council wouldn't pay. You'd have to go to a developer. But Mr Weaver suggested, off the record, of course, that the thing to do is work with the Council to establish a vision. Something that would attract a developer.'

Lesley-Anne was working hard now to remember the exact phrases used. 'Weaver said that sites near Rokeby-on-Bass, where Hugh was thinking of building his model suburb, would be very attractive. If there was also what Weaver called a PDM – a prestige development magnet – it would put this part of West Hiding on the map and draw in key investors.'

'Did this Weaver guy have any idea about the kind of magnet?'

'Well, he's heard that the local football club is looking for a site to build their new stadium.'

'That's soccer, right?'

'Right. And Weaver said that an international consortium is

planning to invest in the club, if it can guarantee a suitable site.'

Calvin pondered this information. In truth, property on this scale was not his "thing". He'd once owned a share in a small condo in LA, a backstop investment he'd struggled to finance at the time. He'd recently sold this share for cash-flow purposes but had seen no reason to share the information with Lesley-Anne. But where his property ownership fell short, he was good at "mind-mapping a scenario to facilitate an overview of connections and projections".

His "thing" was to create businesses that removed as many overheads as possible from the process of transferring money from customers to his offshore companies, then from his companies to his private investment and bank accounts.

This had taken years of accumulated experience, research and development, not forgetting the cost-cutting and downsizing alongside the alignment of new technologies. But he believed he had finally achieved the ultimate business revolution for the single entrepreneur. It was not just a new model, but a working, profit-generating, 'kick-ass' business in operation – Calvin Dewum's 'Alternative Remedies by Distance Solutions', more commonly known as Dewum Online.

The key to his success was the realisation that some members of the public could be persuaded that signature properties of water-based solutions – such as homeopathic remedies, healing water from Lourdes or spiritually enhanced Kabbalah water – could be digitised. This digitisation could then be uploaded to a computer and stored. If a digitised property could be uploaded, it could also be downloaded. You just place a glass of water beside your computer, turn up the volume and run the app. The signature vibrations imbue your water with divine properties. Critics might scoff, but we live in a world of compression and expansion on scales that were unimaginable a generation ago. Now all this was possible. Or not impossible. At a price.

Not everyone approved. The major homeopathic practitioners' associations of the western world certainly did not. Nor did the relevant offices of the Holy See in Rome and the Chief Rabbinate in Jerusalem. In fact, they went further and positively dissed his company's entire raison d'être. They seemed to have a particular bias against his choice of brand name – Holy App.

You couldn't blame them, and Calvin didn't. They had territories to defend and he had no intention of trespassing. He'd been in business long enough to realise that there was plenty of room for all. The marketplace was elastic. He simply guessed that for every ten paying customers who preferred not to part with their money unless they could be assured of the supplier's credentials, there was at least one who'd think 'Hey, what the heck, this download stuff only costs one dollar fifty a throw, so I might as well give it a shot.'

The result had taken him by surprise. Like his clients, he was taking a risk and hoping for a lucky break. Until recently, his aim was to get by, then get out of town when a source dried up. But now his problem was how to stop his income stream being dammed or diverted by other interested parties. A gross figure might sound like an impressive amount, but it was surprising how little a lot can seem when others declare an interest. Given all the variables, he had no idea how long his good fortune might last.

What he did know for sure was that over 11,000 individuals from all over the world now visited and purchased his 'distance solutions' *every day of the week*, providing him with a gross income of over six million dollars a year. His sole overhead was the Dewum e-commerce website, controlled entirely from his laptop. Although he'd never thought of it quite in these terms, he was a modern alchemist, with one great difference between himself and his medieval precursors: where they had failed, he had succeeded in turning garbage into gold. Or, in his case, bitcoin.

'So...' he continued, his faculties closely focused on Lesley-Ann's scheme, 'a suitable site means land where these guys can build a stadium, a leisure centre, an upmarket shopping mall and several blocks of executive homes, I guess.'

Lesley-Anne liked to express her approval in pithy, equestrian terms.

'*That* is a clear round!'

'And, don't tell me...' he was teasing now. 'You not only thought the same thing – give or take a few blocks of executive condos – but you've also done something about it. Right?'

'Yes. Alex Weaver is the Leader of Malvoir Council and he thought the whole thing was a brilliant idea.'

'Of course, he did.'

'By the end of the meeting I let him think the best parts of the plan were his ideas. Even the equestrian centre.'

Calvin was, in his sardonic, understated way – known across the Pond as 'cool' – all admiration and approval. 'And all based on some guys kicking a ball around a field. A sport you and I know nothing about and like even less.' He returned to perusing the 'Forbes Top 100' celebrity list.

'So... you're on board?' she asked.

'Rope in hand and ready to cast off, hon'. It's a new paradigm.' He paused for reflection. 'In fact, a new old paradigm. One that never went away.'

Even to himself he did not admit that this was everything he'd hoped for when he first dated Lesley-Anne back in LA eighteen months earlier: the alliance of his cashflow with her prospects of some serious, grounded, long-term capital.

6/ Reinforcements

Bradley woke his master with a howling bark at half-past four in the morning. Hugh groped about beneath the bed, found the torch, then shone the beam at the barn doors where Bradley was delivering a deafening, maniacal diatribe.

That Bradley would wake Hugh in the small hours was not unusual. A passing cat or fox, the sound of a farmer's quad-bike in the lane, most likely with a snooty sheepdog sitting on the rear platform, or an insolent rodent asserting rights of tenancy, was enough to test his narrow ideas of territorial integrity. But such a sustained broadside was unusual. He was, as the saying goes, beside himself: tail curved like a scimitar, teeth bared, as if he expected whatever was on the other side to burst through the doors at any moment.

There was no alternative to getting up and discovering the cause.

'Bradley! Shush!'

The dog quietened down once his master was alongside but continued to rumble and froth.

'Who is it?'

'It's Jacinta!'

'Hang on. Shut up, Bradley!'

As pyjamas and dressing gown had gone up in flames, he returned to the area around his makeshift bed to augment faded rugby shirt and underpants with joggers, trainers and wax jacket.

He unbolted the barn door. Jacinta was standing outside in her travelling gear with a holdall and several bulging plastic bags in each hand.

'I brought the team. They're outside. Can they come in?'

'The team?' He peered into the pre-dawn gloom, discerning only an amorphous huddle beyond the gate to the lane. This was the team Mary had promised would set his life on an even keel once more. She'd texted him the day before.

Reinforcements en route. J in charge. F 2nd in command. Great workers. Good luck!

'Bring them in.'

Jacinta dropped a holdall and waved an arm like a woman tossing rocks over one shoulder. Then she bustled past Hugh with her luggage, took one look at the state the place had achieved since her departure just forty-eight hours earlier, muttered something in Polish, and headed for the kitchen area.

A man arrived at Hugh's elbow. In the light cast by the distant kitchen bulb he was perhaps in his late twenties, tall and slender with narrow dark features and a serious expression. He was wearing an unlikely suit, almost comically overdressed for the place and tasks at hand. He extended a hand in greeting.

'Hello, sir. I am Feliks. This is…' and he proceeded to name every man that walked through the door, each carrying a prodigious amount of luggage and equipment, his litany punctuated by Bradley's fury at each and every intrusion. '…Ambrozy, Edmund, Henryk, Izydor, Jakub, Josef, Kasper, Mateusz, Szymon, Tadeusz, Tomasz, Urban, Wilhelm, Wiktor and Zygmunt.'

The men formed a ragged semi-circle inside, some of them already glancing sceptically at the accommodation and the scale of their mission, some making a fuss of Bradley who'd reconsidered the nature of the threat they posed with the first offering of a half-sandwich. Feliks hadn't finished the introduction.

'Or, as you say in your country…' here he identified each man with a restrained and rather elegant gesture… 'Andy, Eddie, Harry, Izzy, Jake, Joe, Kazza, Matt, Simon, Ted, Tom, Herb, Bill, Vic, Ziggy and I am known as Phil.'

Hugh was speechless but coming up to speed in leaps and bounds. These men had been in the country long enough to acquire parallel British identities. Apart from Feliks, they all looked and dressed like working men who meant business. Some looked as if they had the physical capacity to tear the place apart and rebuild it faster than a team of Amish on a film set. One of them, Eddie he thought it was, looked like a human bulldozer with arms and legs parked in a tatty blue sweater and a pair of jeans that must have been specially tailored from two outsize pairs.

Feliks seemed to confirm this in his next breath with something that sounded like, 'Eddie is four men.'

'Yes, he is pretty...'

'...and I am the manager.'

Hugh cottoned on. 'Right. You're the manager of this team and Eddie's the foreman.'

'That's right. And Jacinta's the boss. You must excuse me. I speak English with an accent.'

'No, no problem. Your English is very good. The thing is, when Mary told me she was sending a team...'

'I know you expected more. But the women are coming later, when we have fixed the place.'

Hugh conducted a quick count. Sixteen men plus Jacinta. 'How many women are there?'

'Nine women, in addition to Jacinta. Because not all the men are married. I, for example, am not married.'

Hugh was struggling with Feliks's odd mixture of bluntness and formality while also adjusting to the idea of twenty-six total strangers, plus children, occupying his barn. He'd expected half a dozen at the most.

'The thing is…I'd expected maybe two or three families…'

Feliks looked startled. 'No, we are only one family. The Zielinsky family from Silesia.'

'You're all related?'

'Of course.'

'I see. But what I meant was, this is the only place with any sort of roof, though it leaks, and there isn't much space.'

Feliks glanced at the high rafters then directed some words in Polish at Eddie. His gaze explored the full volume of the building before announcing something gruffly in his mother tongue.

Feliks turned to Hugh. 'He says there'll be plenty of room once we're organised.'

'But how long will that take?'

Another exchange that Feliks interprets. 'He hopes before lunch time, but he can't promise.'

Hugh's bemusement was overridden by a hollering from the kitchen area where Jacinta was already cooking breakfast for a battalion. Pans sizzled. She waved her arms and the men followed her every instruction until the table threatened to collapse beneath the most enormous fry-up Hugh had ever seen. Bradley was in his element, taking his big pleading eyes from knee to knee, but keeping well away from Jacinta and her "mother of all bosses" demeanour.

When the meal was over and the plates neatly stacked ready for washing, Jacinta and Feliks called a meeting. She kept order while he led the discussion. Cigarettes were loaded into lips but promptly removed unlit on Jacinta's say-so. Feliks translated key decisions for Hugh's benefit, alternating between a vigorous and sometimes forceful debating style with his extended family and a measured, temperate manner with Hugh.

'We suggest we live here until we fix your house.'

'But where will you... er, *we*... all sleep?'

Pointing, arm-waving and a couple of passionate disquisitions terminated by a guttural intervention from Eddie.

'We'll build a platform for you up there.' Feliks pointed to the rafters. 'And we'll live down here.'

Hugh was about to object that it would take an age. The women would surely protest against living in a barrack room. The summer might be bearable, but the winter would be hell. But he saw that the decision had been reached by seventeen mature and, as far as he could tell, sane individuals. They'd got themselves to The Grey House and organised a slap-up breakfast. What's to say they couldn't repair a barn and a house? But there was a major stumbling block.

'You do all realise, don't you, that I have no money?'

'You didn't have insurance on the house?'

'The new owners of the estate let the insurance lapse and it burned before I could sort it out.'

Feliks didn't bother to consult the others. 'No problem. If we can stay here for free, we'll help you fix your house.'

'But how will you afford to live?'

'We'll get jobs.'

'Where? Doing what?'

'In the towns. On the farms. We'll do any work we can find.' He spoke to the others in Polish, then turned back to Hugh. 'Maybe you can help us get jobs by writing letters in good English.'

'References. Of course.'

'But now we have to start work. Maybe you can show me and Eddie the house, and the other men will begin to fix the barn.'

Hugh had reservations about letting them loose on what remained of his property. He wasn't even sure that they'd all understand directions he gave. But he had to trust Mary's judgement. She was not a woman

59

to suffer fools. If she trusted them, so could he.

He stepped outside with Feliks and Eddie. The old cottage looked sadder than ever in the early morning light, with a fine mist creating the illusion of a still smouldering ruin. Eddie stood amidst the charred debris, in the middle of what used to be the sitting room, and stared morosely at the outline of a baby grand piano sketched in charcoal on the concrete underfloor of this gutted shell.

'Joo play?' he asked, miming an arpeggio with fingers the size of Cumberland sausages.

'I did.'

He murmured what sounded like a curse, then a question.

'He asks how the fire began,' translated Feliks.

'Officially, there was a fault with the boiler, but one of the firemen told me he'd never seen a thatched cottage burn so fast. He thought the fire was set in several places. But it's just one opinion from a junior officer.'

Feliks translated as Eddie nodded knowingly and scowled at the bruised, drizzle-charged sky. Eventually he delivered his assessment of the situation. Aiming this at Hugh with a mixture of compassion for him and contempt for some Unspecified Other, it appeared to be an attempt at English and sounded like, 'Daze farqueue barsta.' But there was no time to enquire further as Eddie turned like a buffalo in a temper and strode back to the barn.

Feliks was about to follow but Hugh detained him.

'Just one question. Why do you wear a suit while the others…?'

Feliks smiled. 'It's simple. British people trust a suit more than they trust a hoodie. Don't they?'

Hugh conceded this was more likely than not, considering the 'team' he led.

'Don't worry. I only wear it for first meetings and formal occasions.'

When they caught up with Eddie, they found him, arms akimbo, legs planted well apart, in an attitude of disbelief. Whatever the other men had intended by all the scraping, thumping and hammering, it wasn't good enough.

To set an example, Eddie sloughed off his imposing-but-leisurely demeanour with a burst of activity. He began by taking charge of the scaffolder's planks the men had discovered in a corner of the barn. Some of them were working in pairs to move these one at a time. Eddie demonstrated the tempo of work he expected by lifting these planks one at a time and hurling them through the air, arcing them as high as well-tossed cabers, until they arrived at the desired destination in a series of ear-splitting crashes and a lingering cloud of dust. Jacinta complained while Eddie hurled, but the job was done in a trice.

Next, he delegated the building of a stairway, two men to saw and two more to hammer the steps into place.

Jacinta meanwhile was overseeing the division of the barn into sleeping cubicles, placing the single men at one end and the married men in the middle so that their wives – when they arrived – would be closer to the kitchen. While the stairway was being fashioned, Eddie was back out to the cottage with four men to see if the downstairs bathroom could be restored as some sort of functioning amenity. A man was already at work on the mains fuse box and another was up a telegraph pole working on the telephone line.

'Do they know what they're doing?'

Feliks explained patiently. He was getting used to Hugh's diplomatic but permanently sceptical tone. 'Joe is an electrician and Matt is a telephone engineer.'

'Are those not good jobs in Poland?'

'No idea. In Poland we were all farmers. Joe specialised in pigs and Matt was our best chicken man.'

'So you mean they acquired new skills in this country?'

'Acquired? Yes. It's a good word.'

Hugh's aim was to elicit information, not conduct an English lesson, so he tried a different angle. 'How long have you been here?'

'I have been here three weeks. I came from the United States. From Washington.' He smiled. 'I'm the family's black sheep. I left to do a Masters in Political Science. I want to go back for a PhD.'

That accounted for hints of an American accent.

'And the others?' Hugh persisted.

'The others have been here about six months. They came from our farms in Silesia. Since Poland joined the EU, small-scale farming is finished in our country. The whole family has to work together if we want to keep our farms.'

'I don't understand.'

'Big money is buying up small farms that are uneconomic. So instead of being picked off one by one, the family drew up a plan. We make enough money together, then we go back to Poland, merge the farms and work out a strategy for the future.'

'Why come here? Why not Germany?'

'Too many rules. It's easier to work and save money here.'

'I see. And the man working on the plumbing…?'

'Vic.'

'Yes… Vic… what did he do in Poland?'

'Everything. But he was always very good at irrigation.'

'Well, quite.... irrigation… pipes… water… plumbing. Why not?'

Eddie was looming nearby and must have understood enough of this q & a to pick up on a certain scepticism in Hugh's tone, for he interjected as a matter of gospel a phrase that would soon become familiar. 'No problem. Heez fix daze farqueue barsta.'

Back in the barn Eddie detailed two men to head for town and buy waterproof tape to fix the leaks in the roof. Then he lifted the entire new staircase into position against a beam and tested each step by stamping on it during his upward progress. Reaching the top, he removed, one at a time, the four six-inch nails held in his mouth and hammered them home. He re-tested the stairs on his way down and found two steps inadequate. This involved much accusation and denial as he repaired the damage with several more nails.

In no time at all the other planks were carried up the stairs and hammered into place until there was a new floor suspended between beams. Then it was the turn of Hugh's sleeping arrangements to get airborne. He watched Eddie hoist the bedstead and mattress aloft using a primitive pulley, but Jacinta refused to let any of the men touch the bedding with their soiled hands, insisting on carrying it up the stairs herself and remaking the bed. That done, half the family stood below admiring their handiwork.

Eddie hammered a protecting rail all around the new platform, stamped about a bit more in his sturdy size 14 boots, then pronounced the structure ready for use.

'Det farqueue barsta good.'

At which everyone applauded, and Hugh realised that all the apparently major arguments were really quite minor. They were, he decided, amicable discussions on the finer points of interior design.

By lunchtime Hugh and his remaining possessions were installed on the platform. Most of his wardrobe had been destroyed in the fire, and he now possessed only the clothes he'd been wearing on his fateful trip to London, plus a cardboard box full of old clothes stored in the barn ready for delivery to the charity shops in town. If he chose to wear these once more – the beaten-up leather and denim jackets he'd worn on his motorbike as a teenager and the ragged, faded jeans – he would blend in very well with the slightly dated look of the men from Silesia.

Mary had not got rid of some ancient furniture she'd found in the house in the 1990s on the grounds that it was not hers. So the men milling about below had discovered old bedsteads, armchairs, mirrors, chests of drawers, tables, kitchen chairs, carpets, cupboards, chests, trunks, cabinets, buckets, coal scuttles and children's toys. They were dusting, beating and hammering these into any sort of communal use they could contrive. They'd all arrived with simple roll-out mattresses and sleeping bags of the rectangular kind that unzipped to make a quilt. Claiming their spots on the floor, they lined up their bedding to create a primitive barracks.

What astonished Hugh the most was their grateful good humour. They were delighted, as if this were some great adventure. And this spirit began to insinuate itself into his general despondency, beginning to see why Mary had suggested these people as some sort of solution to his problems.

But there was no time to dwell on his circumstances. Jacinta was yelling the men to table for large helpings of steaming vegetable soup, and that included him.

Part Two

Autumn

7/ The Vision Unveiled

As usual on the first Saturday in October, the women of the Rokeby Lawn Tennis Club were entertaining the Manley Women's team in direct competition for top spot in the West Hiding over-45s Tennis League.

The Manley Women regularly gave their closest rivals a thumping on the hard courts across town but were rarely prepared for the slippery, faster grass surfaces of Rokeby in early autumn.

There were dark hints of drier courts being watered early on match days, but no official complaints. The only suggestion that foul play was suspected would come at their next meeting in the club house at Manley when some below par scones and cakes were served. The mutterings amongst the Rokeby Women hinted that these were bought, not home-baked in the accepted tradition. Not only that, but they'd been sourced from a notoriously downmarket retail store.

Despite these BOGOF offerings, it was understood on both sides that no critical comments would be made publicly, since looking down one's nose at 'the limited choices of hard-working mothers' was bad form. This was dangerous territory where no Rokeby woman's tennis shoe would ever knowingly tread.

At the break for tea, the women of Rokeby led 5-2 following a series of hard-fought singles. The scones, jam and large helpings of whipped cream were designed to further blunt the Manley Women's athletic advantages, and the players were now about halfway through their five doubles matches.

As so often in recent years the destination of the championship trophy rested on the day's results. With Manley two points ahead in the league table at the start of play, the home team needed to win by a margin of two clear matches. Rokeby had to maintain their current advantage. A win by a single match would not be good enough. They'd assembled their strongest team, and their captain, Tracy Morgan, had teamed up with her fourth best player and selected her vice-captain to play with the third best. It was a calculated attempt to establish an unassailable lead. So far, so good. The top two pairings were both a set to the good. Tracy was about to go a break up at the start of the second set, and her second team was leading three-one. Even their weakest pair had managed to take their first set to a tie-break.

The first sign of trouble came with the barking of dogs. It was distant but unmistakable. A pair of domestic dogs would not be making such a hullabaloo. It was clearly a pack of dogs and getting closer. Tracy's opponent double-faulted. On another day Tracy might have offered to replay the point, but this was the real thing. If you've got a beef, take it to the umpire. Two-love. The dogs went quiet.

It was only when the multiple report of shotguns erupted on the other side of the wood that the tennis players realised what was happening. Not a problem. They would simply have to maintain their concentration. It was the same for both sides. An occasional escaping pheasant whirred past the south side of the courts, belting out the alarm. At this point the women gave an inward cheer to the ones that were getting away and continued with their matches.

But a much nearer volley sent all the Manley players complaining to their umpires. Points, it was agreed, should be replayed. But before the servers had returned to their marks, a deafening double-report on the near side of the wood turned all heads in that direction. Flat-capped figures were now loitering about a hundred yards beyond the net fencing. Birds were coming over.

Blam-blam, blam-blam-blam-roar!

Feathers were wafting down onto court. A couple of these nestled on the top and back of Tracy Morgan's headband, adding a touch of ethnic and rather warlike exoticism to her otherwise immaculate tennis gear. At this point she was four-love up and could smell the silverware, a trophy she'd not won for seven long years.

In the years between, Manley had always been untouchable by the final round of matches. But last year had been the real heartbreaker for the Rokeby team. Tracy had won the deciding match on home territory early in the season, then played the tennis of her life to open up what looked like an unassailable lead going into the final tie at Manley. But her team-mates had crumbled, perhaps at the sight of mass-produced comestibles. Tracy had won her matches, yet still the old enemy won by a single set when the for and against columns were totted up.

It was not to happen again. She'd fought too hard this season to surrender her rightful advantage. She'd soldiered on through back-ache and strapped ankles and just a hint of tachycardia. This was going to be Rokeby's year.

But only if she could quell the disquiet, partially feigned she felt, in her opponents' behaviour.

'Aren't they a bit close?'

'I'm not playing with all this going off.'

Going *on*, thought Tracy. Going *on*. Only a Manley woman would speak the language of the soaps. She approached the umpire's chair and tried to reassure.

'They'll move on shortly.'

'How do you know?'

'Well, that's what shoots do. They shoot the pheasants in one spot, then move on.'

But her opponents weren't buying it, and the other pairings had stopped playing to listen to these exchanges. Some were gathering up tracksuit tops and water bottles as if it were a question of rain or bad light suspending play.

'Did you know there was going to be a shoot?'

'I had no idea. They haven't had a pheasant shoot since Hugh Brooke started running the place…'

It dawned on her that Hugh was no longer in charge and the new occupiers of the ancient seat had screwed up in a way that he never would.

'Anyway, it's bloody barbaric,' said one of the Manley women. 'I can't play tennis and watch all these poor birds being slaughtered.'

Coming from the hardest nut on their team, Tracy suspected this was, to say the least, disingenuous.

'It's not as if it's raining birds…'

This was misguided, as any qualification was drowned out by a deafening volley. A plump cock bird, his wings folded neatly at his side, resplendent in what was now his funeral garb, thumped into the deuce court on Tracy's side, while a hail of buckshot rained down on the corrugated roof of the clubhouse. A hen bird bounced off the net cord and dropped right onto the sideline, throwing up a confusing – 'You cannot be serious!' – mixture of small feathers and titanium pigment.

It was time to suggest a break in play until the storm passed, but then Tracy looked up at her umpire, also the referee for this match. She was examining what looked like a pellet of birdshot No 5 that had bounced off her baseball cap, onto her score sheet and rolled slowly down into her lap.

'That's it. Play suspended. Match abandoned. I shall send a report to the league.' She looked pointedly at Tracy. 'You can appeal as much as you like, but I won't have players and officials put literally in the line of fire.'

The rest, as they say, was pretty much a blur. Tracy didn't bother to change, but strode out into the fields towards the edge of the woods where the shooters were now gathering in mutual congratulation, where the dog handlers and beaters were assessing performance, and where the soft corpses were being laid out in neat rows for counting. She spied her quarry from a long way off. She'd attended the same C of E primary school until the more privileged girl had been sent away to continue her education among her own kind.

Tracy's complaint also began from a long way off.

'Excuse me!'

A few heads turned. Smiles glimmered. A woman in tennis whites, bare legged, in the midst of a countryside cull, was incongruous to say the least. Her purple face looked as if she was about to burst into tears. But surely not over the deaths of a bunch of pretty but essentially semi-wild poultry that would not exist but for the shoot? Such a scenario was almost too much to hope for. It would grace their after-shoot tales for years to come. But, no, her babbling seemed to tend otherwise.

'How could you organise a shoot without informing people who might be affected? We've just had to forfeit our most important tennis match of the season. Would it be too much to ask for an apology and an explanation?'

The woman she was staring at, who almost certainly had no idea who she was, or that she'd ever shared a school classroom with her, looked her up and down with a calm and poisonous eye.

'Whoever you are, and wherever you've come from, you're trespassing. I suggest you f'korff, or I'll have you removed.'

The blur became a head-rage. Knowing that she was legally, though not morally outgunned, Tracy Morgan retired. She collected her gear without bothering to change, climbed into her Mazda coupé and headed for an early shower. On reaching home in the village of Rokeby-on-Bass, she slumped down at the kitchen table with a cup of tea fortified with a drop or several of the stuff-she-usually-kept-for-bedtime, and stared unseeing at the pile of unopened letters, the unwashed crockery from her light, pre-match lunch, and the latest edition of the local paper.

It cannot be denied that she wept. She wept for a season spoiled, for a trophy cruelly snatched from her grasp by the stupidity and thoughtlessness of those who'd never fought for anything, and – yes – at the silence of a house made empty by the removal of her ex-husband to the interior delights of a younger model with rather more time left on her Maker's warranty.

A good ten minutes passed until Tracy's vision cleared and she could focus once more. As she did so, the headlines on the front page of the newspaper acquired definition and meaning.

'Weaver Unveils Vision – Massive Development for the Malvoir Valley – Rokeby-on-Bass to be site of new stadium – Huge Investment Planned.'

At that point Tracy reversed her usual proportions of tea and whisky.

8/ The Vision Delayed

As a regional chess champion in his youth, Peter Wilde recognised a surprising move when he saw one. And it didn't get much more surprising than the headlines in that week's Manley Observer. Either Alex Weaver was sure of his strategy, or he was beginning to believe his own publicity.

Considering the main item on today's agenda, it was alarming to see the Planning Committee barely quorate. Normally, the Labour group dominated with seven members, with the single Tory and Lib Dem members as window dressing. Only a major epidemic could wipe out the Labour majority, or a piece of sublime arrogance.

Old Bob Phelps was in the chair. Peter remembered his work as a local trade unionist campaigning for improved conditions in the workplace and better social care for the elderly. But now Bob was caught between his better nature and loyalty to Weaver and the fracturing metro-leadership in Westminster. He knew that Bob was made fractious by failing health but, in his uncharitable moments, Peter reckoned he'd been fitted with a specially designed pacemaker that nudged him into full consciousness when issues dear to Alex Weaver's heart were being raised.

Ken Rudge was checking sports reports on his phone. He was Alex Weaver's man, and his likely successor if the boss ever decided to take an early bath. Mel Coates, Paul Rogers, Ian Price and Gary Higgs were absent. The first two were probably out on the golf course, or more likely hanging about the nineteenth hole where they seemed to glean so much of their local knowledge.

The sole Tory Councillor, white-haired Robin Smythe-Banks, had come within a thousand votes of being the local MP in the late 1980s.

Bolstered by an adequate pension and addicted to public service, he didn't seem to mind being in permanent opposition. He was, on the whole, forthright and transparent, someone you could do business with. But he also served Alex Weaver in being the butt of many barbs about class. 'It's either the likes of Smoothie-Banks or me.'

The remaining member of the committee was Gwen Mackie, a Liberal Democrat. The youngest at thirty-two, she had a nervous but ambitious air, conscious of her inexperience and always anxious to do the right thing by her principles. It made her, together with Peter Wilde, a less calculable member of the Planning Committee.

To one side of the Chairman sat Michael Wright, Clerk to the Committee, who managed a passable impression of a neutral Council officer.

Despite the atmosphere of a routine gathering, Peter sensed an unusual outcome for today's business. Why, he wondered, was Roger Mason, the Council's Chief Executive, present to observe proceedings?

The initial exchanges were predictable. The chairman treated the Rich and Quick submission as if it were no more than an application for a conservatory extension to a residential property. The magic figures of three-two, representing an automatic majority, must have been fixed in his Bob Phelps's mind. He went round the table, as the appearance of democracy required, asking for views and observations. He began as always with Ken Rudge, as if his rhetorical powers might somehow swamp and drown out any dissident thoughts in others.

'Mr Chairman, esteemed members of the Committee...' Ken always over-egged the formality.

Peter Wilde never blamed him for that, only for his lack of independence. Ken was in the business of hedging and trimming until Alex Weaver bowed out. Whatever followed from that, he liked to suggest, was not spinelessness on his part, but a courtesy towards a great man in local affairs.

'... I believe this development will bring a whole range of long term and future on-going benefits to the people of Malvoir Valley. Twenty-first century facilities, a re-development of our infrastructure, high-profile rebranding opportunities for the town and, above all, considerable employment opportunities, especially for our youth who are on vocational training schemes and who can carry these skills with them into future, ongoing employability. I see it as more than a win-win situation. It's an ongoing win-win-win scenario, with local government, local businesses and, above all, local residents making massive ongoing gains from the development.'

Peter found this kind of performance rather sad. Ken was often reduced to practising speeches on committees where few members of the public could savour his ongoing attempts.

The baton passed to Smythe-Banks.

'I would usually be in favour of all the advantages mentioned by Councillor Rudge but, in this case, I feel they are outweighed by some evident disadvantages. This Council has always regarded the land between Manley and Rokeby as a sort of green wedge. I'm not rigid about this. You'll recall I was in favour of setting aside some of this land to extend the existing business park. That was to encourage proper long-term investment in the town. But if you allow this application, Rokeby castle and the village of Rokeby-on-Bass, two of our outstanding rural attractions, will be swallowed up by urban and commercial development. I believe this committee should reject the application.'

This was predictable since Smythe-Banks represented Rokeby-on-Bass.

On to the Liberal Democrat.

'I object on the same grounds, Mr Chairman. I also notice that an environmental impact assessment has not been carried out. I believe the area is inhabited by some rare species, including dormice.'

The Chairman's gaze came to rest on Peter Wilde. It carried perhaps the slightest glimmer of disquiet, but also a confidence that such a long-time Labour activist would ultimately swallow his scruples and do the required, if not the right, thing.

'I am surprised, Mr Chairman, that an application involving such large sums of investment should be so poorly prepared. It smacks of unprofessionalism…'

This had the chairman and Ken Rudge shifting uncomfortably in their seats. They could deal with accusations of political bad faith, but one of their own was casting aspersions on the competence of Councillors and officers. Yet Roger Mason, the Chief Executive, Peter noticed, betrayed not a flicker of disquiet.

'To begin with, the items mentioned by fellow members need to be addressed. In addition, I notice that part of the land being designated for this development is Council-owned. I would like to know the price being asked on behalf of local taxpayers.'

'That's commercially sensitive information,' asserted Ken Rudge.

'It's also democratically sensitive,' Peter shot back. 'I would also be interested to know how the residents of Manley Town and Rokeby will react to this application…'

'With all due respect, Mr Chairman,' Ken Rudge interjected, 'that is a political point. The residents and their community councils are free to lodge objections if they wish.'

Peter never prefixed his comments with hypocritical references to 'respect' that did not exist. He was as spiky as his greying hair.

'It's also an issue with serious financial implications. If the Council supports this application, it may lead to long-drawn out legal battles.'

'With who?' Rudge was genuinely bemused.

'With residents, landowners and – who knows? – ultimately with the developers themselves. But beyond that…,' he quickly stymied a riposte from Rudge, 'there are practical issues to resolve. The Lower Rokeby sewage works is already overstretched. How will an additional four hundred houses affect the facility? What Section 106 agreements have been made with the developers and retailers to supply adequate roads, some playgrounds, playing fields and perhaps, a site for a primary school since places are tight in this authority?'

'That'll be down to community councils.'

'Not for the first three years. I see nothing in this application to suggest any wide-ranging benefits from this series of developments to the existing residents of the Valley.'

The Chairman looked dumbfounded, as if he'd mistaken Peter Wilde for someone else entirely. But the clerk at his elbow, who'd been dutifully recording these observations, cleared his throat and Bob Phelps's blank expression recaptured that degree of character necessary for the task.

'If you feel we should ask for the application to be resubmitted…'

'With respect, Mr Chairman…,' Robin Smythe-Banks had seen his opportunity, 'I propose that we vote on the application as it has been submitted. Nothing prevents a re-submission.'

Bob Phelps absorbed the implications.

'Could we have a show of hands, please? Those in favour of a re-submission…'

'With respect, Chairman, that was not my proposal…'

True to form, unused to being challenged in any meaningful way and encountering opposition without the equipment to respond or argue the case, Bob Phelps floundered.

'Maybe, but *this* is *my* proposal. All those in favour of advising the applicants to resubmit?'

In the heat of the moment he raised his own hand. Ken Rudge, baffled but calculating, raised his as well.

'All those in favour of…,' Bob momentarily forgot the alternative or its accurate formulation, '… *not* asking the applicant to resubmit?'

Three hands were raised, including Peter's, and Bob Phelps announced the result with a resigned and betrayed expression that turned into a vague notion of a victory achieved by some clever sleight of tongue on his own part. 'Then we resolve that the applicant should *not* be required to resubmit the application. Good, let's get on, we've got a lot to get through this afternoon.'

The other members were perplexed and amused. Peter wondered if Bob had taken his pills that morning.

'Mr Chairman, I believe we have still not voted on the substantial issue. For or against this planning application, as it stands.'

Phelps regarded Peter with one malign eye. The other looked bewildered and fearful.

The Clerk got in close and whispered something in Bob's ear.

'Right. All those in favour of the application…' he gave Peter the full 'class traitor' stare, '*as it stands?*'

The same two hands in favour.

'Those against?'

The same three.

'Any abstentions?'

The others, including Ken Rudge, now wondered if the Chairman could see other figures around the table invisible to the rest of them.

But the Chairman recovered. He'd always been an excellent assessor of results involving one to nine voters and had always announced them in firm and measured tones, as if this were an important qualification for the job. 'Then the application is… *refused.*'

And he brought his gavel down absent-mindedly but sharply on his Clerk's little fingernail.

9 / Last Straws

Lesley-Anne had seen the light. You give an inch and people take the whole biscuit. You go the extra mile and people pull the rug from under your feet. It had to end, and she was ending it now, by mobile, and from the saddle, as she rode the bridleways between Deverill Court and the banks of the Bass.

Her first call was to the secretary of the Rokeby Women's Tennis Club, ending the word-of-mouth, uncontracted agreement that had traditionally allowed them to use the facilities. In normal circumstances she would have cited alternative development of the land, but the team captain had been so offensive there would be no softening of the blow. The courts were Dewum property. Using them had been a privilege, not a right. The Morgan woman could use the public courts in Manley Town – like everyone else – and repent her behaviour at leisure.

Sadly, she had to leave a message with the woman's answering service.

'I don't expect to see you in the vicinity again, except on the public highway.'

On to the next call. To a private investigator. The small businesses using the old stables were a nuisance. That might have been Hugh's idea of a rent-generating scheme, but it was small beer. Lesley-Anne wanted her privacy. The buildings would be returned to their earlier uses as stabling for horses, kennels for dogs and garages for cars. No more white vans at all hours.

'Mr Richards. I have serious misgivings about some of the activities in the business units at Deverill Court. Could you find the time to meet me at 10am tomorrow to discuss ways of discovering what's going on? That's very kind of you. See you then.'

The inhabitants of the dozen or so cottages on the estate were a much easier proposition. Hugh had been very lax with his tenants, who included all sorts of riff-raff. A so-called jeweller who included no jewels in his work; a handful of *soi-disant* writers and musicians; a yoga teacher, a reflexologist, an eco-activist who appeared to have no earned income and fired off letters to the local press about bicycle paths and the supposedly disastrous effects of mobile phones on the bee population; a rustic furniture maker and the widow of a clergyman.

Don Richards, the private investigator, very quickly established that non-smoking clauses in their tenancy agreements were being transgressed. As Calvin had said, 'They may not be smoking tobacco, but I'll bet they're smokin' sumthin'.'

He was, it turned out, not wrong. That accounted for four households. The others were carrying on businesses from home. Hugh had been happy to have them in the village carrying on their various enterprises but had foolishly allowed his estate agent to use a standard contract which forbade running businesses from the premises. Tough. They were out. There was nothing against the widow, yet, but she kept a boisterous black Labrador and there was bound to be something they could pin on him. Worrying sheep. Fouling the green. Noise pollution. There was always some final straw to be found. Deverill Court would return to being a respectable community, free of undesirables.

As Lesley-Anne turned her cantering bay down Fletcher's Hill with one hand on the reins and dialled her current estate agent with the other, she could see the Court nestled in its distant parkland. Informing the agent that she required the immediate transfer of the Deverill Court portfolio, with all its documents and tenancy agreements, to her new estate agent, she recalled another source of dissatisfaction.

What had once been an avenue of oak, beech, chestnut and elm, leading all the way from the foot of Fletcher's Hill to the stables, was now no more than an uneven dozen or so colossi bordering some grazing grounds. Cattle were sheltering in the lee of one great oak. The ground to north and south would be littered with their cowpats. The very notion gave offence. How on earth had Hugh allowed such a desecration?

Lesley-Anne wanted the avenue back the way it had been in her childhood. Recollections of riding up the avenue on her pony first thing in the morning during her school holidays, then turning back into it from Fletcher's Hill at the end of a long day in the saddle, were memories she'd carried with her through the long nights of failed marriages and foreign customs. Besides, what house of any distinction lacked a tree-lined drive?

Tracy Morgan caught sight of her tormentor riding down Fletcher's Hill with one hand on the reins and the other holding a mobile phone to her ear. A woman on a gleaming, athletic bay of sixteen or seventeen hands, wearing a tailored, dark-navy riding jacket, beige jodhpurs and gleaming black boots. A woman controlling a magnificent beast with the confidence of barely perceptible cues.

It was in many ways a rare and impressive sight, a reminder that technology may change, but the fundamentals still hold. A horse like that, and the ability to ride it with such ease, still carried greater status than a Porsche or Ferrari on the driveway.

But the image was spoiled, and Tracy's ire rekindled, by the soundtrack to this rural vision. Carried on the breeze, even from a distance of eighty yards, came that voice barking into her mobile. Peremptory, certain of being obeyed, utterly derisive of alternative views, yet somehow made acceptable by a range of disarming expressions.

'That *is* kind of you.' 'If you could take the trouble.' 'As soon as possible would be the norm.'

Tracy had lived, decades before, with the infant equivalent and never received any credit for her own forbearance.

'I think you'll find that pencil is mine.' 'I don't recall saying you could borrow my eraser.'

The memories came flooding back, and Tracy recognised a watershed moment.

Would she stay or would she leave? If she left, she would get a reasonable price for the house. Certainly, a good deal more than she and her ex-husband had paid way back in the mid-nineties. Even including the sum she'd raised to buy out her ex-husband's half-share, it would yield a tidy profit. Such had been the rise in property values in just a few years. She would be able to go almost anywhere and buy a smaller, more manageable and better situated cottage. She was attracted to the south coast. The literary associations of Lyme Regis had always been a magnet. But if she stayed, she would have to fight this development all the way. And if she lost, her house would be worth far less than it was today. No-one could persuade her that a stadium blocking her view beyond the river could boost its value.

The galloping lady of the manor baying into her mobile had been the last straw. The resolve to think this through calmly and rationally had gone. Emotion was back in the driving seat. So Tracy postponed her walk to the top of Briery Hill, turned smartly about and retraced her steps along the public footpath towards Tinkin's Wood, where every spring she strolled across soft floors decked with snowdrops and celandine, bluebells and wild primrose.

Once home she took off her walking boots, placed them on a mat beneath a radiator in the kitchen, tossed her socks into the washing basket, made a cup of tea, placed the digestive biscuits within easy reach, and stretched for the phone.

'Councillor Smythe-Banks? This is Tracy Morgan from Shepherd's Lane. I'm phoning to say that in my opinion the proposed development at Rokeby-on-Bass is a scandal, and I hope you are planning to oppose it on behalf of all the residents here.'

'I am and I have,' came the reply. 'In fact, I helped defeat the planning application this very afternoon.'

This took the wind out of her sails. 'Ah…'

'But the job is far from done. The developers will almost certainly re-apply, and the Leader of the Council won't risk a second defeat. I imagine he'll make sure all the Labour members of the planning committee are present next time. So, if residents are not in favour, they'll have to get organised and get cracking on petitions and meetings and demonstrations.'

'Demonstrations?'

She'd never taken to the streets. Not once, not even as a student. She'd always suspected that demos were encouraged by people with covert interests. She'd written to the local papers. She'd spoken at local meetings. But she'd never joined an amorphous body of people in the streets bearing clichés on poles. Such gestures had always seemed to her vague and theatrical. They'd never changed her heart or mind. Perhaps she was, after all, a nimby, a conservative, without the imagination to be touched by anyone else's concerns unless they not only touched hers but threatened to undo them.

She switched to more comfortable territory. 'Is anyone organising a petition?'

'Not that I know of.'

'Then consider it done. I'll get back to you by the end of the week and let you know how many signatures I have.'

'Good, let's keep in touch through the email…' Smythe-Banks

hadn't quite mastered the language of modern communication. 'By the way, it may help you to know that there are some surprising people opposing this development.'

'Such as?'

'Peter Wilde, for one.'

'Red Peter?'

'Precisely. So, if you come across any hard-to-persuade Labour supporters who think you represent middle-class nimbys, just tell them that Peter Wilde has serious reservations.'

Red Peter. This information produced a simmering brew of conflicting emotions. Elation that even he, of all people, was opposed. But also some reluctance at being on the same side as the man she'd once overheard calling her husband... ex-husband... a 'prime example of a Little Englander on the make'. The insult had infuriated her at the time, and she'd shot back something along the lines of 'The Wildeman has spoken'. It got a laugh, but she knew it was a cheap shot.

She had also learned to her cost that her ex-husband did indeed possess elements of that description. He was not big in any direction, he was proud of being English in ways that seemed unimportant to her, and the closer he'd got to middle age the more he understood where the bigger, easier money was to be made, never mind the cost to anybody else.

There'd been the fear of failure in his early forties, when he'd become anxious, retiring and clingy. But it only took him a year after being made partner in his mid-forties to discover a penchant for low-slung gas guzzlers and leggy secretaries.

Tracy made a mental effort to suppress this bitterness and went to work on the phone instead. By six o'clock she had a core of activists, mostly regular churchgoers, members of her local reading group and every member of what was unofficially known as the Rokeby Tennis

Tarts.

After an early dinner, she hit the streets, going from house to house in Rokeby-on-Bass. Tackling residents in the old centre of the village with its ancient farmhouses, rectory, almshouses and large, detached residences was child's play. Everyone signed her petition. But the semis that lay further away from the riverbank were a different proposition. They ranged from the simply direct …

'Why would I oppose that? 'Sbout time we 'ad a proper stadium. C'mon the Blues is what I say.'

… to the simply complex, or completely off-topic.

'I know what you mean. It's not right. Big companies coming over 'ere and building whatever they like. It's like with the European Common Union. They thinks they can just ride roughshod over everythink.'

'Dead right I don't like it. It won't be us what gets anything out of it. It'll be them asylum seekers. They'll be working on the building sites and getting paid a pittance and we'll get nuffink. Now, if you 'ad a petition against all this immigration…'

'Good for you. Them planners want their heads seen to. They can pass an eyesore like that, but they wouldn't let me open a burger bar down in the village…'

For once in her life Tracy began to pity would-be politicians who, on this evidence, lived on an intellectual diet of worms from open cans with jagged lids. They had to mortgage a portion of their sanity in exchange for votes.

But she pressed on. By the end of the evening, the time when the populace of Rokeby-on-Bass was barricaded behind its curtains and refusing to tear itself away from the football or the soaps, she had a hundred and fourteen signatures. She trudged home in the dark looking forward to a well-earned cup of tea with a dash of Scotch.

Was it worth it? Was she kidding herself? Wouldn't she be a lot happier selling up and heading for Lyme where she could live out her days re-reading the works of Austen, Hardy, Fowles and, in the privacy of her bedroom, Georgette Heyer?

Her mobile shuddered. Here was a message left earlier in the day. She tapped the right icons and listened. A message left by the Dewum woman.

That was the last straw.

10/ Tribunes Of The People

Jim Phillips was jolted into full attention by the traffic light. Red on his side. Road works ahead. It was about time the Council did something about the potholes. His husband's car had been written off when forced into the soft verge by a speeding van on this narrow lane. A foot on the brake and the edge of a concrete trench had done the rest. Not worth the repair cost. But a Council officer suggested it was a case of driver error and was still withholding full compensation.

Edging forward on green, Jim checked the open lane was clear and accelerated past the long line of traffic cones. There was no sign of pothole repair. Was it a case of a burst water main? Overhead cable work? Hedge trimming? Road widening?

His foot came off the accelerator when he saw the reason. On a winding lane, with steep dips and inclines and a road surface barely wide enough for two large vehicles to pass without scratching paintwork, was a solid white line guarding the stylised image of a bicycle.

Seriously? Long broken stretches of cycle lane around the bends on a road with the highest accident rate in the Valley where no sensible cyclist would venture?

Jim had heard the rumours. A Council taking cash from central government for expensive bike lanes. But instead of laying miles of them in places where they could be useful, someone had decided to paint white lines, declare the box-ticking mileage and take the Treasury's money. How, Jim Phillips wondered, had the difference been spent? And when would anyone ever hold this Council to account?

His husband had often said that if he had a complaint about the cooking, he should step into the kitchen and have a go at doing better. Maybe he would.

Michelle Watson was beginning to tire of her husband's defeatism. He'd lost his oomph. Days, even weeks, spent out on the road selling software that nobody wanted. Then hours slumped in front of the TV.

Apps were the thing now, or so she'd heard. Created by twenty-somethings in their bedrooms. No overheads apart from their laptops paid for by the bank of mum and dad. They may not have their own home – Michelle had hers at nineteen – but they knew what users wanted. Derek, on the other hand, spent half his time creating power point sales material that nobody had time to sit through these days.

'We can't go on like this,' he said. 'We'll be out of cash in six months at this rate.'

'You'd better get a job, then,' she replied.

She knew what his cold stare meant. 'Why don't you make a sacrifice?' he was thinking. But she'd never sell her ponies. Or the stables. She'd spent twenty years setting up that business and she wasn't throwing away all that time, money and hard work. True, income had fallen, but it had always been seasonal. She'd usually broken even – just about, or so she guessed – and there was every chance business would pick up.

Besides, she enjoyed the rent-a-pony business. It was more like socialising than work. And it offered work experience and holiday jobs to teenagers just out of school. At least for the ones who didn't mind exercising, currying and mucking out.

If Derek couldn't find anything better than a shelf-stacking job at his age, she'd have to chip in herself. But it would have to be something that would fit around the pony business. Something flexible, not too taxing. Something sociable that would exploit her flair for persuasion and organisation.

There was an opportunity. Something that might tick all the boxes. People were talking about next May's local elections. Councillors got a basic allowance and there were other opportunities. Her father was a retired builder who knew all there was to know about planning. It was certainly worth considering, unless Derek came up with an ingenious reason to get out of his armchair and make forty thousand a year.

Christine Chivers stared at the contents of her biscuit tin for several seconds and again decided not to take one. She offered one to her granddaughter who shook her head. Sensible girl.

Christine resumed her seat at the kitchen table and stared at the image on the front page of the local newspaper. The local MP and the Leader of the Council – who'd promised to help her, to put matters right, to help her win compensation, if not justice. In the end, they'd encouraged her to accept the lawyers' advice, fobbed her off, refused to fight.

She would never accept that somebody wasn't responsible. Somebody had decided to lay cardboard sheets over the scaffolding boards. To make them less slippery, it was said. And somebody had laid cardboard over a gap between the boards near the top of the building. A gap large enough for a man to fall through.

How was it possible to not trace the course of events in reverse? To not identify the person who had laid the cardboard. To not decide that somebody had failed to do their job. To not determine that's person's employer.

But all the lawyers, officials and politicians had concluded that pursuing the case further would be a waste of public money. Unless she wished to pursue it herself, using her own resources, financial resources she'd exhausted in funeral costs. Mental and emotional resources that she had burned through in the 296 days and nights since the "accident".

'If I was half my age I'd stand for election and try to change all this,' she muttered, staring straight ahead, as if focussing beyond her kitchen walls to a world which confounded and offended her sense of natural justice.

Her granddaughter Charlotte knew what she meant.

'I'll stand, Grandma?'

'What?'

'There's an election next May. I'm going to stand. For Grandad's sake.'

11 / Master Of The Unexpected

The next meeting of the local Labour Party was a humdinger. The Chairman struggled to keep control. Interruptions abounded, points of order flew. A copy of Standing Orders was taken down from a shelf, its paragraphs closely examined and disputed.

Alex Weaver sat quietly through it all with a serene half-smile etched into his features. He'd seen it all. Been there, done that, recycled the T-shirt. The spectacle of these boys squabbling over matters of no consequence appeared entertaining to this indulgent colossus of local politics.

Mel Coates and Paul Rogers had started it all by trying to cover up for their chronic absenteeism.

'Even if I'd been present at the planning committee meeting, Mr Chairman, I would have voted to reject the application for very much the same reasons as other objectors,' claimed Coates.

'That is also my position, Mr Chairman. Therefore, the outcome of the vote would have been the same.'

Peter Wilde registered this as a disingenuous attempt to turn lax behaviour into a principled position. They both knew that challenging the Leader's declared policy carried risks, but this way was better than admitting they were incorrigible saps. The other two miscreants, Ian Price and Gary Higgs, had cast-iron excuses, one involving high blood pressure, the other a dicky heart.

But then Ken Rudge made an ill-advised intervention.

'Even if the result would have been the same had the two members in fact attended, the fact still remains that a vote in favour would have been possible – should in fact have been guaranteed – in the circumstances which actually pertained at the meeting in question.'

He then produced a fairly lengthy ramble through the highways and by-ways of the English language and included a reference to 'an unprovoked stab in the back'.

A reply from Peter Wilde was unavoidable. He'd hoped to remain, like the Leader, aloof. But Ken Rudge was a master of provocation. He wanted a response and he'd get one.

'I was not aware, Mr Chairman, that the vote on the planning committee had been pre-ordained or whipped by the Leader. Members know me well enough to realise that I would have objected to that in the strongest possible terms and, if necessary, resigned my seat on the committee and then explained my position publicly. Now, if this is the reason I was not included in any advance consultations, perhaps the Deputy Leader, or even the Leader himself, would like to confirm or deny.'

In response to Peter's probing, Alex Weaver pursed his lips as code for 'No comment'. Peter smiled in return. For all the veiled hostility between them, they enjoyed the cut and thrust.

'Nor was I aware that members of this Party are obliged to rubber stamp, sight unseen, the results of private meetings between members of this Council and outside interests…' a rumble of indignation mixed with renewed interest. This was getting tasty. 'If the Leader would like to itemise the outcome of meetings he may have had with any commercial interests, and if he would like to give us an estimate of the financial advantages to the local taxpayer, agreed perhaps at these private meetings, then I would be in a position to make a judgement. In the absence of that information, I am obliged, on behalf of my constituents, to vote against anything that might harm their long-term interests.'

Weaver's expression was now in watchful crocodile mode. The sliver of eye that Peter could see glittered in amusement at this futile attempt to draw him out of deep waters.

In any case Ken Rudge was quick to reply, hardly bothering to go through the Chair. 'But there's another duty, and that's to the Party. No one's asking for blind obedience or toeing the line in all circumstances. All the Party asks is for self-discipline...'

A good phrase and one that garnered nods and favourable grunts. These always sounded to Peter like 'Urghuwhuh'. He'd always wondered how many 'urghuwhuhs' before he was thrown out of the Party.

'... and it's not only a question of self-discipline. It's a question of bad faith...'

'Ooo-ooh.'

'Urghuwhuh.'

'...because it's not always the Leader's job to play all his cards face-up *all* the time. It's not possible to conduct the business of local government in that way. We have elected a Leader. He has been invested with the trust of local people. We expect him to go out into the world and make deals on our behalf, often in competition with other councils. We cannot tie his hands. Sometimes we have to have faith in what the Leader is doing.'

'Urghuwhuh.'

Peter raised his hand to reply, but the Chairman ignored him and called, instead, on Gary Higgs of the Dicky Heart. But Peter Wilde was having none of it.

'Point of order, Mr Chairman!'

The Chairman pointedly avoided his eye.

'Mr Chairman! I have been accused of bad faith and I have a right to reply!'

That's when it all kicked off. Whatever else was established over the next half hour had no bearing on the rights and wrongs of voting this way or that on planning committees. If anything, it confirmed that several members were in need of tranquilisers, blood thinners or pacemakers. It was also plain that several sub-clauses of Standing Orders would have to be clarified.

It did not help that Peter Wilde suggested that some unnamed members were behaving like a caucus. This confused the hard of hearing.

'What did he say? A cactus? What's he talking about?'

Peter was obliged to clarify. 'I said a caucus. A cactus is when the pricks are on the outside.'

At this, the pacemakers present had to jolt their owners' hearts back to a steady rhythm.

In the event it mattered little. The Leader was in such an equable mood because he'd already pre-empted any possible outcome of the local Party meeting. He was, after all, a master of his universe. When Party affairs threatened to upset his apple carts he would turn instead to his whip carriers in local government. If Council officers proved obstinate, he unleashed the muscle of local democracy as expressed through the Party. It was as easy as a game of ping-pong.

Weaver slid into his Volvo still wearing the blissful if slightly cynical smile he'd affected all evening and contemplated the bombshell he had waiting for supporters and detractors alike. Even Ken Rudge had no idea.

Just before leaving the Leader's office that afternoon he had placed on the agenda for the next full Council a proposal to make every councillor a member of the planning committee. It stood to reason. Planning decisions of this magnitude were too important to be left to a handful of committee members. Such a dispensation was simply undemocratic. Big planning decisions affected all the wards in the authority. Therefore, all wards should be represented when decisions were made. That his thirty-nine Labour councillors would outvote their five opponents, however many had trouble dragging themselves away from daytime telly, the golf course or the bookies, was a decision the electorate, in their wisdom, had taken three years earlier, and Alex Weaver was the last man on Earth to deny that democracy had its virtues.

12 / English Lessons

Hugh had never been so busy. Reveille was performed by Jacinta with a clatter of pans at five o'clock sharp. Even Bradley gave the impression that this was a tad too early. A full half-hour would pass before he waddled down the steep stairway and got on with the serious business of begging for scraps. In the meantime, the men had got themselves up and taken turns in the outdoor bathroom in the wrecked cottage. The smokers would huddle outside the barn door, hawking and wheezing through their first cigarettes of the day before extinguishing them in the bucket of sand Jacinta had deployed for the purpose.

'No filltee habit in my barn.'

Hugh was impressed by the self-discipline and regularity of their unfilltee habits. Everything was decided through collegiate argument: cooking and washing up rotas, timing of access to the single bathroom, shopping sorties, selection of TV channels, times for lights out.

There were the usual discomforts of barrack room living. The aroma of imprisoned feet newly released, not to mention internal gases lately escaped. These accumulated just below the rafters where Hugh slept. But Bradley slept at the foot of his bed and was perfectly capable of matching a whole barnful of human beings in this discipline. There was some snoring, a few nightmare riders, the occasional outburst from a homesick stress bunny - usually Izydor – and some protracted misunderstandings that required mediation. Otherwise the nights and days passed in orderly endeavour.

'Of course,' said Feliks when Hugh expressed his admiration, 'we have all been conscripts. Except for Izzy and Ambrozy. Conscription ended before they were old enough. I was in the Polish air force, but the others were in the army. You learn to ... how do you say? ... do what you can with what you've got.'

'You learn to make do,' said Hugh, who could see Feliks making a mental note of the expression.

By seven o'clock only Hugh, Jacinta, Feliks and a couple of men remained. The others had all found work. Some on the new roadworks where Eddie was promoted to ganger within days. Henryk and Szymon in a service station washing cars. Wiktor was flourishing as a freelance plumber and took young Ambrozy along as his assistant, while Josef and Mateusz were finding plenty of work as decorators. Kasper, Urban and Zygmunt packed vegetables, dug gardens, cleaned offices and washed glasses in nightclubs. They seemed to work all hours and were often absent when everyone else was going to bed yet always appeared at the breakfast table for Feliks's daily debriefings.

Only Izzy, as he insisted on being called, failed to hold on to a job and instead spent his time helping Jacinta. This relieved her to do various cleaning jobs in nearby villages from mid-morning to mid-afternoon. She'd somehow acquired a mountain bike and powered her way down country lanes several times a day. The rest of the family appreciated Izzy for qualities other than lifting heavy weights from one place to another. He came into his own when the barn was turned into a hair salon and the relatives got free haircuts, or when he picked up his guitar for a singsong, by turns rousing and maudlin. He also spent many hours doing psychic readings for Jacinta, especially when her daughter was about to sit an exam.

It had taken only a few days for the family to show signs of a new affluence. On paydays cash was added to the pool held by Jacinta. Monies were then allocated for housekeeping, personal needs and savings. Everyone had a mobile phone, and Feliks gave Hugh a spare for his own use.

'No problem, I have two.'

Mateusz and Josef appeared one day carrying a used laptop they'd been given by a nightclub owner.

'He has five houses, seven cars, three girlfriends and five laptops,' enthused Mateusz.

Josef then spent the entire evening trying to get Hugh's old broadband service up and running. After much cursing in Polish, which sounded to Hugh like, 'Izsunov beech beatie,' an irritatingly familiar signature tune, followed by a cheer, echoed through the barn. Hugh was back online. Over seven hundred messages were lurking in his webmail, so he waded through this cyber-garbage to find the thirty-odd bona fide communications.

A few were from local well-wishers expressing their sadness at his misfortunes. There were several from former tenants complaining about their treatment by the new landlords. One was from members of the Deverill Quartet wondering why their series of Christmas concerts at the Court had been cancelled. Another was from Isabella, his ex, asking him to remove some clothes from her Knightsbridge flat, as they were emitting some unhelpful *feng shui*. In the circs this was a bonus as he was pretty sure he'd left a decent jacket or two in her wardrobes. A recurring message required him to contact his solicitor *tout suite*, good news unlikely.

The indications had been ominous from day one after the fire, and various old emails confirmed, that the Dewums had cancelled the insurance on The Grey House without informing him. Financially, he was closer to ground zero than the house was physically.

If being back online brought him no immediate comfort, he was able to help his lodgers open bank accounts, apply for credit cards and register their mobile phones. With Eddie riding shotgun, he'd gone to deposit the more than five thousand pounds they'd saved collectively in only their first seven days of work.

The Zielinskys, Hugh soon realised, never missed an opportunity. Zygmunt turned up with a used laser printer discarded by a firm where he cleaned. A large flat screen television was bought from a car boot sale and two washing machines and a dishwasher were rescued from the roadside, to be refurbished and put to work. But the icing on the cake was the arrival of an ancient VW van, complete with bits of straw still protruding from various crannies and holes in seats, that Henryk and Jakub had discovered in a barn.

The farmer let them have it for free but charged them fifty pounds for the ancient registration documents. They summoned Eddie by mobile phone, waited for him to arrive, then chivvied a young farm worker into towing the van to The Grey House while Harry steered and Eddie sat like a Buddha on the engine housing to apply the otherwise non-existent brakes by pulling backwards on an iron stave rammed through the floor and between two beams, thus engaging the road surface below. Other drivers flashed their lights, hooted and waved, trying to warn of sparks flying from beneath the van, but its crew managed to get the ancient jalopy around the by-pass and home before the traffic police turned up.

'Weez mek dat farqueue barsta go,' beamed Eddie.

Hugh got his Land Rover back from the repair shop the same evening. His insurance had covered all but the excess, though his finances were perilous.

'No problem. We'll help,' insisted Feliks.

'But I may not be able to pay you back…'

He was about to add 'for a long time' but Feliks waved away his resistance. 'You're helping us enough.'

The next evening Ambrozy and Tadeusz guided him several miles across country to a pile of slate tiles recently removed from a barn.

'A lot of them are broken,' explained the farmer, 'but you can have the good ones for free… if you shift the lot.'

'That's very generous.'

'A good deal as far as I'm concerned,' said the famer good-naturedly. 'Besides, I heard about your troubles.'

Hugh and Feliks spent the next couple of days loading tiles and towing them back to The Grey House in a borrowed trailer. The barn they'd covered had been so huge there was a good chance they'd easily roof the cottage with slates to spare. Seeing the first shoots of renaissance in his fortunes, Hugh caught the Zielinsky bug and vowed to shrug off his despondency and grasp every opportunity.

Quick to self-criticism, he realised that his life had been one of monumental privilege. The Zielinskys had little but behaved as though life was their oyster. They might have no more than one such shellfish, and no champagne to wash it down, but they gave the distinct impression of believing they could lay their hands on both commodities if a family powwow decreed it. So, Hugh tore a leaf from their book and called in a favour from a former tenant who now ran a sawmill.

'I need to source some rafters at the lowest possible price.'

'No problem. I heard about your troubles.'

Hugh was beginning to sense people willing him back on track, wanting his phoenix to rise from the ashes. Till now, he'd had the distinct impression that he was widely envied and often derided. Moneybags. Butter-boy. Silverspoon six-pack. But now his initials – H.M.S. – referred to Her Majesty's Sinking Brooke, an underdog in receipt of the Brits' traditional support.

Such clichéd musings were dealt a blow when a Mr Goater from the Manley Planning Department turned up to point out that the tiles being used on The Grey House were "inappropriate". The house was in a conservation area and it was Mr Goater's responsibility to make sure that historic houses in the Malvoir Valley were preserved for posterity. The house would have to be thatched, something that Mr Goater knew very well would cost a cool fifty thousand.

Feliks reacted first.

'The tiles are temporary. To preserve the rest of the building during the...' here he was lost for the right words.

'...repairs and refurbishment,' added Hugh.

'Then you'll have to guarantee the temporary nature of the work and its completion within a given time. I'll send you the necessary forms.'

Good-natured though he was, Hugh mistrusted Mr Goater. It was odd that he should turn up in person. Even odder as work on the cottage had hardly begun. It was as if somebody was keeping a close eye on events at The Grey House.

It was Mary who prompted his suspicions further in a telephone conversation later that day.

'But why do they think The Grey House is called 'grey'? It's because it originally had a slate roof. It was only when your great-grandfather decided thatch was the thing that all the houses in the village were thatched. So if Mr Poker, or whatever his name is, wants to restore the building in accordance with conservation guidelines, it should be roofed with slate. It's in the Monuments for West Hiding. Mr Poker should be aware of that. I left a copy in the rolltop desk in the sitting room, so it'll have gone up in smoke. But you can easily get another copy sent out from the archives.'

Hugh crafted a letter for Mr Poker-Goater. 'As I am sure you are aware...' No, that might be unfair. One had to give a man the benefit of the doubt. 'Your informants within the Planning Dept may have failed to inform you that...'

In the meantime, he and the Zielinskys got on with reconstructing the roof ready for the tiles.

'Why don't you put a corrugated roof on straight away to protect the walls? Then we can get on with the work in our own time.'

In his understated manner Feliks was always coming up with measured, constructive suggestions. In this way he was carving out a role for himself as Hugh's right-hand man. Looking back, Hugh sensed this might have been his aim from the outset. For every quibble Felix had an immediate solution, for every doubt a reassurance, as if he anticipated the next question or demur. While Hugh doubted, even now, that this project of rebuilding The Grey House could possibly succeed, Feliks seemed to have his gaze focused way out in front on some distant finishing line.

'Apart from anything else, I have no cashflow. It's all very well for me to provide your accommodation, but…'

'You could give us English lessons.'

'What?'

'We all need English. We can either pay for evening classes at the college in town, or you could give us lessons here. It's better for us to be here. We lose less time. You speak very good English.'

'Well… yes… thanks… but…'

'Take me, for example. My English is OK. But there are some things I still need to improve. I needed help with my MA thesis, for example. And if I want to study for a PhD, my English will be… how do you say… stressed?'

'Stretched.'

'You see? I can't afford to be almost right at that level. So, it's a great opportunity for me.'

'The thing is… I've never taught English…'

'But I've had several English teachers. I can give you… how do you, say? … hints.'

'Tips.'

'Yes, tips. Good, we have started already. I will organise the lessons and a rota. I can have an hour and a half, but most of us won't be able to concentrate for more than half an hour or forty-five minutes. If we say… three learners a day at ten pounds a lesson, that's thirty pounds a day, and more when you teach me.'

Oddly enough, Hugh soon found himself walking around with more cash than ever. Wads of the stuff bulged in his trouser pockets, littered the floor of his elevated platform, found its way into his bed, or got chewed by Bradley, whose favourite game was nosing out and shredding any sort of paper or cardboard.

Walking about with loaded pockets, Hugh imagined, was how some of the heroes of his youth must have felt. Home from school in the holidays, he'd spent an impressionable spring in his thirteenth year hanging about the Bassett Arms, watching the owners of impressive motorbikes flexing their tattooed biceps to alternately lift pints and launch feathered missiles with surprising tenderness at the dartboard. They had no idea who he was, and the publican decided it was better not to tell. But a couple of bikers were sufficiently impressed by all the admiring questions re engine capacity and acceleration that they took him under their wing, ordered him crisps and a lemonade – on one occasion smuggled him half a pint of cider – and paid for it by hoiking a folded wad of notes from a jeans pocket and peeling off a fiver. The gesture possessed a maverick quality and suggested a devil-may-care autonomy. Cash in hand, no questions asked.

The gesture had no similar effect when Hugh mimicked it as a first-year student at university. He soon learned that when *he* peeled off a tenner, it conveyed an impression less of piratical independence than of vulgar *richesse*. But now that his credit card bills were haemorrhaging interest, and he'd begun to dance the zero credit hop like the lowliest of debt-ridden Micawbers, he found the feel of a wad nestling against his upper thigh, or pressing into a seated glute, to be as reassuring as Wilberforce, his childhood teddy bear, long since "disappeared" by Bradley.

Perhaps as satisfying was the knowledge that this cash was earned with honest, sometimes excruciating, mental toil.

Feliks was a joy to teach. He asked intelligent questions, adapted his language in line with Hugh's suggestions, and generally showed application and aptitude. Their two times forty-five minutes often stretched to two and half hours. Lessons were as much conversation as instruction.

However, the other Zielinskys presented pedagogical challenges for which Hugh was ill-prepared, and he soon realised that foreign language teaching wasn't going to be so very easy.

'I like yours country very much.'

'*Your* country.'

'Why your country? This country is yours, no?'

'Yes, this is my country and Poland is yours.'

'Is what I say. Britain is yours country.'

He was soon able to distinguish between the argumentative goats and the compliant sheep but had few techniques to modify his approach.

'Please to tell me, wat is that?'

'No, what doesn't rhyme with cat. It rhymes with hot.'

'Wot?'

'Yes. What.'

'Wat is this wot?'

'No. W-h-a-t is pronounced wot.'

'Aaah! Wat is wot?!'

'Well... um... yes... in that sense, it is.'

'But you spell that like t-h-a-t, yes?'

'That's right.'

'So... why you not say "Wot is thot?'

'Ah... well, yes... I see what you mean. Why indeed? The thing is that English spelling is a bit tricky that way...'

He was usually saved from floundering embarrassment by Feliks keeping an attentive ear on the proceedings. A volley of forceful Polish usually set his pupils on the right path, though Hugh had not the vaguest notion of how this was achieved.

Izzy was his most entertaining pupil, and he'd usually insist on giving Hugh a psychic reading to kick off their classes.

'I feel you have a big sadness, ... a sense of great loss...'

'Hmm,' thought Hugh, 'this one's sharp.'

'... you have some enemies... who have the power... but you also have many friends...'

'Now, where would he get such notions?' wondered Hugh.

'But I see changes... faster than you think... you must be ready for new opportunities...'

'Opportunities,' thought Hugh, bitterly, 'are the only things I do have at the moment.'

'I feel there's something big coming up in your life... all I can see... is a ball... it's in the air... and a net... long, like a fishing net...'

'And I'm the fish,' thought Hugh.

But, in all possible ways, his most challenging pupil was Eddie. It took the whole of the first lesson to discourage a tendency to pronounce –*king* like *queue*.

'He is mayqueue chair.'

'Making.'

'May-KING!'

'Do you like England?'

Eddie sat four-square, like a brick wall somehow encased in dungarees, and assumed what he no doubt imagined was an exemplary manner for a student of Shakespeare's great language.

'I am charMING in England.'

'Um… I think you mean… I am charmed by England. Yes? Or I find England charming.'

Hugh realised halfway through this correction that giving a beginner two structurally different examples was a cardinal error that would return to haunt them both. Eddie considered the conflicting information with an expression of suave concentration.

'Also… I am liked by England.' He smiled. 'Or… I find England liKING.'

At this point Hugh decided to follow Feliks's example. Basic information delivered at a high tempo would serve the purpose better, and he began introducing Eddie to combinations of the verb 'be' and singular nouns.

'I am a man'

'I am man.'

'*A* man.'

'I am a men.'

'*Man.* I am a *man.*'

'I em a MAN!'

'Er… right… OK. He is a dog.'

'He is a dog.'

'Good. She is a woman,' said Hugh, pointing at Jacinta, whose hands and forearms were encased in yellow rubber gloves, a plastic pinafore protecting her clothes, strands of hair escaping from a hairband and obscuring her face, as she heaved yet more wet clothes out of a washing machine.

Eddie's eyes bulged. '*She,*' he declaimed at very nearly the top of his voice, 'is a farqueue barsta goddess!'

The men roared with laughter and Jacinta blushed. Linguistic accuracy, mused Hugh, was easily outgunned by communicative effectiveness. It took a few lessons, but he and Eddie were soon exploring the interrogative.

'Ask me where the hammer is.'

'Where's dat farqueue hammer?'

'Good. Screwdriver?'

'Where's dat farqueue screwdriver?'

'Yes. Fifty pounds you owe me?'

'Where's dat farqueue fifty pounds you owe me?'

'Good. Here's twenty pounds.'

'What you mean? Where's de farqueue rest?'

'Excellent.'

Successful language teaching, Hugh decided, was all about supplying what was needed. There was not a building foreman in Britain who would dare do Eddie and his relatives out of a farqueue barsta thirty pounds at the end of that lesson.

13/ Timing

Alex Weaver regarded himself as an expert in the taxonomy of politicians. He found it hard to imagine that he'd not met and studied just about every sort there is to be found. His favourite type were what he referred to as the "flash boys", the ones who flattered to deceive, promising in presentation and attractive in appearance, but whose outward displays of confidence evaporated upon their first encounter with personal criticism, like a very small saucepan of water above a hot flame. He'd seen many of these come and go, and not without a certain relish.

A close second were the "if-only boys and girls", who love to enlarge on their visions of "how things should and could be, if only...". The first whiff of a ruthless machination, or a complex clause in Standing Orders, would send them scuttling back to their ivory towers. Ideas, Weaver knew, might contribute to the "gaiety of notions" but were useless without the will to stand toe to toe and slug it out for their implementation. And it took a particular blend of qualities and flaws to make that happen. Politics was an unpredictable and unforgiving game, and few could claim its mastery.

Despite this grim assessment, Weaver found much to excite his sense of humour. He was observant and enjoyed demonstrations of the ridiculous, such as principled people simmering in their self-righteous juices, or lowly politicians attempting some tiny coup that was well beyond their abilities to clearly conceive, let alone carry through. Best of all was watching and listening to folk who hadn't the foggiest notion of what they wanted to say, yet had several dozen, consecutive, and sometimes concurrent, ways of saying it. When all was said and done, it was clear to Weaver that the successful politician was a rare breed and one that needed to combine certain qualities in precisely the right amounts and degrees. If pressed for details, the qualities he'd recommend for success were largely his own.

These jagged thoughts were prompted by evidence of a recent deception. His trust had been betrayed and the ingrate was the usual suspect. On only three occasions in his reign as Leader had his explicit party whip been ignored; on all three occasions ignored by the same man. The result of the vote on the Rokeby stadium planning application – thirty-eight to six, a crushing victory for his motion – was neither here nor there. The arithmetic should have been thirty-nine to five.

No serious gardener can tolerate a tall, hardy weed in one of his flowerbeds. It can lead to underground root expansion and the eventual choking of all nourishment to the best blooms. No leader who wishes to remain in charge can condone the flouting of his line by the lowliest of his legions.

The remedy, he knew, was simple. Uproot the offending weed and throw it on the steaming compost of history. That's why head gardeners employ underlings like Ken Rudge. One of the great benefits of power was the delegation of heavy work to subordinates. What was the point of being surrounded by supporters, dependants and sycophants if he had to sully his own reputation with the blasted or soggy remains of other people's careers? That, after all, was the whole point of Ken Rudge. A nod was as good as a wink, a raised eyebrow as good as a subtly mouthed epithet.

As soon as Weaver had completed his final meeting of the day, he would arrange to have the party whip withdrawn from Peter Wilde and a candidate found to contest his Council seat at the next election. As far as Weaver was concerned, Wilde was finished in the Party. He was, quite simply, a man in denial and, in many ways, a composite of all the weaknesses Weaver had ever detected in local politicians. The worst of Wilde's sins was that he had never worked out some way of seizing real power. That in itself said it all. If he'd been any good, he'd have been in power by now, but he wasn't. Why prolong an evidently vain and ineffectual career? Weaver could see the headline already - 'Weaver Tames Wilde Streak'.

Peter Wilde was considering his options over a late afternoon pint at his Wild Hill local, 'The Shoot and Duck'. He would often retire to a corner and cogitate with the Guardian crossword as cover. No one disturbed him.

1 Across – Co-operative place of learning about one in place (10)

4 Down – Willing on finish leading to conclusion (7)

There were plenty of people willing the end of his career, and he'd spotted the minimal nods between Weaver and Rudge as the result of the vote was announced in the Council Chamber. It used to be said that a dog was allowed one bite. This was his third. Allowing this to pass would suggest a weakness in Weaver, and weakness was the last shortcoming a man such as Weaver could allow.

It was a pity, he mused. Weaver had a few decent qualities. He adored his wife, even to the point of believing she possessed great taste in soft furnishings. He was indulgent to dogs and children. He had belatedly grasped the rudiments of football, even if it only appealed to him as a route to influence and association with money. He even tried to cloak his authoritarianism in the guise of mateyness.

Peter Wilde liked to be fair, but those were the only redeeming features he could dredge from the deep silt of memory. Rising to the surface with these nuggets were also the political corpses of several friends. Highly literate men and women pulverised by the tracked vehicles of political cliché. People of sensibility bludgeoned by pejoratives. The well-heeled and well-meaning ground down by class hatred. Women ignored by patronising oiks. The collegiate outmanoeuvred by the tactical use of previous minutes. The creative gavelled into silence. The ethically-minded by-passed by some covert agenda.

It had to be faced. He and the local Party were poles apart. The recent vote on planning permission for the Dewums' land had shown that a single whip would crack the yes-men and women into voting for something they doubted, even abhorred. A few would even retract their previous convictions by means of some inept and semi-literate rationalisation.

'I believe the scenario of the situation has altered, Mr Chairman, …'

The local Party had become a different beast under Weaver's leadership. The benign Labrador had become a nervous Rottweiler. How had it come to this? How had Weaver morphed from a working man's representative in the early Eighties into a man in denial and an apologist for the status quo in 2015?

But there was no riddle. Wilde had witnessed every example of the man's tacking and jibing over the years. He'd started off as republican, unilateralist, Eurosceptic, anti-Thatcher, anti-global, anti-devolution, anti-euro. As the wind changed direction among the party leaders in Westminster, he jibed, making sure the wind was always behind his slowly advancing career. So now he was not unfaithful to the monarch, a defender of the UK's nuclear weapons, as pro-EU as any metropolitan progressive, an apologist for some of Thatcher's reforms, except her opposition to the euro, which he argued for joining. Until he didn't any longer, when the new Labour PM opposed it.

Over the years, Weaver's most entertaining performance on policy came on the question of proportional representation. He had shifted his position on this so often that Wilde had compared the Party to a male dance partner swinging around the ballroom floor at a dizzying tempo with members like Weaver trying to keep in step while travelling backwards in six-inch high heels.

'PR would cement a progressive left-of-centre alliance and keep the Tories in permanent opposition,' Weaver had declared in the late nineties.

'If you bring PR into Westminster, you'll have right-wing nationalists as MPs in Parliament undermining support for your beloved EU, not just doing that as MEPs in Brussels.'

'Don't be daft, Peter. PR broadens and legitimizes democracy.'

'Is that right, Alex. Just remember when the balloon goes up that it took less than seven per cent of the vote to present the EU with our Nigel Farage and what's turning out to be a Trojan horse inside their citadel. Be careful what you wish for.'

'Farage is an asset for us. He splits the Tory vote. By contrast, your constant whingeing doesn't split our vote, Peter, because our local majority is so big, and you are just an irritating splinter.'

There was some truth in that, as things stood. So where could he go now, with Weaver going rogue and the national party appealing to the self-reported identities and lifestyles of the comfortable? Certainly not to the Other Lot, the Tories. A few years earlier he might have considered the Lib Dems, but they'd lost credibility by failing to move beyond pressure group status to become a genuine, national party.

The alternative was to declare himself an Independent, an accurate description but never one to covet. A political party at least offered the company of foot soldiers prepared to fold and deliver leaflets, pay their subs, raise funds, cajole the wavering supporters and keep their ears to the ground. Unless as an Independent he held the balance of power, life would resemble a village without a pub, or a married man suffering… well, never mind, there were pills for that sort of thing, as junk emails reminded him daily. The point was that he would have even less power than now.

As things stood, he was able to change the small things that mattered. Weaver might refuse to discuss the overall regeneration of the Malvoir Valley, but he'd never been foolish enough to interfere when Peter set about righting wrongs for his Wild Hill constituents. If he went Independent, Weaver would erect procedural bollards all over the place, starve his Wild Hill ward of cash, place developments elsewhere. Such were the norms of local politics in the Valley since Weaver became Leader. The only way being an Independent would count for something would be to turf the Party out of power at the next election. But how to overturn a thirty-nine to five majority?

That much was politics. What about principle?

He was deeply fed up with the tribalism. In a town like Manley, where the Party had been in power since the year dot, there was no hope of getting anything done if your district didn't vote the right way. The few suburbs that didn't return a Labour councillor never got a swimming pool or a new library or proper cycle lanes. As far as Weaver was concerned these people were privileged and therefore not entitled, while he was a modern Robin Hood. Which was odd considering that Weaver must now be quite a lot better off than the people he accused of being toffs. Quite how he'd amassed so much capital, consumer goods and frequent flyer miles was beyond anyone's ken. Delving into the details could easily result in a writ. But Wilde had his suspicions. On that basis alone he ought to be proclaiming his independence and organising some solid opposition.

But it didn't stop there. He was convinced that Weaver hadn't given up his Westminster dream. Malcolm Woodbridge, the sitting MP, had disappointed many in London and the Valley with an unexpected show of political conviction. He just would not accept that globalisation was good for all. "The man's a wooden bridge to the past" was Weaver's feeble joke.

At this rate the local party would be deselecting the incumbent and looking for a new candidate. The Rokeby development could be well underway by the next general election. Step forward Alex Weaver, local political genius, backed by all the powers that be in local affairs. Big-shot business people would back him out of gratitude, and quite a few local government officers would be only too glad to be shot of him. And Alex would finally get what he'd always wanted. Not that it would do anyone else much good. That wasn't the point of politics as far as Weaver was concerned.

Peter uncapped his pen, pondered and filled in the squares for 1 Across. C-O-L-L-E-G-I-A-T-E. Then he pulled the latest edition of the Manley Observer from beneath The Guardian and re-read the main story.

THE BATTLE BEGINS.
Action Group Formed to Fight Development

A historic local village has become the focal point for opposition to the proposed stadium and retail development in the Malvoir Valley. The newly formed Greater Rokeby-on-Bass Action Group (GROBAG) has vowed to protest the multi-million project all the way to the House of Lords if necessary.

Chairperson Tracy Morgan claims that GROBAG has a growing petition, with over three thousand signatures so far and many more to come.

'The Council Leader,' she declares, 'needs to be aware of the strength of feeling, not just in Rokeby-on-Bass, but right across the Malvoir Valley. We are not against the development as such. We are against it destroying a local

beauty spot which has been a superb amenity for so many Valley residents.'

Responding to a charge of nimbyism, Tracy Morgan added, 'There are plenty of other sites where it could be better located. At the moment, the project as proposed looks like a fig leaf for a large, upmarket housing development. If the Council were really concerned with housing needs, there are far better ways of satisfying them.'

Council Leader Alex Weaver has rejected this assessment. 'I can understand the concerns of some Rokeby residents. But, as Leader, I have to concern myself with the long-term interests of all residents with regard to future employment opportunities and housing requirements. The wider benefits of this proposal for the entire Malvoir Valley are manifest.'

Peter returned to his national newspaper and downed the last of his pint. He chewed briefly on the end of his pen before filling in 4 Down, E-N-D-G-A-M-E.

Then he rose to take himself to the offices of the Manley Observer where he would announce his resignation from the Party in favour of independence, before Alex Weaver had time to announce a party meeting to have him expelled. To retain credibility, timing was all.

14/ A Wobbly Chair

GROBAG's first campaign meeting was barely ten minutes old before Tracy was hankering after the little house on the seafront she'd renounced in favour of this battle.

'I think we should dress up as dormice and picket the Council buildings.'

'I think you should stand well clear of the Council buildings and I'll bring my tractor in with trailer with a coupla tonnes a' silage and spray the blimmin' place.'

'And while you're at it, aim your sprayer through the Chief Planning Officer's windows. That place is a scandal.'

'I see what you're saying, but that's another question entirely, and it may be worth another tonne of silage, but it'd 'ave to be a different consignment altogether…'

'As you know, I don't advocate violent protest of any sort. Instead, I feel we should be informing the people of Malvoir Valley about the environment we're about to lose and the alternatives to concreting over the landscape. I had a book published last year called 'Sussing It Out' and I think we could make a start by distributing the introduction as a booklet to all households in the county…'

'What we need to do is unite. If we are united we can fight. We have to show that the government is playing fast and loose with our future. And I don't mean my future… I'm too old for them to worry about… I recognised that when I lost my pension in 1991 and the government didn't want to know… but never mind that… I'm talking about the youngsters' future… they're the people we need to be thinking about… and if we are prepared to fight for them, they'll unite with us. But you've got to be united in order to fight…'

It was clear to all eighty people in the hall that Gerald Corby was far too nice a man to be in the chair. It was also clear to him. He would purse his lips and begin to raise his hand as if on the cusp of intervening, but would then allow a speaker to ramble on, or allow another to butt in without going through the Chair. His indulgent smiles spoke volumes about forbearance but did nothing for the brisk dispatch of business.

Tracy could have stood for Chair but calculated that the organisation needed efficiency and drive in running its day-to-day business. Anyone could orchestrate a meeting, or so she thought. Gerald Corby looked the part. You could imagine him making the right impression in the movement's press releases and campaign literature. Tall with aquiline features, well-groomed and neatly dressed, with a clear voice and equable manner. Yet he was somehow lacking in cold steel.

As a half dozen contributors who were not out of love with their own voices held forth and drove the meeting into obscure byways, the silent portion of the assembly exchanged glances, rolled their eyes, or cast them down in case there was something of greater interest happening to their shoe laces. It dawned on Tracy that a feeble hand on the tiller could run the most seaworthy of boats onto the rocks.

She raised the pencil that had so far not recorded a single item of interest. 'Mr Chairman, could I move that we stay with the agenda and those who wish to speak go through the Chair?'

As the majority in the hall let out a collective murmur of approval, Gerald Corby cast her a look of gratitude mixed with fear. Tiny beads of sweat were forming on his upper lip.

'Thank you, Tracy. The item is, suggestions for recruiting more members. Any ideas, please.'

'If you're united you can always get more members...'

The hall groaned and Tracy stepped in quickly.

'Yes, thank you. Through the Chair, please…That gentleman over there has had his hand up for some time. I'm sorry I don't know your name.'

'Jim Phillips. I don't normally get involved in action groups, so I don't have any experience. But it seems to me we need a big hitter or two. I know we have Robin Smythe-Banks on our side but, with respect, he's a member of the Conservative Party. You'd expect him to oppose the development. It would help our cause if we had someone closer to the wheels of power who is also opposed. As it happens, I was in the pub the other day chatting to Councillor Peter Wilde, and I got the very distinct impression that he would be willing to become an outspoken supporter. If he did, I think we'd pick up quite a few more members…'

Tracy noted the suggestion but kept her counsel as the discussion flowed back and forth on Councillor Wilde's merits and shortcomings. But she found the suggestion dispiriting. Red Peter. Wilde with Zeal. She could see it all. The people's uprising against the developers becoming politicised, losing its freshness, however chaotic, and finally selling out in some unhappy backroom deal. She'd rather go for a leisurely swim near a sewage farm.

But Gerald had suddenly discovered a Chairman-like tone. 'All those in favour of approaching Councillor Wilde?'

She counted forty-three hands.

'All those against?'

She counted thirty-eight. Just as she thought. Peter Wilde would split GROBAG right down the middle. But Gerald was addressing her.

'Would you write the letter or make the call, Tracy?'

'If I must.' She made another note. Contact the Wilde man.

'Any other suggestions?'

Liz Greyve-Traine, the author of "Sussing It Out", only needed to meet a Chairman's gaze for permission to speak. Like most of the assembly, Tracy knew her by name and sight, and often came across news of her latest publication in the Manley Observer. She was published by her husband, Mick Greyve-Traine, who ran a small publishing firm, largely financed from lottery funds and regional enterprise monies.

Together they'd become a local 'power couple'. Their main interest was 'green issues' and saving the environment, if not the world, for future generations. Although Tracy was all for this – how could anyone be against? – she couldn't help feeling that she'd prefer to be saved by people with a little less notion of their own virtue. She'd even tried reading one of Greyve-Traine's books a few years ago and couldn't fail to notice that in portraying the injustices of the world, the lens of the overworked prose always refocused on her.

'I'm quite happy to bring my writing expertise to the campaign and I should be able to mobilise a couple of hundred environmental activists across the Valley. Of course, we can bring in more from outside, if necessary.'

The hall buzzed its approval, but Tracy couldn't help putting a damper on all the mutual love.

'Mr Chairman, may I ask if that includes a commitment to bringing in members with their membership fees?'

But Liz Greyve-Traine, for all her apparent New Age credentials, was a consummate politician. 'I couldn't speak for the individuals involved, but I'm sure each and every one sympathises with the aims of this action group.'

Sympathy buys precious few leaflets, thought Tracy. And she'd noticed that Mick Greyve-Traine wasn't offering to donate any printing costs to the cause. But, at meeting's end, she lined up dutifully alongside the Greyve-Traines and the rest of the GROBAG officers for the Manley Observer press photos. Quite how Mick and Liz managed to get themselves in the centre of the shot was a mystery, but it clearly worked for them.

As the remaining clusters drifted away, Gerald Corby hung back.

'I don't think I'm the right person for this job after all, Tracy. It needs someone with better management skills.'

It was, she recognised, an honest assessment by an honest man. There'd been moments when she feared the focus of the action group was already fraying, beset by sectional and personal interests: militant farmers, sound-of-their-own-voicists, bandwagon merchants, even literary opportunists. If all that wasn't enough, she was now tasked with finding a new Chairman, and getting in touch with a man she loathed to beg for his support. She foresaw an evening of lonely recuperation, with a highland spirit in one hand and a re-run of "Strictly Ballroom" on the box. She really should have plumped for that cottage by the sea.

Part Three

Winter

15/ Hunkering Down

The mildest of autumn weather continued through Halloween, past Bonfire Night and was threatening the Christmastide with balmy nights, unseasonal insects, bewildered birds and bushes in bud. But the cold fingers of the north wind reached out one night in early December and froze all living things back to a natural order of frostiness.

The inhabitants of the Grey House barn woke shivering, a condition the two stoves working around the clock were powerless to improve. An icy wind howled through the gaps and knotholes in the wooden walls. The same clothes were worn indoors as out, and a family meeting determined that the barn would have to be insulated. As a first step, materials were collected from near and far. Hugh preferred not to ask too many questions about provenance. Normally he would not have allowed "liberated" supplies on his property, but he'd noticed of late that almost everyone else was drinking at the trough of undocumented perks. At worst he'd be no better than the norm.

In any case, he was beginning to enjoy his new lifestyle. Although he'd experienced a certain sort of competitive camaraderie at school, it had lacked personal warmth, while the Zielinskys treated him as part of a common project.

'It's more than that,' said Feliks. 'We think of you as part of the family.'

It was them against the world. For generations their family had learned to work together against many a deadly foe: German and Russian imperialists, home-grown collaborators, German and Soviet totalitarians, home-grown informers. Their farmlands had been looted by waves of armed gangs with or without recognisable insignia and official warrants. The Zielinsky peasants had learned how to hobble horses temporarily against requisitioners, camouflage their grain supplies, hide their young men from the military press-gangs and their women against the natural appetites of men with guns.

They were cheerful cynics, quick to suspect and scrutinise everybody else's motives, but without losing their zest for life. Saturday nights were a perfect example, when the home-made vodka, made in a stainless-steel sink liberated from a skip, was served in tiny crystal glasses. These were raised to Hugh as their host and the Zielinskys proceeded to drink themselves into oblivion, but not before passing through various stages of eloquence, elation and voluble incoherence. Even Jacinta would join in, drinking fruit-flavoured versions of the hooch, but never reaching more than a giggly stage, knowing that a few hours later she had to rouse sixteen overhung wrecks, who either had to get to work on time or attend early morning Mass in a shriveable condition.

In drink, each man transformed into some parody of himself. A few began to squabble, hector and screech. Izzy would at first shrink into his shell and gaze around the table at these antics like a cuddly koala, but switch suddenly into an all-singing, all-dancing adolescent bear in charge of festivities. Eddie would plant his imposing rear-end on a bench and regard all the fuss with a disapproving and quizzical air, moving only to raise and lower a tiny glass barely visible in his great fist.

Only when he finally rose from the bench were the effects of the hooch made plain. He would sway like a rhinoceros caught in two minds, his great feet stamping the floorboards to establish some sort of equilibrium, then lurch suddenly this way and that, people on either side raising their arms to avert the full consequences of a crushing experience, only to see him turn on something larger than a 5p piece and make off in a completely unexpected direction. The placement of each foot became one narrowly averted nose-dive after another. He made the return journey look like a ferry passenger staggering towards his seat in a violent storm.

Only Feliks maintained his usual show of dignity and did his best to protect himself and Hugh from the constant refills and endless toasts. Even then, they would greet each other the next morning with sheepish smiles and the croaks of hard-won experience.

The change to working on the barn meant that progress on the house was postponed. Eddie insisted on a quality job, which meant the exterior planks had to be detached and a waterproof membrane tacked across the framework before the planks were replaced. This stage had to be carefully planned and swiftly executed during the daytime when most of the men were at work elsewhere.

Hugh pitched in, discovering that he had as much confidence as the others in mounting a ladder, working level with the eaves to jemmy loose the planks or nail them back in place. All his life he'd been trained to discern requirements and give orders. Now he found himself being told what to do in barely comprehensible language. The splintered fingers, bruised thumbs and grazed elbows were minor wounds gratefully received. He also noticed that a job well done was more satisfying than a job he had to appraise with a critical eye. He wondered how much of the critique he and his ancestors had dished out to servants, employees or contractors was habitual, not objective.

Once the outside boards were replaced, other teams spent their evening hours rolling out the variously thick and discoloured rolls of insulation. Their hues varied from bright yellow to 'old barnyard', evidence of diligent scavenging by the Zielinskys. There were two long nights of further hammering as the interior cladding was nailed into place, but by then the men were taking off their pullovers indoors, complaining of the warmth and urging their relatives to feed less fuel to the stoves.

Though work on the Grey House was delayed for more than a week, Hugh was not disheartened. He was beginning to believe. The slate roof was now in place and the Chief Planning Officer had been informed without turning up in person or responding with an injunction. As far as Hugh was concerned, he could now take as long as he liked over the interior renovation. Once the Zielinskys had moved on, as they undoubtedly would, he would find a job, maybe train as an English language teacher, and travel the world for a while. He would always have the Grey House to come back to. The Zielinskys had shown him that life could go on very well in imperfect conditions. His house didn't have to be a model of what a country cottage was meant to be. If anything, it was an aspiration, an almost blank sheet that he could inscribe. In that sense he'd been liberated from that larger inheritance he'd had to constantly improve and at the same time conserve for future generations. Gone were the accusations of betraying his stewardship.

Even so, he could hardly bear to walk to the high ground overlooking Deverill Court. A concrete-block wall was being erected around the old stable yard. How could any Planning Officer allow such a desecration? The last of the small businesses had been evicted and the paraphernalia of enterprise removed. The office and workshop interiors were being stripped out and replaced with stalls and half doors. Skips and builders' junk littered the yard. The yellow digging arm of a JCB hung above the west wing like a metalled mantis. Just out of sight was the large pit that he'd heard would soon be a private swimming pool with its accessories of hot tubs, whirlpools, saunas and barbecues. He knew that the oak tree planted in the garden by his Grandmother on the day of his birth had been grubbed up to make way for the pool. How had that escaped the eagle eye of the planning officers? And just south and beyond the new pool area, in plain view, lay what was rumoured to be an indoor tennis court, although its concrete-block walls and corrugated roof could just as easily be a shed for battery-raised chickens. No doubt the walls would be plastered and given a lick of whitewash, but such a building on such a site demonstrated an astonishing elasticity in the interpretation of planning regulations.

Perhaps it would look neat once all the work was completed, the scars in the landscape smoothed over and healed, but Hugh felt that Deverill Court was taking a step back into the past and cutting itself off from the local community. It had once been a County seat giving employment to many. Hugh had tried to retain that role by offering work and accommodation to people with deep roots and permanent connections to the rural economy, even if much of modern farming was now performed by specialist contractors who travelled many miles between jobs. But the drab new wall around the stables was a shift in direction. The Court was about to become a gated residence, cut off from its surroundings, its assets unshared with local people. As Mary had suggested, when he was just old enough to appreciate the point, every house, great or small, mirrors the character and personality of its owners.

A small glimmer of hope appeared one day in the person of Tracy Morgan turning up at the barn to recruit him to an action group. She caught him and several of the Zielinskys in full insulating mode, looking like farm labourers from an earlier era, their hair matted with dust and cobwebs, their hands grimy, their faces smudged and their clothes emitting clouds of sawdust at the slightest contact. Hugh and Tracy knew each other well from tennis club and charity events, but her swift glances around his new abode betrayed unease. This didn't stop her stepping into the barn, accepting a cup of powerful coffee, served by Jacinta Polish-style, and delivering her pitch.

'GROBAG,' mused Hugh. 'What seeds are you planting?'

She rolled with it, not remotely offended.

'We're mostly a bunch of old bags who intend to get bigger.'

'To achieve what?'

'Stop this whole development. It's clearly a fig leaf for all sorts of things. The developers want to maximise their return from so-called executive-style houses. There's hardly any social housing and there's absolutely no need to put it in Rokeby-on-Bass. Your scheme for an eco-village was just what this area needs, but they're going for the old-fashioned gravy train model. It'll be cheap materials with fancy facades, no green design built in, and no infrastructure for years to come until the local community council is able to solve all the problems the developers wash their hands of...'

'That's fighting talk.'

'Of course. Slugging it out from the baseline. That's my game.'

'How many signatures on the petition so far?'

'Six thousand two hundred and twenty-three.'

'Not bad.'

'And they're still coming in at a rate of about two hundred a week.'

Hugh thought for an instant. 'Just a mo. I want you to meet someone.'

He came back with Feliks who'd taken over Hugh's place at the top of the ladder and had just dislodged an old bird's nest with the top of his head. Despite his appearance, he shook Tracy's hand gravely and addressed her with an old-world charm and a transatlantic-European drawl.

'This is Feliks. He has a Master's in Politics. He's fascinated by elections and political processes. So, if you need any practical help and advice, he's your man.'

She looked sceptical – Feliks did after all have the remains of a bird's nest in his hair – but she gave him a chance by outlining the aims of the action group in a slow and clear tone of voice, her gaze locked onto his features for any signs that she was speaking too quickly or using unfamiliar words.

When she appeared to have finished, Hugh turned to Feliks.

'Did you understand any of that?'

He cottoned on instantly.

'I think Tracy's looking for classic action group strategy and tactics, combining high-visibility protests and major-impact publicity to exert leverage locally and nationally. In addition, the factual case has to be watertight and capable of rebutting counter-activity by the proponents of the development scheme.'

Hugh turned to Tracy. 'Do you think he'll do?'

Her eyeballs, he noticed, were suddenly available for a complete inspection. 'Well… we can't afford to pay anyone on a professional basis.'

'You wouldn't need to pay me.'

'But it would be a lot of work.'

'It would be good work experience in my specialist area.'

Tracy handed over a card with her home address. 'It's our headquarters at the moment. Come to tea one day when you're free.'

'Go tomorrow,' said Hugh. 'We've got plenty of hands for this job.'

'Tomorrow, then.'

It was agreed. Hugh could tell that Feliks had at last found an outlet for his real passion. They saw Tracy to her car.

'Lovely to see you again, Hugh. I wish I could say the same about my meeting this evening. I've been instructed to recruit Peter Wilde to the cause.'

'Ah… yes…' said Hugh. 'I remember his last election slogan. "Wilde for You". Best of luck.'

16/ Innocence And Immortality

The atmosphere at Rich and Quick's presentation was heady. An exclusive country hotel. Designer images of stadiums and housing estates lining the walls. Directors, senior partners, civil engineers, architects, chief execs, lawyers, landed gentry, sports club chairmen and their managers with a few high-profile players. Plus the press pack, and one politician – himself. Alex Weaver didn't want too many of those trying to elbow their way into the group photos and he'd made sure not to publicise the date of the press launch to Councillors.

The big-screen power-point presentation by the senior architects of Glance & Sein was pregnant with all the buzzwords. The estate would be green, sustainable, communal. The spine road that joined it to two major roads would be TDE - transport-delivery-efficient. The variously shaped crescents and cul-de-sacs would maximise available space constraints while delivering optimal outdoor amenities. Best practice analysis of functional services allocation would deliver a combination of topmost community benefit combined with maximised privacy preservation.

A rapt audience hummed, murmured and sighed its approval as each computerised image flooded the giant screen to illustrate a point. A round of applause greeted the virtual tour of a similar stadium designed for an Austrian city. Phrases like "cutting edge", "21st century" and "high-tech" punched through the power ballads and reverberated around the conference hall. How could the teams playing in such a stadium not march out of the small time and into the bigger leagues?

At the reception that followed, Alex Weaver sipped his champagne and hovered at Gerry Quick's shoulder, happily acknowledging his friend's accolade as "the man who started the ball rolling".

'There's every chance it'll all be named after 'im. Should be. Scandal if it's not.'

The film crews and photographers were close at hand. Not only was he posing for photographs, but he was also being asked to sign autographs alongside footballers, models and WAGs. He was even making eye contact with an elegant redhead in charge of the undernourished mannequins.

The only downside was that Barbara would certainly see the results in the papers and want to know why she hadn't been invited. He'd have to claim ignorance. Thought it was simply a straight business presentation. Blame Gerry Quick. But somewhere in his heart Alex Weaver was glad he'd come alone. This was now his natural stage. This is what he'd worked for, his legacy.

He glanced once more at a bird's eye view of the proposed estate. He imagined its northern side following the curves of the River Bass, its southern end striking like an arrow's head into the greenery between Rokeby-on-Bass and Rokeby Castle. In soft focus it could easily pass for an italicised '*W*' etched into the landscape. Weaver Stadium in Weaver Town. His mark was very nearly made.

'Hello, I'm Janine.'

It was the redhead. Tall, stunning, green-eyed. He was caught in two minds. Be flattered, or play the incorruptible man-'o-the-people?

'Alex Weaver. But I'm not a celebrity. Just a Council Leader.'

'I know. Gerry Quick was telling me how all this was your idea.'

'Well, I suppose it was, in a way.' Uncharacteristically, he tried a lop-sided, self-effacing smile, with mixed success he felt, and made a mental note to stay away from unfamiliar self-projections.

'You don't remember me, do you?'

He looked more closely, ransacked his memory. 'No, I...'

'That's all right. It was a long time ago and I was very young.'

Slight panic. He'd kissed a secretary or two at Christmas parties, but that was by mutual consent and way back in the eighties and nineties when it was still sort of acceptable and not likely to land you in court, or up before an employment tribunal.

'You were handing out prizes at our school sports day. I was victrix ludorum.'

That far back? When he was a community council mayor and schools had competitive sports days.

'So,' he said, still fazed by her physical presence, 'you were a Manley girl?'

'Not particularly,' she grinned, 'just quick.'

'No, I didn't mean…'

She reached forward and touched his arm. 'It's OK, I know what you mean. It must be the oldest joke in town.'

'Probably.' It was unnerving. He could feel himself blushing. Alex Weaver turning pink. That hadn't happened since… well, never mind. He needed to recover quickly. 'So, what have you been doing since school?'

It was her turn to manage some embarrassment. 'Oh, you know. Went into modelling. Did a bit of TV. Got married, unmarried…'

Promising, he thought.

'… then I started my own modelling agency.'

'Based locally?'

'No, London, of course. But Gerry asked me to do this gig.'

Of course, he thought, Gerry was a regular talent-spotter. He *would* know a woman like Janine. All of a sudden, Weaver was overcome with an aversion to his own metier. There were too few Janines in local politics to keep life interesting.

'Can I get you another glass of champagne?'

'No, thanks. This is sparkling water. I never drink when working.'

She leaned forward confidentially. 'What I'd really like… is a slice of Ma Grady's lardy cake.'

'Ma Grady. She's still there, you know. Still going strong.'

'I heard. Gerry told me. I used to haunt her little café. I bet she remembers me.'

'Well, why don't we go there right now? She'll still be open.'

She thought about it for a moment. 'OK. I'll get my assistant to get the girls safely back to London.'

He watched her walk away. The body of a ballet dancer in high heels. He felt light-headed, as if he'd had more than a single glass of champagne. A speck of guilt landed in his euphoria, but he ignored it. A slice of lardy cake in a twee café with a former Manley schoolgirl? What could be more innocent?

17/ A Walk On The Wilde Side

Tracy was bristling long before she arrived at the pub, her reluctance for this meeting expressed in her selection of clothes. She'd spent half an hour trying to balance dressing up against a carefully considered dressing down. After all, it was a meeting in a pub on a notorious housing estate just two bus stops from a medium security prison.

To make matters worse, her "appropriate" wardrobe no longer fitted. Zips closed on a deep breath in… and slipped a couple of inches on the exhale. So she dithered until twenty minutes to seven, till there was only time to pull off her indoor cardi and throw on a battered wax jacket. In effect, she was saying she couldn't care less what anybody thought of her, far less about making a favourable impression on Peter Wilde. Though she did revisit the bedroom to insert her favourite earrings – a question of self-respect.

She'd much rather have stayed at home to watch a repeat of "Northanger Abbey". Instead she'd lost valuable time battling with her old TV's unreliable record function. She could have seen the wretched man earlier in the day at his local "surgery" – a ridiculous, self-aggrandising word for a politician to use – but he couldn't guarantee her more than five minutes; or so he claimed.

'We've got a housing association crisis in Wild Hill at present.'

So she'd agreed to drive in from the green and pleasant land of Rokeby-on-Bass and make her way to a pub called "The Shoot and Duck" on the edge of Wild Hill. The names alone added a roughly cut serrated edge to her unease.

She half-expected to find a carpark full of souped-up Fords with dubious main keeper records but found instead half an acre of asphalt boasting a single, rather sedate-looking Rover of pre-Chinese vintage.

She felt exposed and lonely as she passed beneath a pub sign depicting a mallard and a gathering of eighteenth-century country gentlemen armed with fowling pieces. Looking in through one of the ancient sash windows she spotted her quarry sitting alone in the lounge bar beside the glowing embers of an open fireplace and reading a newspaper.

'Sorry, I'm late.'

'No problem. Only just got here myself.'

The half-consumed pint beside the newspaper belied this assertion. He was holding her hand in a firm, warm handshake, which her brain decided to file as "surprisingly unclammy".

'What can I get you?'

'Oh…' It was so long since she'd been in a pub. 'I'll have half a bitter.'

'Manley Best or Manley Mild?' He noticed her hesitation. 'A pretty good year for the mild. I'd recommend that.'

'A mild then.' She wasn't at all familiar with men who knew their beers. Her ex-husband had been a wine expert. Self-appointed. Always insisted, with a disdainful air, that the Manley Brewery produced liquid soap. She remembered with a degree of shame how she used to smile along like an accomplice in snobbery. Until, that is, she'd finally rumbled his pretensions.

'Can I get you anything else?'

'No… thanks. I've eaten already.'

'Right… ,' he placed her glass on a coaster. 'Well, we're all alone here. How can I help?'

She wasn't sure if he'd recognised her. Surely, he hadn't forgotten their heated exchange, even if it was many years before? But there was no hint, around his rather crinkled and friendly gaze, of defensiveness or recrimination.

'As you know, I'm secretary of GROBAG and I've been instructed

139

by the members to approach you and ask if you'd join or support our cause.'

She'd expected a knowing chuckle and an evasive refusal. A putdown even. After all, she represented the countrified persuasion and he the town centre. Her world was fresh air and farmer's markets while, in his province, youthful, tee-shirted denizens of the night made it impossible for people like her to visit after nine o'clock, first by trying to drink the town dry then misinterpreting the many TO LET signs along the High Street.

'Well, straight off, as a Councillor, I couldn't join. That would make me ineligible to vote on this matter. But that doesn't mean I won't do whatever I can to help. The development in the Rokeby area would affect the residents I represent here in Wild Hill, so I'm free to take a view.'

He seemed straight and sincere, which made her all the more suspicious. Was it true that he wanted the housing to be built near Rokeby-on-Bass and the stadium in Wild Hill? That's what some GROBAG members were saying, but she decided against confronting him with this allegation at an early stage.

'You mean, you'd help unofficially? Because we've got a superb political consultant on board. Someone trained in the US.'

She didn't know why she was saying this. Quite unnecessary, and not entirely true. She had no idea if Feliks Zielinsky could write accurate English, let alone organise a credible campaign.

He smiled. Still warmly, but perhaps with a hint of scepticism. 'Yes, I heard. You'll need all the skilled support you can get. But try to hang on to the initial enthusiasm, though you're bound to lose a few fairly quickly. Are you putting yourself up for the chairmanship?'

'We have a chairman already.'

'I thought he was thinking of resigning?'

'How do you know that?'

His smile was suddenly apologetic but not ingratiating. 'I don't mean to be intrusive. It's just that everybody knows everything in local politics. People who know me go to all the meetings...'

'And they report back to you?'

'Not report, exactly. But we meet up at lunchtime and the gossip does the rounds. It's the way it works. Your beer all right?'

Unused to mixing business with the smaller pleasures, she hadn't even tasted it. She took a sip. 'Yes, very... Mmm... yes... rather good.' It really was. A pleasant surprise. 'I'm sorry, you have to realise that I'm not a professional politician and I've never been involved in anything like this before. So I'm bound to come across as a political...,' she was about to say 'virgin', but thought better of it, '...ingenue.'

'The best sort of politician, in my view. Unsullied. Asks all the right questions. But I know what you mean. It's a rough old business and you need skin as thick as a rhino's hide. A lot of good people can't stomach it.'

She wanted to ask if he therefore considered himself a good or not-so-good person, but they were straying too far into the personal. They were bound to hit the personality buffers sooner or later. Stick to business.

'As you have so much experience, I'd really appreciate advice.'

'All right, then.' He took a long draught of beer. 'To begin with, put yourself up for the chairmanship. You're the one who's galvanised this opposition and you've got the qualities to take it forward.'

'Why on earth do you think that?'

'Two things. I've followed the local sports pages over the years and I've a pretty good idea of your leadership qualities.'

She nodded. There was no flattery in that. It was perfectly justified. 'And the second?'

His smile widened boyishly and there was a definite twinkle in the eye. 'I recall being on the wrong end of a fairly withering putdown some years ago...'

So, he hadn't forgotten. But she felt this was getting a little too chummy for comfort. She could have admitted to the embarrassment she'd felt at the time but wasn't sure how wise it would be to become too friendly with Peter Wilde.

'I seem to remember you deserving it,' she replied.

This delighted him. 'I'm sure you're right, though I don't remember what prompted it.'

'You were rude to my husband.'

'Perfectly good reason. You sprang to his defence. I think I've learned to stick to facts these days. It's better to play the ball not the man. So, I apologise now to you and your husband.'

Was this mildly tongue in cheek?

'Accepted for my part, but I've stopped passing on messages to my ex-husband.'

'I see. If I remember he was secretary of the local Conservatives at one time?'

'He was. And I was a member, too.'

'But not anymore?'

'No.' She was ashamed to admit that she'd been only, as it were, a sleeping member. As soon as her husband started sleeping with someone else... . I was too sheep-like, she thought, too stupid for words.

His gaze suggested empathy and, God forbid, some understanding of her thoughts. 'Emotions ran high in those days, and a lot of people said things they regret now.'

'True.' She was thinking of her ex-husband's triumphalism. Of how he would punch the air at TV images of policemen arresting environmental activists. Or jeer at the sight of good men and women trying to make a case for fairness. 'But the world ain't fair, matey,' was his constant, mimicking refrain.

'Another half?'

Astonishingly her glass was nearly empty. 'No, let me get them. Then we need to get down to business.' She hoped her manner suggested an end to all the chit-chat. 'A pint for you?'

'No, just a half. I have more work waiting at home.'

She watched the barmaid pull the creamy brew and was reminded of her days at university, the only time she'd ever been a barstool fixture. Happy times, on the whole, and the time she'd felt most fulfilled.

'Well…,' she began, returning to their corner. He'd placed a couple of fresh logs on the fire and was now pushing them into the right positions with a poker, demonstrating, she thought, his status as a regular in "The Shoot and Duck". '… I hope you don't mind my picking your brains like this.'

'Feel free.'

'Right. Let's suppose I'm elected chairman… woman… person…'

'I still say chairman, whatever the gender.'

'Right. I'm elected. Then what?'

'I think you have a problem with discipline at meetings.'

'How do you…? Oh, I see.'

'Yes, I had a verbal report on the last one. Look, all organisations need procedural rules. I can jot down some Standing Orders. It'll just mean that the usual suspects can't dominate meetings and waste everybody's time.'

She was chastened. That's exactly what happened.

'I'll send them over by email. Copy them up for the next meeting and put them top of the agenda.'

She was taking notes.

'Introduce me to your consultant and I'll brief him on local conditions and what kind of leaflets to produce.'

'We've done a leaflet already.'

'You'll need one a month, at least, and you'll have to print off swift reactions to any major developments.'

'I'm not sure we can afford it.'

'Then you'll have to raise funds. I'll email some ideas. Your consultant will know what I mean.'

As he rattled off a long list of practical suggestions, she couldn't decide if she was daunted or energised by all the things that needed doing.

'The important thing is focus. Don't worry about setbacks or successes along the way. The only thing that matters is getting this development stopped in its tracks. One favourable decision means nothing. There will be appeals and counter-appeals. It'll run for years. You've got to be prepared for the long haul. I've seen it time and again.'

She stopped scribbling, pen poised. 'Why do *you* want it stopped?'

'Because I think it will end very differently to the way it's being presented. My guess is that there'll never be a stadium. There will only be a housing estate built to mediocre standards, with over-priced properties. There could even be a development company that files for bankruptcy as soon as it's completed, so the Council will have to pick up the bills for all the uncompleted infrastructure.'

'No, wait a minute…that's much worse than even I suspected. Why do you believe that?'

A wry grin. 'I can't say, because I don't want writs thumping into my palms. Don't get me wrong, there are plenty of decent politicians out there, and some very good property developers for that matter. I'm not blindly ideological about this. That would be a stupid position to take. Let's just say I have experience of the people involved in this instance.'

He was about to say, 'And I've heard that the presentation to the press was glitzy but full of conditional language. Lots of woulds, coulds and shoulds.' But he bit his tongue, fearing the writs. They'd clean him out. He went instead for a general observation.

'The Malvoir Valley looks the way it does because landowners have the upper hand. The Stourvilles have industrialised the southern valley piecemeal because they don't live there, and their main business is extracting rent. Now we suddenly have two landowning families in the Valley who need serious injections of cash. So, we locals will just have to put up with whatever they decide. They usually get what they want in the end, and if they can get the likes of Alex Weaver to smooth their path so much the better.'

It wasn't what she wanted to hear. Surely, it couldn't be – shouldn't be – that easy for the moneyed will to override the popular won't. There had to be some other reason for his opposition.

'Is this also something personal for you?'

'If you mean my rivalry with Alex Weaver, no. I think Alex is misguided. I've no hard evidence that he's corrupt in the usual... in the worst sense. If we're lucky, it'll be a different kind of corruption. He's been seduced by his own ambition. Which can be a good thing in a politician. But sometimes it leads to terrible consequences for the public at large. If I thought this would lead to lots of good things for most people, I wouldn't object. In fact, I was a supporter of Hugh Brooke's eco-village. If that was on the same site, I'd be a supporter and we'd probably be on opposite sides of the argument...'

'But I'm not a nimby. I'd support an eco-village, too. Even... *especially* in Rokeby...'

His expression hardened sceptically, then softened into acceptance. 'What do you reply when people call you a nimby?'

'Well… I… what do you say?'

'Depends on the circumstances. But, in this case, I'd say I wouldn't mind good developments in my back yard, but I oppose badly thought out developments in my face. That would make me a NIMF, unlikely as that is for me. Much more plausible for you.'

If he was trying to flatter, she was determined not to nibble the bait. But she started writing down NYMPH in large capitals on her pad, then twigged what she was doing, crossed it out, and wrote NIMF – Not In My Face.

'But, for me, it's not just about a new housing development. It's about life under Weaver. He's keen to build houses and a stadium. But we've never had decent sports facilities in the Valley, not even a full-size athletics track. Where are the bicycle lanes, the paths for ramblers, the kiddies' playgrounds, the youth clubs, the public spaces? Where are the real attempts to introduce green solutions? I mean, the ones that vested interests might not fancy?'

His eyebrows were cocked, challenging her to tell him where all these worthy initiatives could be found. But she knew that, even in the good times, demand had far outstripped supply.

'And where's the democratic accountability, the real consultation? The way things are under Weaver, we might as well appoint the boards of supermarkets or building companies to run our local government.' He paused. 'Sorry, I'm going off on one.'

'No, really, it's … interesting.'

This was no lie. He was speaking her mind, too, although these were ideas she'd never framed outside the workings of her own indignation.

'It's a habit I'll never tame.' He smiled. 'Look, as things pan out, I'll tell you what I suspect, if the evidence can bear the weight of my suspicions. But we'll need to trust each other.'

So, she thought, he doesn't trust me either.

'But there's one thing you need to prepare for, if you really want to stop this thing.'

He paused as if she was bound to know what he meant. But she didn't.

'There's a local election coming up next year. In May. Put up Independent candidates right across the Valley and try to get Alex Weaver out of power.'

'But that's not even a possibility, is it? I mean, mathematically. He's got a huge majority.'

'He has now. But the margins in local politics are elastic. About a third of voters actually vote, often fewer. They don't know what they could be voting *for* in local politics, so they stay away in droves. But if they take a dislike to something or someone, they'll turn out. It's so much easier to get people to vote *against* something. And in sufficient numbers to prove that Weaver's so-called majority is a house of cards.'

It sounded impressive, but so did most orators speaking an unfamiliar language. She regarded him as she would a tennis opponent practising a devastating service swing without a ball. Once a ball was introduced the service usually revealed itself as a hopeless donkey-drop.

'Are you serious?'

'Perfectly. There are forty-four seats on the Council. A combined opposition would need to capture twenty-three. There are five at the moment, six with me. You need to hold those and win seventeen more. Nine wards haven't had a contest in the last fifteen years. No one stands against the sitting Councillor. But if you can make it a contest between indignation and complacency, it's do-able.'

'But standing for Council is the last thing I want to do. And I think that applies to almost all the GROBAG members.'

'Then you'll get the local governance you deserve. If Weaver has a majority, he'll run rings around any action group standing in his way.

147

He's got all the local big boys on his side, and a few national ones as well. You can't stop a heavy roller with a daisy chain.'

Driving back across town an hour later, her mind was sifting impressions. He was much less prickly than she'd imagined, though she hated the spiky hairstyle. Old goat served up as young buck. Had that been achieved on his own instructions, or had he let some trendy hairdresser loose without supervision? At some moments he was like a large cuddly bear, but with a watchful gaze backed up with some sharp critical faculties. She'd felt he was sizing her up. As a woman? Or as an equal, a co-campaigner? Hard to tell. And he seemed intelligent, or was it just experience combined with cunning? Again, she simply couldn't say. Was he genuinely trying to help, or was he trying to impress? That phrase he'd used as they walked to her car. 'It's not what people say, it's what they do. Keep a close eye on that.' And a tinge of shame at wanting to pry just a little.

'So, you're off home to do some more work?'

''Fraid so.'

'And what does Mrs Wilde think about that?'

'You mean the first or the second Mrs Wilde?'

'Well… I mean the current one.'

'There is no current. But the first and second did have very decided views… clearly.'

'Sorry, I had no idea.'

'Well, we don't, do we?'

She wasn't sure if that was a putdown or just a wise comment on marital complexities. In any case, it provided a clue to the more general puzzle. He must be a difficult man to live with. At least, not an easy one. But whatever her misgivings, she was looking forward to their next meeting to map out strategy and tactics, though she was feeling a little queasy about doing this over a kitchen table with a disaffected

Labour councillor who wasn't a member of GROBAG and a Polish migrant doing who-knew-what.

'Only the final result counts,' Peter Wilde had repeated.

'You mean the end justifies the means?'

'You misunderstand me. Strategy is always worked out by small groups. As chairman you could ask anyone for advice. Then you put it to the vote in the appropriate forum. If they don't like it, they can vote against.'

'So GROBAG is also a form of elective dictatorship?'

'Not at all. Your members don't stand to keep or lose their jobs if they dissent.'

No, she thought. Just lose a lot of sleep and their peace of mind. If there was one thought that would keep her awake at nights, it was the thought of standing as a candidate for Council. She hoped and believed that idea would wither on the vine. Peter Wilde would have to realise that very few people burned with that sort of desire.

18/ Peeling Onions

It had never been Calvin Dewum's intention to live through a British winter. The idea – the deal – had been that he and Lesley-Anne would spend half the year in Britain and half in California. But his flight to warmer climes was being delayed by holes in the ground. British contractors, who claimed that roofs would be on by October, were still standing at the top of craters and staring downwards with expressions of abject insincerity.

'We had another digger break down yesterday.'

Calvin had heard so many similar excuses he was now able to decode their meaning through the smokescreen of local accents. At first, he was infuriated.

'I don't wanna hear it. Just get somebody's – *anybody's* – ass over here and get this job done!'

At which point the contractor would strike an attitude of extreme sensitivity and take offence.

'There's no need to start swearin'. We're doin' our best, in't we?'

'Are you *serious*? This is your *best*? If that's so, then God help this country.'

He was quite sure he'd heard one man, waddling away in what Lesley-Anne called a "huff", muttering, 'Bloody Yanks'.

Another refused to conduct further business with him and insisted on speaking only to his wife.

'It's not a good idea to upset tradesmen, darling.'

'Why the hell not?'

'Because they have the power. At least at this point in the procedure. We won't find another swimming pool contractor in this area. If we want to hire another, he'll have to come further and cost more.'

'You mean these guys can hold you to ransom like this?'

'In a way, yes. But once the job's finished, we'll have the power. He'll want to be paid and I've been keeping records of all his promises, written and verbal. We'll just withhold a portion of the payment, and if it goes to court, my records become public knowledge. It'll be his call.'

He admired her foresight and tactics, and the thought of shafting the pool man sent a laser beam through winter's gloom. But it could not make up for the disappointment of life without a heated pool and a jacuzzi. The tennis court was up and running, but the roof had already sprung a leak leaving a large and permanent shallow puddle on one baseline. He did not share Lesley-Anne's enthusiasm for riding in all weathers. He enjoyed a canter through sand dunes and along beaches in balmy weather, but hacking through cold wet mud was not his "cup of tea".

It wasn't that he didn't enjoy sports. He'd made a special effort by becoming a patron of the local soccer team and going to some of the home matches. Reg Barton, the Chairman, had taken him under his wing, on account of his "forward looking approach" to selling land for the new development.

'We're gonna make this club big, Calvin. The new stadium's gonna kick-start football in this area in a big way. We're gonna have a junior centre of excellence…'

But even transatlantic Calvin could tell the difference between a Championship, level-two side, with ambition to join the Premiership and a team like Manley Town trying to get out of level six. The Manley players were all hustle and bustle. 'Geddit inna box!' And it worked for a while. Four hundred rain-drenched souls in a leaky concrete and corrugated iron stand could justifiably chant 'One-nil to d' Manley Town!' for several weeks in a row, but then came the visits of some teams with a thinking midfielder or two who played it neat and simple and made the Manley hurly-burly boys look like bouncers on ice.

The Chairman shrugged off three straight home defeats. 'The players are too keyed up about the FA Cup. It's all about experience. The manager'll have to sort it out.'

But the Conference side that turned up to play Manley in the first round of the Cup was managed by an ex-England playmaker.

'Nah, he was a handbag player. Couldn't tackle. His team'll be the same.'

As it turned out his team didn't have to do much tackling. They kept the ball and found the most devastating angles. Nil-six. A lotta goals in one handbag.

Reg fumed. 'That was the worst refereeing performance I've seen in a long time. I'll tell ya, I'm gutted. Gutted!'

Within a week he'd done a deal to bring in a couple of Albanian former internationals.

'Now we're talking. This club's going places.'

Calvin couldn't work out how on earth Reg Barton had captured the signatures of internationals from anywhere. Getting a former Liechtenstein striker with a record haul of three goals in a hundred and five internationals would have been an accomplishment. But Albanian football was no pushover, so these signings must have been genuine feats of persuasion. Maybe, Calvin mused, Reg Barton had more to him than your average British landfill entrepreneur. Even so, dreary home league matches, watched from the terraces in a cavernous shed, were proving an unattractive draw, and Calvin's short burst of interest in soccer was exhausted.

His only true recreation was playing electric guitar in the sound-proofed studio attached to the tennis court. The walls were not finished ('My plasterer's little boy's got a sore froat' – or some other pathetic evasion), but he could turn up the amps and give 'Born in the USA' some serious wattage. All he needed now were some band buddies. Trouble was, all the guys he met in the local pubs thought he was offering a break into the big time. They saw money and "backing" and opportunities to record an album and get themselves on YouTube. He just wanted to hang and cut loose in his own backyard. He tried finding some older, professional guys who were into rock 'n' roll, but the solicitors and accountants of Manley Town seemed more interested in gentler pursuits and quieter music.

Eager to get matters settled and leave for LA, he urged Lesley-Anne to apply some diplomatic pressure on the local movers and shakers. Rich and Quick had confirmed their intention to buy the second tract of land but were dragging their feet on a contract.

'They haven't agreed what the terms should be,' Lesley-Anne explained. 'Nothing's legal till both sides sign off on that. Maybe they think they can pressure us on price.'

'They can do that?'

The head Councillor guy confirmed the possibility when he came to dinner with his wife. Their arrival posed some interest, as Calvin was certain he'd seen Alex Weaver with quite a different woman at the last football match he'd attended. Even though he hadn't seen them touching, their body language suggested an intimacy several steps beyond acquaintance or family relationship.

But Calvin had no time for Weaver's domestic arrangements. He was looking for answers. Answers that would release him westwards, lickety-split. His urgency had alarmed Lesley-Anne, who made him promise to curb his critical instincts and let her ask the questions. Apparently, they required British nuance, which he was still grappling with as if it were an entirely different language.

'Do you foresee any hitches in the process, Alex?'

Calvin thought this a nice touch. Lesley-Anne would never

invite a Councillor to dinner in normal circumstances. Back in LA their guests had been major fixtures in the State legislature, even the occasional national figure such as a Congressmen or Senator. On one occasion she'd even sat three places away from former Governor Schwarzenegger at a charity event. Now here she was first-naming a local councilman.

'Nothing serious. There's some public opposition, but there always is when the project's big enough.'

'So, you don't think this GROBAG movement is a threat?'

'To be frank, I wouldn't call it a movement. It's a temporary coalition.'

'But the local Greens getting together with Conservatives, Lib Dems and Independents … that's an alliance with some clout, isn't it?'

'On the face of it, yes. But being a coalition is its fundamental weakness. You can peel the layers away.'

'Is that what you're planning to do? Peel it like an onion? Sounds eye-watering.'

Calvin appreciated Lesley-Anne's subtlety. She was one of the toughest females he knew, but here she was playing with Weaver's sense of knowledgeable manhood, prising him open like an oyster.

'Not to *my* eyes. No… and this is completely off the record, of course…'

'Of course,' Lesley-Anne assured him. 'Anything you say here stays within these walls.'

'I'm sure that's the case. These things can be delicate.'

Calvin hoped that Weaver's desire to impress would get the better of his judgement.

'In this case, the Greens are probably the easiest layer. There are fractures in their ranks already. Personality clashes mostly. Prima donnas. It's the holier-than-thou syndrome. They don't have the discipline of other political parties. The fractures will become a split fairly soon.'

His manner suggested he could say more but preferred to be guarded and discreet.

'The Independents are next easiest. There are always people in it for the money. Sad but true. Hold out the prospect of a Council seat and a committee chair and you'll soon draw them away. And we now have an ex-Party man in amongst them. He was a divisive force with us. God knows what he'll do to them. Especially when he comes up against the natural conservatives within the organisation. I'd love to be a fly on the wall at their meetings.'

'It sounds as if they're ready to fall apart.'

'But what else can happen? The Council has given planning permission to the first tract of land. National government is pressuring local councils to build more homes. You've made the second tract available for purchase in line with our verbal agreement. As I understand from Steven Rich, the contract for that is almost ready to sign.'

'Almost, perhaps. But there is some wiggle room at this stage, isn't there?'

'It can happen that various matters continue to be negotiated. But that's a commercial matter. It's not a local government issue, except when the council is one of the commercial partners.'

Calvin couldn't hold his tongue at this point. He assumed that Lesley-Anne had done the diplomatic work and the way lay open to approach the pressing question. He tried hard not to sound harsh.

'Continue to negotiate? Sounds like a major difference between US and British practice. I don't think you could modify a price after hands have been shaken on a deal in the USA. Not unless you wanted to make some lawyers even richer.'

But there was no bridling from Weaver. He was astute enough

to see why he'd been invited to dinner. 'It may not be the best way of doing things, I agree. And maybe developers find themselves in a strong position these days. They've built up reserves of land and cash. They probably feel they can wait. A lot of the people they deal with need to sell quickly. They know they can exert downward pressure on prices. Not in your case... our case..., but it's routine behaviour.'

'Well, I hope it's not,' said Lesley-Anne. 'It's just that we value our routine as well. If we can't wrap things up, we'll have to shelve sale of the second tract. We have to be back in California by mid-December at the latest.'

Calvin recognised this as knife-edge stuff. It was a spontaneous ploy they'd never discussed, but it had the desired effect on Weaver. He paused with a freight of lamb provençal on his fork, then lowered it, regrouped, raised it once more to his mouth and chewed. He's a man who counts to ten before saying something he'll regret, thought Calvin.

'I can only speculate, but there are a lot of parties involved in this project. There are the football and rugby clubs, the supermarket, their various financial backers and lawyers. It's like solving a jigsaw puzzle. All the pieces have to come together. My guess is that the developers are wary about any of the stakeholders delaying things or even pulling out. They've got a lot of juggling to do. And the fact that we need to be discreet about the second tract of land probably slows things down even further.'

Calvin suspected moonshine, but Lesley-Anne accepted the point.

'Well, there won't be any indiscretion from our side.'

This also served to restrain Calvin's frustration.

'But, all things considered, for a project of this size and complexity, the signs are good,' Weaver assured.

'That's good to hear...,' Lesley-Anne began but couldn't resist underlining her grounds for complaint, 'even though the agreed date for finalising the second contract with us has been missed.'

'It's not ideal, I agree. To be fair to Rich and Quick, these delays tend to be factored in. Delays are par for the course and they're using their best efforts.'

'Best efforts …,' came back from Lesley-Anne as a doubtful echo. 'I see. But it is disappointing.'

She was still being equable, probing around the edges but really making a statement. Pass on the message, she was saying. Either honour the verbal agreements, or there could be no deal.

Weaver maintained his composure, but she'd driven home her point.

Before he could respond, his hostess was switching smoothly into a lower gear. 'But I do apologise,' she was smiling at Barbara Weaver, 'I shouldn't be talking shop, should I? Calvin's far better than I am at chilling, as he calls it. Have some more wine… Now what do you think? Shall we take dessert and coffee in the drawing room? I think Calvin's got the fire going in the fireplace…'

'Is that where I was supposed to start it, hon'?'

At this, Barbara Weaver let out a chuckle that unsettled Calvin. It sounded spontaneous, even warm, but her eyes hinted at impatience and a knowing disapproval. She'd hardly said a word since arriving, and Calvin had taken her for the dutiful, retiring wife, at least in public. But maybe she was one of those who saw more and spoke less and wasn't taken in by attempts at throwaway wit.

19/ Brother

By the middle of December Hugh was back in The Grey House. His Polish lodgers were expecting their wives and children for Christmas and needed every inch of space in the barn. This prompted a sudden surge in renovation work until he was invited to move his bed from the platform in the barn and into what used to be the living room in the cottage.

It was in effect a bedsitting room with a functional bathroom, a microwave and a hotplate. The rest of the house was still mostly storage space for building materials and tools, though the makeshift doors and windows were tight against the elements and the roof was water-resistant. In any other circumstances this would have been depressing, but he was not downcast. Far from it. There was simply no time.

He still took his meals with the Zielinskys, though his English language students were now able to visit him and have their lessons in relative peace. Bradley slept at the bottom of his bed as usual, but spent most of his time in the barn sniffing out mice, ripping up any paper left on the floor, and begging for food with eyes that suggested he hadn't been fed for a week.

Hugh also spent most of his waking hours in the barn. Ever since he'd joined GROBAG and become a peripheral member of the secretariat, there was rarely a free moment. Feliks and Peter Wilde devised the strategy over multiple cups of coffee. There were leaflets to compose and deliver, notices and minutes of meetings to distribute, demonstrations to organise, fundraising events to arrange, and a constant stream of publicity to devise.

Feliks had been frank from the beginning. 'I need your English language skills.'

And Hugh had been happy to oblige. Especially when he saw the initial efforts from GROBAG members trying to craft campaign leaflets.

'Its shear madness to build on a flood plane.'

'We don't have to tow the line.'

'Its important to maintain moral given the bearfaced attacks from Alex Weaver.'

Feliks was dumbfounded. 'Maybe we Poles aren't that useless after all. We could also spell that badly.'

So Hugh set about rendering the newsletters into passable English. Tracy Morgan's gratitude was oceanic.

'I was tearing my hair out. I just don't have time.'

In truth she didn't. The circles beneath her eyes seemed to get larger and darker by the week. She was struggling with her weight – comfort eating – and, although she brushed up well for a formal occasion, her hair was often unkempt from standing out in all weathers waving placards or door-stepping residents. But her attitude, Hugh thought, was steely, as on the last day of the tennis season when there was still all to play for and nothing else mattered.

Thanks to her efforts, the GROBAG petition had almost eight thousand signatures, though active membership had sagged to fewer than a hundred. Dozens had lapsed as soon as the amount of hard work required had become clear. But the money was trickling in. Membership raffles, demonstration whip-rounds, car boot sales and direct donations kept the publicity campaign just about solvent. If they were still short of the odd 'pony' to finance another leaflet, the organising committee coughed up the cash and rarely bothered to reimburse themselves.

Hugh took proposed texts by email, translated them into recognisable English and printed them out. Tracy and Peter Wilde would read them and propose further changes for 'political' reasons. The file was then sent to the printer and Hugh would collect several thousand leaflets a few days later.

When Hugh left the barn there'd been a scramble for the vacated platform, but Feliks had put a stop to that and requisitioned the area as GROBAG Operations HQ. He set up a large tabletop on trestles and somehow acquired half a dozen treacherous chairs. There were several maps and charts propped on tripods. Neat piles of undelivered leaflets were arranged at one end of the table while a computer graced the other. Tracy, Feliks and Hugh spent hours here organising their next steps and Peter Wilde would occasionally turn up to offer advice.

There were times when Tracy and Hugh felt as if the other two were communicating in a secret language.

'The football club has to be making a loss, so where is Reg Barton getting the money?' Feliks would ask.

'They seem to be establishing a new market in the west of England. Not Bristol, of course. That's established. And Birmingham's spoken for. But there are opportunities. Manley was left alone for a long time. Till the new prison opened.'

And Feliks would nod as if he understood the full implications of this cryptic reply.

'But on another subject,' Peter might say, 'have you identified your candidates?'

Tracy sighed. She'd finally cracked and agreed to stand as a candidate in the local elections. Not only that, but she'd taken on one of the biggest tasks of all. Challenging Ken Rudge in his ward, his fiefdom. Her only consolation was the certainty of losing.

'If I got elected Councillor, I'd embrace the heaviest boulder I could lift and throw myself into the Bass.'

But it was an important task. Taking on the deputy wolf in his lair.

She had to fight as if she could win. No wavering in public.

She soon learned that there were quite a few would-be candidates raring to go and with an inflated opinion of their qualities. It was uncanny how those least likely to impress a neutral observer were the first to volunteer. They were also the least willing to do any real work and expected Tracy, Feliks and Hugh to yoke themselves to some imaginary chariot and pull them to victory.

'Who's going to deliver this lot?' they would ask, regarding a modest pile of leaflets.

'We thought you,' Tracy would reply.

'But how many's that? It would take me a week.'

'Hardly. We delivered three hundred each last night. Time flies, once you get going.'

'But… I've got other commitments…'

These same self-appointed champions of the people were also uncannily astute in choosing smaller wards requiring less work. Some were as small as five hundred households, while Peter and Tracy were faced with wards four times that size.

'A leaflet every fortnight before Christmas,' insisted Peter. 'There will be about twenty per cent of people who give a damn, people who are hopping mad. Your leaflets will give them hope. They'll begin to think there's some point in actually voting or changing their allegiance. Some might even see the point of active involvement.'

So, they had trudged the streets of various Malvoir Valley districts, braving the horizontal drizzle being blasted up the Bristol Channel and swept on to the Midlands. They all had "folder shoulder" and "leaflet finger" – the twinges caused by repetitive folding, and a callous between first and second knuckle continually grazed by the thin aluminium flaps covering most Manley letterboxes. Hugh now knew, more by feel than sight, the steep unlit steps that could tip a leafleteer head-first into a wheelie bin at the bottom. And the houses with dogs that would launch themselves at the door to snap at fingertips trying to insert a leaflet in obedience to the sign on the outside that said 'Do not knock or ring doorbell. Baby sleeping upstairs.' And the houses with children that would see him coming and be waiting inside the door for whatever he was bringing, only for a collective and derisive groan to rise from the dwelling once they'd unfolded it and glanced at the header.

Then there were the households where the leaflet would be pushed straight back out again. At first, thinking that they must have somehow stuck to his fingers, Hugh inserted them once more, only for leaflets to reappear miraculously and silently as if he were trying to operate an automatic ticket dispenser. The householders, he concluded, were standing on the other side and making their feelings known in a mute and insulting fashion.

But there were also supporters.

'Good on yuh. 'Bout time that lot got sorted. You standing for Councillor?'

'No, just delivering.'

'Pity, we need to shift that lot outta there.'

'Why don't *you* stand?'

'What? Me? Nah… don't have time.'

Peter Wilde had repeated time and again that nobody should announce themselves as candidates just yet. And certainly not in print. Otherwise calculation of election expenses kicked in.

'Legally you can only spend so much during the election. So, you want to make the most of your allowance once the election's been officially called.'

Hugh guessed something unpleasant was about to take place when the other three – Tracy, Peter and, above all, Feliks (whom he'd

162

foolishly assumed to be his friend) – shifted uneasily on their chairs at GROBAG HQ, cleared their throats, glanced warily at each other and assembled their hands in what looked like a prelude to prayer.

'The thing is, Hugh…' said Tracy.

'Oh, God,' he thought.

'The thing is… that Peter thinks…' at this point she glanced at him to confirm that he was indeed the originator of whatever piece of horror was about to unfold, 'that we really need someone to stand against Alex Weaver…'

'Holy shit!'

At which they all laughed.

Peter Wilde took over. 'We don't expect you to win. But the candidate's got to be articulate and plausible.'

Hugh was aware of the flattery. The only plausibility he'd ever been granted was as a landowner, and that had been supplied by the plain visibility of the land he was supposed to inherit. The grounds for that had been, in every sense, removed. As for articulate, he'd had an excellent nanny and an expensive education. Both had struggled, with limited success, to overcome a childhood stammer, natural hesitancy and lack of self-belief. In many ways, Alex Weaver would be his nemesis. A grammar schoolboy with vim and vigour, nous and sinew. Up against the charmingly mild-mannered, independent school specimen.

'The thing is…' he replied, 'I see no personal pleasure and not much political advantage either. He'll characterise me as a toff and portray me as a tosser. Won't he?'

Tracy and Peter's poker-faced silence confirmed an accurate assessment. But Feliks was smiling.

'Weaver hasn't faced an election for almost twenty years… yes?' He turned to Peter for confirmation, which he gave with a nod. 'We need to give him a battle to fight and this will distract him from the war.'

'I know Weaver,' said Peter. 'He'll take it as a personal affront. Just to see another candidate's name on the ballot sheet in his ward. He'll divert activists away from other wards to make sure he wins. It won't look like it, because he's got the hard man act down to a T, but it'll be a form of panic.'

Feliks waved at the empty barn below. 'And we will help. You will have more leaflet deliverers than any local candidate in history.'

'And a terrific writing team,' insisted Peter.

Though Hugh quite liked Peter Wilde for his forthright and surprisingly warm engagement with his fellow man, his reasons for relishing the battles to come were clear. He had an axe to grind. The same applied to Tracy. She was now leading a team, and Hugh had often wondered if there wasn't a god or goddess of tenacity that possessed certain people - Tenacitus, Tenacia? – so that winning became more important than the cause.

Of the three, he was more inclined to trust someone who had very little to gain beyond a sense of doing the right thing. He looked into Feliks's eyes and saw gentle but realistic encouragement. His nod was a slightly sideways affair as if to say, 'It won't be pretty, but it'll be worth it in the long run.'

'All right. I'll do it.'

There was relief, but no euphoria.

'I know how you feel, Hugh,' Tracy consoled. 'Call me when you're feeling suicidal. We'll probably coincide. I blame my evil genius.' She jerked her head sideways at Peter Wilde. Hugh and Feliks imagined, perhaps, that she was joking. But Peter had known which argument would weaken her resolve.

'Not standing as a candidate is like a team captain walking off mid-match with the scores level.'

'Don't try to take advantage,' she'd replied. But his point was kryptonite to someone of her competitive spirit. She knew it straightaway. More annoyingly, so did he.

Hugh had noticed how Peter's mouth took on a surprisingly tender configuration on the rare occasions when he did smile. He was doing so now in response to Tracy's good-natured but not entirely barbless tease. She was already looking at the next item on her agenda and appeared not to notice.

And that's how Hugh, the ultimate political virgin, was selected to take on Alex Weaver, one of the wiliest operators in local politics. It was said that even the local MP felt uneasy in Weaver's presence; that Weaver had an array of channels to official and unofficial power too numerous to predict, decode or counteract. Rumour had it that political rivals had been neutered, officials framed, and local businessmen damaged at his instigation. But of hard evidence and witnesses there were none.

On the other hand, Hugh knew that his life had already been reduced to a pile of sawdust by the termites of Chance, so felt there was little left to lose. He might as well lay his reputation upon said sawdust, set a match to it and burn through whatever remained of his self-esteem. His life was buggered anyway.

This item of self-knowledge had been underlined recently when Isabella turned up unannounced. She'd been having second thoughts, it seemed. But they were quickly dispelled by a glimpse of his new circumstances. The still half-ruined cottage with its damp-rubble odour. The barrack-like barn occupied by a platoon of foreigners speaking an incomprehensible language. The atmosphere redolent with the preparation of stuffed cabbage leaves on an industrial scale. Her spanking new, Range Rover Evoque was as out of place as a royal carriage in a breaker's yard, and she quickly began to backtrack from her original story. 'Came to see you' quickly became 'was passing on my way to see a cousin'.

Notting Hill girls like Isabella might be able to pass off Deverill Court as peripheral Cotswolds, but the barn qualified as hicksville with a Slavonic flavour. After a few perfunctory, bulging-eyed how-juh-do's, while suspiciously sipping one of Jacinta's cups of caffeinated TNT, Isabella was on her way. Her visit had surely implanted a settled conviction that Hugh was irredeemable. Lost to civilisation as she knew it. Beyond the pale. He'd not see her again, he was sure.

Yet hers had not been the only fastidious assessment taking place. Once they'd realised that Isabella was less interested in their existence and more concerned with escaping these defective surroundings, Jacinta and Feliks began to view her with a critical gaze of their own.

'She's stuck up,' Feliks declared, watching her Rangie recede up the lane.

'Stuck up where?' wondered Jacinta.

True, thought Hugh, with a mix of sentimental regret and liberation. Though the heritable wealth of Isabella's parents supplied their daughter with a vast choice of goods and services – such as the lady's-club-on-wheels that she was driving – this came with a very long list of duties, obligations and rules. If you had to ask to see this list, you were clearly embedded in the wrong social layer. Hugh was now free of all that and was happy to choose his own friends. Such as Jacinta and Feliks.

The latter was in his element. Until a month ago he'd been a fish out of two waters. Away from the Poland he'd grown up in, and far from the USA that had taken him to its meritocratic bosom. But now he was free to organise, motivate, initiate and execute. All of which he did with measured aplomb. If the GROBAG cabal decided something should be done, it was. Timetables blutacked to the wall decreed how many leaflets should be delivered, where, by whom and when. Ticks in red marked all the jobs accomplished. More than that, Feliks demonstrated how to play people like musical instruments to get a job done. Sometimes like a bass drum, with flailing arms and booming monosyllables; sometimes like a snare, with a rat-a-tat-tat of unanswerable logic; sometimes like a melodious flute, lulling his unwitting helpers into drowsy gullibility. He was clearly, thought Hugh, a leader of men.

He often wondered if he was himself being played like an instrument – and if so, which one? But he was still convinced that Feliks considered him a close and intimate friend. More like a brother, really. The sort that Hugh could have done with much earlier in life. As for how Feliks regarded him, he could only suppose that Feliks sometimes needed a little relief from the high-tension relationships he had with the rest of the Zielinsky clan.

20/ Hotting Up

Some days are special, and this, thought Alex Weaver, was turning out to be one of those feel-good days. He began by picking up his new Jaguar XF with its 3.0 litre V6 diesel engine and leather seats. In some ways it had been an impulse purchase, out of character for a man of the people. He was so taken by the look and feel that the salesman took the risk of offering him the more expensive *Sport* version and sealed the deal. Jags, after all, are made for the elite on the move at speed. They ooze a certain authority. Only those who have "made it" can afford one. The Volvo had been fine for a long time. Dependable, solid, safe in every way. But it was also a foreign car, whereas the Jaguar was made in Britain.

There would be a certain amount of grief from Barbara. She wasn't that keen on expensive surprises she hadn't planned herself. But he reckoned he was due one of his own. He'd always been frugal about cars. An engine, four wheels, a chassis and five seats was all you required. Who needed expensive styling and daft amounts spent on marketing? Or so he'd always said back in the mid-seventies when he'd gone to great lengths to buy an imported Lada. That was before he saw the writing on the wall… 'Buy British or lose your credibility, Councillor'… and switched to anything built in Britain. Until all those firms went belly-up or were taken over by German and Japanese makers. After that, anything Swedish seemed to combine reliability and the moral high ground. These days the picture was… well… more complex. Cars no longer said much about your politics or social attitudes. That was all gone. Gone to what, he couldn't quite say. But people bought cars from all over the world, even the USA. They now said less about what you thought than about your credit rating.

Barbara would hate the Jag. He knew it. She still harboured ideas about elitism and 'where-the-money-really-comes-from'. The faster the world changed the more she relied on traditional attitudes. 'Earn money, pay your bills and save at least twenty per cent,' she would say to their grown-up daughter. Had she not laid eyes on their credit card statements recently? Weaver was paying the interest online, so perhaps not. If nothing else, ignorance preserved his wife's quaint notions of thrift.

Barbara had stopped thinking about how the world was changing, and it was changing fast. Almost anyone with a full-time job and a house could buy a Jag these days, or a starter Jag at least. The days were long gone when a bank manager would look you up and down in his office, check out your accent, and decide if you were the right sort to be owning a certain make of car or a house in a certain part of town. Financial deregulation had introduced democracy, and there were a lot of people who didn't like it. In that sense, Weaver felt it was almost his duty to own a Jag and flaunt it. Had not Marx written that one day people would be rewarded each according to their needs? And who was there to adjudicate what those needs were, if not the individuals themselves?

The reactions of his colleagues as he drew up outside the Manley Party Social Club spoke volumes. Intellectual confusion on the rights and wrongs of owning a Jag was writ large.

Ian Price looked stupefied. Then his phiz rearranged itself into an expression of mild disgust.

'Orright, Ian?'

Pricey forced a reply through lips as tight as a rubber seal. 'I'm fine. But you seem better.'

Ken Rudge saw and understood it all. 'Bought yourself a mostly Ford, have you?'

'Yeah, one made in this country. Right, what was this meeting you wanted? I've got a meeting in London at lunchtime.'

'Having lunch in London and perhaps having a meeting afterwards?' Ian Price's question was almost a demand for specific information.

'Since you ask, Ian, it's a funeral first, followed by a meeting in the late afternoon, and I'd rather not be late for either. Is that OK with you?'

The meeting went quite well after that, though Weaver made it plain he couldn't see the point. Grown men worried about a few pamphlets coming through doors in their wards, as if the world as they knew it was about to end.

'What worries me,' said Ken, 'is the Greens splitting the vote. And the Lib Dems could mop up a few. You know what they're like.'

To give him his due, Ken could always be relied upon to see the crucial point.

'You're right, Ken. The Greens haven't been happy. But I'll be making an announcement next week. That's what my meeting is about this afternoon. And this is completely confidential. If this gets out ahead of time, it can only have come from this meeting. A German company is interested in putting up forty wind turbines on Heath Edge. I've met with some prominent local Greens and they're prepared to drop campaigning for GROBAG if the turbines go up.'

And that was that. Economic investment, jobs and a contribution to fighting climate change. GROBAG and the other parties would be knocked right off their stride and the Greens would split right down the middle. The deputation that had called this "emergency" meeting were a bunch of doubting Thomases, but they all acknowledged his supremacy.

'You got to admit it. 'E deserves 'is Jag,' said Mel Coates with a reptilian grin.

So, there he was, swishing along the M4 towards his appointments in London on a cool, sunny winter's morning with hardly a cloud in the sky. He was still annoyed at how his fellow Councillors had said farewell, with waves and smirks. 'Ta-ta!'

That aside, whatever it meant, life had never been better.

Life, Tracy kept trying to remind herself, could be worse. But it would help if others could step outside their own concerns and see the bigger picture.

'But, Michelle, you live in Underhill East. Your shop is in Underhill East. Why do you want to be a candidate in Underhill West?'

Michelle was the friend of a friend. Tracy had begged her to turn up at demonstrations, even before GROBAG was formed, just to make the numbers look more impressive in local press photos. Now she considered herself a fixture, one of the original members, and therefore with more clout than any Joan-or-Johnny-come-lately.

'Because I have more friends in Underhill West. I know I can win there.'

Her voice on the speaker phone was beginning to sound insistent and shrill. She was claiming a 'right' to stand where she wanted.

'OK, Michelle. We'll get back to you.'

'With good news, I hope.'

There was a very distinct 'or else' lurking in the hope.

Tracy appealed to the others in the room as she tapped off.

'Can you explain that?'

'Easy,' said Feliks. 'Underhill East is a big ward. Fifteen hundred households. Underhill West has five hundred and four. She wants less work, less risk.'

Tracy pursed her lips, scandalised by a calculation that hadn't occurred to her. 'If that's the case, she can't have it, and that's that.'

'On the other hand…,' Peter Wilde intervened, 'shopkeepers are often the best candidates. Everybody knows them, and if they aren't in the habit of short-changing their customers, they have every chance of winning. I suspect she'll win wherever she stands.'

Felix agreed. 'Even if her written English is worse than mine.'

'Far worse. Not sure it even qualifies as English. She'll need lots of help with the leaflets.'

'Then Jim Philips will have to stand in Underhill East,' said Tracy, 'even if he lives in Underhill West. It seems daft.'

Hugh was generally reluctant to comment where the others seemed to have much more experience, but he was sure of his ground here. 'On the other hand, Jim is prepared to do the work. I don't think he'll mind if we just explain how things are.'

'You'd think he ought to mind.'

'True, but he's not that sort. He used to organise charity events at the Court. He just gets on with it. He's a great organiser, good talker, no BS.'

'Right, then,' said Tracy. 'Michelle's down for Underhill West, and Jim for the East. Who's next?'

'The Greyve-Traines,' said Feliks. 'Liz wants to fight Rosemead and Mick wants Presthill.'

Peter intervened. 'Presthill's not a problem, but I don't think anyone should stand in Rosemead. That's one of the few real chances for the Tories and they came close last time. Their candidate next year owns two nursing homes in Rosemead. That's about a hundred and twenty votes.'

The others looked shocked.

'You mean…,'Hugh began, 'the old folks don't get breakfast till they've put their crosses next to the right candidate?'

'What I mean is, there are entry phones on all the main doors. I doubt we'll be able to deliver leaflets to any residents directly. And the postal vote will be tied up for sure. Even sixty of those hundred and twenty votes will make all the difference in a tight race. They only lost by twelve last time.' His amused expression was challenging anyone to refute this reasoning. 'I suggest Liz fights Monkton. There are plenty of young, green-minded couples living there.'

Tracy had to admit that she couldn't manage without Peter's local knowledge. What he didn't know about the Valley was hardly worth knowing.

At the end of the meeting, Hugh and Feliks left for the printers to collect more leaflets. Peter lingered.

'Bit of a diva, our Michelle,' he ventured.

Was he reading her thoughts?

'A goodish list, though,' he continued. 'I'd be on the fair side of grumbling if I didn't keep a hold on myself.'

'Don't spoil things. I can't take too much excitement.'

'Don't worry. It'll get worse. But you've got a good core of candidates. As for those two,' a twitch of the head indicating Hugh and Feliks in absentia, 'they are terrific.'

'I know. Surprising, isn't it? I mean Hugh. I don't think I know anyone so completely unassuming.'

'No ego. Gives the impression of being his own worst critic. Wouldn't stand a chance in politics.'

'But he *is* in politics.'

Peter smiled ruefully. 'True. He is now. But doesn't stand a chance. Not against Weaver. Pity really. There ought to be places for people like Hugh.'

'I'd have thought you'd be dead against people like Hugh.'

'Me?' He looked genuinely hurt. 'How could I be?'

'Really? You? A supporter of the upper classes?'

'You read me wrong, Madam Chairman. I don't draw that sort of distinction. As I see it, there are various classes, but they're not based on socio-economic criteria. For me, there are people who do the right thing for the right reasons regardless of wealth. And these include people like Hugh, and Feliks and... you... I think.'

'I thank you for that hesitant vote of confidence.'

'You're welcome. And then there are a lot of other people who do all sorts of things, right, wrong and neutral, for entirely selfish reasons, whether they're aware of it or not.'

'People like?'

'The usual crowd. People with more success than substance. It's easily done these days. People pay more for presentation than performance. So, you always risk ending up with more façade than foundation. A bit like our Michelle.'

'You have a bad feeling about her, don't you?'

'Just a quiver or two on the old antennae.'

Part Four

'Tis the Season to be Feisty

Fa-la la-la lah
La-la-la lah

21/ Visitations

The festive season brought three visitations to the Grey House barn. The first was by Mary and her partner, Sir James Mansfield, QC. They arrived while Jacinta was rationalising the Zielinskys' jean pool, the long kitchen table littered with denim in various stages of disintegration and repair.

'Such a surprise!' Jacinta exclaimed.

Hugh was on the platform, trying to make a leafleteer's verbs agree with his nouns.

'Didn't want to make a fuss. We knew somebody would be at home.'

There was no mistaking the warm briskness in the voice.

'There you are!'

Hugh was coming down the steps. Seeing his former nanny looking superbly turned out in a natural-white coiffure, immaculate wax jacket and pale-blue twinset, made him acutely conscious of his own appearance. Jacinta had insisted on tidying the frayed hems on his best jeans, so they were somewhere on the kitchen table and he was wearing a spare pair he used for carpentry around the cottage. His old pullover, rescued from a black plastic bag, was fraying at the cuffs and elbows.

'Hugh! You look wonderful!'

'Hardly…'

'Never mind that.' She knew, as usual, what he meant. 'I mean, the gleam in the eye. Isn't it wonderful what Jacinta and her family are doing here?'

Anyone else would have noticed the meagre space allocated to each member of the family and concluded that they subsisted in a squalor of dispossession. But Mary had the knack of assessing work in progress.

'And this,' she said, turning to introduce him, 'is my friend... James.'

Hugh remembered the slight build and the round, impish features. Sir James had always been the sort of person grossly underestimated on first impression. The unwary were wont to take him at face value.

'Good to see you again, Hugh.'

Hugh couldn't remember being properly introduced in the past, even though Sir James had been a feature of the countryside, walking or biking the lanes on an ancient rudge with a panier mounted on the handlebars. That made him look eccentric, but woe betide the driver who cut him up at a junction. Close up he had the appearance of an animated Toby jug, perpetually good-humoured, but fearsomely intelligent. His soft, smooth hands spoke of a lifetime of doing little physical work. The contrast with Mary, a model of brisk achievement, whether planting trees or peeling potatoes, was stark.

'I've been in the wars, y'know. Otherwise we'd have been here before now.'

'Nothing serious, I hope.'

'Serious enough but could have been a good deal worse. Could have been without Mary, for one thing.'

He beamed in her direction, but she was off with Jacinta making tea and unwrapping the cake she'd brought.

'Fruit and nut, Hugh. Still your favourite?'

'Much missed.'

'Reminds me of national service,' said Sir James, looking around the barn as they sipped tea and nibbled the cake. 'But I suppose you do without the morning and evening parades.'

'We have morning sit-down parades.'

'Ah. So you have a sergeant-major?'

Fingers and thumbs indicated Jacinta.

'It's my firm belief that no enterprise can function without one. It would be like a lawyers' chambers trying to operate without a senior clerk. Or an independent school trying to get by without matron. I remember once...'

'You know,' interrupted Mary, 'I think we ought to say right away that we're here for a very specific reason.' Her smile suggested that Sir James was a raconteur who could easily forget his original purpose.

'Of course, m'dear. You tell 'em. You're more succinct than I.'

'But it's your idea.'

'Yes, but you gave it your stamp of approval.'

Hugh marvelled at their joshing regard.

'Well... to keep it short... I got James to read your local press to bring him up to speed on what's been happening, and he thinks there's a weakness in the Council's position regarding the land...'

'The sale of Council land to the development...' added Sir James.

'Exactly. Now James thinks that the Council may have agreed a low price for its piece of land. But that wouldn't be in the public interest...'

'Local taxpayers' interests...'

'Exactly. So, if that is the case...'

'Quite likely the case...'

'... then what you need is for someone to make a counter bid for the Council land...'

'... offering a much more enticing price.'

'... and that will smoke out the price the Council is being offered and test the developer's appetite for the deal...'

'For a deal at genuine commercial rates.'

'Exactly,' Mary concluded.

The pair looked satisfied with this scheme, but Hugh had spotted a flaw.

'I don't know where we'd find someone ready with a counter-offer.'

'Ah, no…' Sir James turned to Mary. 'You omitted that vital point, my dear.'

'I did.'

'For the sake of suspense, I think.'

'The punchline is that James is prepared to make a counter-offer to the Council.'

'B-b-buh…,' Hugh was both stunned and animated, like a bee that's flown into a windowpane. 'But the land is worth millions.'

'Certainly,' agreed Sir James, 'At the roughest guess it would be worth at least two million and possibly as much as three.'

While Hugh recognised this as an accurate valuation, it was not in his nature to ask a man where on earth he proposed getting access to three million nicker. These days his upper cash limit could be calculated by the size of wad he could squeeze into a trouser pocket.

'The point is that the stock markets have been doing awfully well for the better part of three decades, and I've got some spare knocking around and, more importantly, I have a couple of old friends who trust my judgement – poor suckers – and they're willing to come in.'

'Though you should point out,' Mary hastened to add, 'that they will probably never need to spend the money.'

'Quite. It's the threat of the cash that's important.'

'But,' mused Hugh, 'suppose the Council is being offered close to that already. Won't there be a bidding war?'

'There's always that possibility. But I worked in commercial law and my guess is that these people are winging it. They're in it to make a killing. Our airports aren't nose to tail with private jets from people on small margins. But a big profit often means having a mug somewhere in the chain. And the local taxpayer is always an easy victim.'

'Rarely regarded as a victim at all,' added Mary.

'That's so. Therefore, in the perpetrator's view, a clever and victimless gambit.'

So far, Feliks had sat quietly through these exchanges. That was often his way. Listen, evaluate, then offer a simple course of action.

'We should try to find out what price the Council has been offered.'

'That would be a definite plus,' Sir James agreed. 'Though I don't know how you might discover that. It's usually treated as commercially sensitive. But making a counter-offer public through local media might force them to show their hand.'

'But there's something else,' said Hugh. 'Just a suspicion. A touch of paranoia, perhaps. But the Council property is a such a narrow slice of land that I wonder why the developers need it at all.'

'How big is it?' asked Sir James.

'About ten acres in total. About half a mile extends along the north bank of the river Bass. But only about three hundred yards would join up to the land the Dewums have sold to Rich and Quick. My concern is that the other five hundred yards, if the Council sell that part, too, could be a wedge into more estate land.'

'But that's not in the planning application,' said Feliks.

'No, but I have this feeling. Why would the developers buy a narrow band of land five hundred yards long that they don't appear to need for the project?'

'It would be a perfect way to increase the housing element in future,' Sir James speculated.

Feliks regarded Hugh with renewed respect. 'It's worth following up.'

After tea, Mary and Hugh crossed to the cottage to inspect the remains of the old house and beginnings of the new. Hugh was surprised at how lacking in bitterness she was at the crime committed against her once beloved home. Perhaps she was trying to keep up his spirits.

'It'll take time, but I know you'll make a good job of it. Restoring things was always your forte.'

'A useful talent to have if you've got something to restore. The estate was a life's work in that sense. But I'm not sure what I'll do when the Zielinskys move on.'

'Ah, yes. What will life be without them? I know what you mean. They turned up in Somerset and transformed more than one concern. There was a daffodil farm, a pottery and a local laundry. But it cost them a small fortune to rent anywhere to live. So you're a godsend from their point of view. But what about you? Let's see…'

Mary strolled back and forth for a while, passing across one threshold after another, perhaps trying to recreate the old place in her memory.

'Well, you could always try to marry someone from the monied set. That was the way your ancestors kept themselves going. They used to marry British heiresses. But then they had to look elsewhere, and your great-grandfather married an American with new money. Your father's marriage to an American was for love, but there was no lack of cash. Who knows? You might find a super-rich Chinese girl who also adores you. But I don't know if the Chinese regard us British as entirely respectable.'

'Apart from anything else, I'm landless, cash-poor and don't have a title. So, I was thinking of getting a job.'

'Now, that is a novel idea. Though your father, I understand, was beginning to dabble in property in the south of France before he died. Though that's not quite the same as an early-morning-to-midnight job, which is what it takes these days to succeed in most occupations.'

She was ribbing him gently but unmercifully.

'I was thinking of teaching English as a foreign language, perhaps. Renting this out when it's repaired. Travel abroad.'

'Not sure that's a good idea, darling. The pay and treatment are abysmal. You can't tolerate injustice. Something would have to give.'

Yes, of course. The Zielinskys were so kind they'd turned the teaching job into a pleasure. Others would not.

'Something practical,' suggested Mary. 'Something in the open air. I always see you in the great outdoors, Hugh. Getting things done, making things happen.'

She was right, as usual.

'I do love being outdoors, but I've lost my desire. Can hardly bear to walk around here anymore. I take Bradley for walks on the other side of the Valley. I never go near Deverill Court.'

'I know what you mean. We thought of having a drive round the village, but I took one look at that hideous wall they've built around the stables…'

There was no need to continue; they knew each other's minds so well. Mary walked into the remains of the sitting room.

'I always thought that wall could be knocked out to create one big, beautiful room. You could do it now. I imagined French windows giving access to the garden. I spoke to your grandmother about it once, but it was never a priority. Too much else to be done.'

For all his grandmother's virtues, Hugh knew that she'd been incorrigibly old school. Why undertake works on an employee's cottage? That would have been her instinctive reasoning.

Mary read his mind. 'You know Hugh…,' She hesitated in broaching a delicate subject, 'I still find it hard to imagine your grandmother willing the estate to Lesley-Anne, of all people.'

'I examined the will and other documents. They all seemed in order. I knew my grandmother's signature. It looked genuine.'

'I just think there might have been some… underhandedness.'

'But what? Grandmother was lucid to the end. A little forgetful, maybe, but compos.'

'So everyone tells me. But I remember you grandmother's views on Lesley-Anne and the way she conducted her affairs… in all senses. I can't imagine how or why she changed her mind in her last weeks of life.'

'Perhaps she thought Lesley-Anne would protect the estate better than I would.'

'Very doubtful. The fact is, your grandmother and Lesley-Anne had a challenging relationship, to say the least.'

Mary pondered how much she wanted to reveal. Lesley-Anne's conviction that she should have inherited as her father was the older son. His death as he pursued teenage trespassers in his Bentley. Deliberately driving over their bicycles, heedless of damage to his car and the presence of his wife in the passenger seat. A bike frame getting caught in a front wheel arch and locking the steering mechanism. The limousine careering straight ahead and into a swollen River Bass.

Two months later, Hugh's parents boarding a Pan Am Flight bound for New York. On their way to attend a family funeral and return in time for baby Hugh's first Christmas. Air traffic control losing track of the plane over Lockerbie in Scotland.

Hugh knew the last part and had learned to place it in the context of de Broche family history. Ancestors executed for heresy or treason during the reigns of Henry VIII, Mary Tudor and James II; bankrupted by over-exuberant investments in the seventeenth and eighteenth centuries; cuckolded and deserted by their spouses; maimed or killed on the battlefields of Waterloo, Mons and Imphal; one de Broche second-lieutenant killed by a falling horse being unloaded at a Crimean port. He knew something of his ancestors' fatal heroics and follies, the loss and return of their lands, the medals and incarcerations handed down on the whims of monarchs and magistrates. But his grandmother had tried to withhold the knowledge that Lesley-Anne's main inheritance from her father, one that had cascaded down through previous generations, was a cast-iron self-righteousness and a red mist that would descend with alarming regularity. Despite the tragedy, her father's death had been something of a relief to his own parents and the passing of the torch to Hugh's father had been an opportunity to "breed some rationality into the line".

Mary had heard those words from Eleanor de Broche's own lips. She had married in and seen up close what the molten layer of choler could achieve: from tantrums to rages, from vengeful and fruitless litigation to the accidental manslaughter of a wife.

Added to Lesley-Anne's cantankerous streak, Mary guessed, was the experience of exile, like those British colonials who'd carried on the old ways long past their best-before dates "back home".

'I do recall an atmosphere about the place when Lesley-Anne came to stay,' said Hugh. 'There was the time she got me to retrieve pheasants when her dog was too lame to go out.'

'I was furious, and so was your grandmother. Your arms and face were covered in scratches from brambles and your clothes caked in dried blood and feathers.' Mary simmered. 'That woman never had a maternal bone in her body.'

The indignation pitched her, haltingly, in a new direction. 'You know, James and I have spoken about this... and he thinks that, as I'm clearly obsessed, I may as well pursue it...,' Her tone and smile revealed again the tenderness of her relationship with Sir James ..., 'We think... I think... you should challenge the will.'

'On what grounds?'

'On the grounds of its unlikelihood. James says that once you get the proceedings going, you're in a position to dig out evidence if any exists. If you do nothing, it will just stay buried.'

'Even if I wanted to, there's the small matter of legal fees.'

'James will do it gratis. And he needs a challenge. He had to give up his various chairmanships when ill, and there are only so many cryptic crosswords and difficult sudokus.' She placed a hand on his arm. 'We really do feel we're in this together. Sir James and I spent some memorable years here. We can't bear to see the place traduced like this.'

It suddenly struck Hugh how their fortunes had been reversed. There'd been a time when Mary had to count every penny: repairing her clothes, growing her own vegetables, turning down the thermostat on mild winter days. But now she could afford a life of affluence. She wore tasteful but understated clothes, her trim, petite figure the result of a fully active life. Her hair was neat, her earrings an expensive gift, perhaps. She was like... what?... a graceful silver birch in full leaf. But she still lived modestly. She and Sir James drove a small, economical hatchback. No overbearing, automotive statement for them. They were, quite clearly, what Feliks liked to call "a class act".

'I'll think about it, Mary. There's so much going on at the moment.'

'Let me know after the holidays.'

As they headed back towards the barn Hugh couldn't resist a spot of mischief. He stopped and looked as serious as a headmaster detecting smoke signals from behind the cricket pavilion.

'By the way, Mary... are you and Sir James married?'

'No,' she said, not missing a beat, 'still living in sin. We decided against. James has two children and five grandchildren. There's a good deal to inherit and we didn't want to give them any cause for concern. What would I do with it, anyway? I've no one to pass it on to. But,' she gave him an arch smile, 'I know what you meant.'

'It's just that I grew up never giving your emotional life a second thought, except where it affected me. I probably imagined you didn't have a love life and didn't need one.'

'Until I met James, I pretty much thought the same.'

When they re-entered the barn, Feliks and Sir James broke off what looked like an intense discussion.

'It's getting late, my darling,' said Mary. 'It's a long drive back. Oh, look at that...'

She'd left her shoulder bag on the floor and Bradley had rummaged through it. Paper handkerchiefs were chewed to mush and a cheque nibbled at the edges.

'Who's a very bad dog?'

'Bad' was an adjective that Bradley's doggy-brain, thanks to constant repetition, recognised as a negative enforcer. He looked suitably abashed and cute, while the final six inches of his tail dispersed other contents of the bag in various directions.

'Pig dog! In your bed!' roared Jacinta, and Bradley slunk to his basket.

'My fault really,' said Sir James. 'Should've been paying attention. He's a lovely dog, really.'

Bradley recognised the change in tone and began raising himself from his place of exile.

'No! Why do you English treat dogs like children?' demanded Jacinta, waving the hapless Bradley back to his proper place.

Sir James considered this proposition carefully.

'Yes, you're quite right. We do indulge the beasts. Silly habit, really. But he is a *gorgeous* creature, don't you think?'

Jacinta's high dudgeon gave way before Sir James's mischievous humility. 'I know,' she howled, frowning and grinning at the same time. 'He begs with his eyes. Like a no-good husband.'

The goodbyes were brief. Mary had no liking for protracted farewells.

When they were gone, Hugh took Bradley for a long walk by the river. He hadn't passed that way for months, unsure what he would say or do if he ran into his aunt or the husband.

He'd heard the tales of leases terminated and tenants evicted. There were also rumours of a vicious gamekeeper called Mr Paradise. He guarded his flock of semi-tame pheasants against ramblers and dogs with a combination of pithy abuse and physical assault. A Labrador had been shot in front of its owner for the capital offence of being off its lead and nosing around in a ditch.

But there was a new mood building in Hugh. Losing the estate was one thing, but now he was having to stand aside and watch land being sold off as part of a get-rich-quick scheme. As far as he could tell, the profits were being used to fund trivial pursuits. Grandmother would never have wanted that. In moments of resentment and despair, he'd wondered if there hadn't been some underhand business with the will, but now it was starting to form as a serious question.

His grandmother had always told him, in moments of disagreement, that she could pass on the estate to the person she thought best equipped to maintain the inheritance. They'd bickered about his "new-fangled" ideas – his tenants were "loopy" and even "undesirable" – and he had assumed that her ingrained conservatism had found the notion of Lesley-Anne as owner of Deverill Court less challenging.

His aunt had no children, so the inheritance would pass to him eventually. He would have to serve a longer apprenticeship. That, perhaps, is what Grandmother thought as she put pen to testament.

But now that his inheritance was about to be turned into a gated residence surrounded by expensive, "executive-style" homes on a dormitory estate, he was becoming less reticent about what he might say to Aunt Lesley-Anne and her current husband.

The second visitation came in the form of nine wives and eleven children arriving on a Ryanair flight from Katowice on the 20th of December. Szymon knew a fellow-countryman in the coach-hire business, so commissioned an ancient Volvo coach with driver to transport half the clan to Stansted. They trailed a smoky route across country, leaned on the barriers in mounting expectation, then hugged their loved ones to within millimetres of fatal constriction as soon as they emerged from the sceptical embrace of Her Majesty's Customs.

The journey home was delayed by two separate Friday night snarl-ups, so they relieved the boredom by unwrapping a few Christmas comestibles, the liquid items proving popular. By the time it reached The Grey House the party resembled a busload of triumphant football supporters.

Jacinta was furious – she'd been in a mounting mood of irritation for several days – and demanded to know what they meant by being so late, jump-starting Christmas, getting sloshed and not appreciating that her massive vat of food was being burned in the bottom after so much continual heating. Did they think she was born to stand around for hours stirring their stew? Two of the new arrivals had to take her to one side and calm her down. She reappeared red-eyed but managing a smile.

'I'm sorry,' she said to Hugh, just about the only person she hadn't verbally abused in the past half hour, 'but Christmas is difficult sometimes.'

Hugh was understanding but, in reality, clueless. The last thing in the world he was equipped to manage was a moody explosion. Indirectly he was fascinated by the whole Zielinsky family show – the tears, the remonstrations, the shouting – but never relished the one-on-one confrontations. He had to maintain a distance, attracted, as it were, by recoil.

There were now another twenty names to familiarise himself with, though it was taking some time to work out who was married to whom. The women at one end of the table seemed closer and more intimate with each other than with the men. The children, on the other hand, were less clannish, centring most of their attention on Bradley. They petted, stroked, patted and hugged him. He, in turn, licked, nuzzled and fixed them with his quizzically demanding, grinning stare until they hit upon yet another game to play. He also begged shamelessly at mealtimes, concealing himself expertly beneath the table and keeping well clear of Jacinta while he snaffled any scraps being offered or dropped.

The meal over, the family settled down for an operational meeting. Feliks translated for Hugh's benefit.

The big day was not the twenty-fifth itself, but Christmas Eve. Necessary victuals and presents had been smuggled past the budget airline's miserly baggage allowance in coat pockets and waistbands. There were more bottles of vodka than at a British student's graduation party. There were jars of hand-plucked wild mushrooms, berries, pickles, fruit juice, sauerkraut and poppy seed. Clean dry hay would have to be found from somewhere so the barn floor could be strewn in the traditional fashion. But the biggest headache of all was where to find enough fresh carp for the evening meal. Turkey and goose were anathema: the meal had to be meat-free, and the traditional carp was in short supply all over the country.

'I can supply carp,' asserted Hugh impulsively.

The entire barn fell silent.

'You can?' asked Felix with unconcealed scepticism.

Hugh couldn't account for this rush of blood, except that it was born of defiance. He knew very well where carp could be found. In different circumstances he could have waved his hand through a window and told his friends to go and get as many as they needed. But now his wits would have to substitute for his rights of possession.

'Tomorrow evening,' he said to Felix. 'You need them alive, right? And a bath to keep them in until dinnertime?'

The assembly looked mildly offended. 'No,' said Feliks. 'That's the Lithuanian way.'

'Sorry. So just freshly caught. How much do we need? In terms of kilos?'

It took five minutes to decide on a figure of twenty kilos of filleted fish, or three to four large carp.

'Not a problem,' said Hugh with a devil-may-care confidence.

Once the meeting was over, half the inhabitants packed their bags and phoned for a stream of taxis.

'Where are they going?'

'They are the married couples,' Feliks explained. 'They're off to a travel lodge for a bit of privacy.'

It was only then that Hugh noticed gargantuan Eddie's wife was the most petite of the women, a mere slip of a forty-something who was ordering him about like a big sister. Where were his clean socks? Did he have his sponge bag? Wouldn't he be leaving that bottle of vodka behind?

Feliks noticed Hugh's direction of gaze. 'You would think that he is the hammer and she the nail,' he said. 'But, believe me, it's the other way round.'

Calvin was frankly bored and frankly was the way he expressed it.

'If it would only goddam snow. Gimme winter. But the weather in this country is kinda like… hermaphrodite. Neither one thing nor the other. Can't tell from one minute to the next if it's autumn, winter or spring. And don't mention summer. There is no such season in this country.'

If Lesley-Anne had been of a different disposition, she would have realised that Calvin was not blaming her for everything from British business practices to the Atlantic weather system. But she was feeling poor, despite the almost one and a half million that Rich and Quick had paid for the first tract of land towards their project.

She couldn't work out where most of that money had gone. Yes, there were the new building works, the payments on the new Range Rover, the Land Rover and the costs of keeping a thoroughbred, but it was the constant drain of smaller payments – a thousand here, a thousand there, the wages of estate workers – that depleted her cash pool.

For his part, Calvin knew that his wife had received one point two million for the first tranche of land. But he'd picked up hints from bar-room conversation, confirmed by Google, that she'd been ripped off. There was something called 'planning permission' that had handed Rich and Quick multiples of added value. He found it hard to believe, given her confident manner, that his wife had been played for a sap by a bunch of two-faced Brits. Slimey-limeys. Anglo-shysters.

Feeling defensive, Lesley-Anne's impulse was to lash out. Calvin's was to triple-underline his complaints, and so began a period of sustained marital bickering, like distant thunder somewhere over the horizon.

They began with the drip-drip of veiled dig and counter-accusation. Pressure was released as a hiss or a squawk, then escalated suddenly into the storm breaking directly overhead in the form of prolonged bouts of screeching and baying.

Mortified and exhausted, they realised that a third party was to blame. Rich and Quick had sent no terms and conditions for the second tranche of land. As a result, there was no contract, therefore no imminent bank transfer.

Lesley-Anne felt that this was her money, her chance at independence. Capital was all very well, but it needed a sluice of ready cash to keep the estate functioning. Bills for all the works were piling up. The tennis court and swimming pool contractors were making demands. Her bank was jittery about extending the estate's overdraft yet again. New tenants for her cottages were in short supply. Council officers were sending warnings about the maintenance of footpaths and the reinstatement of signs. She was even struggling to keep the stables working smoothly.

Being a full-time estate manager had not been part of the plan. She'd intended to live the life she'd always imagined. A life of outdoor pursuits dictated by the seasons: shooting, skiing, sunbathing. Horse riding was a lifelong passion that could be satisfied all year round and in any place. Dealing with petty matters of fence repair and rent collection was neither her wish nor her strength.

The problem was that people were hopelessly inept or inefficient. Even if she paid them to do the work - and she did, quite handsomely in her view – they seemed incapable of getting the simplest things right. She had tried the tactic of regular follow-up calls using calculated, vigorous language, but to no avail.

'Folk are dumb, hon',' was Calvin's considered assessment. 'They don't get it.'

While she was inclined to agree, this conclusion spelt disaster for her lifestyle. She'd tried hiring estate managers, but two had already slunk away in quick succession, tails between legs, at the first sign of her frustration. Well, maybe after the second outburst, possibly the third.

'I reckon we should call their bluff,' said Calvin the morning after the row before. 'Let's suggest that the second part of the deal is off. Let's head for the sun. Give 'em the idea that we don't need their money. We can sell the land to someone else.'

She winced inwardly at his use of "we". He had his own money and plenty of it. But his point was sound. If her land had achieved planning permission for one scheme, there was no reason why another should not take its place.

'Then let's go,' she said. 'After Christmas. When we're back, we can look for other buyers.'

'Damn right. We'll teach these guys a lesson. No one messes with us. Assholes!'

Though the phrasing was typical of Calvin, it was said with uncharacteristic force. Something had been making him tetchy, and not just the weather. There'd been much horizontal drizzle of late and he was unused to evenings drawing in well before five. She would often hear the faint buzz and whinge of his electric guitar from his not-quite-sound-proofed studio. He would be in there, ear defenders muffling the decibels and hammering away to Led Zeppelin. Letting off steam was good, thought Lesley-Anne, though so much steam to be off-let was not a comforting thought. The steam was beginning to have a scalding, wilting effect on their relationship.

She was surprised, too, that he suddenly had no urgent wish to holiday in California.

'Let's go to Europe. Somewhere remote. They got skiing in

Scandinavia, right?'

'I usually ski in Switzerland.'

'I heard there's not much snow. Scandinavia's fine. Snow they'll have, and plenty of.'

The thought of understated, egalitarian resorts did not appeal, but she'd be happy enough if Calvin was content. His cash would be needed to meet the bills in the new year. Deverill Court was beginning to fret upon his nerves and, she sensed rather than reasoned, he was therefore entitled to the sort of holiday he wanted.

The same afternoon, with the sun low in the sky, Hugh entered the barn to collect Feliks for a fishing expedition. The interior was sweet with the aroma of mulled wine; oranges speared with cloves hung from the beams; Jacinta was sizzling something in a vast pan. She summoned him.

'I have a favour to ask.' Hugh wasn't sure if her eyes were red and swollen from chopping onions or a prolonged bout of weeping, but she sounded weary. 'My daughter is coming from Holland on December twenty-five. She's coming to Heathrow. Can you collect her for me?'

'Of course. Aren't you feeling well?'

Her eyes flashed at this insult to her customary fine fettle. 'It's no problem.' But then she relented. 'I have to fix too much. It's nice for me if you go. And your car is not likely to break down.'

This was clearly a reference to the Zielinskys van, which had somehow contrived its MOT. It managed short runs with up to ten passengers but sounded like a jalopy and smelled like a cross between a steel works and a fish and chip shop.

'I'll be happy to go.' This was no lie. He needed a job, a task, a quest, to fill the barren wastes of a Christmas Day in exile from the Court and all that had once been familiar.

'You sure?' demanded Jacinta.

Under pressure, her genuine concern could sound threatening, but he'd learned to regard this with charity. She'd spent much of the morning closeted with Henryk's wife, who'd helped develop Izzy's psychic powers and was clearly regarded as the family seer. There'd been a lot of business with cards, coffee cups, and something organic that had attracted Bradley's interest.

'No, really. I'll be very happy to collect your daughter.'

Having lured workaholic Felix from the platform, Hugh guided him across country using the public footpaths interspersed with stiles. He noticed that some of these were insecure or falling apart, unserviced by the landowner. Gates had dropped on their hinges, wire fences were sometimes slack or even breached. The signs of dilapidation were already there and, if allowed to go on at this rate, would put the estate back to where it was when Hugh first took over.

But he was now on a different sort of mission. Quite different. He kept a sharp look out for the gamekeeper, though his informants claimed the man stuck to the main thoroughfares or obvious byways, not caring too much to master his brief in the copses and spinneys, the dips and the dales. His aunt, he was informed, would have set off for California a couple of days earlier, so no chance of encountering her. Even so, he kept Bradley on a tight leash. No point offering an excuse to protectors of property.

Hugh was now an outlaw and looked the part in his old biker's jacket, worn blue jeans and black, steel-capped builder's wellies. Feliks looked a little more respectable in a wax jacket and a Barbour fleece he'd found in a Manley charity shop, his suit trousers tucked into Hugh's old Hunter wellies that fitted well if he wore a second pair of socks. He was becoming, thought Hugh, quite the country gentleman, an appearance the GROBAG campaigners found reassuring. But this would cut no ice with the new enforcers at Deverill Court.

They reached the summit of a ridge and found themselves looking down on parkland. The high chimney stacks of the Court were visible to the west. They'd skirted the main grounds to reach the far side. Hugh pointed to his left.

'See the lake?'

Feliks nodded.

'It's fed by the river and is full of carp and trout. We can't go to the side closer to the house, obviously. It's open ground and we'll be seen. But the water's deeper on the other side, where the lake water rejoins the river.' He pointed to his right. 'There's a footpath along the bank. We can fish from there.'

'But…' Feliks looked incredulous, 'we have no fishing rods…'

'Here…' Hugh unzipped his jacket. 'Years ago, when I was a teenager, I met a bloke in a pub who told me how he poached fish in these waters. 'Course, he didn't know that I was heir to the land and owned the fishing rights.'

'So you caught him?'

'No, I let him be. He was OK. Bought me my first underage pint. I used to see him sometimes, but I made sure he never saw me.'

'So why don't you ask him to do this?'

'Haven't seen him for years. Must've moved away.'

Feliks giggled. It was a sound Hugh had never heard before.

'What?'

'You were a big landlord. Now you want to steal from your own place. It's an example of English irony, I think.'

But Hugh was rummaging. From inside his jacket he pulled an empty beer can wrapped in fishing line and secured by a hook. From his jacket pockets he pulled two neatly folded canvas bags with shoulder straps. These he handed to Feliks. From his trouser pockets he took a pair of black leather gloves, from an inside pocket a tin with a selection of baits and boilies. He brandished the beer can.

'This is the most important piece of gear. It acts as a float and has two lengths of line. I've tied the weights and the hook to the shorter line. We chuck the can in the lake and let it drift downstream. I hold on to it by the end of the longer line. We walk along the path. If we get a bite, I pull it in. That's what the gloves are for. To protect our hands as we pull. We put the fish in the bags. If we've got a fish, you hide it in the bag beneath your jacket. If anyone comes along the path, I let go of the line and the can goes on its way. So, it looks like we're just two men going for a walk. When the person is out of sight, we send Bradley in to retrieve the can, and we start again.'

'And if somebody comes and sees us taking a fish from the water?'

'Then we're stuffed.'

Feliks considered this for a second or two. 'OK.'

As Lesley-Anne had spent hours online booking her last-minute ski trip, she took a later than usual afternoon ride. It was nearly dark by the time she reached the rise overlooking her parkland. From that height she was able to hear a barking dog, then spotted two men hauling on an invisible line. Mini-explosions on the surface of the water traced a reluctant capitulation, the fish only visible once it was flapping on the bank. The identity of one poacher was given away by the dog, an over-indulged mutt that needed taking in hand. The identity of the other intrigued. Rumours had been rife for weeks of the Polish-American breathing new ideas into the otherwise naff campaign of the

GROBAG wimmin. He'd been seen on the streets of Manley suburbs with Hugh, stuffing letterboxes with their tacky, rabble-rousing literature. She stared hard through the twilight gloom. She couldn't be certain, but it was a fair assumption. Her nephew's upright stance and long stride were other clues as the poachers skedaddled in the direction of The Grey House.

Lesley-Anne pulled a grim smile. If it was Hugh, he'd come clean the instant he was accused, such was his nature. That he was her nephew made the crime less excusable. He'd had an easy ride all his life, but he didn't have a grandmamma or a nanny to hide behind now. That he would have to pay for his feeble, impressionable character had only been a matter of time. What was he thinking of, giving houseroom to a tribe of foreigners and consorting with riff-raff?

Predicting the effect of her telephone calls to the police reignited Lesley-Anne's relish for a fight. Her life had been put on hold long enough by a renegade family member and a bunch of busybodies who ought to have had no say whatsoever in private matters. Where did people get off thinking they could dictate who could sell which land and to whom?

That Weaver character had said that legalistic management techniques were sometimes needed to get the right results in a democracy. She would call him when she reached home and suggest he support his impressive theory with some practicable ideas. Such as arranging to have her nephew banged up over the holiday. That should rearrange the misbegotten whelp's ideas. The thought alone warmed like a tumbler of mulled wine.

The third visitation arrived on the day before Christmas Eve. It was the boys and girls in blue. More specifically, an armed response squad, weaponised and bullet-proof. Hugh was roused from sleep by tyres braking hard on gravel followed by imperative hollering. Bradley went berserk in response to some foreign presence beyond the door. By the time Hugh was dressed and outside – with Bradley shut indoors – the yard was alive with swirling blue lights and the crackle of radio communication.

'Anything wrong, officer?'

He was addressed by an anonymous but civil helmet.

'Very much so, I'm afraid, sir. Are you…,' he consulted a document, 'Hugh Montgomery Sholto de Broche?'

'I am, but I prefer to be known as Hugh Brooke.'

There was muttering from the helmet as the hand made a note. 'Prefers to be known as… Is that Brooke with to 'o's and an 'e'?'

'It is.'

The helmet ceased muttering while scrawling and snapped into official mode. 'Then I must caution you that…'

The form of words seemed interminable as Hugh racked his brains for any possible cause. It had to be a mistake. At long last the officer reached the pointy end.

'You were observed poaching on the Deverill Court estate, sir. With an accomplice. We also have reason to believe that the people occupying this barn are involved in people smuggling.'

Hugh's smile, raised by the charge of poaching, was replaced by concern for his friends being rounded up in the barn.

'That's ridiculous!'

'Don't become emotional, sir. This is an arrest. Save your efforts for the police station.'

'Then can I just speak to my friends and tell them to keep calm?'

The officer was a decent man and led Hugh to the barn door.

Feliks, dressed in suit and tie, was doing his best to placate his relatives. Jacinta was trying to wrench her arm away from a black-clad officer while dishing out abuse in Polish. If this were the nerve-centre of a sex-slave ring, she was the only candidate for Madam. Hugh stood beside Feliks and spread his arms, palms down, urging calm.

'The police are only doing their job…' Feliks translated into Polish. 'Somebody has made a malicious accusation. We must go with the police quietly and it will all be sorted out. Don't worry. Nothing bad will happen.'

The commanding officer was grateful but not entirely convinced.

'We need to know where the other women are.'

'They're at the local travel lodge…'

'Right!'

'… with their husbands.'

'Ah. Well… we'll have to bring them in, too. We'll need names.'

'No problem.'

At this, the commander looked less than certain of a successful mission.

A solicitor acquaintance of Hugh's loyally abandoned his family at holiday time and quickly established that while the fishing rights technically lay with the estate they were still registered in Hugh's name.

The plaintiff was a Mrs Dewum, who had not boarded a plane for California after all but had been out riding at twilight on the day in question. From the cover of the woods beside the bridleway, she'd observed two men, one of them her nephew, helping themselves to her fishy capital. From precisely where the other accusation originated could not be confirmed. At least the police were not prepared to say.

But it was soon established that all the inhabitants of The Grey House barn were EU citizens with bona fide passports, driving licences, bank accounts, tax records and employers willing to vouch for their hard work and good behaviour.

They behaved impeccably, though Eddie's wife had to act as a release valve to his pressure cooker while the police officers doing the interminable paperwork eyed him nervously. Hugh and Feliks spent their time estimating the cost of this futile operation to the taxpayer, not to mention inconvenience to the police.

As the family left the building *en* masse, the arresting officer confided to Hugh. 'Off the record, sir, we're not comfortable with this. Not comfortable at all.'

In the taxi on the way home, Feliks reflected on Mrs Dewum's behaviour. Not content with wresting the inheritance away from her nephew, by whatever means, she was now adding venom to the proceedings. If Hugh had been prepared to give her the benefit of the doubt before, she was revealing a set of vengeful motives now. Her gloves were definitely off. She had decided that the Malvoir Valley was too small for them both. One or the other had to go. Given her advantage in assets, Hugh was the moveable commodity.

While his resources might be a lot smaller, Feliks pointed out that Hugh's roots in this place were deeper. He had allies. She was close to friendless, and local gossip suggested she complained constantly about this lack of companionship. But in order to *have* friends, said Feliks, you have to *be* one. It was an axiom bred in the bone and passed from one generation of Zielinskys to the next.

'That Aunt of mine…,' muttered Hugh.

'Yes?'

'Bit of a b really.'

'No question.'

They understood each other perfectly.

For Tracy Morgan, the usual antidote to Christmas misery *sans* husband, *sans* family, was a package holiday to a Muslim country. She could explore business-as-usual out on the streets of Morocco or Tunisia, but also enjoy some aspects of Christmas abroad at the hotel. But the past few months had been so exhausting that she was looking forward to a few days of solitary bliss. She'd bought the goose, laid up the Christmas pud, rolled, cut and assembled the mince pies. The drinks cabinet had a goodish selection of single malts, ports and Irish cream. There were nibbles, snacks and chocolates, a Radio Times with her choices of film, TV and radio circled in red ink.

She was looking forward to waking an hour later in the mornings and leaning back on her pillows with a cup of tea in hand and the Today programme on the radio. Her cottage would be a haven, an oasis of peace as she recharged her batteries for the new year. There would be long or short walks, depending on the weather, and she'd come back to a smouldering wood burner that she could coax back to red heat for the rest of the evening. She would then recline in her armchair or laze on the sofa, a glass or mug of something always close to hand, never mind if she was putting back the few pounds she'd lost during the recent weeks of frantic leaflet-folding and letterbox-stuffing. At the same rate, the next four months would see her slim as a sylph, albeit of the squarely built variety.

That was the dream. The reality was the telephone constantly ringing, with several recorded messages and texts from her ex.

'Thought I'd call round to drop off some books that I'm pretty sure belong to you.' ... 'I've been getting messages from old friends of yours trying to track you down and they found me first.' … 'I've come across an old memory stick that must be yours.'

Her replies amounted to, 'whatever you can't send as email attachments pop in the post.'

These clearly didn't satisfy as he turned up on her doorstep the day before Christmas Eve and she let him into the house, more from fatigue than desire, having run out of energy to make up a plausible excuse. She noticed how he ran a possessive eye over the cottage.

'You've repainted the kitchen.'

'Of course, I've bloody repainted!' she thought. But she counted to three and said, 'I was tired of the pistachio.'

He lingered, poked his head into the sitting room and adopted a generally approving air while she wondered what he really wanted.

'You're looking well,' he ventured.

This politesse was fatal to her resolve and she found herself offering a cup of tea in the spirit of 'OK, let's go through the rituals and get this over with'.

She was about to reciprocate on the "well looking" when he took her place – his old seat – at the kitchen table and rested his elbows on the surface like a customer in a café considering the ambience and décor.

Despite the attempted bonhomie, he looked lean, even shrunken. His hair was greyer and the eyes ever so slightly haunted, like a man who'd just recovered from a fit of weeping.

'So, what's new with you?' she asked.

'Not much. Same old, same old. But what about you, trying to turn the world upside down.'

'Meaning?'

'This campaign against Weaver's stadium.'

'Do you disapprove?'

'Not at all. Good on you for having a go, even if you don't win.'

'You think we won't?'

'Well,' he shrugged, 'too many interests backed by too much money. They usually get their way.'

Her reaction to this hackneyed statement surprised her. Instead of irritation it conjured a deep sadness, for him not for herself. It wasn't so much the sense, as his tone of knowing defeatism. It saddened her to think that his success, such as it was, with all the perks and bonuses, was built on knowing when he was beaten. He would always go with the flow and float where the cash was deepest.

'Well,' she said, trying to shorten the conversation and the length of his stay, 'we'll give them a run for their money.'

Yet he stayed for hours, accepting another mug of tea when she was trying to introduce a full stop, then *not* declining the polite but reluctant offer of a drink then, damn-it-all, either sitting and watching her eat her dinner or acceding to a "bite" himself. Three-thirty became six-fifteen. They'd covered every almost every topic known to "small talk": his golf elbow and dodgy ankles; the family lives and mini-scandals of people he assumed she knew from his place of work but either couldn't remember or had never known; the latest survey on his Mercedes and the MOT on his prospective new house – or the other way round; changes to his diet thanks to his wife's obsession with a popular TV-nutritionist.

She turned in desperation to a discussion of his family's Christmas arrangements, hoping he'd be reminded of some urgent task at home. But this gave him an excuse to lament the dullness of his existence, suffocating in his new, extended family, with little escape but playing golf and attending the horse racing at Chepstow and Cheltenham. His life, apparently, was just one horror after another as he faced the rigours of an early, affluent retirement.

Just as she was running out of conversation and thinking that his greying but still blond hair against the wine-flushed pink of his cheeks reminded her of nothing so much as scrambled eggs and salmon, he made his move.

It looked for a moment as if he were going for the bottle, but his hand passed beyond and grabbed her arm just above the elbow. In a fraction of a second his face was next to hers, pursing and gulping like a goldfish, while a wetness poured into her lap. It was the wine that he'd managed to knock over on the kitchen table.

The point at which she really minded came when it was clear he knew about the wine but couldn't be bothered to halt his grotesque attempts to plant a kiss on her mouth.

'That's an £18 bottle of wine!' she yelped.

He understood prices, if not values, and stood suspended in mid grope, giving her enough time to lean backwards to a worktop and pick up a jointing knife.

'Not for you,' she grinned, 'though you never know...' She pushed the knife blade into the neck of the bottle and lifted it vertical, saving a last glassful.

'Sh'only tiles,' he said, childishly absolving himself and demonstrating that he'd been drunk all the time. He must have been at it since lunch time, downing his Dutch courage, then managing to hide it till the urgent moment arrived.

'The thing is, Chris...'

'No, the thing bloody *isn't*...' He was cross now, like a sheep that's seen a dog.

'I'm afraid it very much is. First, you're married. Second, what makes you think you can come crawling back? And, third, it wouldn't work anyway.'

'There's shumbody else, isn't there?'

She was amazed and annoyed that he could make this sound like an accusation. It ought to have been a miracle that there wasn't "shumbody else" in her life.

'Why would you think that?'

'It's that bloody man, isn't it?'

'I know lots of bloody men.'

'I mean that Wilde bloke. How could you be attracted to that... that *commie git?*'

'I didn't know I was.'

'I've heard the rumours. They're all over Manley.'

'How would you know? You don't live in the Valley, let alone the town.'

'Word gets about.'

'And BS gets sprayed around. It guarantees stink not truth.'

He was temporarily stunned by that and she was impressed by her own soundbite. Writing for campaign leaflets might have something to offer after all.

'That bastard. The thought of him being with you. In this house.'

'What has that got to do with anything?'

'I effectively paid for this cottage.'

Her expression was a blend of amusement and outrage. All the desperate measures, all the overlapping, low-paying jobs she'd taken after he'd left, flashed through her mind. The flyer deliveries, the cleaning jobs, the shelf-stacking, the driving instruction, the exam marking and the French to English translation that finally gave her pleasure and financial stability. But she didn't want his pity.

'I bought out your share,' she said, anger simmering beneath her matter-of-fact delivery.

'But you could never have bought this cottage in the first place. Not on your income.'

She leaned back and assessed him. He was almost a foot taller, yet he seemed as small as his line of argument, a point that seemed to dawn on him as well.

'Let's say that was the case,' she conceded. 'But I never entered this cottage – *in the first place* – with the intention of breaking my marriage vows at the first sign of my spouse's depreciating bodywork. You left me for a new model and now you want me as some sort of on-road, off-road, tax-free classic.'

He started mumbling something about that never being his intention, but she cut him short.

'You and I have responsibilities elsewhere and you should get back to yours.'

She felt a dreadful blend of pity and fury as he slunk towards the hallway. But the compassion evaporated before he'd even finished his next sentence.

'I always suspected you'd end up sinking what we worked for in some losers' enterprise. I hope you're only giving them time, not money.'

This attempt at high-mindedness floundered as he tripped just outside the door and almost went sprawling.

'Mind the step that you claim to have effectively bought, yet somehow forgot!' she called, slamming the door and driving home both bolts for effect. Then she skipped down the hall to make sure the back door was secure.

It wasn't until she'd mopped the wine from the kitchen tiles that she wondered just how close she'd come to a nasty experience.

She'd sensed something vulnerable in Chris on opening the door. Now she shuddered at the timid choreography of his slow advance towards a desperate lunge. As always, his first concern was with his own needs.

But now her arm ached where he'd grabbed her. He'd never laid a finger on her when they were married. His treatment of women back then was less schoolyard bullying than an abject, couldn't-help-himself mentality. Was he changing? Had he developed a mean streak? Where, she wondered more generally, were the men who could rest easy in their manhood and live comfortably with a woman?

He phoned the following day to excuse himself but not, she noticed, to apologise.

'… had a bit to drink… went over the top… it doesn't happen often… can't remember it ever did… but at least you can't fault my taste, heh, heh… give me a call when you get a minute… you're probably monitoring this call, right now… anyway, have a good Christmas… I'll be mired in the same old same old…'

Damn right she was monitoring her calls.

Hugh's first Christmas in relative penury was turning out less depressing than expected. Even the memory of an early morning police raid, with its sinister aspects turning comical, could not destroy his pleasant memories. Here he was, tooling along the M4 in his Land Rover – recently serviced and MOT'd by loyal mechanics – and happily reminiscing. It mattered nothing that the big day – the 24th – had been alcohol-free according to Polish custom. Not that he'd volunteered to undergo the same twenty-four-hour fast as the Zielinskys until the twelve-course meal on Christmas Eve. The carp was a huge success rendered unmuddy by Jacinta's cookery skills.

As an only child in a three-person household with Nanny and Grandmamma, Hugh had missed out on the delights of big family gatherings. He was enchanted by the raucous after-dinner atmosphere as the children ripped into their modest but graciously received presents.

He was so taken by the bonhomie that he decided to join them at the midnight *pasterka* in Manley's St Mary's Catholic church. He mused that such devotion, unfuelled by alcohol, was now unknown to the vast majority of his countrymen. He witnessed Eddie solemnly wishing health and happiness to a man he'd recently threatened to throw over a hedge. As this was the head of a rival Polish family competing for the same work, this was the traditional spirit of Christmas in action. And the singing! He was now humming one of the tunes, the words a mystery, in clear danger of developing an earworm.

He'd asked Feliks to come along for this ride, but the man had grinned sheepishly and declined, saying it was better he did this alone.

But why? Was his pick-up not a popular member of the family? Why did no one want to go with him? What was Jacinta's daughter like? All his questions were met with a sly smile – quite unlike Feliks – and the unhelpful prediction that he would find out soon enough.

Heathrow was the expected postmodern purgatory, with its various levels of animated suspension. He found a good vantage point at the barrier outside ARRIVALS and settled down to wait.

And wait.

Flight delayed.

Delayed again.

So he squeezed himself onto a crowded bench.

And waited.

Alex Weaver was miffed. On holidays past they'd stayed at the same hotel as Gerry Quick. But now, for some reason, he and Barbara were booked in at the four-and-a-half star Turtle Beach. The year before last they'd been all together at the five-star Colonial Club. There was a half-star difference. What did it mean? What did it signify?

Sure, he'd been pestering Gerry Quick about the Dewums' threat to pull out of the land sale, and that barrage of emails, texts and calls might have offended Gerry's sense of command and control. But this was big stuff. Playing it too cool could wreck the whole scheme. Surely Gerry wouldn't punish him by downgrading his booking by half a star? The thought he held on to was that Gerry would never be so small-minded. But why had this hotel failed to achieve the full magic of a fifth star?

'It must be all the kids,' he said, scanning the beach with its highly organised and well-staffed activity groups for the different ages.

Barbara raised one eyebrow a millimetre to indicate she'd registered the remark but did not shift her gaze from her paperback whodunnit.

'A younger clientele,' continued Alex, persistent in trying to solve this private mystery. 'Young accountants, bankers, professionals, people like that. But with kids. The younger generation. They'll graduate to the Colonial in time.' A couple of infants ricocheted past their loungers intent on reaching a game being played with a large plastic ball on the beach. 'But not soon enough for my liking.'

Barbara had been a social worker when she first met Alex, and habitually rejected any suggestion that small children could ever be a nuisance. She lowered her book and addressed him in measured tones.

'Alex, I think this place is splendid. I'm enjoying it. Nobody is bothering me. The service is excellent, the staff are helpful, and the room is great. I don't want to be anywhere else. The only person causing me any concern is you. Couldn't you just lie back, close your eyes and work on your tan for an hour or two?'

'That's easy for you to say.'

'It would be even easier if I didn't have to say it. Look, we're seeing the Quicks tonight. We're having dinner. All will be revealed. Or maybe not. In the meantime, I'm very conscious of having a freebie in the lap of luxury. And I'm feeling just a bit guilty because we're not spending Christmas with my daughters, one of whom needs me.'

'Like a baby needs a rattle.' Weaver could not yet forgive his youngest child for gently mocking his forty-year commitment to the Party. ('Fried eggs and bacon, Dad. The hen was involved, but the pig was committed.')

'No, Alex. Not remotely like a baby of any kind. Like a recently separated young woman needs a caring mother. And I elected to come here with you because I thought you needed this holiday. But, as soon as we get back, I'm going to spend at least a week with Judy and try to make up for lost time.'

'So, I'm time wasted, am I?' Weaver thought but did not say.

He was a past master at tipping Barbara into one of her righteous moods, and she was approaching the brink. After thirty-three years of marriage he had a pretty good idea where the tipping points lay. One of these was saying what needed to be said about their over-indulged offspring.

But there was no advantage in priming Barbara for a ding-dong. God knows there'd be material enough for her to work with if she ever… It didn't bear thinking about, so he leaned back on his shaded lounger and raised a hand to summon a waiter. The Caribbean drawl and promise of another Hemingway Daiquiri would mask for a few seconds the incessant shrieking of tiny – and not-so-tiny – tots in the pool.

After four dreary hours there is still the hope of release. After six comes the cold certainty that life on planet Earth is a series of elaborate but third-rate practical jokes. After seven, there is the caffeine and sugar rush brought on by yet another cup of something warm. Hugh had stopped leaping up each time the sliding doors released another planeload from the calculated mercies of Immigration and Customs. He listened instead to the lingo, only stirring when the greetings were in Dutch, until the ETA receded further. The hands on his watch had gone beyond the stated time on three occasions, but the magic word LANDED failed to appear on screen. The next time he looked, the ETA had shifted another forty minutes into the future, then three whole hours.

Jacinta was sending him texts every thirty minutes.

What happened?

He texted back, trying to convey a relaxed joviality.

Delay delayed.

But there was no relaxing Jacinta. *Where's plane? Still in Amsterdam?*

He stood in the queue to ask and the story filtered back from head to tail.

Flight diverted to Toulouse. H

Please txt me the minute she arrives. J

He fetched a burger in a box, bought a newspaper and ransacked every supplement. He filled a rubbish bin with the paper cups, wrappings, paper napkins from various snacks and his discarded reading. He experienced the initial symptoms of supersizing his body through boredom. Another manufactured bap with mayo-nauseous filling, another barely intelligible announcement, another surreptitiously altered ETA and he'd seriously lose the will to go on. For the first time, he began to suspect the Zielinskys' motives. Why subject him to this all on his tod? After all, this female was *their* relative.

He was about to contemplate a most uncharacteristic mental slur on his fellow human beings, by attributing to the Zielinskys a belief they had never entertained – 'After all I'm not their bloody chauff…' – when he was interrupted by familiar cries.

'Daar ben je!'

'Eindelijk!'

'Hek is gek geweest!'

He glanced at the monitor. Beside the flight number was the magic word. But… why?… how?… when? No matter. He was up at the rail holding his piece of cardboard with her name in block capitals. ŁUCJA ZIELINSKY. He'd practised her first name without much success, making it sound Sloane Rangerish – Woose yah, Wooze yah – until Jacinta suggested he stay mute and hold the cardboard at a viewable height.

The passengers were now being disgorged in knots and clusters. But no single girl in need of a chauffeur. Clusters scattered, then gathered once more but the Dutch was mixing with the unmistakable tones of Transatlantic English.

Then he saw her. No question. Dark haired. No taller than her mother, but… well… a lot chunkier, and with an athletic spring in her trainer-moulded step. Wearing sports gear of a predominant white. Her thighs and broad shoulders filling, stretching, rippling the hi-tech material. Her complexion a little encumbered by the exertions of adolescence, but there was a spirited, bright-eyed freshness in all her movements.

Hugh held his card a little higher and further away from his body. She saw the movement. He smiled. She met his gaze and smiled back.

'Excuse me.'

He turned. Smiling at him from the other side was an entirely different woman. His synapses italicised and repeated the phrase as it echoed through every cell in his body. *An entirely different woman.*

'Erm…'

'I think you're waiting for me,' said this other apparition.

'You're Loose-ya?'

She smiled compassionately and held out her hand. 'Call me Lucy.'

'I'm… er…'

'Hello, Er. But you're supposed to be Hugh,' she grinned. 'Meet me down there.'

And she pushed her trolley with its considerable baggage towards the open space where the barrier ended.

He'd noticed her before, of course. 'Of course' because everybody had noticed. He'd clocked just about every good-looking woman that came by – not in a leering, laddish way, but just as you do if you're a casually observant, heterosexual male – but he would never have thought any of them, and particularly this one, was destined for his… his what? … his up-picking. He'd seen her passing by chatting happily with a largeish bunch of other people. A whole family, possibly two. They were coming up now, shaking her hand, pecking her on the cheek, wishing her a pleasant holiday. And suddenly they were wanting to shake Hugh's hand as well – every one of them – then more waving and farewells.

'You travelled with friends?' he asked.

'No, never met them before. But we had time to get to know each other.'

'Can I push that for you?'

'No, thanks. I need the exercise. I've been sitting all day. But you – you poor man – you waited all that time? Alone?'

'Yes.'

She frowned and pouted. 'My mother!'

'What about her?'

'Oh… nothing…' Her frown changed to a luminous grin. 'Is there somewhere to eat? I'm very hungry. Did my mother warn you? I'm always hungry.'

'No, she didn't say a word.'

'Really? She's told me everything about you.'

'She has? What... exactly?'

'Exactly, I don't remember. But just that you're very nice... too nice... and very reserved. She thinks you're a typical Englishman.'

'Ah... not good?'

'No, very good. She told me that if you were ten years older, or she was fifteen years younger, she'd marry you.'

'Ah... well... but I'd have to agree first.'

'Which you would.'

'I would?'

'Oh, yes. There are only two people who can resist my mother. One was my father and the other is me.'

As she pushed her trolley into a lift, he couldn't help noticing the long, silky, dark hair, her green eyes, her determined, amused expression as the wheels of the trolley rebelled against a slight elevation but finally surrendered. Probably like everything and everyone else, thought Hugh. It wasn't that she was a classical beauty, more an electrifying presence. It had to be the eyes, he decided. They seemed to engage the world with a limitless and playful curiosity.

'Where's the restaurant?' she demanded as the lift rose to the car park.

'Can you wait forty minutes?'

'Never.'

'Oh...'

'No, seriously... I'm joking. Of course, I'll wait. Where are you taking me? Not a service station? I've been warned about those.'

'No. I know a pub just off the motorway.'

'Good food?'

'Not bad.'

'That means 'good' in your language, yes?'

'Yes.'

At that moment both their mobiles rang.

'That'll be my mother.'

'Not both, surely?'

'Both for sure. She has two phones. One is only for calls to and from me.'

He stared, and she seemed delighted as the significance of this sank in. Then, quite seriously, 'I think we'd better answer,' she said.

His imperfect comprehension drowned in the Polish deluge that followed, but he held the phone obediently to his ear and visualised Jacinta holding a phone to each of hers. She was clearly overwhelmed and relieved by the arrival of her daughter. To his phone she directed a few words only - 'Thank you, Hugh. You are a wonderful men' – a plural compliment he accepted with singular grace.

'It's a wonderful hotel,' said Barbara. 'We love having the younger families around. Don't we, Alex?'

This fib required an extra effort of concentration from Weaver, but he thought he pulled it off with ease and grace with a fishing expedition attached. 'Great. Love it. Whose idea was it?'

Gerry Quick always said that politics was no game for him, yet he was in so many ways more of a politician than most of Weaver's fellow Councillors.

'My secretary…,' deflecting responsibility from himself. 'I told her… something classy…,' reflecting nothing but good intentions… 'but close to here…,' acknowledging a question begged. 'I thought…

this trip… considering what's going off in Manley, it'd be better to keep things separate.'

Weaver relaxed inwardly at this. The thought was good. You could never be too careful. He decided to reciprocate.

'Sorry about all those texts and calls, but that woman's been on at me all week. And then the husband started.'

That he was referring to the Dewums was understood.

'Some people don't know they're born,' Gerry declared. 'Trouble is, it's not my department. Stevie Rich is dealing with the money. Another seven hundred grand might not seem much to the Dewums, but it's not funny money to us. Let's face it, there's an election in May. What happens if you lose control of the Council?'

Weaver threw up a chuckle from the pit of his stomach, 'Well, that's not gonna happen.'

'You say that, and we all hope you're right. But we can't afford to be cavalier…'

Weaver knew he'd learnt that word from Steven Rich. When he was a scaffolder he wouldn't have known a cavalier from a roundhead screw.

'… the Dewums wouldn't take such a risk, so why should we? Anyway…' Gerry shrugged off the subject with a small show of irritation, '… let's drop the shoptalk, eh? Now, who's gonna join me in champagne and lobster?'

Silvia, his wife, always ready for a party, slipped her arm through Barbara's. 'C'mon, darlin', we're gonna be full of something tonight, but I don't know what.'

This demonstration of her own wit made her hoot and screech. As Gerry leered suavely in response, Weaver suppressed, as he often did, a desire to kick him in the groin and lift Silvia's dress above her head and tie it in a knot.

'What are you having?' asked Lucy.

The Christmas Day platter was a no-brainer but expensive. On the other hand, Hugh was feeling expansive for the first time in many months. 'Turkey with all the trimmings.'

'Mm... lots of calories. If I have the sea bass, do you want to share?'

'You mean...?'

'I get a taste of your turkey and you have some of my fish?'

'Sounds good.'

'We'd better not drink alcohol. I'm not supposed to drink and you're driving me. My mother would kill us both.'

Her smile was disarming. Normally Hugh would have baulked at having his decisions made for him, but he had a clear sense that Lucy knew what she wanted and usually got it. She was larger than life, high maintenance and direct, which was a change from, say, Isabella, who was only one of those. He felt comfortable in Lucy's company and the edge of her decisiveness was softened by a mischievous sense of humour and a surprising self-awareness.

'It's probably none of my business,' he began, 'but your mother hasn't been in the best of moods recently.'

This put some lead weight in her buoyancy.

'There's going to be a big scene,' she began. He waited patiently for an explanation as she lost her composure for the first time in his company, fiddled with a bracelet, tucked a truant strand of hair beneath her hairband. 'I've told her I want to give up the volleyball.'

Hugh's expression churned out a series of question marks.

She laughed. 'I know. Probably the whole family thinks I'm crazy. There's nothing wrong with volleyball. I've enjoyed it a lot. But my architecture course ought to take all my time. And, anyway, I'm starting to get physical problems. I'm only one metre seventy-six. That's shorter than most players, so I have to work harder to compete. And I've been playing competitions and tournaments since I was six years old. Fifteen years.' She made it sound like a lifetime.

'What's your mother's problem with that?'

'It's the Olympics next year.'

'And?'

'I got into the national team and she thinks I'd be crazy to miss out.'

'You play for … ?'

'Poland, yes. The last couple of years. When I'm available. You know, no exams and so on.'

'And your mother thinks volleyball should come first?'

'She thinks I should give it one more year. And being an Olympian is good on a CV.'

'Is she going to pressure you into changing your mind?'

'Not just her. The whole family. They're very patriotic. They'd never pass up such an opportunity. But …' her eyes took on a steely glint, '… it's *my* aching joints, *my* exam results and *my* life.'

'Fair enough,' said Hugh. 'You stick to your guns.'

'Stick to my… gums?'

'No, guns. Don't give in.'

'Ah.' She pondered this encouragement for 'no surrender' then countered. 'And what about you? Do you stick to your guns?'

'How do you mean?'

'My mother told me you let your aunt… how do you say?… step all over you.'

'Walk.'

'What?'

'The expression is walk all over me.'

'OK. So, does she?'

'How can she? I hardly see her.'

'But she stole your property. Didn't she?'

'No. In law, she inherited.'

'But you can fight her using the law.'

'Maybe.'

'So, why don't you?'

Her manner suggested he was being a wuss.

'It's not that easy.'

'I wasn't saying it was easy. Fighting back… I mean, resisting… is never easy. But it's possible.' She was watching him closely now, making it seem as though any respect she might have for him rested on his reply. 'Isn't it?'

He was annoyed that his business was being relayed to barely known people in other countries, let alone parlayed in the Malvoir Valley. Even more, that his resolve was being called into question. Taking on the Dewums in court and losing could sink him into unfathomable levels of debt. The American husband was rumoured to be a multi-millionaire who could hire the best counsel in the land. But here was a Polish sophomore urging him on as if this were about winning the next point in a ball game.

'Put it this way,' he said. 'I'm taking the best possible advice.'

She smiled. 'How very English.'

He returned the smile, thinking, 'How very Zielinsky.'

She was egging him on to pick a fight with a courtroom full of heavyweight lawyers while apprehensive about a tiff with her mother. While his lower cortex yearned for a closeness to this woman, his frontal lobes were yelling that it would never work. Be impressed at first sight, repent at leisure.

She excused herself before dessert arrived and, as he watched her interrogating the in-house signs, trying to work out which way to turn, he noticed that almost all other eyes in the pub were watching her too. Then they glanced at him, wondering, he guessed, how such a striking apparition came to be in his company.

Weaver saw her approaching from some distance away. He spotted her over Gerry's shoulder, marching towards their table, his gaze attracted at first by a pair of strong, long, chestnut-brown legs in a short black skirt. Then he noticed the way she held a black diamanté clutch bag and the way she bounced just a little on her five-inch heels. Unmistakable.

As if he was reading his thoughts – or had eyes in the back of his head – Gerry changed the subject.

'Oh, by the way, there's an old acquaintance of yours staying as well. Janine Appleby. You remember Janine, don't you?'

Weaver paused, lobster-greased fingers halfway to his lips.

'Oh, everyone remembers Janine,' laughed Silvia. 'With legs like that…?'

Her laughter sounded like a petrol mower at work about two gardens away, while Gerry's was more like a jack hammer. Both impressions grew more distinct as their speech became more slurred. Weaver feared this was going to be 'one of those nights', as Barbara called them. Gerry Quick had never lost that desire to get hammered from time to time, even if his lubricant of choice had changed over the years from best bitter to Scotch and now champagne. That said, the man rarely lost his native cunning.

'Yeah, you remember, Alex. Used to be a bit flash over the hurdles. She told me you gave her something once…'

Silvia's faux outrage was like gravy pouring onto a pure white tablecloth. Diners at neighbouring tables were beginning to take notice.

'... a prize on school sports day...' continued Gerry, masterfully directing this scene.

'I'm glad you clarified that,' said Silvia, her mock indignation pacified.

By this time, she was right there, at the table and being introduced.

'You remember Alex Weaver, don't you?' Gerry was saying. 'Leader of Malvoir Valley Council.'

'Yes, of course.' A perfectly polite handshake, no hint of more than cursory recognition. And another one for Barbara as Weaver watched both women carefully. Frank smiles, straightforward eye contact. The only one here that Weaver could never quite read was Gerry Quick. He always had the look of a wily gator who fancied himself a comedian.

'Will you join us?'

'No, thanks very much. I've got a date... in the bar... mustn't be late.'

And before Weaver had stood up properly it was time to sit down.

'Join us for breakfast love...' said Gerry, '...if we're up before eleven...'

She smiled over her shoulder, recognising the impossibility, and was gone, heading towards the outdoor bar where the young people played all night.

'Lovely girl,' said Silvia, for once growing serious. 'Such a hard life.'

'Yeah, that's another reason we thought of separate hotels,' claimed Gerry. 'Thought she needed a break. So, we said, stay with us. Poor kid. She spent most of yesterday crying on Silvia's shoulder.'

'What's the problem?' Barbara had a social worker's instinct for solutions to "issues".

'Can't say. I'm not even allowed to tell Gerry. Enough to say it involves the usual suspects…'

Weaver looked up to see Gerry smiling that lopsided smile of his that always seemed the same, whether he was laughing at one of his own jokes or celebrating a multi-million deal. But of one thing Weaver felt certain. Gerry *knew*. And if he was certain that Gerry knew, he also suspected that he had foreseen, organised and manipulated the whole thing. There was nothing innocent about Janine. She'd not only been around the block, she'd rented the corner shop as well. Janine knew precisely what she was doing. And so did Gerry. In fact, Weaver began to wonder, in a wild succession of mental speculations, whether the ingenue here wasn't Silvia. The message from Gerry was clear. Don't rock the boat, mate. 'Coz you're tied to the mast. To an experienced politician like Weaver this was not a startling conclusion – politics is often a hierarchy of tied hands and sealed lips – but he resented this new twist in his relations with Gerry Quick.

'We're taking her out on the boat tomorrow afternoon,' said his tormentor. 'Come and join us. I know you'll get along like a house on fire.'

'Love to,' chipped in Barbara, pre-empting Weaver's reluctance.

Neatly played, he thought. Gerry knew Barbara's addiction to sad cases. He was playing her like a dog that spied a biscuit.

'You are beautiful!'

How Hugh would have loved Lucy to be holding his head in her hands and uttering those words, but it was Bradley upstaging everybody else. He was gazing adoringly into Lucy's eyes, his mouth open in his usual tongue-lolling grin, his whole body gyrating in passionate pleasure at this new acquaintance. It did not matter that the entire family was still awake, hanging on Lucy's every word, or that her mother was holding back her tears and trying to gauge her daughter's most immediate needs – for tea, coffee, food – or that Hugh was being bombarded with a barely comprehensible story about the police – but Bradley was determined to make another friend for life and had, as usual, succeeded.

'What is your name? Are you a boy or a girl? What are you trying to tell me?'

Jacinta soon ran out of patience and ripped off a long stream of Polish annoyance. Hugh could guess what she was saying.

'It's only a dog, for God's sake!'

This had no effect whatsoever on Lucy.

'But he's so gorgeous!' She turned to Hugh. 'Is this your dog?'

For once he was more than willing to take full responsibility.

'But don't fall for his looks. He's that type. Give him an inch and he'll take a mile.'

This warning, Hugh could see, was wasted.

'Oh, I want him on my bed.'

Another volley from Jacinta.

Hugh retreated with his mug of tea to the end of the long table and observed. The return from Heathrow had been one of the most enjoyable car journeys of his life. He couldn't recall a minute of tongue-tied silence. They'd chatted and nattered as if they'd known each other a lifetime. He had, at any rate, belied Jacinta's report of being reserved.

But Lucy seemed to have this effect on all and sundry. Children were begging to be taken into her lap and petted. The women clustered around in the interrogative mood. The men ribbed her and accepted the entirely expected ripostes with a boisterous grace. Tadeusz said something that earned him a swipe on the arm from Jacinta, but a sympathetic defence from Lucy. Everybody loved this girl, he could tell. Somebody, one day, would be loved by her in return. He hadn't had the courage to ask if there was such a somebody already.

The Quicks had reached that stage of the early morning where only the deafest ears could bear to be within twenty yards. It was quite possible that too much alcohol affected Gerry's hearing, for he seemed convinced that only his loudest boom could be heard, while Silvia could only concentrate on a single face, as if any movement of head or eye would scramble her faculties completely. Her chosen point of focus was her husband's mouth, and she gazed upon it with a wonderful concern and concentration, as if truly deaf and reduced to reading his lips.

Weaver had never had the courage to call a halt to proceedings when Gerry was on a roll. It was a case, he knew, of seeing it through to a loud, incoherent, staggering finish.

'Trouble wiv you, Alex… you tolerate people…'

'Yeah, well I have to…'

This was an ill-advised response. The last thing he wanted was some reference to his being an elected politician in the hearing of other Brits abroad. The thug, so carefully concealed beneath expensive clothes and a perma-tan, had a habit of headbutting his way to the surface when Gerry had poured a bottle or two down his neck.

'Nah, you don' 'ave to. You just tell me wot needs doin' an' I'll make sure it gets sorted.'

'No need to worry. I've got all that well in hand.'

'You 'ave?'

'Oh, yes. There are people back there who'll wish they never poked their little heads above the parapet.'

Gerry leered in what looked like lopsided appreciation. 'I look forward to the results wiv anti... antishi... antipipaysh.... . You know wot I mean.'

Feliks approached and sat beside Hugh. He nodded at Lucy's back.

'She's special, yes?'

They watched her unwrapping her presents, the delight she showed at every little gift, the heart-warming hugs and kisses liberally given as thanks.

'Very.'

'I thought it best for you to discover yourself. Too much praise in advance can prejudice people. But it's hard to exaggerate in her case, I think.'

Hugh wanted to ask if she had a boyfriend but suppressed the question.

'They were here again this afternoon,' said Felix, wearily.

'Who? The police? What for this time?'

'Looking for stolen goods, they said.'

'Did they find any?'

'They found an old tennis ball that nobody could account for. Until Bradley jumped up and claimed it.'

'Did they apologise again?'

'They did, unofficially. They said their information had appeared reliable.'

'I wonder what they'll be told to look for next.'

'Who knows? But now it's time for us to give you our present, I think.'

One important tenet of Peter Wilde's practice of modern political activism was that you need to work harder when your opponents are putting their feet up. He knew that Alex Weaver would be taking his fourth 'well-earned rest' in twelve months in some exotic spot overseas. The Council's Chief Exec would be in the South of France as usual and the Director of the Planning Department, Peter's destination this morning, was beginning a period of compassionate leave. If Peter's knowledge of staffing practices was accurate, only a middle-ranking officer and a couple of juniors would be in the office on the twenty-ninth of December.

But he was wrong. Angela Middleton, the Office Manager, was there, guarding the counter like a modern-day Hydra. Peter had always suspected she was a creature of the powers that be – Alex Weaver and Roger Mason, the Chief Exec. Asking her for the files he wanted was likely to be counter-productive, so he took a flier.

'Is Sarah at work this morning?'

'Yes.'

'I just wanted to check how her mother is. I visited about a week ago after that nasty break-in…'

But Angela Middleton had no interest in his ward responsibilities and interrupted. 'I'll get her, and you can ask her yourself.'

Sarah Woodcock had been a student at the old Manley Tech, before it became part of the University of West Mercia. Hardworking, pleasant disposition, good results. Could have gone on to a prestigious university but stayed in Manley to look after her ailing, single mother and help two younger brothers through school. 'Keepin''em away from the two Ds,' she'd say. Drugs and the dole.

'Councillor Wilde,' she smiled. 'Always on the job.'

'I wish. But I can't say I'm glad to see you working. Shouldn't you be putting your feet up?'

'Dream on.'

Despite her usual perkiness, he detected fatigue. There were grey-blue circles beneath her eyes, as if she were nursing a baby through the night.

'What can I do for you?'

'Just wanted to check with you on your mother's situation.'

'Yes, she told me you'd been round to see her.'

'Second break-in this year..'

'... it's getting worse around there. I wish she'd move, but...'

'... hard to find a suitable flat...'

'Exactly.'

'But I'll keep trying.'

'I know you will.'

'And, as I'm here. I just wanted a quick look at the files for the Rokeby-on-Bass development.'

Her face blenched at its mention and her lips tightened. 'Take a seat.'

He hoped, of course, that she'd manage to bring all the files and avoid any interference from her boss. But it wasn't to be. Angela Middleton must have been watching the closed-circuit monitor because she emerged from the Chief Planner's Office – Philip Goater's domain – and insisted on seeing which files were about to be handed over.

'No, you can't give that one out.' It sounded like a reprimand and Middleton drew the olive-green document wallet from the pile. 'I'll take that back.'

Sarah came around the counter towards him with the dozen

remaining wallets and a resigned smile. He got up to help her with the load.

'I'm glad Angela's on the ball,' she laughed. 'More than my job's worth.' She shifted her body slightly as if to block the view from the CCTV camera. Pulling a wallet from the pile, she placed it on top and held it in place with a forefinger. 'You never know.'

He joked along. 'It's always worth trying. Though I don't think I've ever found anything out of the ordinary in one of these.'

'I should hope not. But it's bound to happen one day, isn't it? Law of averages.' She tapped the folder once more, then turned away. 'Have fun.'

He looked at the wallet's title. Discussions towards Section 106 agreements, MVC / RQC. This was most unpromising. MVC was Malvoir Valley Council. RQC was Rich and Quick Construction. The 106 proposals were the promises RQC had made for adding community benefit. Pavements, drop-down kerbs, children's playgrounds, perhaps a location for a new primary school. Though Peter – and every other Councillor – guessed that only a fraction of these promises would be honoured before the three-year handover period ended or the construction company went into voluntary liquidation. He opened the wallet anyway, just to remind himself of the airy good intentions that would precede the hard sell.

He sifted, flipped and scanned. Half his life seemed to be spent noting and assessing local government papers. If he'd entered into academic work wholeheartedly and spent as much time examining primary and secondary sources, he could have become one of the better-informed British historians in his special subject. But activism had got the upper hand.

Sometimes his regret felt as large as a well-fed, under-exercised heavyweight being wrestled into submission by a scrawny flyweight.

The position of senior academics was still to be envied. Delegating the grunt work to graduate students. International conferences in faraway places. Even the common room in the University of West Mercia had its jet-lag corner. He wondered if it was too late to make his mark. If he threw in the political towel and got down to writing a book or two. He could recover from his loft space all those notes he'd made on 'Churchill and Stalin: Empire Lost, Europe Restored'. His second wife had intended to burn them, but he'd saved and hidden them in the nick of time. She'd incinerated his collection of Wisden instead.

He paused in his casual flicking and went back a couple of documents. His brain had been in background automatic mode, as it usually was when memories of his second wife intruded. But it still registered something unusual. And there it was. A letter. Person to person. It was unusual among documents of this kind. A personal letter from Steven Rich to Alex Weaver.

'Dear Councillor Weaver...'

As he read and grasped the nature of this document, he knew that he ought to be showing no outward sign of special interest. Instead, he continued turning over other documents in an attentive but detached manner while he absorbed all the implications. He knew what he'd like to do with these bombshell revelations but was trying to work how to do it.

There could be no doubt that Sarah knew about the letter and was determined to let him see it. She must have taken it from another wallet – one he would never normally be allowed to see - and placed it in this one. And she hadn't been joking in the least when she mentioned her job's worth. If anyone could prove that she'd deliberately leaked this document, her career in local government would be over.

He couldn't simply pocket the letter and take it to the Manley Observer. That would be stealing. And he couldn't just announce his discovery to the world. That would lead the powers-that-be to Sarah. He had to find a way of releasing it, like a caged bird, into the democratic ether to be admired for its astonishing plumage.

Under the guise of reorganisation, he built the binders and wallets into a low wall at the front of the desk. He could see one CCTV camera in the corner of the room high up to his right. Trying to make his every move as unhurried and natural as possible, he took his mobile phone from a coat pocket and selected a function while appearing to read and reply to a text message. A brainwave. Returning to the piles in front of him and, in apparently choosing a new wallet, he dislodged the letter so that it fell to the floor. In stooping to retrieve it, he took aim with his phone camera and took a snap of the page where it lay.

There was no reaction from anywhere behind the counter, so chances were he'd be able to leave the building unchallenged. On the other hand, there'd be no way of denying how he'd come by this information. The CCTV footage would almost certainly be used against him. He just hoped that any number of Sarah's colleagues could have misfiled the letter before he got to see it, so that her tracks could be obscured.

He took his time, not paying any real attention to the other documents. Finding a second juicy piece of information in this lot would carry odds higher than those in a national lottery.

Much of this time he spent wondering how much his life would be turned upside down by this discovery. There were plenty of people he could turn to when the time came. But in cases like this there are always people you prefer to lean on, if only you could. If only they would let you. If only they wanted you to.

He went through the charade of handing the wallets back to Sarah, pretending he'd found nothing of note. She was ashen with anxiety, either because her risky ploy had failed or, possibly worse, that it hadn't. The consequences either way could be dire.

'Thanks for your help, Sarah.'

'You're welcome.'

'And as far as your Mum is concerned, and everything else for that matter, don't worry. It'll turn out right in the end.'

'I hope so.'

Out in the car park, he considered who to phone first. He weighed the obvious choice against the long shot, but only because he was on the verge of another gamble. In for a penny...

He found the contact on his phone and touched the screen.

'Tracy... Happy New Year, well almost... I'm phoning because I may need your help...'

There was something quite different about Barbara. She was famous for her briskness, but there was now something icy about her homebound preparations. Especially in this warm climate, where 'brisk' and 'tight-lipped' are failures of cultural awareness. She packed her bags and his, left the hotel for twenty minutes to buy a blouse she'd had an eye on for several days, stamped her postcards and left them at hotel reception, then ordered a taxi a good hour before it was needed.

'What's the rush?'

'No rush,' she replied in a tone that suggested much was being left unsaid.

'I wanted to have a quick word with Gerry before we left.'

'I wish you wouldn't.'

'Why not?'

'I'll tell you on the plane.'

Now he was sure there was something awry. What had she heard? Who'd told her? Had it been spelled out, or had she overheard a conversation? It was important to know but pressing for information would only confirm whatever it was she suspected. And when had she come by this information? They'd all been together last night and a good deal of the early morning, too. There'd been no hint of a storm brewing, though there was always the women's loo – reportedly the place where many a husband's fate is sealed. Had Barbara and Silvia gone there together? He couldn't recall. Barbara had certainly gone visiting – they all had, and several times. He'd had to accompany Gerry to make sure he didn't go to sleep mid-stream and brain himself on the china furnishings as per their last holiday together in Menorca. There'd been ample opportunity for someone to slip Barbara a piece of poisoned tittle-tattle at that point. But she'd not said anything overnight, given no hint of spousal outrage.

He would just have to sit tight and suffer. Gerry knowing all about his missteps was one thing; he was a bloke, and the whole point of such inside information was to keep it mum. But Barbara knowing was unknown territory. Would he face a roasting desert or a freezing steppe? Before they'd be sitting comfortably enough for the truth to reveal itself, there would have to be several hours of airport transfers, mega queues and other stationary tedium.

At long last, they were fastening seatbelts. Barbara snapped hers into place.

'Well, thank God for that.' She leaned back in her seat and released a heartfelt sigh which nonetheless carried a serrated edge.

'Thank God for what?'

She shifted in her seat as if bracing herself for a telling delivery. 'That is the last time I ever want to go on holiday anywhere near the Quicks.'

'Eh?'

'Are you serious? I don't mind the drink so much. Anyone can have a skinful from time to time. But Gerry Quick just gets worse with age.'

'That's just Gerry.'

'Just Gerry? Those lousy jokes, told in that loud, ranting voice of his? People like that could do for you one day, Alex. Do for us both, if truth be told. You're supposed to be in a progressive political party, and Gerry Quick is just about as reactionary as they come.'

So that was it. He breathed a huge, inward sigh of relief. It was only Barbara rediscovering her interest in politics. After several years way out on the Consumer Spending wing of the Party she was coming back to basics. If she was serious, it wouldn't be a comfortable ride – Barbara had always been well to the left of his more pragmatic approach – but it was a lot less scary than the scenario he'd been imagining all day. Like Barbara, he was looking forward to getting home, but for entirely different reasons.

Hugh's Christmas present was the best ever, and it also explained why the Zielinskys had been so keen to exile him from The Grey House for a whole day. Felix later gave him a blow by blow account of how they'd purchased the piano from a publican, transported it to the barn, kept it out of sight till Christmas Day, then arranged to have it tuned while he was driving to Heathrow.

He was rusty but willing. The WAGs had been instructed to bring sheet music for Polish dances, and the bedding was rolled back to the walls to create a dance floor. Hugh found the Mazurka familiar, but he was on a steep learning curve with Krakowiacs, Kujawiaks and Obereks. Eddie threatened to stamp lumps out of the floor in a Polonaise, and it looked highly likely he might launch his petite wife into the dark night beyond if he didn't keep a firm hold on her hand.

It was here Hugh had full evidence of the Zielinskys' physical staying power. It seemed they'd never stop, dancing in relays and keeping the piano player fully occupied. When they'd had enough of the traditional Polish fare, Izzy demanded a jive and grabbed Lucy as his partner.

'You're a bad man,' she scolded Hugh after the third number.

'Why?'

'I thought you would never stop playing.'

'I thought you didn't want to stop.'

She shrugged. 'Yes… and no.'

In the days that followed, Hugh was more than happy to keep the children amused by banging out 'Old MacDonald' or 'Yellow Bird'. He called it an English lesson, but was really hoping that Lucy would join in, as she often did, whenever she could detach herself from the maternal embrace of Jacinta.

The requests poured in from breakfast till supper and Hugh had to learn a number of Polish tunes in short order. In all honesty he was trying to find the route to Lucy's full attention by way of music. Dance music was fine, and the children's songs worked, but resulted in almost all her attention being diverted to the infants. She wasn't crazy about folk or pop, but more engaged by jazz or blues. He was beginning to fear she wasn't so very interested in music at all, until he turned to music he knew by heart. Bach and Chopin turned her pensive and a little misty-eyed, so he would choose his moment, then do his very best impression of Lipatti playing Bacarolles, Partitas and Nocturnes. It was nowhere close to the god-like Dinu – his teachers all agreed he'd never practised enough between ages twelve and eighteen – but music was the only place he lost his hesitancy. The notes were given, and he knew what he was aiming at, though he rarely, if ever, achieved the sublime.

'Do you play an instrument?' he asked Lucy.

'No. My Mum took me to ballet and tennis. Add schoolwork and there was no time for anything else.'

'It's never too late.'

'I will try one day… At least, I think I will.'

'Why not today?'

He scootched along and had her share the piano stool while he taught her how to play the lower line of Grieg's "Morning Mood" with three fingers.

'See? You're a natural.'

He couldn't fail to notice how, insisting on her incompetence, she briefly placed her arm around his back and onto one shoulder. But she did that to everyone. Always touching, always playful, always natural.

He wondered if his playing could convey what he felt, since he knew he'd stumble clownishly, hopelessly, if he tried to give those feelings a voice. So he contented himself with playing, or following her and the children down footpaths, while she conducted group singing. He'd never felt more like old man von Trapp trailing after a troupe of family singers. Nor could he fail to notice Feliks sometimes watching him with a detached and amused interest, as a replete spider might observe yet another hapless fly.

22 / And It All Kicks Off

Being met by the press at Heathrow airport would usually be a mark of celebrity, though it helps if there's a press pack and not a solitary journeyman from a local rag. To be fair – as many a Manley saying begins – he was from a regional paper, the daily West Hiding Echo, rather than the humbler, weekly Manley Observer. But a single journalist in need of a story is similar to a lone supporter at a football match. The players can hear every word being bellowed, while a crowd or press pack would present an indecipherable roar or a waspish buzz.

'Councillor Weaver… is it true that your Council has offered 3 million pounds worth of land to a private developer for less than the price of a three-bedroomed house? And is it true that eventually the proposed development is for twice the number of houses put to the Planning Committee?'

'What are you talking about?'

'A copy of a letter has been sent to the local and national press…'

The memories of eight lazy days in the lap of luxury at a Caribbean resort were erased in an instant. Multiple images and key words flashed through Weaver's brain in a split second. Betrayal, a leak, deliberate, calculated, an inside job, maybe incompetence, malice aforethought… Peter Wilde.

'I wouldn't know. I've been on a well-earned holiday.'

The journalist was waving the edition in his face. 'Would you like to read the article and comment?'

'No, thanks. I'll just get myself home. I'll catch up with work once I'm there.'

'Is that a no-comment?'

'It's a refusal to be jumped all over for answers to questions I know nothing about.'

'Are you then denying that there is such a letter?'

'I've no idea which letter you're referring to.'

'So, you accept that there could be such a letter?'

'Good try, but no cigar. Call me tomorrow when I've had time to find out what you're getting so excited about.'

'Does this mean that you don't know what is going on in the Council's planning department?'

Barbara added her weight to the luggage trolley and turned it hard left towards the lifts.

'Goodbye.'

But the midday crush in ARRIVALS meant they were still well within earshot as the reporter rang in with his story.

'He says he doesn't know which letter I was referring to. Won't make a comment till tomorrow. Yeah... make of that what you will.'

Weaver had reached that stage in life when he could feel his blood pressure rise. It had come on in the last couple of months, especially when certain people came into view. Peter Wilde was by far the worst culprit, but that Morgan woman and the rest of those GROBAG merchants could produce a surge. Even a Ken Rudge ramble brought a flush to his temples and a tug in his gut – or was that his chest?

He saw it all clearly and in technicolour. Peter Wilde somehow suborning a council officer to give him a document. Of course, he knew precisely the letter the hack had been referring to. It had to be Wilde. Only Wilde would have the guts and the gumption – give him his due – to take it to the Press.

But this time, he'd overplayed his hand.

'You drive,' said Weaver when they reached their car in the multi-storey Long Stay. And without a second look at this famous gateway to a nation's holiday dreams, he started working his mobile phone.

The Dewums had passed the same way six hours earlier and were completing their journey. This included two separate, hour-long delays on the motorway as crash debris was removed to the hard shoulder. Calvin was in a less than amiable mood. The narrow, traffic-jammed, three-lane motorways symbolised what he called "this tight little island".

He'd benefited from anonymity in the sparsely populated, forested spaces along the Norwegian-Swedish border. But this did not dampen his resentment of a general ambience he dubbed "more sleepy hicksville than smart society".

Lesley-Anne had struggled with the shortness of the daytime and the raucous incomprehensibility of the night. By lunchtime on their second day they were both longing to be elsewhere. But as they rarely spoke about their feelings, preferring to critique the world about them, they had no idea that they shared an emotional failure to identify Deverill Court as "home". Certainly, Lesley-Anne was looking forward to a gallop around the grounds on her favourite bay, and Calvin was keen to visit one of the greenhouses, but it was becoming little more than the place where they currently lived.

Both were eager to check the pile of mail in the hall. The cleaner had, as usual, divided it up into "his" and "hers". Lesley-Anne searched in vain for a payment notification from her bank. Her mood was further dampened by a final warning from the local council to repair no less than five stiles on public footpaths across her land. Her last estate manager had resigned just before Christmas, complaining about her rule to always have his mobile phone switched on. He'd been her second appointment in just three months, and she'd had to promote Mr Paradise the gamekeeper to general manager just to make sure her horses got basic care over the holidays.

Why weren't people prepared to do a decent day's work? Her

phone rule was to prevent malingering in some distant part of the estate. Besides, when she wanted something done she wanted it done now. What was unreasonable about that?

Calvin took his pile off to his study and stayed cloistered for half an hour. He'd noticed the unmistakable colours of an envelope from the US Inland Revenue Service and another from the Homeopathic Society of America. When he returned to the cavernous kitchen, he was unable to conceal a certain irritation, and chose to blame the "damned English cold" for his peevishness. He knew Lesley-Anne was itching to get back in the saddle, and he'd be left all alone in this damp, ancient pile, and nobody he knew well enough within miles for an "exchange of information" over a stiff Scotch. He wanted to be back in the States, but the contents of those envelopes had strongly suggested the time was not right. These lifeless, tomb-like, capital-devouring rooms would have to be his home for the foreseeable future.

If Calvin Dewum was regretting the absence of human companionship, Peter Wilde had the distinct feeling that his home was overcrowded. Heavy-soled boots and shoes were tramping around his living room, office, kitchen and bedrooms. There were two police officers in the back garden going through his composting bins.

'I'm afraid we'll have to take away your computers, memory sticks and mobile phone for further analysis.'

'No problem,' Peter said from the armchair that had been his only refuge since mid-afternoon. 'Could you give me a chit signed and dated by you, with the time you began work on them this afternoon and for when you are now taking them away.'

'I don't understand, sir.'

'I want a receipt and a record of the times for when you have taken over my computer equipment and phone.'

'We're not obliged by law, sir…'

Bob Miles, his good friend and solicitor, was sitting opposite.

'Then we'll write one for our own records, and you can either sign or refuse to sign it.'

'I don't understand the point, sir.'

'Not necessary.'

The officer's reddening cheeks made their way out to the police van. A female officer followed with his computer tower and laptop. Bob leaned towards Peter.

'Any reason?'

'I won't deny what's on the phone. It's politically damaging to Weaver, and I can claim I did it in the public interest. But someone might try to smear me with other stuff on the laptop. Everything on it is backed up to the web. But in three places, not just one. I deleted two of the backup icons and suspended their operation. If anything is planted on my hard drives or memory sticks after two-thirty this afternoon, it can only get backed up in one place on the web. Anything genuinely mine, and not a plant, will be backed up in three places, not just one.'

Bob was impressed. 'Bloody hell, Peter, you sound like an old hand.'

'Something I picked up leaning on a bar having a pint. It's always worth doing.'

The senior officer entered the room.

'Find anything interesting?' asked Peter breezily.

The officer smiled in spite of himself. 'Nothing out of the ordinary. But we may have to come back tomorrow, or any other time for as long as the investigation continues.'

'Do you have a charge in mind?' asked Bob Miles.

'We have reason to believe there may be stolen property on the premises.'

'What sort of stolen property?'

'Property belonging to the local Council.'

'And what prompted these suspicions?'

'Information received.'

'If you mean,' said Peter, 'that I may have more records of documents politically embarrassing to the Leader of the Council I can assure you I have, but none of them have been stolen. They've just been accumulated over the years and they're already in the public domain.'

The officer took the point. 'As I understand the matter, we're more concerned about documents of a highly confidential nature and that includes photographs of documents.'

'I understand,' said Peter. 'But you'll understand that I have to make judgements as an elected representative. No hard feelings. Say hello to Alex Weaver when you report back.'

But this bordered on sarcasm and Peter regretted the lapse.

'It's not for me to say hello to anyone, sir. I know it's a cliché, but I am just doing my job.'

'I appreciate that...' but he couldn't let it go. The experience was too trying, even if he'd expected that knock on the door as soon as Weaver hit the tarmac at Heathrow. 'I'm sure you'll show equal enthusiasm on behalf of the new Council if the incumbents are defeated in the local elections.'

The officer's mouth remained unsmiling, but his eyes could not quite defeat a twinkle of sympathy. 'We do our best in all circumstances.'

Which is what Feliks also did as he yet again restrained his relatives and patiently laid out all the passports, driving licences, Polish ID cards, National Insurance records and PAYE slips on the long table in the barn. Meticulous to the core, he'd insisted that his relatives keep every receipt, pay slip, credit card statement and mobile phone bill they'd ever had in the UK. After the first police raid, he'd refined the system further. There was not the remotest leeway for suspecting any possession in the barn to have been stolen. The officer leading each investigation had been different, and Feliks wondered how many such officers there were, before they all accepted that the Zielinsky clan were as clean as a whistle.

But now an officer was approaching the table with a holdall.

'Sarge, something here.'

It was a bag of white powder in a self-sealing cellophane bag.

'Whose is this?'

'It belongs to my cousin. She's not here at the moment.'

Lucy had gone for a walk with Hugh.

'Are her documents here?'

'No, she's only been here for a few days. She's on holiday too.'

'From Poland?'

'No, from the Netherlands.'

This caused a minor stir.

'And what does she do in the Netherlands?'

'She's a student.'

'Studying what?'

'Architecture.'

'I see. And do you know what this powder is?'

'No, you'll have to ask her… or maybe her mother.'

Jacinta was sitting by the stove with her arms crossed, looking resigned. Feliks couldn't help thinking this mood would not last. She looked contemptuously at the bag and spoke to Feliks in Polish.

'She says it's talcum powder.'

'This much? Why is it in a bag?'

Jacinta made Feliks translate although she'd understood the officer perfectly well.

'Sports people use it all the time. Doesn't he know that?'

Feliks preferred to leave out the rhetorical question in his translation. But just as he was losing patience with the officers' comical suspicion that they had finally found something of note, Lucy returned with Hugh.

'Oh,' she said with a huge grin. 'You're here again.'

'I beg your pardon?'

Her smile was disarming.

'My relatives were telling me how somebody is always sending you round here to harass them.'

'We don't regard this as harassment.'

'Oh, I'm sorry. My English is not good. I hope I haven't offended you.'

'We're not offended…'

'You're not. But have you ever found anything? I mean, three times you've been here, no?'

'I've only been here once.'

'But your colleagues have. It must be such a waste of your time. Aren't you offended by the person who keeps sending you here?'

'Information received is what brings us here.'

'But someone has to give you the information, no?'

'Well, yes… but what I want to know is… is this your bag?'

'Yes, it's one of them.'

'And what is this?'

'Powder for my feet.'

'Your feet?'

'Yes, I'm a volleyball player and like lots of volleyball players I suffer with my feet. I get athlete's foot, so I have to use a ton of this stuff every time after I take a shower.'

'I see. But I thought volleyball players use talcum powder for their hands.'

'Some do. But I use chalk on my hands when I play. It absorbs the sweat better.'

'I see. But we'll have to take this away for analysis.'

'OK, I suppose I'll have to get some more at the supermarket.'

Hugh and Feliks were both thinking more or less the same thing: that her candour had demonstrated to this officer once and for all that this entire operation was a wild goose chase with a serene and unruffled swan gliding along at the end of it.

Needing to show some conviction that their cause was just, the officers stayed for another hour, poking about and getting their dog to sniff in this or that corner just one more time. But even before half that time had passed, they were accepting cups of coffee from Lucy and Hugh. Feliks had involved the senior officer in a detailed comparison of community policing in the USA, Poland and the UK, while the dog handler opened the barn door and let his animal loose to play with Bradley, who for once got as good as he gave.

Half a mile away as the barn owl glides, the Dewums were going to bed early, and Lesley-Anne had made the all too common mistake of taking a pile of official letters to bed. 'Knocking a job on the head' rather than 'leaving well alone' was her mantra.

Sitting up in her twin bed – well separated from Calvin, as he insisted she regularly dreamed of riding to victory in the Grand National

– she adjusted her reading glasses on the end of her nose and drove a silver letter knife under the flap of a classy looking envelope. She slit it open, removed and unfolded the correspondence and perused the first page. She was hoping this would be, say, an opportunity to buy shares at knockdown prices, or an invitation, finally, to join the West Hiding County set at dinner or a field sport. But the content switched her emotional mode from "general disenchantment" to "vengeful panic".

'That little shit!'

'Whad?!'

'That little speckle of spit! That… that… two-faced, whingeing little scumbag!'

Calvin already had plenty of unpleasant news to digest and was doing so privately, without fuss. He was now sipping rum and lemon with honey – for the first signs of a cold – while sucking on his sixth Rennie of the evening, hoping this would keep the heartburn at bay.

'He's challenging the will!'

'Who?'

'That Hugh-shaped turd of a nephew!'

'What, you mean he's…?'

'Yes! Started proceedings!'

'Well, what the hell? Where's his case? He hasn't got one. Big deal.'

There were times when Lesley-Anne's genetically programmed reactions got the better of her judgement and her love – whatever that might mean – for a man. She turned on Calvin like a long-fanged feline and hissed.

'Isn't it obvious?! This means we can't do anything with the assets or investments until the case is over!'

Calvin had to admit that this put a more urgent gloss on the matter, but he was as offended by her tone as by her nephew's malice. It took a while before he would acknowledge her presence, opting instead to calm his pulse rate by visualising an enormous cone of soft Italian ice cream just like the ones his Papa had bought him on visits to the beach back in the early seventies. This was his version of transcendental meditation and it worked – to a degree. In no time at all his heart rate was down to a hundred and twenty-eight.

But there was still a fraught night ahead. Every time he was on the threshold of slumberland he would hear Lesley-Anne tossing and turning. Just as she was falling asleep he had to go pee, yet again. In no time at all, so it seemed, it was six-thirty, and Mr Paradise was passing below their bedroom windows in his pick-up with the grumpy old diesel engine. Like lovers grown together through custom and familiarity Calvin and Lesley-Anne's reactions, pronunciation aside, were identical.

'Oh, Gahd!'

'Oh, Gord!'

Although this chorus sounded like despair, it was in many ways and at many times the saviour of their brief marriage. 'Gord' and 'Gahd' were their champions, the names they would turn on their tormentors as they tried to fight them to a standstill. They'd done it before, though not in such urgent circumstances, as this was the first occasion their right to do pretty much as they pleased was being challenged. But their invocations of 'Gord' and 'Gahd' were likely to bring grief into many another life, if precedent was any indication.

Even as the Dewums surfed their storm waves of wakefulness, the ripples of Gord and Gahd's anger were already producing an effect a few miles away, as Peter Wilde tried and failed to sleep through the continual nuisance calls. He could have removed the plug from its socket, but he preferred in a perverse way to taunt his tormentors.

'We're gonna screw you, Wildey.'

'Nah, I'm not your type.'

'You mouthy bastard. We'll put a stopper in that bastard mouth of yours once and for all.'

'Never mind that, say hello to Alex Weaver from me, and tell him to buy you a thesaurus to widen your vocabulary.'

'You're going down, Wilde.'

'Hoping for some company?'

There was some satisfaction in having the other man slam the phone down first. But back he would come. Judging from the accents and intonation Peter reckoned that three men were being paid to harass him through the night. This was the level of politics that few voters realised was often the lot of an elected representative, especially one who challenged the culture.

'Tape your letterbox up good and tight, Pete, m' boy.'

That was the threat that kept him awake from four o'clock onwards. There'd been a few cases of petrol poured through letterboxes and set alight in Wild Hill over the years.

When the phone rang at seven, he was about to ask if they didn't have jobs to go to, but it was a different voice entirely.

'Sorry to call so early, but I know you get up at the crack of dawn. I thought about phoning last night, but I only heard last thing and didn't want to disturb you.'

'It wouldn't have mattered. You would have made a pleasant break from the anonymous threats.'

'Oh, my God. Are you serious?'

'Deadly.'

'And it's true that the police raided your house?'

'Yep. Went through every cupboard and drawer, took both my

computers, my mobile and a whole stack of ring binders.'

'Is it that serious? I mean, what have they charged you with?'

'Nothing, yet. But it says a lot about how serious this is for Alex Weaver. I've only seen him react like this once before, and that was when a naïve young journalist in local radio mentioned a rumour about backhanders in Electoral Services without any hard evidence.'

'Oh, yes, I remember that. What happened to the journalist?'

'No idea. But he stopped being a journalist, that's for sure.'

There was a long pause, then, 'Look, I don't think you should… I think you should take a break from your place and… well, you can come and stay here… if you like. Till things calm down.'

'That's very kind of you, Tracy. I'll pack a suitcase.'

23 / Takeaways

Any GROBAG member entering the village hall would have detected a hum of excitement missing from recent meetings. Perhaps, as a cynic might say, it was the sense of a New Year and New Possibilities before they beat themselves senseless against the walls of reality.

There was Tracy Morgan leafing busily though a ring binder. There was Peter Wilde, looking surprisingly untroubled at the centre of a chattering ruck. On opposite sides of the hall stood two smaller groups with the Greyve-Traines, Liz and Mick, as their respective focal points.

Tracy Morgan began the meeting with a proposal to alter the agenda. Liz Greyve-Traine was asking to make a speech. The change was accepted, and Liz rose to speak from the floor.

'Thank you, Chair. Before I can continue as a member of this organisation, and therefore before I can continue in my role as Media Coordinator for GROBAG, I have to ask members, and anyone thinking of standing as an Independent candidate in the May local elections, what their views are on the current Council's proposed siting of a wind farm on Heath Edge.

'I am a committed campaigner for sources of renewable energy and in my view the proposed wind farm would make a significant contribution to the reduction in greenhouse gases. If the consensus of the members here is in favour, then I feel I can continue as a member of GROBAG. However, if a majority of members are opposed, I feel I must resign my own membership. The takeaway for me is that the long-term benefits of sustainable energy outweigh the short-term considerations of local politics.'

She means, Peter Wilde guessed, that the regional subsidies towards her eco-activities and the grants towards her publications would be at risk if she opposed Weaver's wind farm scheme.

Tracy Morgan picked out Peter Wilde to respond.

'Could I say, Madam Chairman, that plans for such a wind farm are at the earliest possible stage. Nobody in the Council has been informed that such plans exist. All we have are the statements of the current Council Leader made to the press. This may be no more than a political manoeuvre intended to split our independent movement.'

But Liz Greyve-Traine needed an answer. She needed to secure her monies before May, thought Peter. She'd begun her eco-warrior's memoir and applied for a grant of twenty thousand pounds so she could take time off to complete the work and have it published. A draft chapter had been deemed "exceptional" by the arts committee.

A vote was taken on whether the meeting needed to take a decision now. It decided not by a large majority.

'In that case, I resign with immediate effect,' announced Liz Greyve-Traine in sepulchral tones. 'And, I have to say, I'm disappointed by members heeding the advice of someone under investigation for illegal activities, thereby undermining the whole purpose of this organisation. And I should add that I do not wish to be involved with any protest that benefits from the services of unpaid immigrant labour.'

She was followed from the hall by a dozen supporters who made a good show of removing themselves with indignation held high.

'Scandalous!' snapped one.

'A misleading waste of our money,' intoned another.

'Not so much a GROBAG as a SHRINKBAG,' crowed one former supporter as he slammed the door behind him with unnecessary force.

As the hubbub settled, Tracy tried to reassure members that defections were inevitable under pressure. On the key issues, the earlier speaker was mistaken. No charges had yet been brought by anyone against Peter Wilde. On the contrary, the Leader of the Council was the one who needed to answer questions arising from the 'Planning-gate' letter. Hugh Brooke's helpers were all entirely legal. To prove it, they'd had to endure three police raids over the holiday period with no charges brought.

A vote was called on whether the former members should have their contributions repaid. After a short debate, the idea was voted down unanimously.

'Any member wishing to be reimbursed should at least make the request without indulging in libel and slander,' was the telling comment.

Mick Greyve-Traine begged to make a statement.

'I would like to thank all GROBAG members who've called me over the past few days to pledge their unerring support. It can be no secret that political developments over the past few weeks have placed an unbearable strain on my relationship with Liz, and it can be no secret that we have decided to go our separate ways. That's the nature of public affairs. If you feel strongly enough, you have to stick with your principles, no matter what the cost. Liz has made her decision – and I have made mine. My political home is GROBAG. Hers is 'Manley Green'. We won't know which takeaway has been the right choice until May the sixth. But whatever the result...'

And so on and so forth. While Mick emoted, Tracy looked out from the platform at a smaller but more determined collection of GROBAG members. It was just as Peter had predicted. The softer, outer layers would peel off in the heat, but the core would be hardened for the battle ahead.

24/ Bargains

In spite of all the music, dancing and laughter over the holidays, the atmosphere in the barn promised a thunderstorm. Everybody felt it. Even arch-diplomat Feliks and fearless Eddie kept their counsel, restricting themselves to cautious glances, gauging the mood of the main combatants.

It began one morning after breakfast when Jacinta decided that her cooling-off period was over and that she was not cool about her daughter's decisions and general behaviour. Understanding not a word, Hugh could only read the body language: Jacinta like a storming sea, Lucy like a cliff face, losing chunks here and there, but too substantial to lose the war.

They had clearly fought similar battles in the past. Lucy would barely react to each wave as it came crashing in. She sat over her laptop with a third mug of coffee, her back to her mother, who was bustling about in the kitchen, making the point perhaps that *she* didn't have time to sit her life away while others enjoyed their holidays. And though her shoulders were slightly hunched, Lucy seemed to know what the next line of attack would be. She saw it coming and had her answers prepared. The waves beat against the cliff and eventually subsided, only to gather once more far out to sea and come hurtling in with even greater force.

Hugh was appalled. He'd never been involved in such a gargantuan contest of wills. His disagreements were carefully modulated negotiations based on a certain awareness of his place in society. When necessary, the language would be pointed but essentially harmless, like a fencer's rapier, and never used like the cresting wave in a Channel storm.

From time to time the cliff would tire of the constant battering and rise from the table, announcing that it was going for a walk. Adding insult to injury, Lucy would take Bradley along for company. Tears would follow when Lucy was safely out of earshot.

'You see? She prefers the company of a dog to her mother!'

Any family members not at work would gather and place their arms around Jacinta's shoulders while trying to reason and placate.

By the third day, the storm, apart from occasional gusts, seemed to have blown itself out, and Lucy invited Hugh to join her on a walk.

'I'm sorry you have to hear all this.'

'It's OK. I don't understand a word.'

'Maybe that's worse. It's just noise to you.'

'I feel bad for you both.'

'The trouble is, she can't see the big picture. She thinks I should be like the rest of the family, but a hundred times bigger. They'll work like hell, make a lot of cash and get what they want back in Poland. Bigger farms, bigger houses, a bigger business. They think playing international volleyball and qualifying as an architect is like being a super-plumber. As if it'll make me millions.'

'They surely don't think that.'

'Not exactly,' she conceded. 'But they've all made sacrifices to get me where I am. I'm trying to tell them I can have a good career, just not in the way they imagined.'

'Does your mother understand that?'

'Oh, she understands all right. Part of the problem is getting some of the others to understand and accept it.'

This made sense. Hugh had detected a certain coolness in some of the women towards Lucy. Perhaps they thought she was spoiled. In spite of all the quarrelling, Jacinta was always making sure her daughter had what she needed, serving her freshly squeezed orange

257

juice, making sure her prime beef was cooked just the way she liked it. The other women had to shift for themselves and their men in crowded, difficult conditions.

'I met a woman here yesterday,' said Lucy, changing the subject. 'On a horse. She shouted at me and told me to put the dog on a lead.'

Hugh grimaced. 'I think I know who that was.'

'Someone you know? You should tell her to mind her language. She was very rude.'

'I'm sure she meant to be. That was my aunt. The one I'm fighting with over the inheritance.'

Lucy stopped walking. 'If I'd known that yesterday, I'd have pulled her off her horse.'

He grinned.

'I'm not joking.'

'I'm sure you're not. But it wouldn't have helped your case or mine. As Feliks would say, our anger has to be channelled into becoming cool, calculated, strategic and tactical.'

She giggled. 'Feliks! I wonder if he's really a Zielinsky. My mother thinks he was – what do you call it? – a changed baby in the hospital.'

'A changeling.'

'A changeling! Beautiful word. There's something of the angel in it, I think.'

Hugh couldn't help thinking there was something of the angel in her.

On the fourth day, mother and daughter came to an arrangement and fell into each other's arms. Lucy told Hugh about it on their next walk.

'I try to stay injury-free. I play volleyball for six months. I do as well as I can. If I'm chosen for the Olympic team, I'll do my best. Then I retire from the sport. No more, it's over.'

'Is that what you want?'

'I'll be fine. I'm young. Six months will go past in a flash. Feliks will be my agent for any photoshoots and interviews. It'll help pay back the family for some of my university fees. That'll make me and my mother feel better. And maybe she won't feel she has to work so hard all the time.'

The benefit of this peace deal to the atmosphere in the barn was marked. The raging sea was transformed into a summer beach. The children charged about with gusto, the women gossiped, the men displayed. Izzy lifted his guitar from its case and filled the air with a melancholic frenzy. Only Feliks seemed entirely unmoved by the changes.

'The outcome was calculable,' he said. 'I have seen too many family arguments. I know how they start and how they finish. My advice would be to lay out the two negotiating positions at the beginning, wait three days while the parties think about them, then reach an agreement without all that sound and... what do you call it?'

'Fury.'

'Exactly. But to propose such an idea would involve a three-day argument. So I don't bother.'

'What I don't get,' said Hugh, 'is why all the fuss about the volleyball?'

'There's money to be made.'

'How?'

Feliks was surprised by his lack of understanding. 'Look at her. Interviews. Photoshoots. Commercials. She's the poster-girl for volleyball in Poland, maybe for the whole Olympic team.'

Hugh willingly followed Feliks's gaze. Of course, she was.

On the last day of Lucy's holiday, she accompanied Hugh and Feliks stuffing leaflets through letterboxes in Manley Town.

'You don't have to do this,' he said before setting out. 'It'll be deadly boring.'

'I'd like to. I need the exercise. Sitting around arguing with my mother is not the best training for an athlete.'

She giggled at Hugh's photograph on the leaflet. 'Very serious!' She chuckled at the earnest prose. 'Very statesmanlike!' And she argued with Feliks about the whole approach. 'He's a young man with ideas. Not a political stiff!'

She insisted that she would take photos for his next leaflet.

'Ha!' said Feliks.

'Um…,' said Hugh.

'What?' asked Lucy.

'If you can get a photograph of this man where he doesn't look as if he's trying to smile with a fishbone stuck in his throat, then you're a genius.'

'I *am* a genius. We'll do it later.'

They warned her that they would never manage to deliver 1,500 leaflets in a day. She demurred and Feliks winched his eyebrows skywards at this naivety. But they were to be astonished. Her walking pace was their scurry mode. She was astonishingly quick off the mark and wasted no time on the turn. She left Hugh to chat to passers-by about the terrible state of the world and got on with delivering another fifty leaflets while he stumbled through conversations with total strangers.

He didn't have the heart to tell her that most householders would think her offerings as welcome as little puddles of dog-sick on their doormats.

'I don't stand a chance, you know.'

'Why not?' she demanded.

'One, I'm no politician and two I'm basically shy. I end up stuttering and stammering at people.'

'It's true, you're not a typical politician, which is a very good thing. But you never... what do say?... statter and stummer with me.'

'No, I don't do either of those things.'

And she flashed him her most devastating smile as she turned into yet another front garden.

'You start over there,' she ordered pointing across the street.

He obeyed, guessing that his speech impediment would return in a flash if he began pondering the whys and wherefores.

25 / House Share

She had tea with breakfast, he had strong black coffee. She read The Times, he read the Guardian. Of an evening, she curled up with Jane Austen or Georgette Heyer, while he settled down with Philip Roth or John Rawls. If they listened to music, she preferred the Beatles and Mozart, while he'd choose Sonny Rollins or Richard Strauss. She squeezed the toothpaste tube in the middle, while he worked methodically from the bottom. She tapped and peeled the narrow end of her hard-boiled egg, while he sliced straight into his soft-boiled egg with a spoon. When she suggested watching *Mamma Mia – The Movie*, he replied that he'd rather "open his veins". She was a night owl, he was a lark.

On the surface of things, she'd had a great deal in common with her ex-husband and *that* hadn't worked. So this – as far as it went – looked doomed to failure.

And yet…

There was in his presence an easiness and a lightness that seemed entirely natural. For all their differences there were no battles of wills. He merely got on with his life, and she with hers. She made her tea, he made his coffee. Without a word, one of them would begin making the dinner and, afterwards, one would begin clearing away. But neither seemed to notice who'd done what or how often. There was a seamlessness to their time in the house, like two people sharing the space, yet never getting in each other's way. She was messy, she knew, and he was tidy. He would "square" her pile of papers on the kitchen table and she would manage to "jumble" his just by being somewhere in the vicinity. But not a word of complaint was uttered.

The difference between being around her husband and sharing

the house with Peter was, she realised, in the conversation. Peter was always interesting because he was unpredictable. Even when she knew he would say something funny, the phrasing would take her by surprise. Peter had timing and intonation and a willingness to explore the peripheries of the serious or the absurd, while her ex-husband had a tin ear and stuck doggedly to clichés.

'Alex Weaver is making a lot of noise in the local press,' she said one morning.

'Alex has heard the call of the Jaguar. He's abandoned his old habits for life in the jungle. Now, he's like an ageing joyrider spinning his expensive tyres. But you get used to the noise and the smell will pass.'

He was amazingly insouciant about his own predicament. Faced with prosecution on a raft of charges, from the theft of official documents to breaching another's privacy, her ex-husband would have been as taut as a cheese wire but as brittle as a strand of glass. At first she thought Peter was putting on a brave face, then she wondered if he wasn't a Buddhist.

With her own more mundane troubles he was a blend of patience and anxiety. A hint of RSI? He knew an excellent osteopath. A touch of indigestion? He knew a safe remedy with no side effects. Trouble with the car? He knew the best-value mechanic in town.

In the kitchen he conjured quick, tasty meals.

'I got heartily sick of the pre-cooked same old same old, but I couldn't be arsed to spend the time.'

So he did a pasta sauce with tinned tomatoes, butter and onions. White fish from frozen in crème fraiche with saffron. Onion soup with wholemeal bread and cheese. Preparation time – about four minutes each.

By the end of a week she was trying hard to find a serious fault. He didn't smoke, but there *was* a hint of foot odour. He never seemed drunk, but he could polish off a bottle of wine by himself. He did his own washing but persisted with the spiky hair. That did bug her.

'Have you ever thought of changing your hairstyle, Peter?'

'About eight years ago was the last time. My stylist promised that the sticky-up look would divert people's gaze away from my beer belly.'

That was it! The paunch.

'You could jog that off in about six months.'

'Or I could keep it for buoyancy in the swimming pool. Jogging would wreck my knees, ankles and hips.'

He said this with his customary clear and disarming delivery – somewhere on the crisp side of booming. It was a voice she was beginning to enjoy. But she concentrated on the paunch for a couple of days, in the hope that it might repel and save her from doing anything foolish at her time of life. She quite liked her life after all. She was comfortable yet had a purpose. Life was quite as full as it needed to be.

And then he went away for two days and three nights. To Birmingham. To visit a relative, he said. And the house seemed aggrieved. The kitchen sulked in the mornings, empty and devoid of that rich coffee aroma. The bathroom seemed colder, the living room softly chiding. She kept the radio on all day, to fill the house with voices. Even while she was composing leaflets or addressing envelopes, the muted TV was on in the background, to create the illusion of company. She even thought about getting a kitten or puppy, anything to fill that void. He'd be back shortly but, any day soon, the police would restore the crime scene that was his home, and he'd be gone.

26 / A View To A Coup

When Alex Weaver set off for the monthly Party executive meeting, his wife went too. This was unusual. Barbara hadn't been to a Party exec for twenty years or more. She always attended the fundraisers, the socials and sometimes the AGM, but the execs were for hardcore members. Newcomers, who might have novel ideas, were never encouraged. In fact, the unofficial policy of the Party was to make executive meetings about as exciting as the seasoning process for wood. In extreme cases, when a newbie refused to throw in the towel out of sheer boredom, Party members would go through the motions at their usual venue then reassemble in a member's living room for the real meeting.

But they could hardly try that on Barbara. She knew the form and, in any case, knew how to make herself popular by being forthright but charming. Weaver suspected that members gave her at least half the credit for his success in local affairs.

'But why are you coming? You're not a member of the exec.'

'But I'm a Party member and I have the right to observe meetings. Now, are you going to take me or do I have to drive myself?'

So he took her in the Jaguar and endured her sighs about the unnecessary expense, the excessive dashboard technology and the seat material. 'I hope some poor animals weren't murdered to support our backsides.'

Weaver feared the evening could go on in this vein, with his wife sniping from the sidelines. But what he feared most was that she'd somehow got wind of something: something beyond the well-publicised garbage in the newspapers.

This fear intensified when she received a warm reception from other members.

"E needs all the support 'e can get,' joshed Mel Coates, and the general hum of assent was interspersed by a couple of distinct sniggers. Sniggers and their associated forms of disapproval were, as Weaver well knew, a bad sign. He'd risen to power on a gently seething cauldron of cackles when his only rival for Leader back in the old days had finally burst a blood vessel at the sound of their constant simmering.

In line with his suspicions, Minutes and Matters Arising were hijacked by a proposed change to the agenda.

'Before we go on, Chairman, I'd like to hear the Leader of the Council answer questions about the recent stories in the press referring to alleged private correspondence between him and a firm of developers regarding the proposed development at Rokeby-on-Bass.'

There followed a half hour discussion on whether or not the Chairman should allow this change. Normally, Weaver would raise a procedural objection and have the idea scotched in a trice. But the feeling of the meeting was not in his favour, and the man in the chair, Ian Price, might well have engineered the whole thing in the first place. The meeting was not short of members willing to second the motion.

'In that case I rule that we shall hear from the Leader of the Council.'

He rose, trying not to look at Barbara, who was sitting at the back wearing a quizzical frown. He didn't want her doing this. She ought to be at home, buying designer bedspreads online, or whatever it was she'd been doing these last two decades.

'In that case, Chairman, I will issue a brief statement...'

'No!' This was Mel Coates, a man who owed him everything: his selection as a candidate, his place on committees, his unexamined expenses, *everything*. 'The motion was for the Leader to answer *our* questions.'

'That is the case, Councillor Weaver. First question, please?'

And so it began.

'Is there a deal in place to sell the Council land for a very low price with twenty per down and the remainder to be paid over three years?'

'There is no such deal.'

'Has it been suggested?'

'Why is the offer so low?'

'How much is the Council land worth?'

'Why was there a private letter in the first place?'

'What was your response to the letter?'

'Is it true that the Council has received an offer of £2 million from another private consortium, and is the Council not bound to accept such an offer as being in the best interests of local taxpayers?'

He knew the pitfalls. You had to predict the next question so as not to find yourself impaled on an earlier answer. You had to watch where you put your leading foot but also know where the one behind was placed. Steadily does it. Keep it brief. Leave some room for a sidestep.

'There was no official proposal ... As it was not an official proposal, the price proposed cannot be characterised as either high or low ... Any offer made is covered by commercial confidentiality ... The Council land has limited value as it lies adjacent to the river and is known to have drainage issues, not to mention access issues over inadequate road surfaces on one side, and a dangerous, decommissioned bridge on the other. Thanks to the criminal activities of a former member of this Party, we all know that there was a private letter... The newspaper that received a copy of the letter was wise not to print it, but only to refer to its contents in the broadest terms ... The letter was private and stolen from Council files ... As it was private, it received a private and confidential response, one that contained nothing detrimental to the interests of the taxpayers of this authority ... But the person who sent the letter was given to understand, by me and in no uncertain terms, that these matters need to be conducted through official channels … The fact that the letter was available in a local government archive is proof that there was no intention on the part of officials or me to mislead or to conceal negotiations…'

That, he knew, was a clinching argument. Who was going to call him a liar?

'And, finally, I am as aware as anyone that there has been a counter-offer for the land. It is for an impressive amount. But we have to ask ourselves, is this done entirely for political motives, or is there a positive purpose behind it in terms of suitable use of land for economic development? That remains to be seen before everybody goes overboard at the prospect of large sums of money in Council coffers. It may prove to be no more than one of the most expensive spoiling bids in local history.'

Even under pressure he had to admit he was pretty smart. He was giving the impression of a man answering questions on the hoof, but he'd been thinking this through all day. Over breakfast, at the wheel of his car, during the Chief Executive's briefing on arrangements for the election. During lunch at the Holiday Inn near Heathrow airport, when Janine claimed to be insulted by his lack of concern, his distance.

It was the first time they'd met since Barbados, and he'd promised himself it would also be the last. No one shafted Alex Weaver. Always a shafter, never a shaftee be. He refused to believe Janine's protestations of real feelings for him, resisted her sad tales of a life lived in the cage of modelling, escort servicing, or teetering on the brink of junkiedom. He couldn't afford to be dabbling with her world, which he saw as being a much darker shade of grey than his own.

'But don't you see?' she entreated. 'It's all part of the same world. Gerry has got his hooks into both of us.'

'No,' he protested. 'It's not the same. I build things, direct things, improve people's lives.'

He couldn't bear her scorn at that, nor her sadness that he did not represent a way out for her. His respectability was another country to which she could no longer gain a visa. There was nothing more he could do for her. She'd have to stick with Gerry Quick.

He hardened himself to her distress, wished her good luck, and set off back to Manley to put his career back on track. A couple of wagonloads had shifted sideways, nothing drastic, nothing that would derail the whole consignment.

As things stood, Peter Wilde had done him a couple of huge favours. First, by resigning from the Party and not being there to ask the killer questions; secondly, by making himself a hate figure. The members pestering him now were brown-trousering themselves at the prospect of losing their seats. How he despised them. Fighting tooth and nail, backstabbing and betraying, conniving and cabaling. And all for a basic nine thousand a year. Without their 'nice little earners' they'd be sunk, back in the job market where most of them wouldn't stand an earthly. It would be more merciful to put them out to pasture, point them towards the allotments or the public golf courses where they did superb impressions of overfed goldfish in the club pond.

Barbara had her hand up. What the hell was she playing at?

'Is there any...?'

Weaver interrupted. 'Point of order, Chairman. Is the member a member of the Executive?'

'No, just a Party member with the right to speak, but not to vote. Go ahead, member.'

Weaver was not deterred. 'Point of order, Chairman. According to standing order 17, members may only speak if asking a stand-alone question, not a supplementary.'

Hubbub. Confusion. The Chairman leafed through his papers

trying to find his copy of the new, updated Standing Orders. He wouldn't find it as he'd never had it. Weaver had made sure that copies were not yet printed, and the online version could not yet be found on the Party's website. Lost them, in other words. Promoted them for the time being to somewhere in cyber space.

Barbara was smiling tightly, knowingly.

'No worries, Chairman. The Leader often quotes from Standing Orders, but more in hope than expectation.'

This brought gasps, stunned laughter, shock and delight.

'In that case, member, please go ahead.'

And she did, swiftly, before her husband could draw breath for his next objection.

'Is there any truth in the rumour that the Dewums' inheritance of Deverill Court and its land is about to be challenged in the courts?'

His own wife! What was she playing at!? That's the sort of question Wilde would have asked.

'And, if that turned out to be true,' she continued. 'wouldn't that mean that the sale of land to Rich and Quick, along with their development of the site, would be called into question?'

'I've not heard that rumour. If there was any truth behind it I'm sure all the parties would have been in touch with my office.' He tried his exasperated yet endlessly patient Leader's manner. 'There are always difficulties, negotiating points, people taking positions, floating options, trying to gain the advantage by crying wolf. I've seen it a thousand times. But this is just about the biggest development in the recent history of Malvoir Valley. And there are bound to be spoilers, moaners, opportunists, nimbys and rumour-mongers,' he added pointedly, 'queuing up to take potshots…'

'But if any party pulls out, the project's dead in the water. Isn't it?'

Weaver swung around to face this interrupter. His eyeballs flashed and swelled and flared, signalling a round of 'Shut-up Gym', which might have been designed as a physical workout for opinionated old folk. This would begin by members taking turns to stand and say, 'You can sit down and shut up!'

'Me sit down? You sit down!'

'Both of you, shut up! If you want to speak, you can go through the Chair.'

'Don't point your finger at me. And you can shut up yourself.'

'He'll point his finger at whoever he wants. He's the Chair, so you can sit down and shut up.'

And so it went. If the sheer boredom of these meetings didn't drive away the young, a five-minute burst of 'Shut-up Gym' would do the trick. And this is precisely what the old boys and the few girls intended, just as surely as the behaviour of middle-aged tennis club members used to deter the young, the fit and the talented from daring to rise above their station. Being able to play didn't mean that you would be allowed to play. As Bob Phelps had so memorably said to Peter Wilde at his very first Party meeting, 'Ability is a serious handicap in the Party, unless it's allied to iron discipline.' Which Phelps had demonstrated by nodding off during the ensuing debate but coming round just in time to vote with the majority.

This particular round of 'Shut Up Gym' saved Weaver from any motion about his current crisis being proposed.

'Let's get on, shall we? We've got to discuss candidates for the elections. We're short of candidates in Hensley, Overchurch and Mitcheldean Upper.'

The Chairman knew this would create a stir.

'Mitcheldean Upper is my ward,' objected Jamal Ashoor.

'There's no such thing as a right to a ward. If you want to stand you must submit your name to the selection committee.'

'But I'm the Councillor for that ward, and Mayor of this town.'

'Election for one electoral period doesn't guarantee any member the right to stand during the next election period.'

'Since when, Chairman?'

'Since always.'

'I see what's going on...'

'There's nothing going on. Rules are rules.'

'Only when they're invoked. Who decided my candidacy was going to be challenged?'

'You decided that yourself!'

This was an unwise intervention from the back. Although the Chairman was too shrewd to be drawn, Mark Given was a hothead.

'And how did I decide that?'

'You've been in the papers these last two weeks saying what a good bloke Peter Wilde is, and you wonder that we notice?'

'I just said what everybody knows to be true. Peter is a friend of mine. He's been chairman of his community council three times as well as a Malvoir Councillor for many years. He should have been town mayor long ago. He's done good things for his ward and the town. That's all I said. I respect him, even if I regret that he's left the Party.'

'Well, if you feel so strongly, maybe you should consider your position.'

'What? As the existing Mayor of this town? The Party wants their own man to be thrown aside? That'll get some good headlines.'

Although Weaver had a lingering objection to Jamal Ashoor – he could never quite put his finger on the reason – he recognised a dangerous and unnecessary step that could be used against anyone in future, including him.

'Unless there's a named challenger to Councillor Ashoor I don't see why he should have to go before a selection committee again. That's not been our practice in Manley Town.'

'Then mebbe it's time it was.'

Weaver turned to stare hard at Mark Given. 'Is there anyone standing against you in Chorfield?'

'No.'

'Then are you going before the selection committee?'

'No. No one's demanded that.'

'Then I'll demand it, in the name of fairness.'

It had to go to the vote, much against Weaver's inclination and mood. He was tired, needed a good night's rest; he could do without this formalised bickering – but he won by 15 to 13, a close call which indicated a growing opposition in the ranks. But no one would be facing covert de-selection on his watch. If the malcontents wanted that, they'd have to do it in the open and not hide behind selective rules.

'Right,' said the Chairman, 'that leaves Hensley and Overchurch.'

No takers. Everyone knew that the boundary changes instigated by Weaver to strengthen his hold on Manley Central had left these neighbouring wards with less social housing, fewer semis and more detached dwellings with conservatory extensions. In other words, he'd sacrificed them to the aspirations of the Tories and the leafleting zeal of the Lib Dems.

Then a hand went up.

'I'd like to fight Hensley.'

It was Barbara. Once again: what the heck?

'You can fight it, but you won't win it.' This might have sounded blunt, but Ken Rudge was trying to be helpful.

'But it's important to try, don't you think? A big party like ours, not seeming to care?'

The murmurs of approval were the sort of noise usually reserved for her husband. Her name went forward.

Weaver remained silent for the first mile of the journey home, but Barbara knew what he meant.

'There's no need to be like that,' she declared.

'I didn't say a word.'

'Precisely.'

'I didn't know you cared that passionately about Malvoir politics.'

'I do. Always have. But now I think the Party needs every little bit of help it can get. In any case, what will we do if you lose your seat in May?'

This did make him laugh. 'Don't be daft, love. Who's going to challenge for Leader? Ken Rudge? I know things about Ken, and he knows I know. Mel Coates? His brain is the size and general shape of a golf ball with the same number of regular indentations where the grey matter failed to develop.'

'I didn't mean losing the Leadership of the Council. I meant losing your seat.'

'Whuh?! Whuh-huh?!' This was hilarious to Weaver.

'Why not? It looks as if you'll have two rivals this time. They could mobilise opposition to you.'

'Don't be silly, Barbara. They're both complete novices.'

'Aren't you a novice? When was the last time you fought an election?'

'It's not about that. That toff, Hugh Brooke, is being taught the realities of power, and that Mellors chancer will wish he'd never moved to the Valley. I've got dirt on both. Brooke exploits migrants and

Mellors has a dodgy offshore bank account.'

'That's all right then. The voters will see who can throw most mud and vote for you. Maybe you could find a way of making *me* drop out of the race. Since you obviously don't like the idea of me running.'

He relented as he always did in the end, though this was not about tiling or curtains. 'There's no point being daft. If you want to run, then run. Only know what it involves. The Tories have a good chance there. And they'll go for you because you're my wife. So be prepared.'

'I think I can handle them.'

'Glad to hear it.'

27 / The Chink In The Charmer

The city of Birmingham turned out to have quite a hold on Peter's time, and Tracy found herself alone for three weekends in a row. It wasn't that she minded. Peter was a single man who lived like a lodger in her cottage. The relationship may have looked intimate to outsiders but was nothing of the kind behind closed doors. He had his bedroom, she had hers. They sat opposite each other at mealtimes, and never occupied the same sofa in the living room.

After a glass of wine too many, Tracy may have kicked off a bit of friendly banter bordering on the flirtatious…

'Nice tie, Peter. Multi-hyper-coloured.'

… and he was always happy to respond in kind…

'Matches my complexion.'

But they never exchanged verbal affection for an experiment in wandering hands.

If he had business in Birmingham, she had no business feeling abandoned. She would simply get on with jobs she'd been neglecting in favour of politics. Plant those bulbs. Buy in the compost for her tomatoes. Tidy her inbox. Label her DVDs. Keep her zero per cent deals up to date. Sign up for that jive class (some hope). Take up knitting.

This last gave rise to insurgent thoughts about how she might be turning into her mother. Except, of course that her Mum had been just that: a mother. Barring a miracle, Tracy never would be, a fact she'd accepted long ago, when the man in her life had withheld the 's' while on his way to becoming her 'ex'. But, provided daughters are willing to look back with dispassion long after the event, mothers have lessons to teach. Her mother had been adept at "keeping herself busy". Marriages "in pickles" could produce, along with preserves, many flavours of home-made jam, freshly baked bread, elderflower champagne, much redecorating, and a more than sufficient supply of cardigans.

So Tracy sat facing the telly, immersed in a Poirot, a Morse or an Austen – one row plain, one row pearl, one row plain, one row pearl, one row pearl, one row…bugger! – and tried not to imagine what sort of business Peter might have in Birmingham, and whether it involved socialising and with whom.

A few brief txts suggested he was preoccupied after his first weekend away, but a lot happier after the second. She was expecting him back on the Sunday night of the third weekend and had roasted a particularly fine leg of organic lamb sourced from a local farm, but he never turned up. Not entirely surprising. He did sometimes overnight at his own house, especially if he had an early meeting at College or in Council the following day. It was, she kept telling herself, none of her business.

But it became so on the Monday morning when the post arrived. Inside a foolscap envelope addressed to Tracy were two photographs on A4 printouts. One of Peter, champagne flute in hand, beaming at a young woman while his other hand rested on her bare shoulder. He was being Peter-as-usual, gregarious, funny. She was tall, dark-haired, buxom and in her mid-thirties. Stuck to the other photograph was a post-it note.

This is what your boyfriend gets up to in Brum.

Nothing else. No signature, no date.

The other image has Peter with his arm around the woman's waist. She's leaning in towards him, with a mischievous grin. Neither are looking at the camera that took the photos. They probably had no idea it was there.

Tracy did the right thing. She put photos and envelope through the shredder that Peter had advised her to buy for, as he put it, "her own protection". Then she threw the shredded remains into her wood-burning stove. If the photographer, or whoever it was who'd paid for the images, wanted to ruin their relationship, it would not work. There was no relationship to undermine. Peter was entirely unconnected to her, except as a political ally. That is what he would remain: a colleague, no more, no less.

Driving back from Birmingham alone, Peter did something unusual. He switched from Radio 3 to Radio 2 and started singing along to the golden oldies. The lyrics were mostly a mystery these days, though the tunes had the power to reawaken some of the most heartrending memories of youth, but he felt ready for them now. Ready to face the past.

The most recent weekend had worked out as hoped and calmed his worst fears. His self-esteem was very nearly fully restored. He could now face whatever the world wanted to launch in his direction: prosecution, huge fines, even imprisonment.

He'd delayed too long, should probably have said something as early as last week, but was now resolved to paint Tracy the full picture. Aloneness had become almost second nature over the last few years. He'd established routines, put up fences around his deeper feelings, but also built in little side gates to let himself out from time to time, or let others in. But the essential Peter Wilde was a fortress – well, more like a modest keep – built against the ravages of later middle age. If he had to be alone, he'd cope.

The trouble with that approach is that it can place too many bolts on the doors. By the time they're all shot back and the door is open, the person outside will have gone. It may have happened once or twice already, though his dithering back then might now turn out to be a blessing. But he mustn't let that happen with Tracy.

He thought about driving straight there, but it was late. Turning up at bedtime was probably not the best move. He wouldn't be able to keep his mouth shut. Then they'd be up half the night, either trying to come to terms with a new happiness or dealing with guilt and disappointment.

He had to be fair, measured, considerate. He'd phone to say he was back. Well, maybe not. It was almost midnight. He'd phone first thing tomorrow morning. Well, maybe not first thing. She'd taken to delivering her leaflets before breakfast, much like the postal service of old. But he'd phone mid-morning. Make sure she was free in the evening. Then he'd go over to her place and broach the subject at dinner... no, take her out to a good restaurant... she loved Thai food... and tell her what he felt... had been feeling for weeks... ask her if... if what? ...never mind, he'd find the right words when the time came.

In the event, he lay awake most of the night, listening to cats going through his neighbours' rubbish bins.

On the other side of town, Tracy found it hard to sleep and got up twice to make cocoa. She sat at the coffee table in the living room, listening to the tock of her grandfather clock and trying to induce sleep by unravelling some knitting which mocked her with its single missed stitch.

Methodical as always, Peter stuck to his plan and phoned at ten-thirty that morning, only to get Tracy's answering service for both landline and mobile. He knew she often monitored her calls but had never – so far as he knew – done this to him. By midday he was phoning her closer acquaintances.

'Saw her this morning in the post office. Definitely around.'

He drove over to Rokeby-on-Bass after work, but the house was in darkness. They had an understanding that he would let himself in through the back door with a key she'd given him, but only after phoning ahead. Stuck to the door was a note.

Peter,

Am out. You can pop the key through the letterbox.

Part Five

Spring

28 / The Skirmishers Deploy

A visitor to Manley and the Malvoir Valley in the first week of March would never have guessed a community in the grip of the most exciting local election in living memory. There were not yet any posters or stakeboards to laud the candidates or even declare their names. Unlike elections in warmer climes there were no competing megaphones playing the parties' chosen music and haranguing each other from headquarters on opposite sides of the street. Only the most observant outsider would have noticed the occasional leafleteers, mostly middle-aged or elderly, trudging the suburban streets, sometimes accosting other pedestrians, sometimes engaging in brief conversation, but mostly stuffing letterboxes with leaflets that would get dumped in rubbish bins within seven seconds of being picked off doormats by occupants.

But in the Manley Central ward, fortress of the Council Leader, things were different. To begin with, the great man himself was little seen. In fact, he was having some trouble finding volunteers to write, print and deliver his election literature. He'd doled out many a long lecture to other Party underlings over the years on how to address local voters but hadn't had to do it in his own interest since 1995. Assuming that he was in some way calling in a favour, he approached Ken Rudge on the subject from an oblique angle.

'You could get some leaflets printed up for me along with yours, I guess.'

'No can do.'

This bluntness caused one of those bodily heat waves that started in his solar plexus – he hesitated to call them hot flushes – and set off palpitations in his chest.

'Wodja mean?'

'There's an election. I'm stretched to the limit as it is. You used to say that every candidate had to take responsibility for their own litrutcher, right?'

That was right, but Weaver had never thought this line of argument would come back to haunt him. He mentally placed a very large black mark against Ken Rudge's name and moved straight on to another member who had every reason to do his bidding. Tom MacDonald was a promising first-time candidate.

'Tom, I was wondering if you'd like the chance to gain experience?'

They both knew what he meant. So Tom MacDonald burned more midnight oil crafting Alex Weaver's campaign leaflets while his wife and baby slept.

He and Weaver had a few heart-to-hearts about the impact of certain paragraphs, but on the whole the Leader was pleased. Tom was a dab hand at digital photography and shot hundreds of frames of Weaver standing in front of swimming pools and recreation centres, shaking hands with pensioners, nurses and doctors (now wash your hands), or playing keepie-uppie with youthful footballers (now wipe your shoes). The results, Weaver reckoned, were far more interesting than the images of would-be councillors pointing downwards at potholes or upwards at malfunctioning streetlamps.

On the other hand, he was shocked by the invoices, even though he took full advantage of a 'tame' Party member in the printing business. Worse was the knowledge that the costs were being doubled by Barbara's first forays into politics, and that it was all going on the plastic.

He earned over fifty thousand a year but could never break even. Had it not been for the Jaguar and the recent holidays he'd have been jabbing a finger at the credit card statements and making noises about 'stuff having to stop'. As things stood, he'd just have to get re-elected, accept the increase in the Leader's salary, and max out the expenses while tightening his belt. There was also, at the back of his mind, the thought that Barbara might get elected after all. Once in, there was every chance she would find herself a cabinet seat or a committee chair. That would solve their financial worries for years ahead – provided she didn't start agitating for a larger barn conversion somewhere else.

He soon discovered that getting the leaflets written and printed constituted barely half the battle. He now had sixteen hundred leaflets sitting on a shelf in his garage. At first, he thought 'no problem' and recalled his first years in local politics, out in all weathers, knocking on doors, engaging in lively discussions on street corners. A doddle.

But after an evening of trudging the tarmac, being barked at by the politically ignorant such as dogs and underage youths, or blanked by residents he thought would be enthralled by his message, he returned to the Jaguar – left discreetly in his designated parking space at the Town Hall – and reflected on the fourteen hundred leaflets still undelivered, not to mention the wide-ranging ache in his lower back (perhaps Barbara was right about him joining a gym – there might even be a few votes in it). But dominating these were the memories of cold, even hostile glances from people unwilling to respond to his perfectly friendly approaches. People, he mused, had it too good. They'd forgotten or had never experienced the battles of the past. They didn't know the sacrifices others had made for the two or three cars everybody now seemed to have in their driveways and the several pieces of oblong plastic in their wallets.

He wondered who he could persuade to deliver his leaflets. Barbara would oblige, but she was getting on with her own electioneering with such easy relish he was almost ashamed to hint at his own difficulties. If Rudge wasn't prepared to deliver on past favours, he couldn't expect more from the other smart alec councillors such as Price and Rogers. Well over half the candidates were a liability and that only left the likes of Tom MacDonald to get the job done.

But Tom – or his wife – was wising up, for suddenly there were thrice-weekly baby-sitting duties. Back in the day, a candidate who had to do women's work wouldn't last two minutes in Malvoir politics, but "looking after kids" now ranked as a cast-iron excuse.

In the end Weaver turned to an old friend outside politics. If there was anyone in town who knew where to find a crowd of young, strapping lads it would be Reg Barton, Chairman of Manley FC and director of Manley Landfill "Unlimited", as the local joke had it.

'Leave it to me, Alex. Ship the leaflets over and I'll get it sorted.'

And why not? Reg wanted his new stadium and understood the hidden costs.

With the back-aching, heel-blistering matter of delivery dealt with, Weaver could turn to the politics. He now had just one opponent, Hugh Brooke, after the other newbie, would-be independent Brian Mellors, had wisely dropped out of the running.

Like Reg Barton in another field of endeavour, Weaver's inclination was to play the man not the ball. Toffs-out-of-water were an easy target. They floundered about, not knowing a shin-pad from a jockstrap – until it was too late. He'd already helped to create the distinct impression around town, mostly through reports in the local press, that Brooke was a rogue employer of East European labour who'd been attracting regular attention from the police. One such depiction would usually be enough, but the multi-barbed image of social privilege, sharp practice, exploitation of people in a weaker position, and encouraging foreigners to do local people's work was bound to snag Hugh "the Broke" on at least one prejudice per household. Why, even his own grandmother had judged him unsuitable to inherit according to family custom.

The Lib Dems had made the toff's job harder by putting up a 'paper' candidate. One that wouldn't canvass but just send two mail shots in the week before polling. The Lib Dems knew they had no chance of winning but could not resist the 'puffer fish' tactic of trying to make themselves look bigger than they were. So, even if Mellors the Independent had quit, the Lib Dems would come along to split the vote.

Therefore, job done. Weaver felt it was hardly worth his while to read and critique "the Broke's" literature. He'd leave that to his assistant.

So it was that instead of elderly campaigners strolling the pavements of the Manley Central ward, delivering their unloved bumf with liver-spotted, arthritic fingers, there were packs of young men in jackets of a style so common to each group that they constituted a uniform.

The first group wore tan bomber jackets of a distinctly seventies cut, while some of the rival team wore equally short, black leather jackets boasting vertical or horizontal stripes on the sleeves. Unlike their counterparts in other wards they did not slow down, linger on doorsteps to elicit a householder's political allegiance or engage passers-by in chit-chat. They were there to deliver as many leaflets as quickly as possible.

From time to time these groups would encounter each other on the streets. One lot, seeing the other, would usually elect to tread a different route until the opposition was gone. But occasionally they would turn a corner and come face to face. This was more than a little awkward, for they were not Britons, trained to deflect a delicate situation with a wry smile, or at most with a lively example of sportive wit, graciously acknowledged on both sides, at least until the other was out of earshot. These were men passionately concerned with their own notions of patriotic self-esteem, which they could insist upon with the several pounds of well-honed cutlery concealed about their persons.

So far, the evenness of numbers had led to no more than some flicked airing of the steel, an underhand flourishing, a cutting of air, and a considerable number of terse injunctions that were both incomprehensible to the other side yet perfectly understood. There were no witnesses to the weapons, though an elderly Mrs Jenkins at number 42 Holly Bush Road claimed, upon questioning, that she may have seen "scissors" or "large keys" being brandished. Her failing eyesight made closer police investigation unlikely, but each side took the precaution in future to leave its bespoke jewellery at home and carry well-sharpened screwdrivers instead.

If these men's commissioners had suspected any of this, they'd have been "horrified" in the manner of folk who rarely, if ever, laid a finger on another person approximately their own size. Alex Weaver knew that Hugh Brooke could rely on what he called "a pack of young Poles" to deliver his leaflets. But he had no idea that Reg Barton, Chairman of Manley Town FC, would supply him with a small army of young Albanians.

The fallout had its private and public dimensions. In private Alex Weaver phoned Reg Barton.

'Bloody hell, Reg! Who are these people?'

'Sorry, Alex. I'll have a word.'

'Have two while you're at it.'

Since every setback is an opportunity in politics, he had Tom MacDonald craft a letter to the Manley Observer.

If anyone else has evidence of weapons being carried by leafleteers in the Manley Valley, of intimidation or threats of violence, then the police should be informed and the perpetrators identified. Until then, candidates should not make general, unsubstantiated accusations in the media that could be regarded as an attempt to smear other candidates.

While on the subject of the law, I should point out to Hugh de Broche, and anyone else involved in campaigning, that every leaflet must carry details of who has printed the material and on whose behalf. Anything less could result in criminal proceedings.'

In a barn near Deverill Court, Feliks Zielinsky considered this letter.

'It's – how do you say – disingenious.'

'Disingenuous,' said Hugh.

'Nobody on our side has made any accusation about anyone carrying weapons and we carry all information about the legal publisher. He's using the letter to make accusations against us.'

'What do we do?' asked Hugh.

'We rebut. It's your right.'

'Are you sure…?'

'I'll write it. You correct the English.'

'Fine.'

Before the evening's leafleteering, all members of the extended family were assembled and soundly berated.

'Are you crazy? Who decided to take knives?'

'Are *you* crazy?' countered Tomasz. 'Those Albanians haven't just got blades, they've got guns.'

'Have you seen guns?'

'I saw one of them holding a gun ready in his pocket,' Ambroszy declared.

'What? You saw the gun itself? Or just the shape of a gun?'

'Of course, it was a gun,' insisted Jakub. 'They run the drugs in and out of this town. You think they don't have guns?'

Feliks was prepared to concede the point. 'OK. But from now on, no weapons. Not even a screwdriver or a Stanley knife. The police will be watching you like hawks. They have special powers now, so they'll stop and frisk you.'

For presentational purposes, Feliks organised a fashion makeover for his leafleteers. The black leather jackets with the stripes would have to go. So, too, the well-worn jeans. To this end he made careful notes at the next GROBAG meeting on features of British dress code for respectable-looking activists.

The streets of the Manley Central ward over the next few days experienced a period of perplexed calm. The young Albanians continued much as before, apart from leaving their weaponry at home. But to the untrained eye a familiar group had retired from the scene to be replaced by men in wax or tweed jackets, fleeces or light overcoats. Some wore ties, while one or two sported cardigans. There was the occasional flat cap, one or two angler's hats with paraphernalia and, as far as footwear was concerned, not a trainer in sight. Even the Albanians were confused, until they spotted these apparently quintessential Britons piling into a VW van for their journey back to base.

29 / Bggr

The atmosphere at the Grey House was electric. It pulsated with activity: as a building site, a political HQ at the height of an election, a night school, and a workers' dormitory.

Hugh revelled in every enterprise, up with Jacinta at the crack of dawn and into bed long after the night workers had left for their shifts. He attended meetings, demonstrations, and what Feliks called 'cabals'. He wrote and distributed leaflets, wrangled with candidates, trudged the streets of Manley. He drank too much coffee, wolfed down Jacinta's versions of beef stew and chocolate cake – 'You have to build your muscles' – and was asleep almost before his head hit the pillow.

He'd imagined the English lessons would tail off as his guests gained proficiency, but the opposite happened. The more they learned, the more they needed. Izzy was now attending a hairdressing course at Manley College, thanks to Peter Wilde's support, and needed to practise a whole range of vocabulary as alien to Hugh as a bushman's knowledge of edible roots: extensions, A-line bobs, disconnection, feathering, the Jekyll and Hyde.

'This is a kind of normal look that becomes something totally 'out there' when you change the separation…'

'Parting.'

'Thank you. Change the parting and uncover the cut underneath.' Izzy stared at the top of Hugh's head.

'I can do one for you if you like.'

'Try it out on Eddie first.'

Henryk, Kasper and Jakub now wanted long lessons as a small group. If they learned the correct words and pronunciation for petrol, diesel, pizza bases, parsnips and gin, they also wanted to know how to describe origins, production methods, pricing and recipes. The lessons grew longer, not shorter, the explanations more refined, and there were periods when Hugh did ten hours of teaching six days a week.

Mr Groves, his accountant, raised eyebrows in despair. 'I was hoping you'd have a few years without any tax liabilities. When you managed the estate, there were all sorts of ways to offset income against expenses. But this... this is cash. In *hand*. With hardly any *overheads*.' He frowned and released a long breath through one side of his mouth, as if Hugh had performed some elementary blunder – *earning* money - thereby singlehandedly undermining Mr Groves's reputation for reducing his clients to paper penury. He retained Hugh as a client, despite his misfortunes, and this was his reward. 'If you were *paying* these people to rebuild your house, we'd stand a chance.'

Hugh had never really believed in his heart that the Zielinskys would make good on their promises. But the house now had a water-tight roof, which meant all the beams, rafters and joists had been repaired or replaced and the slate tiles laid. Until the moment of completion he'd never fully understood that hackneyed phrase "a roof over one's head". And the Zielinskys hadn't resisted Mary's suggestion that he knock out a wall to enlarge the sitting room. They hadn't baulked at the notion of tall French windows and a larger prospect of the garden. Eddie had rolled his gaze around the walls and ceilings, thumped a door jamb with the flat of his hand, and chuntered to himself for half a minute. From then on, the job was as good as done.

It meant that Hugh had to return once more to the barn while all the builder's dust hung in the air, but this time he decided to bed down with the family, claiming a spot between Szymon and Henryk who worked most nights, then plied him with questions first thing in the morning concerning, of all things, organic farming methods.

But Hugh did not mind. There wasn't a man in the barn who

smiled and twittered at breakfast. Nor a woman. A grim breaker of fasts respects the rule of "caffeine first".

The grimmest was always Feliks, who looked for the first half hour like a man with severe indigestion. He'd taken over Hugh's sleeping station on the platform and gallantly offered to hand it back. But Hugh recognised the right man in the right place. The platform was now awash with leaflets, charts, schedules and battle plans. The slightest action of a careless hand would upset the perfectly controlled chaos. One end of the table was always kept clear, but the rest, underneath and on top, was occupied by heavy boxes and paper piles, stacked as tight as sandbags and adding to the siege mentality of the GROBAG cabal when it met at the other end.

Living in the barn, Hugh could enjoy the Zielinskys' increasing affluence. There were now two televisions served by a satellite dish. A large flatscreen model was set up against the wall furthest from the kitchen, and this area became the sports stadium where the men would cheer on their favourite football team, not surprisingly the one owned and raised to the English Premiership by a Polish émigré. By contrast, the one they loved to hate was owned, produced and directed by a Russian oligarch.

Jacinta had the other TV in the kitchen so she could follow her favourite soaps while doing the chores. There were no battles over which channels to watch as there were now several laptops connected to Hugh's broadband. On a Sunday afternoon, following Mass and Sunday lunch, the barn looked like a youth hostel occupied by a tribe of lounging, ear-plugged techies. The clothes and footwear were new and noticeably trendy. Only Eddie and Jacinta stuck to their more Spartan ways.

'It's more important that Łucja has new clothes,' Jacinta would insist while darning a hole in a cardigan. 'And have you spoken with

Łucja today?' she demanded of Hugh.

'Not yet.'

Which was sometimes a lie, as he knew Jacinta could be touchy if she thought her daughter was favouring another with the first fruits of communication.

In fact, Hugh and Lucy were in touch at least twice a day and praised creation for the inventors of txting.

'Match for my club team today.'

'Let me know how it goes.'

Later.

'What is it you say in English? Bggr? Lost match. 23-25, 21-25, 25-19, 25-22, 13-15. Hurt wrist again. DON'T tell Mum.'

'FYI, we check results online. IMHO better to tell your mum about wrist.'

'Bggr. OK.'

But for every message delightfully received, Hugh experienced an equal diffidence. By comparison to Lucy's, his prospects were earthbound. While she was travelling Europe with her university and club teams, he felt riveted to the ground by circumstance. If he'd had his inheritance, he could have flown anywhere to watch her play. On the other hand, if he'd kept his inheritance, he'd never have met her. He wondered if she cared. Or whether there was bound to be someone out there – wealthier, more bulging in muscle and aerobic capacity – who'd prove a better match.

As far as challenging his grandmother's will was concerned, there appeared no more hope than on the day the will was read. His solicitor was as fatalistic as Mary and Sir James Mansfield were hopeful.

'There's no *in*substantial evidence, let alone anything *sub*stantial so far. Looks like a lost cause, I fear.'

But Sir James demonstrated why he was so often likened to a

terrier at the Bar.

'Who had access to your grandmother during her last days? Was there a maid? A nurse? A doctor? A cleaner? We need evidence as to your grandmother's mental state. Find these people and elicit their memories.'

But Mr Cashin, the solicitor, was less eager. 'Beginning an enquiry of this kind with no more than the *hope* of payment from an eventual legacy is not an *attractive* proposition.' In other words, not worth his time and effort. He was secure enough in this opinion to repeat it over the phone to Sir James. Who contacted Hugh.

'Solicitors unprepared to take even the slightest risk on behalf of their clients are generally of the less than useful variety. Allow me to contribute to your fighting fund. A thousand pounds to get started. But only if you find yourself another solicitor. I found lawyers like Mr Cashin deeply irritating when I was at the Bar. I wouldn't wish to subsidise them now that I'm retired.'

Reinforced by Sir James's "bag of sand" Hugh approached the firm of Bight and Maym, whose junior interns were on basic salaries that allowed them to live at home and share the occasional pint in a pub. On the other hand, commissions on successful outcomes were generous. These juniors were, as a consequence, what Bight called "keen" and Maym called "hungry". They even had the look of ravening canines with muzzles constantly scenting the breeze for the nearest morsel.

Within half a day, one of them learned that a Mrs Dewum had ordered three thousand pheasant poults costing almost eight thousand pounds from a Wiltshire hatchery a fortnight after she had returned to England and seven months before the earliest possible delivery date in June the following year. She had paid the deposit using her husband's credit card.

'Your grandmother had months to live. Would she have agreed to a pheasant shoot on the estate?'

Hugh was astounded. 'No. In any case, I was managing the estate and I wouldn't have allowed it.'

'So, Mr and Mrs were planning for a pheasant shoot months before the new will was signed. We'll dig deeper.'

The spadework threw up a John Belcher, who'd made a verbal agreement to become Mrs Dewum's gamekeeper before she bought the poults.

'She asked me to keep it discreet, like, but I wish I'd turned her down. She was clueless about bird welfare and in the end paid me less than half what she promised.'

The spades were augmented by diggers, and exploratory holes became excavations.

'Mr Brooke? Could you pop down to the office this afternoon? There's something I'd like you to hear.'

This "something" turned out to be an interview with his grandmother's GP. One of the scenting dogs had caught a waft on the breeze and committed it to a sound file on his mobile phone.

'Mrs de Broche was a little agitated on one occasion when I visited. Might not be important. But she was becoming wary of her niece's husband. Said he'd taken over care duties as her niece was always out riding or shopping. Of course, she didn't understand a lot of what the man said. He's American, apparently. And he'd started dealing with her post. She didn't like that at all.'

'Would you vouch for this in a court of law?'

'No need really. I like to keep notes. One can never be too careful these days. If I'm obliged to release them, I will.'

'There!' exclaimed Mr Bight. 'Examples of unusual behaviour

worthy of further investigation. Whatever you were paying Cashin and Cashin, it was a hundred per cent too much. Your next move, I suggest, would be to employ a firm of private investigators. We need to know a little more about your aunt and her husband.' He was offering Hugh a business card. 'It's your decision, of course, but you couldn't do better than Hackett and Pearce. If you'd prefer me to instruct them, I'd be more than happy.'

Though Mr Bight smiled a good deal, his every word seemed packed with cold intent. Hugh handed him carte blanche to pursue the investigation, along with another five hundred pounds' worth of encouragement, while silently praying that no one would ever approach Messrs Hackett, Pearce, Bight and Maym with a grievance against him.

30/ One Rule For Them…

Lesley-Anne was puzzled. Every morning for the past few days her husband would enter the breakfast room and, without quite meeting her eye, would emit - for that was the only word she could conjure for such battery-powered feebleness… *emit* what looked like a miniature, lopsided smile. She might have identified this as a grimace – a grimace of pain indicating a doctor's deadly diagnosis that he was trying to keep secret – had it not been for a trace of ingratiation in the mouth and fear in the eye. These were the emotions – like careless fingers on a hair trigger – guaranteed to touch off the "tongue-lash" impulse located somewhere at the back of Lesley-Anne's skull.

She'd also noticed that Calvin was letting his hair grow longer at the back and hoped this wasn't an attempt to reinstate the ridiculous, plaited, would-be hipster pig-tail he'd sported the first time they'd met. It hadn't lasted long. A few "lost in the moment" tugs while making love had presented him with a choice: lose the tail or lose the soulmate. Any sign of its reappearance would signal a change in their soul mateyness.

She'd come to recognise that allowing these impulses free rein had consequences for herself, so she bore this smile and this straggly hair even though they touched her like heavy-grade sandpaper on a tender part. But there was no facial expression that could irritate her quite so much. If a man has something to say, he should say it. This man clearly had something he was longing to say. What, she wondered, was he waiting for? How long would it take before he mustered the courage?

Lesley-Anne was no stranger to sudden revelations that shook the foundations of her relationships. Calvin Dewum was, after all, her fourth husband. She hoped he would also be the last. But this first-thing-before-porridge-type-smile was placing this ambition in some jeopardy.

'Any news?' she barked one morning.

He was startled. For many mornings past she had watched him closely, as if she somehow *knew*. 'News? Nothing special. And you?'

This counter-question usually saved him further trouble. Lesley-Anne rarely needed a second invitation to offload her latest anxieties. When they first got together, he quite enjoyed her outbursts and referred to them as "spontaneous". He realised now that while she defied theories about British "reserve", he often wished she'd conform.

'If you mean bills and demands, there are plenty. Some chap from the Department of the Environment, Food and Rural Affairs is swamping my office with idiotic requests and instructions. They're telling me what to grow in the fields, and how to mow around them, and what condition the gates are supposed to be in, and when the hedges should be trimmed, and it's just ridiculous…' Deep down, she knew that much of this would have fallen to her leasehold farmers. If only she hadn't pushed them into surrendering the leases by what she called her "steely renegotiations" and they called "unreasonable demands".

When Calvin had first met Lesley-Anne, some two and a half years earlier, he'd formed the impression that here was a supremely competent woman, and competence was what he needed in a companion. He was tired of fragile consorts and needed, he decided, someone more robust. That she was potentially rich had added to the attraction. But these references to her "office" were alarming. It was, in truth, less a filing station than a storage facility, where correspondence was placed in drawers and rarely, as Calvin would say, "actioned". Even he, a self-confessed indoor person, who spent most of his life seeking air-conditioned protection from the elements at latitude 34, had noticed that the fields on the estate were looking overgrown and weed-infested. Where were the farmhands who were supposed to keep 'em neat and tidy? If he were her, he'd fire them on the spot.

Only to hear that she'd done just that, but much earlier and for some other misdemeanour, like not responding instantly to some demand. Trouble was, farming was starting to get profitable again. These farmer guys were doing OK from the land they owned or worked, and they could pick and choose the jobs they did. Lesley-Anne blamed it on some European guy called Kapp.

'They don't have to do an honest day's work. The EU pays them to do nothing and we have to finance it from our taxes.'

The mention of taxes increased Calvin's heart rate and rendered his innards a little more gooey. He was tempted to seek solace for his current troubles, and where better than in the soft bosom of a spouse's understanding? But "soft" and "bosom" did not accurately describe Lesley-Anne's attributes, which tended towards the spiky.

Unable to face the porridge and waffles that sustained his wife in the saddle most mornings, he retired to his study. But even this was no refuge. In the bottom left-hand drawer of his imported teak, roll-top desk sat a pile of official letters that induced a combination of rage and fear in equal measure. Injunctions, instructions, rulings and demands. It felt as if he had some of the world's most powerful people snapping at his heels. Cardinals, chief rabbis, general secretaries, CEOs and tax inspectors of both the US Federal and Her Majesty's governments, all requiring detailed replies to impertinent questions. Just because he made a buck or two from harmless substances.

Why weren't they out chasing the real crooks? There were billionaires who had lower tax demands than he was facing. Words like fascist, Nazi and authoritarian ripped through his cognitive faculties like buckshot at short range. If certain people had acted on their promises, he would be well free of all such problems. At the very least, he'd be able to afford lawyers to keep these intrusive jobsworths off his back. But the international tax lawyers he sounded out cost thousands of pounds an hour!! One rule for the rich, another for the honest toiling classes.

He would sometimes sit for hours wrestling with alternative solutions, all of them, it turned out on closer inspection, quite hopeless. There was, he decided, only one way out. The second part of the land deal had to go through. And this time they had to get full benefit from the uplift in value when planning permission was granted. These people had taken Lesley-Anne for a ride on the first tract of land. She could have got three or four times the amount they paid out. But he wouldn't blame her for that. No point weeping over an upturned milk truck. But it was time those Rich and Quick crooks put up or shut up. He had a good mind to… Well, maybe not, but somebody had to start kickin' ass around here. He'd abandoned so many unpromising scenarios in his almost four decades of entrepreneurship that he was never short of a Plan B. But if Plan A involved the transfer of three to four million pounds sterling, it was worth giving it his best shot.

His dander up, he set off to find Lesley-Anne and tell her exactly what they should be doing about these goddam people. He positively flowed along the corridors and down the main staircase, knowing that if she was already in the saddle, he wouldn't see her again till lunch, and his nerves would have to withstand hours of fretting.

As luck would have it, her horse had cast a shoe and she was still at the stables. There would be no riding today. The local farrier had relegated Deverill Court from the top to nearer the bottom of his client list. Calvin knew nothing of this but caught Lesley-Anne in a similarly molten frame of mind.

'Honey, we've gotta get that money!' he exclaimed. 'I've had it up to here.' He indicated the bridge of his nose with a low-flying salute.

'I couldn't agree more!' she exclaimed, her face coming up fully flushed from a hoof-examining position.

They explored, during the next few minutes, a full alphabetical list of expletives – the a's, the b's, the c's, the f's – and concluded by promulgating an action plan of bullet-pointed, finger-jabbing severity. Points one to seven concerned actions their chief tormentors would have to take if they were to avoid the direst consequences.

'I know things about these people,' fumed Calvin. 'I've seen what they get up to. They're gonna deliver on this deal, or I'll make arrangements to have their mugshots all over the internet.'

In a calmer mood, Lesley-Anne might have urged more caution. "These people", as Calvin called them, operated in spheres that she despised but barely understood. They employed modes of self-promotion and protection that were less comprehensible than, say, the biophysical study of heavy vapours. But there was something about a man in full apoplectic mode that she found stimulating. In this sense, her Calvin was restored.

'We'll get that money!' he snapped. '*Your* money!'

'*Our* money!' she replied, underlining the exclamation mark with a slap of riding crop on booted calf. She stood poised for a few moments, wild-eyed and nostrils dilating, examining his features for evidence of total commitment, like a horsewoman demanding to know how genuine her ride would be.

He knew that look and glanced quickly around for a newly cleaned stall with plenty of fresh hay.

While Lesley-Anne and Calvin renewed their vows in a stable, surveyors were at work in the fields between Fletcher's Hill and

Deverill Court. They were not employed by Rich and Quick, but by Malvoir Valley Council. Their task was not to survey for the building of a stadium or new homes, but for the laying of a new drive between the main road and the Court. It was one of the side-deals that Lesley-Anne had struck with Alex Weaver. I sell some of my land for your prestige project and the Council pays for a new drive. Justified to the Planning Committee as a traffic safety measure to replace an existing junction. Passed by a large majority. Estimated cost: £200,000 per 100 metres. Distance from road to house: 357metres.

31 / A New Breed

Tom MacDonald was a novelty in Malvoir Valley politics. He earned less than his wife, made beds, vacuumed carpets, warmed milk and changed nappies. They were things he did on principle, not because he enjoyed them. Needs must. His wife was a nurse and bringing in decent money. Not enough to afford two holidays abroad every year, but enough to pay the mortgage and cover the bills. Meanwhile, he was down to part-time in the local PriceCutta supermarket doing a job he'd never imagined when receiving his Upper Second in Economics.

'You would have got a First, Tom, if only you could have suspended your need to seek truth with a capital T. Economists create their own reality.'

When neighbours and PriceCutta customers learned he was standing for the Council, they mostly wished him luck and told him things he was glad to learn.

'I'll vote for you, lad, no danger. We need proper working people like you on the Council.'

It was a gamble, but he had a chance. He'd done his background research, chosen his target ward with some care, produced his leaflets in large numbers, and set up the infrastructure that every modern councillor needs – a home office, a laser printer, a website, an online presence. But more than that, he was known on the street, had put in the miles and done time on the doorstep.

What he hadn't accounted for was being leeched on by Alex Weaver. The demands were constant. Leaflets, posters, letters to the local press, posts on social media. Kim, his wife, was becoming fractious.

'But you've got enough of your own stuff to do. I hardly ever see you these days. It's not fair.'

'You're right. It's not fair. He's using me.'

'So why don't you tell him that?'

'Because he'll slash my political tyres if I make a fuss.'

'Is it worth it?'

'It is.'

It was an honest answer and she trusted Tom's judgement. She knew he would never risk her and the baby's welfare on an ego trip of his own.

Although Tom accepted the burden, he found it increasingly irksome.

'I thought those leaflets would have gone out by now.'

Weaver would issue these irritable observations without even looking at him.

'These are the new ones you wanted. The others were delivered last week.'

Without the slightest hint of gratitude for a job he could never achieve himself at such levels of flowing prose and efficiency, another demand would follow.

'And what about that letter to the Manley Observer?'

These letters – rebuttals, prebuttals, disclaimers, denials, justifications, accusations, evasions and general self-promotion – were the straws that were slowly breaking the camel's back. Tom understood the importance of getting the message across in the media, but Weaver was the kind of politician who thought that media coverage was both the means and the end. He genuinely seemed to believe that saying was as good as doing. Every favourable press story was a "result".

But Weaver was now fighting the battle of perception, shoring up his image as it came under attack from deadly facts. Even though the media did not yet have wind of the most damaging information, Weaver was becoming desperate, demanding that Tom produce reams of cosmetic verbiage for everything from the Manley Observer to the Residents Association newsletters. He even griped about the photos being used.

'Why did they choose that one? Would you trust the man in that photo? They must have taken better photos than that.'

Now he wanted Tom to attend every event with his own camera and be solely responsible for the images released to the press.

'What do you mean, you can't? You work part-time.'

'The editor won't wear it. It'll be a union issue.'

This was more than a little disingenuous, as Tom knew very well that newspapers had long since ignored the unions, but he also knew Weaver would find it hard to buck the union argument. He wasn't that far removed from his old Party roots.

'But how do I stop them publishing these photos?'

'You can't.'

That was the closest Tom came to open revolt, but he knew that a bust-up could not be far away. If he was ever to get on in Manley politics, eventually making his way to the national scene, he'd have to find a way of dealing with Alex Weaver. And the easiest way was to have Alex Weaver deal with himself. The sooner, the better.

A helpful source of information opened up as a result of Weaver's constant demands. Sally Prior had been editor at the Manley Observer for a generation and was known for her wondrous memory. So swift and accurate was her recall that she'd been banned from playing the quiz machines in every pub within a fifty-mile radius. And among all that general knowledge and cultural trivia were memories of conversations with Alex Weaver dating back to the 1980s.

'So, you're Alex's new doormat, are you?' she asked.

Tom had been speaking to her by phone for several weeks, delivering his ghosted letters and opinion columns by email attachment, occasionally phoning her at Weaver's behest to complain about perceived bias in her editorials.

'You recognise the suckers, do you?' he replied, trying to dilute her scepticism with banter.

'Oh, I've seen them come and I've seen them go. I could count seven, not including you. Talented young men who do lots of hard work for our great leader, but don't ever seem to get the rewards they deserve.'

'You're not a Party supporter, then?'

'Me? I've always thought so. Never voted anything else. Yet. But I've never thought of Alex as being a true Party man.'

'So what is he, then?'

'Alex? I suppose I'd have to call him a Weaverite. And what are you? A Party man or a MacDonaldite?'

He was intimidated but also encouraged by her forthright manner.

'I'd like to make a difference if I can.'

'Ah! Not afraid of the cliché that betrays an unpopular seriousness.'

'Should I be?'

'Perhaps not. The trouble is, everyone says that, even people who've long since lost all credibility.'

'But I mean it.'

'I'm sure you do. But you need to say it in a different way.'

'Any ideas?'

'Plenty. But I shouldn't waste them on Alex Weaver's stuff. He's had his chance. But you get yourself elected, and we can sit down one day and talk it over. Not that I'm offering to set aside my editorial independence. But I like young people with just the right amount of earnest idealism. I'm frankly fed up with the flash boys and girls, who think that policies and narratives are one and the same.'

32 / Teaching An Old Dog New Tricks

'There's not much I can do.'

'But he's a mate... m'friend...,' persisted Gerry Quick. He hated it when his partner came over all minging-monging "objective" and tried to teach him about the construction business. Young Stevie Rich! Who hadn't known the difference between screeding and scumbling when they first met. He thought they had something to do with hill walking. 'He'd just like to know that the Dewums are gonna get summat in advance.'

Steven Rich's metal-frame glasses glinted in the late afternoon light. His large office windows overlooked the depot where the company's vehicles parked overnight. He preferred it to the view from the front of the building over the picturesque canal basin. It gave him and his employees the sense of a watch tower with a wide field of vision.

'In advance of what? Money is transferred when all the conditions are agreed and all the documents signed.'

'But the Dewums sold the first lot on the basis of the second sale going ahead.'

'If they want more money, they can sell the other plot to someone else.'

'But that would scupper a big part of the whole project! And the profit.'

'The whole thing's scuppered anyway, Gerald.' Rich waited for signs that his full meaning had sunk in. 'Retail stores are dying a slow death and that football club can't sustain the sort of stadium they're planning. The sums just don't add up.'

'But it's a clear-out in retail,' Gerry offered. 'For the folk who over-invested.'

'No, it's bigger than that. If we go ahead, it could finish us as a business. But if we're smart, we could come out ahead.'

'How's that?'

'Drop this project and bank the land. Add the Council land and we've also got a riverside location. Then wait. We build houses when the time's right. In the meantime, we look at projects with more profit, less risk.'

'Such as?'

'Student accommodation. There's a lot of liquidity in the international student market. They don't want old-fashioned study rooms. A lot of them want the sort of town and city centre apartments they have back home. It's a high-value, growing market.'

'OK.' Gerry was relieved that building was part of the plan and his input was still required. 'What do we do about Alex? We can't hang him out to dry.'

Steven Rich played for time. 'You know him best, Gerald. What would you do?'

'Normally, you'd want to tie him in tight, but make him a decent offer as well.'

'Can you do that?'

'It depends how he reacts. But, yeah, I can hold him close. But you do the spreadsheets, so the offer is up to you.'

'That shouldn't be a problem. Alex has been solid all the way. He deserves a bonus.'

'Fine. Let me know and I'll set up a meeting with him.' Gerry stood and flexed a stiff left knee. 'So, how bad are the markets?'

'Very bad for some. If you've got shares in retail, I should clear out.

Or you could short the shares of a company like Greensville and clean up.'

'Short?'

'Yes, I know people in the City who are planning to short Greensville and Tatum.'

Gerry rolled his eyes on his way out. 'Good luck, to 'em, I guess.'

In fact, he quite liked the idea of borrowing shares he didn't own, selling them, then buying them back when prices hit rock bottom to pocket the difference. Stevie Rich might have inherited a modest, debt-laden building business in his early twenties, but he'd turned it around and shown that he could out-think a ferret. He was also generous in passing on useful information to his mates. Gerry was sorry for Alex and his prospects, but he'd understand there was nothing personal about business decisions. At least, he hoped he would.

Steven Rich watched from his office window as his big-bodied, stiff-legged partner crossed the yard to his Mercedes convertible. He'd inherited Gerald as a co-director from his father, and the question of how to free himself from the relationship was never far from his thoughts. He recalled the evening of his sixteenth birthday, when his father had come home late from work ashen-faced after more than one bank had refused to extend the company's credit lines. He was desperate for cash to stay afloat, and Gerald Quick, scaffolder of choice to Malvoir Council, had plenty.

Quite how "good old Gerry" had accumulated so much property and cash was never clear, but Rich was gathering intel from reliable sources about his past and current associates. Directors of the two rugby clubs once slated for a move to the proposed Rokeby stadium had dropped broad hints about Reg Barton and his connections to shady Balkan businessmen. Thumbscrews couldn't induce them to sign their names on the same contract as 'Reg the Wedge'. There were even rumours that he was involved in illegal betting on Manley Town's match results.

Sharing this with Quick would have set off warning lights in his partner's brain. For which there was no need. Chess pieces can be moved with minimal fuss for maximum effect.

Rich would never forgive the big-name building firms for killing off their small and medium-sized rivals in their scramble for bigger profits. The major banks were sometimes as bad in putting their boots on the throats of people working at ground level. But it was not impossible for a dispassionate intelligence to play these people at their own game. It wasn't important to win big: just winning a thin slice, and then another, was revenge enough.

As he turned from the window and back to work, Steven Rich blessed his father's memory for insisting that their business premises remained physically separate from Gerry Quick's scaffolder's yard by a distance of several miles.

33 / I Have A Dream...

The reality of a democratic contest came bearing down on a long list of Malvoir Valley first-time candidates in the first week of April. It arrived in the form of headshots, group photos, nomination papers, election expenses and a manifesto.

Worst of all were the nomination forms. It would be hard to imagine official applications better designed to deter new blood. Instructions were not so much opaque as vertiginous. They could disorientate native speakers of the English language to the point where readers might wish to slip away down a cliff face or throw themselves into the void beyond the cliff edge where no officialese existed.

But once the forms were signed and delivered to Electoral Services, election expenses kicked in. Peter Wilde harangued fellow Independents on the importance of keeping strict accounts and not straying over the spending limits, however unlikely this might seem.

'If it's a close race, Alex Weaver's people will be going over your expenses with a microscope. All our rivals will notice the number of opposition stakeboards going up on what they consider to be their patch. Record every single one as an expense. Write down your car mileage for every trip. All your stationery and computer expenses, photography costs, all your meals when you're out canvassing, all the buttonholes you buy during the campaign, everything. And, finally, if you've got any skeletons in your cupboard, now is the time to pull out of the race. You can do it quietly. You can decide you don't want the hassle. But do it now, because Alex Weaver will take full advantage in the week before the election, and he'll make sure any negative stories hit the main pages of the Manley Observer in the few days before polling.'

There were some mutterings at this, and some uneasy glances to this side and that, but no one was clearly on the point of withdrawing.

'Above all, make sure your computers have the best malware detectors you can afford and never open an email attachment you don't trust. The last thing you want to do is download the software that one of Alex Weaver's mates will no doubt be sending to all other parties' candidates. If you do, you could be sending out porn with every email you write.'

Gasps of outrage and incredulity.

Feliks then set about arranging the Independent Alliance photoshoot outside the Council Offices. Thirty-eight hopefuls and one incumbent milling about in their best togs and apparently doing their utmost to ignore or misinterpret instructions.

There was an added delay as Peter urged the photographer to wait. With his phone clamped to one ear, he warned the Alliance that he had "incoming".

This turned out to be Jamal Ashoor, the Mayor of Manley Town and, until recently, a member of the majority Party in the Valley. He came striding down the ramp from the Town Hall's main entrance, his mayoral chains of office in place, and joined the Independent Alliance.

'You wouldn't believe what Weaver's just said to me,' he blurted.

'I can imagine,' said Peter. 'But don't worry about him. You're surrounded by friends and allies now.'

This produced a loud cheer from the ranks which increased as passing motorists honked their horns.

Recognising the visual impact, Feliks and Peter placed the Mayor and his insignia in the middle of the front row. The Alliance was mainstream now and whatever Weaver had said to Jamal, he'd regret it as soon as the A3 colour leaflets hit the doormats.

Peter thought this coup might thaw Tracy's cool manner towards him over the past few weeks. But she remained a model of distanced professionalism.

'Nice work, Peter.'

'Thank you. I was wondering…'

'See you at the planning meeting tomorrow.'

'Right.'

He'd been hurt but mostly perplexed since the "give back your key" moment, but now he was resigned. Tracy didn't want a relationship. He'd outstayed his welcome at her cottage. She must have sensed his feelings and decided that the icebox treatment was the best policy. He'd get over it. It wasn't the first time. Hearts mend, and the occasional pint, or four, of Manley Mild wouldn't hurt.

The photographs appeared on the colour leaflets that went through doors a week later. By this time the candidates of all parties were looking forward to the day after the elections, when there would be no piles of election literature on the kitchen table and no depressing prospect of yet another walk around streets where most people still did not know your name or what you stood for.

'Yeah, well, it's a choice between you and UKIP, I reckon.'

'Look, if you're thinking of voting for UKIP, don't vote for me.'

'I'll vote for anyone I fancy.'

'Not for me.'

'Are you telling me who to vote for? If I want to vote for you, I'll damn well vote for you. 'S'none of your business. You'll get my vote whether you want it or not!'

No more nights slaving over the wording of a new leaflet or news sheet, no more grim-faced spouses wondering where it would all end. It would end on Thursday, May 7th, except for the count on May 8th, and except for the commiseration party on May 10th – not to attend that would be ungracious. By 11th May life would be back to normal. Alex

Weaver would be back in power, probably with a reduced majority, and life would go on.

Until then, the dreams and night terrors would continue. Jim Phillips regularly dreamt that he was kitted out in full combat fatigues and loaded down with a forty-pound backpack containing Michelle Watson's leaflets. She cycled beside him, lashing at the back of his legs with a length of washing line.

Michelle Watson dreamt that she was walking along a deserted street being laughed at by every concealed inhabitant. Mick Greyve-Traine dreamed of enormous wind turbines sucking in vast black clouds from the Atlantic and creating a permanent swirling storm over Manley Town. His soon-to-be ex-wife, Liz, roamed the hillsides calling soundlessly across an unpeopled landscape like a gulping fish.

Tracy Morgan usually dreamed of tennis, but the nature of the dreams was changing. Where sleep had conjured nightmares of her signature forehand ballooning well wide, she was now hitting the lines. On the other hand, so was her faceless, nameless opponent, and she spent what seemed like whole nights running full tilt side to side, back and forth, stooping forwards and stretching backwards. Until the sweat poured and the seams of her sports gear began to disintegrate in a flood of bodily secretions. Stretching for a sliced serve, the stitches gave way and she had to wake up in order to avoid a serious clothing malfunction and forfeit the match.

When Peter could no longer stand the late-night abusive phone calls, he would sleep at a local travel lodge. Thanks to thin walls, his neighbours would be disturbed by his unconscious imprecations, maniacal laughter and chuntering counter-threats.

'I've often wondered if unpleasant people dream of being on the receiving end,' Tracy said one day at a planning meeting in the Grey House barn. 'Or do they only dream of dishing it out?'

'I should think Alex Weaver thinks it beneath his dignity to dream,' Peter replied.

'I never mentioned Alex Weaver.'

'No, but what you said made me think of him.'

This was a little harsh, for Alex Weaver did indeed dream. He often dreamed that he was lying on his back, fully dressed under the bedclothes, arms by his side. He found that he was unable to rise, but different people would occasionally rush in and pull back the duvet.

'You've got to stop lying around, Alex. You've got to get up!'

He couldn't, but would be saved by his mother coming in, replacing the bedclothes and calming him with a soothing singsong.

'There, there. Alex needs his sleep, doesn't he? Back to sleep you go.'

Sometimes – and somewhat alarmingly – it was Barbara tucking him up once more. She would pat his head, then turn towards the door, where Gerry Quick was waiting for her with a wolfish grin etched into his leering features.

On the other side of town, one of his main opponents had developed a nocturnal stutter. Hugh Brooke could not get through a single night without taking several hours to complete a one-minute statement to the press. In the highly amused crowd behind the reporters were his braying aunt and her honking husband.

'C-c-come on, Huh-huh-huh-Hugh!' they roared, stoking up universal derision, until a monstrous version of Bradley leapt in from the side and sent them all packing.

It was as good as a wake-up call, with the real Bradley licking his face and luring him back to a world where the dog chased pheasants and he – for the time being – chased votes. For both of them it was futile behaviour. Bradley had never caught a pheasant in his life, and Feliks had done the polling that showed how an Independent and a

Lib Dem candidate split the protest vote to guarantee a win for Alex Weaver. It was, quite frankly, a relief.

34 / The Thing Is…

Alex Weaver could always tell when his good mate Gerry Quick was about to deliver bad news.

'The thing is, Alex, we're pullin' outta the Rokeby-on-Bass business.'

'You mean, buying the second tranche of land?'

'Nope. The whole project as planned.'

'Houses as well?'

'The lot.'

Those two little words delivered an asteroid strike to Weaver's world just below the equator in his very own southern hemisphere. It sent his whole planet lurching away from its customary orbit.

To his credit, Gerry had foreseen the effect.

'Nah, nah, listen. We're pullin' out now. But it doesn't mean the deal's off. It's just the economic climate, Alex. There's a lotta stuff goin' down the tubes. This credit crunch is turning out to have a long tail. Never ends. Retail property's a nightmare at this junkcha.'

When Gerry started using words like "juncture" Weaver knew he was quoting Steven Rich, though this was a good reason for paying attention and suppressing his own fury at being hung out to dry.

'If we tried to build the stadium and the houses now, we wouldn't get very far. The banks have had all that quanti… quantititty… y'know, all that free money, but they're not giving it to the likes of us for lower league stadiums. Even if we did persuade the banks to finance it, we'd end up with more than one white elephant. Probably two. Everythink's in trouble. The football club's stuffed. You must know that. Their debts are getting out of hand. Call it over-investment, whatever. No bank will lend it another cent till they can show a profit, or the economy turns round. And retail parks? Forget it.'

'All right, Gerry. Just suppose it does turn out as bad as that…'

'It has already, Alex…'

'All right. Fine. Let's say it has. I just want you to know the effect on me.'

'I understand that. Really, I do. And that's why Stevie Rich an' me have been putting a package together…'

At last something promising. Falling backwards as he was at some speed, a fallback position – with padding – would be good.

'The thing is, we go ahead and buy the Council land. That shows intent and good faith that we'll come back and build summat on that site in the future…'

'When will you buy it?'

'Now, right away, as soon as you can sell it to us.'

'Before the elections?'

'Like I said, Alex, whenever you say.'

'But there mustn't be a word of this till after May 8th. I mean about the build not going ahead.'

'I swear. We'll go on as if everything was normal.'

'What about the Dewums?'

Gerry lowered his voice to show he understood the delicacy. 'The second part of the land deal with them is off. Besides, they were getting greedy. Started in on Stevie Rich about us conning them about values after planning permission. They wanted four mill. But like you said, we need to string it out.'

'Am I right in thinking you and Steven Rich are moving into land acquisition and out of building?'

'We're not moving out of anything, Alex. We're just making sure we don't risk our assets. We've got to choose our projects. But there's more than that. I've spoken to Stevie Rich an' we're agreed. Whatever happens in the election, whatever happens next week or in the next ten years, we know your qualities. So, there'll always be a place for you as a special consultant to the firm. Top expenses, the lot.'

This was, in its way, worse than the deal being pronounced dead. This was, even for Alex Weaver, the sure sign of failure. Worse than that, it suggested he was in no position to do anything other than sell out to people like Gerry Quick and Steven Rich. Every politician of note walked that line, between his principles and his self-interest, but every one of them preferred to believe – preferred to have enough evidence to argue – that they stayed firmly on the side of integrity.

'Thanks for the thought, Gerry. And pass on my thanks to Steven Rich,' Weaver was aware that his tone was icy, 'but there'll be no need. If we all stick to the same hymn sheet, the Party will be back in power, and we can all go on as before.'

'Exactly. You can rely on us. Won't breathe a word. There's only three people what know about this. You, me and Stevie. What the Dewums don't know they can't cause a rumpus about. It'll be smooth as…,' he cackled briefly, 'I was gonna say a baby's bum, but I'm thinking Janine's legs.'

Alex struggled to see the funny side while recognising this as Gerry's segueing between talking business and preparing for a night on the tiles.

'Give over,' Gerry persisted. 'No harm meant. If anything, I'm the one who should be upset. You disappointed the poor girl.'

'How's that exactly?'

'She's fair struck on you, then you go and dump 'er.'

'*I* didn't dump *her*. Aren't we forgetting that little episode at New Year?'

'Nah, she was just keeping you interested. She's a good girl, is Janine. She wouldn't two-time anyone. Give 'er a call sometime. She'd be really pleased. Even better, stick around for half an hour and she'll be here.'

As so often in Gerry's company, Alex experienced a number of emotions at once. Irritation that he was having this sort of adolescent conversation with a grown man. Resentment that a few moments impulsiveness had put him in this position. Frustration that his mate – which does not always translate as friend – had manoeuvred him into a position of weakness. But also a frisson of excitement that it might be just as Gerry was claiming: that Janine really did have a soft spot for him. Not to mention that surge through the body – what was it? adrenaline? testosterone? – launched by the very thought of seeing Janine again. Who knows, maybe, after the election, when the status quo ante was restored, he really could have his cake and eat it.

'Right, then,' Gerry downed the rest of his single malt in one. 'Let's get 'em in. Whatchoo 'aving, Alex? On me.'

There came a point in every social encounter with Gerry these days when his eyes would glaze over. The sure sign of an alcoholic, along with the pouches around the jaw beneath the ears. In one sense it was fortunate Weaver had insisted on meeting well away from Manley Town. The downside was he'd almost certainly have to drive the man home. A couple more shots, or five, and Gerry would have as much trouble locating his car as driving it.

35 / The Local Rag

Sally Prior knew well enough that the month of local elections was the busiest period for a local newspaper. This was also the most exhilarating run-in to a local poll she'd ever known, even if it was overshadowed by a general election on the same day. Just as, she reflected with some bitterness, the owners of the Manley Observer were planning to close down the print version and make a dozen reporters and other staff redundant. It was looking like the end of an era. All the more reason to go out in a blaze of controversy and sensation. Show 'em what they'd be missing.

To begin with, there were a lot of fresh new faces, candidates for public office who had no idea of the tedium and administrative straitjackets awaiting them if they did get elected. But there were also delicious scandals winning airtime on regional and national news.

No one had firmly established what happened the night Alex Weaver's car went off the road near Swindon. There were suspicions that Weaver had been at the wheel while somewhere between squiffy and pickled. But he and the other two persons in the car vehemently denied it. Gerald Quick, on his own admission, had been several points above plastered on the boozometric scale. On no account, he insisted, had he taken the wheel. Their version was that the third person present, a woman in her mid-thirties and well known to police in London and the Thames Valley, had agreed to drive both men home in Weaver's Jaguar.

But why had said automobile departed the highway where it ran surprisingly straight for the best part of four hundred yards? Weaver and the young woman asserted that Quick, in the front passenger's seat, had made a sudden, unprovoked lunge for the driver and/or steering wheel. That the lunger could remember very little, if anything, of his actions gave some credence to the lungee and the other witness, Alex Weaver. The only point of negligence, therefore, was that the driver should have placed the very nearly unconscious member of their party, Gerald Quick, on the rear seat so as to avoid any tendencies for lunging.

She – a certain Janine Roberts – countered by claiming that the relevant party was so opposed to riding in the rear that the balance of risk pointed towards the action she had in fact taken. Which was to allow the inebriated Gerald Quick to travel in the front passenger seat.

There was plenty of time for readers' letters to arrive and be printed. Such was the interest in all things electoral that Sally Prior had taken a decision to increase the comment and letters section to two double page spreads.

Under the leadership of Alex Weaver, Malvoir Council has made life a daily hell for drivers. More and more roads are designated as 20 and 30 mph zones. Parking spaces in the town centre have been reduced by a third in the last twenty years, while the parking fees, not to mention the number of fines for parking and speeding offences has doubled.

But while soaking residents for what is really a tax on mobility, the Leader feels free to play fast and loose with his own rules. He should consider his position.

I would like to know the terms on which Councillor Weaver associates with prominent members of the business community on such occasions.

Does he claim expenses? Are council taxpayers footing the bill for these nights out on the town?

At the very least, one might think that he could conduct these social occasions within the Malvoir district, so that our publicans, restaurant owners and their staff could at least feel the benefit.

Our Council Leader often uses his comment column in this newspaper to lecture the rest of us – Council employees, council taxpayers, trade union members, et cetera, on our responsibilities. The greatest of these, it seems, is to recognise the need to live up to them, rather than insist on our 'rights'.

Isn't it now time for the Leader to explain precisely why he was socialising with a major contractor to the Council in the company of a known provider of escort services?

Elected politicians are fully entitled to private lives on the same terms as anyone else in this country. The evening in question may have ended with an unfortunate incident, but this does not seem to have been the fault of Cllr Weaver.

If the rest of us had to account for the company we keep or be held responsible for all the actions of our friends, relatives and acquaintances, we would end up criminalising the entire country. If there has been no criminal activity, there should be no witch-hunt.

Alex Weaver phoned Sally Prior.

'Why are you printing this rubbish?!'

'Because it's in the public interest.'

'But it's nobody's business!'

'As one of the letters points out.'

There was no specific counter to that, so Weaver gave her a broadly ranging diatribe on privacy, editorial responsibilities, financial probity and political bias.

Sally heard later that he'd then phoned Tom MacDonald and torn a final strip of patience from that young man's long-suffering body.

'What the bloody hell were you playing at with that letter?'

'I did what you asked.'

'But you were supposed to draw attention *away* from certain things, not train a bloody spotlight on them. What did you mean by "particularly unfortunate incident"? "Does not *seem* to be at fault"? "Account for the company we keep"? "If there has not been criminal activity"? What was wrong with "*When* there is no criminal activity or intent?" Are you trying to dig my political grave, lad?'

If Weaver had not slammed down the phone, Tom would have been hard-pressed to avoid a "yes". As it was, he decided there and then that Alex Weaver was part of the problem, and nowhere near the solution.

He did not know for a week that Weaver would have his name removed as candidate for Fairfields.

'Carl Gibbons impressed the selection committee more. Nothing to do with me.'

There was just one vacancy left, in the Appleton ward, where the Lib Dems usually agreed to stand down to give the Conservatives a free ride. All Tom's work in Fairfields was now utterly wasted, and he'd have to start from scratch in a ward where the Party just about squeaked home, even with a following wind.

Alex Weaver was now in housekeeping mode and fairly satisfied with his work. He had a "squirrel" inside the Manley Observer offices and knew all about Tom MacDonald's cosy chats with Sally Prior. A little wing-clipping never did a cocky young candidate much harm in the long run.

As for another matter, all he Gerry and Janine had to do was stick to their story. No one had been seriously injured. No other car had been involved. The Jag was a write-off but comprehensively insured. To Barbara he insisted that Janine was one of Gerry Quick's acquaintances. Didn't she remember her from that night at the Colonial? She did indeed.

'I'm just glad the damage wasn't any worse,' she said as Weaver left to arrange, with his Chief Executive Officer, the sale of eight acres of Council land to Rich and Quick Construction Ltd for a deposit of one hundred and fifty thousand pounds with the remaining six hundred thousand to be paid over two years. Steven Rich had understood the need to increase the price and make the deal more attractive to Council members and the public.

While Weaver reconstructed his 'front' and began to believe quite firmly in emerging intact from his troubles, Sally Prior had to disconnect her home telephone to avoid all the hate calls, none of them traceable and some delivered in foreign accents. She took her revenge by printing a long letter from Peter Wilde.

'In line with the spirit of the times, we are plagued, not just with stories, but the facts of celebrity-style misdemeanours, shady property deals, serious allegations of corruption against would-be representatives and a major deficit of democracy and accountability. All of this just when we should be discussing town regeneration, poverty, education, decent health care and illness prevention. Our contributions to the war against global warming in this local authority have been feeble...'

Tracy had once been turned off by these long lists of things nobody in their right mind could be against, but she now found herself strangely roused by Peter's political passion (though she was keeping well clear of any other kind). He cared little for himself, wanted for nothing beyond his basic needs and a few pleasures like a good read and a watchable film from time to time. But he was ardent about the plight of others when such ardour was unfashionable. She could see amusement in the eyes of local residents when Peter cornered them in the street.

'I've got me 'ouse and me four b' four. Why should I bellyache?'

There were times when she wanted to familiarise the foreheads of such people with a forehand, a backhand and an overhead smash, but was learning how to deliver these in more closely reasoned arguments.

'Because your four-by-four was probably overpriced, it's more polluting than you think, and your home could be unsellable if it's built with cladding or on a flood plain.'

Wide-eyed stares.

But this local election was like the Rokeby women's tennis team trying to play in a league or two above their level. They'd fight hard, might even win a match, but the shots they faced were heavy and carried too much spin. She'd made a lot of enemies, quite a few friends and got to know some fascinating people, including Sally Prior, but she'd be utterly relieved when it was all over.

Sally Prior had commiserated in the friendliest possible way when Tracy expressed these feelings off the record, but she was too professional to offer any hint of present relief. In politics, only time will tell, and the long run is far too long for most.

36 / When The Day Finally Comes

To say that election day dawned would be an exaggeration. The horizontal drizzle that had swept across the Irish Sea, then Wales in the early hours, had now reached the border country. Daybreak came glowering across the Malvoir Valley like a badly bruised face.

Even before the morning had achieved its dark slate sogginess, the inhabitants of the barn at the Grey House were up and about. It was no hive of activity, more like a badgers' den of shuffling endeavour. Hugh was convinced that Feliks had either slept in his suit or not slept at all. They nodded grimly at each other like civilised humans who'd not had breakfast. The others were helping Jacinta with the meal, queuing for the bathroom, or gathering the right clothes for a sodden day ahead. Hardly a word was spoken. The bags of election day flyers were by the door, each with its list of target streets, each flyer with its final appeal to voters. Most would end up in the bin unread. This much they knew. Now they were going for the twenty or thirty voters who could make a difference.

There were similar, though smaller scenes, in many parts of Manley. Peter Wilde had driven over to Rokeby-on-Bass to help Tracy with her final delivery. But she'd already hit the streets, so he went and helped young Charlotte Chivers in the Milltown ward. He then planned a quick sortie to Wild Hill to target a few households of electoral 'floaters'.

As there was no election worth the name without a racket, Peter had borrowed a bullhorn from a well-wisher. He calculated that Ken Rudge would be the Labour man with the motivation and the megaphone, so he planned a trip back to Tracy's Collerton ward to shadow Rudge's car and bellow counter-messages.

Not that Peter had told Tracy of his plans. He guessed that making such a din was beneath her dignity. She'd also made perfectly plain her complete indifference to any help from him.

Well to the north of town, Alex Weaver was still asleep and would remain so till eight. He no longer saw the point of last-minute campaigning and none of his senses detected Barbara rising from her twin-bed to slip from the house before five-thirty, looking, it has to be said, immaculately coiffed and her clothes carefully chosen for a waterproof, yet elegant, effect. She would stroll her ward till nine, waving at constituents on their way to work, having breakfast with members of the Residents' Association, and handing out leaflets from beneath her large bell-jar umbrella. Then it was down to the polling stations, standing outside greeting well-wishers, encouraging supporters or waverers, and generally trying to look like a winner.

In the neighbouring ward of Underhill East, Jim Phillips was out alone, as he had been for most of the campaign, delivering the last of his flyers to the biggest ward in the Valley. Past sixty years of age, his shoulders ached from folding leaflets, his knees and ankles throbbed from all the uphill walking, and the arthritic knuckles of his right hand were raw from all the scraping contact on letterbox flaps. He guessed that just a few streets away, Michelle Watson was still abed, her tiny ward of five hundred households easily serviced by her husband and three sons, with just a single polling station to grace throughout the day. Jim would be running a home-to-polling-booth taxi service for his more elderly supporters, while Michelle's husband had hired a minibus. Jim had run up a small overdraft to fund his campaign, while Michelle had barely noticed her outgoing costs.

In balmier weather, Underhill East and West were normally visible from Monkton, where Liz Greyve-Traine had run an exemplary campaign. She had sent out a call for support to all the environmental groups in the region and drafted in helpers from as far afield as Manchester. Resplendent in colourful walking gear, solid boots or handmade shoes, and topped off with many a piece of knitted headgear, they were mostly young, in contrast to many of the other candidates, grey of hair and slow of limb. Not content with mere leaflets, Liz had decided that every household deserved a free copy of her latest book, 'Hoping for the Best, Preparing for the Worst'. There were still many delicate discussions to be had with her ex-partner and co-publisher regarding royalties, but Liz felt that the long wrangles by telephone would be well worth it, provided as many residents as possible fully understood the disaster awaiting if they didn't get those four wind turbines up on Heath Edge. Privately she was furious that Alex Weaver had somehow allowed the proposed number to be reduced by ninety per cent, but some were better than none.

Mick Greyve-Traine's Fairfields ward was situated on the other side of town. Now castigated in Liz's circles for backsliding on renewable energy, he'd had to rely on a group of new friends and allies. Allowing Liz to live in their jointly-owned house had been the noble course, so he'd rented a tiny two-up two-down at the heart of an area he'd barely visited in twenty years. Number 2, The Railway Cuttings had become home and campaign HQ. Posters went up in the downstairs windows, and he organised tea and coffee mornings for anyone who wanted to drop by. As a result, Mick became expert in the affairs of the elderly and teenagers. The elderly because they popped by for long chats, and youths because they stopped briefly to pop bricks through his windows. But he talked with all and sundry and sent letters to the Manley Observer on ways to help pensioners, deter youth crime and deal with dog mess. On this polling day he was free of shuttle duties because his elderly supporters had sorted out their transport among themselves. The burden of delivering his last-minute leaflets – "Vote for a Weaver-free Zone" – was relieved by a few impressionable youths who'd offered to despatch these for "the man who stopped to chat even though you smashed his windows and slashed his tyres". Only one lad had been so bored by the task that he'd hoiked literature, map, bag, the lot into a tributary of the Bass.

Jamal Ashoor's campaign had run right to the wire with last-minute print runs and unexpected hitches. He knew that membership of the Party had protected him from a certain amount of anti-Arab feeling in the town. Despite the general sympathy for Syrian refugees, not everybody would boast of having Britain's first Syrian councillor and town mayor.

Now that he'd severed ties with the Party, he was fair game. He tried not to think of the votes of no-confidence posted through his letterbox, courtesy of anonymous residents and their dogs. Or the terse injunctions painted on the front wall of his semi-detached house overnight. All he could do was try to shield his dependants and hope that once he was voted out, these attentions would stop.

But he would not go quietly. 'The pressure involved in being a member of the local Party in Manley is like being turned into a banana,' he declared on Malvoir FM radio. 'You join them green, they do their best to turn you yellow, then they try to bend you to their will.'

At least his final act as a Party Councillor could be defended in any company. He persuaded the Chair of the Planning Scrutiny Committee to propose that the decision to sell Council land near Rokeby-on-Bass to Rich and Quick be referred back to full Council. Every member of the scrutiny committee saw the danger of lost votes for themselves if this land sale turned out to be controversial.

The decision came so late in the day that no one expected this parting boot-to-groin. Now the sale could not be completed until after the election. It probably would, as soon as Alex Weaver was back at the helm, but Jamal's conscience was clear, and the committee members had put themselves in the clear by sitting firmly on the fence.

By six-thirty on polling day, newsagents across the Valley were open and taking in the latest edition of the Manley Observer. Few had time to stop and read front pages at that hour, but this morning's edition warranted a few seconds' reading followed by the forced exhalation of breath, cynical snort or barked guffaw.

Peter Wilde was, typically, the first candidate to see it. He'd marched into a newsagent's in Milltown while Charlotte Chivers was buttonholing voters on the other side of the road. She had no idea why he was grinning at her from the shop doorway.

Peter would have sent Tracy a text message, but she'd changed her number recently and had somehow neglected to tell him what it was. She wouldn't get the news until her hairdresser, driving past on her way to work, wound down her window and shouted.

'Have you seen this morning's paper?'

A member of Jamal's mosque called to him from a corner shop and waved him in to read the front page. Jim Phillips received several texts to his mobile urging him to buy a copy of the Manley Observer double quick. Michelle Watson didn't bother, as she rarely read a newspaper, and anyway the edition with her photo in it had been published the previous week. Peter Wilde phoned Feliks to tell him the news, which was swiftly relayed to all the Polish leafleteers.

Alex Weaver hadn't seen the paper as he was still in bed. Barbara hadn't seen it because her closest helpers hadn't decided when to break the news.

The front page was dominated by a grainy black and white image and its caption. '2:14am, Evebury High Street, a mile before this vehicle left the road and crashed.' The luxury car was made less glamorous by the grey blur achieved by a speed camera and its flash.

It was not so much the speeding offence, on an otherwise deserted main street in the middle of the night, that created this sensation – who had never done that? – but the identity of the driver. There, in the passenger seat, was the semi-conscious, head-back, mouth-open figure of a man resembling Gerald Quick. This was just as the hapless passengers had reported to police a little later. But the identity of the driver was quite other. Far from being a female, it looked distinctly like Alex Weaver doing a very good impression of a startled rabbit, and who, it was also established at the scene of the subsequent accident, was not so much 'over the limit' as 'twice around the dial'. The only person legally capable of taking the steering wheel that night could be seen leaning forward from the back seat as if quizzing the driver. This was clearly the female who later claimed to be the person at the wheel when the car left the road.

Ken Rudge heard the news as he arrived at a polling station to cast his vote. Red-rosetted helpers clapped him on the back, and he sensed that this was his time. Who else would now stand in his way to lead the Party after this election? He was also relieved that he'd not been tempted to undermine Alex Weaver and hasten the man's exit. Why risk stabbing Weaver in the back when the man was so capable of doing that to himself, expert contortionist that he was?

37/ The Count

Helen Steele was in waspish mood. She had set out a line of chairs between the counting tables and stage where the ballot boxes were stored, to circumscribe an area where mere mortals such as candidates and Councillors should not trespass. But the rosetted and accredited hordes in the Leisure Centre's Main Hall imagined their badges entitled them to wander at will, to mope and exult, mingle and chatter.

'Where are you going?'

'To join my colleagues.'

'Don't you see the chairs?'

'I do.'

'Do you think I put them there to amuse myself?'

'I couldn't possibly speculate.'

'They are there for a reason.'

'Chairs usually are.'

This did not improve Mrs Steele's disposition.

Jim Phillips reached his destination by another route.

'Blimey, who's that?'

'Head of Electoral Services,' said Peter Wilde. 'Used to be a teacher. One of those officers that treats Councillors like children. I take her foul temper this morning as a good sign.'

The late night-early morning general election count had been fraught. For the first time since 1922 the voters of the Malvoir Valley had flirted with electing a Tory. And they would have if they hadn't split a protest vote between the Conservatives and the Liberal Democrats. Malcom Woodbridge squeaked home by 992 votes. During his acceptance speech he bemoaned the austerity policies of the Coalition government for creating a hostile environment for working people instead of solving the economic crisis by pinning the blame where it belonged, on the predatory rich. But once he was off the stage he planned a beeline for Alex Weaver to poke him in the chest and call him a 'money-grubbing globalist' who cared nothing for the Party or for working people. But Weaver was nowhere to be found, so the reinstated MP had a go at Ken Rudge instead.

'Tell that mate of yours he's a liability. And he's finished. I'll make sure of that.'

Ken Rudge's features attempted a combination of innocence and incomprehension.

'Weaver's not a mate. Never was.'

At the count for the local election, Peter was caught in two minds. While he longed for a change in the Malvoir Valley, he mourned the change across the country overnight. It was expected that no party would win an outright majority in the general election. That a hung parliament in Westminster would produce another coalition of Conservatives and Liberal Democrats. But the Tories had won a majority for the first time in eighteen years. Everything he'd battled against in all his years in politics looked set to take over in Westminster. Perversely, the same would happen in the Valley if Labour won the Council.

Why, he wondered, did the people who now ran the Labour party so dislike the working classes? And why did they think that working people, with no capital, low credit scores, mounting debts, jobs exported overseas and few prospects, would not vote for anybody else who appeared to care for their plight? He'd been in the Party for decades and the entitled apparatchiks who'd taken it over had driven it belly-flopping into the sea while partying at the controls. Shortly afterwards, the Liberal Democrats had dived in nose first while holding the map upside down.

Peter looked around the Hall, a scene he lived for. Clusters of women and men wearing red, blue, gold, white and green rosettes. Press photographers hard at work. Sally Prior leading her team of young journalists, conducting interviews, assessing the mood in various camps, eager like everyone else for the count to begin. Within Helen Steele's stockade the officers were counting ballot boxes, checking paperwork, making sure all procedures were beyond reproach. The Chief Executive, a man that Peter Wilde had clashed with on many occasions, was doing his level best to appear impartial, professional, aloof. Yet, to Peter, here was a man inextricably linked with the actions of the Weaver regime. If the Party survived, he'd survive. He knew where the bodies were buried.

The counters had been up half the night verifying the ballot papers. Peter had been there too, trying to assess the outcome, and noticed that one of Collerton's boxes had somehow got taken to the wrong table. Tracy's votes were being collected and verified as Independent in another ward where the Party was certain to romp home. As usual, Peter suspected foul play, and there had been a brief kerfuffle between him and Helen Steele. The Independent monitors then stopped gossiping, fetched more coffee from the vending machines and applied themselves to the scrutiny process. The Party boys watching the local verification had looked distinctly green about the gills following the general election result but seemed in better spirits by four in the morning.

'Not even close,' mocked Gary Higgs.

'Glad to see you're keeping your pecker up,' retorted Peter. 'There is life after politics, you know.'

'I wouldn't need to know. How's life with your lady friend?'

If Higgs meant Tracy, he was way behind the gossip curve.

'Can't complain. I don't need to ask about you. I get all your news from your wife.'

Gary knew it never paid to exchange banter with Peter Wilde and turned away with a leering grin showing more pain than conviction. But he was certain of re-election, an impression he'd gained from watching closely as ballot papers were scrutinised by the scrutineers with a keen scrute.

This morning Peter Wilde watched Gary Higgs passing from one group of Party members to another. The cliques and groups in the hall were like the trainers and managers of sportsmen just before a competition, watching each other closely for signs of nerves, defeatism or weakness. Amongst the Party folk there were clearly worries about certain candidates. Everybody was trying to calculate the effects of yesterday's local front pages and any spill-over from the national mood.

Sally Prior had managed a morning scoop, but by midday every paper, online news service, TV and radio programme in the region was covering national news of the general election. How many people were reading, watching or listening to the local news? Of these, how many voted? And of those, how many cared whether a bloke drove a bit too fast and downed a tipple too many? As Peter Wilde so often said, 'One person's ignorance is another person's triumph.'

The bloke in question, Alex Weaver, was still nowhere to be seen. But there were rumours of his presence at a police station giving evidence to Thames Valley officers. Nor was Ken Rudge a smudge in anyone's peripheral vision. He was awaiting news of the results. If all appeared to be going well, he would arrive to lead the celebrations and receive the plaudits. In the meantime, Gary Higgs was trying to look like a potential local leader, his tentative advances directed towards a group of women huddled around Barbara Weaver. Peter thought she looked composed but not untroubled, and far more of a class act than Gary Higgs would ever be.

Among Independent Alliance candidates the feeling was one of noble failure. Their scrutineers the night before had been inexperienced and unable to give a clear account of likely outcomes.

'Got a few,' said Jim Phillips. 'But not enough.'

'Same here,' said Mick Greyve-Traine. Unlike Liz he'd decided to retain the double-barrelled name until after the election to avoid confusing voters. 'Did OK in a couple of districts but pretty much wiped out in others.'

'How about Tracy?'

'Too close to call,' said Peter.

'But it's been a great experience. Not that I'd want to go through that again.'

'I think I'd top meself if I actually got in, which I won't.'

'If you do get elected, can you get out of it somehow?'

'I think I've won,' declared Michelle Watson. 'By twelve votes.'

Peter Wilde and Jim Phillips exchanged glances. Her ward was so small she and her husband had been able to count votes during the verification process, behaviour that was universally frowned upon.

'But there are thirty-six postal votes,' Feliks pointed out. 'They don't get opened till later this morning.'

Feliks was there as a "special overseas guest observer" on a pass wangled by Peter through a contact in Electoral Services, but without passing beneath the gaze of Helen Steele. His observation checked Michelle's confidence and confirmed her view that Feliks was a person she neither liked nor trusted. How someone like Hugh Brooke could be associated with such people was beyond her comprehension. He must be, as her husband suggested, a "trailer toff", which she thought a brilliant play on words.

Said member of the upper-class ne'er-do-wells had been surveying this unfamiliar terrain with some charity.

'These people seem to know their onions,' he said to Feliks. 'Can't think what I would have to offer.'

'Your lack of arrogance would be a beginning.'

'Mm, but it is a lack, isn't it? And based on ignorance. I mean look as those guys,' he indicated the group including Gary Higgs and Mel Coates. 'I heard them discussing precepts and service provision and goodness knows what else. Sounded as if they command the detail.'

'You mean their command of detail is why this town looks the way it does?'

'Pity you're not a British citizen, Feliks. We could do with someone like you.'

'Then British people like me should stand for election.'

Hugh couldn't fail to notice how Feliks lived and breathed politics – a psychiatric condition, perhaps. Peter Wilde was much the same. Looking about the hall he guessed that eighty per cent of the people there were dedicated politicos. The rest were strays, sucked into the fray with good intentions, but unlikely to survive the cut and thrust to gain a foothold on the greasy pole.

Peter was thinking much the same, but from a different angle. You could easily tell who the fresh faces were. They were all Independents milling about happily like a wedding party before the event. They would have no responsibilities beyond the festive occasion, or duties such as consummating the marriage and keeping it going through good times and bad, not to mention children, teenagers and in-laws.

In contrast, the Party crowd looked like a funeral cortege hoping for a resurrection. The Conservatives were buoyed by the general election results but appeared quietly resigned to their usual fate in the Valley. The Lib Dems were putting a brave face on national rejection, perhaps in denial about accusations of betraying their supporters while in coalition with the Tories. The few Greens rose above it all by looking wonderfully casual yet knowing. In their midst, holding court, was a confident-looking and single-barrelled Liz Greyve.

At last – just three minutes late – came a rush towards the counters as the ballot boxes were brought out and the contents poured onto the tabletops.

The first result was for the Appleton ward, where Tom MacDonald's margin of victory was as tight as expected, the Tory candidate losing out by fifteen. The Party celebrated with a raucous shout, but Tom was sensible enough to look both pleased and chastened.

Next up was the Boreham ward. Another win for the Party. With Biscombe uncontested, the party already led by three seats and it wasn't yet nine-thirty.

'Don't look so worried, Peter. Your stuffing's on the way,' called Mel Coates.

'A turkey would know, Mel.'

Tracy shifted uncomfortably. She'd never liked sledging in women's tennis and hardly saw the point in a sedentary occupation like politics.

'Can't we just ignore them?'

'You're right. Sorry.'

The Collerton ballot boxes were next up and the Indies moved in swiftly to ensure fair play. A few Party members joined in, knowing that this was a key ward. If they could send Tracy Morgan packing, their troubles were over.

After twenty minutes it was on a knife edge.

'The postal votes could swing it.'

Feliks was looking pale and tense. He and Peter had slaved over Tracy's postal vote strategy, making sure she personally got in touch with every resident that might request one. Ken Rudge would have tied up a lot of the trades union and council employee votes, unless some had revolted in the privacy of the voting booth. Felix and Peter had targeted people who might vote for her as the most likely challenger to Labour. They'd hammered home the message that feeling frail, being on holiday or working away could not serve as an excuse for not voting. Every vote was going to count.

But as the reckoning proceeded it was clear the Lib Dems had also made inroads and were splitting the anti-Rudge surge. The Independent Alliance had always feared that Weaver's antics would give all parties hope of doing well, so cancelling each other out and letting Weaver and his cronies back in.

By eleven o'clock Dornley had gone to the Party but Mark Given had surprisingly failed to live up to his surname by losing to the Lib Dems by eight votes in Chorfield. His disappointment was more vengeful than contrite, and Lib Dem rosettes bristled at his downfall.

By eleven-fifteen, Tracy was a hundred and fifty-two votes down before the postal votes were brought forward. Ken Rudge was in touching distance of victory and his main sidekick, Ian Price, could be heard phoning him with a progress report.

'Yep. 'S in the bag, Ken.'

'Close but no cigar,' scoffed Mel Coates across the counting table at Peter Wilde.

'But your fat lady hasn't sung, yet.'

This was also heard by Helen Steele. Had Peter Wilde been a schoolboy he'd have been docked a hundred votes for insubordination and smart aleckery. But it was Tracy's cool, patient, unflinching appeal that calmed Peter down.

'I really could do without that sort of thing.'

'Sorry.'

He really was. More than that, he couldn't fathom why Tracy was still being such an Ice Queen. He'd racked his brains, replayed almost every conversation they'd ever had and lain awake at night wondering how he could recover lost ground. All he could imagine was that she had a) met someone else, b) heard some damaging rumour or c) believed that he really was guilty of criminal behaviour in stealing Council property and was going down. But whenever he tried to engage her in conversation, she found a reason to turn away, sit down, stand up, or catch a lift with someone else. There were times when he felt sunk without a Tracy.

Peter had barely uttered his apology when Labour picked up an unexpected seat as Barbara Weaver took Hensley by sixty votes. The Tories and the Lib Dems had failed to come to an agreement and had split their vote. The Party greeted this bonus with a roar of approval. It had to be admitted that they did loud and boisterous better than any rival. To everyone's astonishment, Barbara was in tears – of joy or relief it was hard to tell – and the Party had recovered its single loss so far.

Ken Rudge must have been lurking nearby, as he turned up within ten minutes, but only to watch as he garnered thirty-one of the postal votes to Tracy's one hundred and ninety-four. Both candidates stood ashen-faced as they absorbed the news that she had won by eleven; he watching his political career, such as it was, swirl away down the plughole of false expectations, she watching her dream of a tranquil life, leavened by tennis, recede into the never-never.

'There's gotta be summat wrong,' exclaimed Rudge.

'Recount!' urged Mel Coates.

So recount it was.

The Lib Dems had unveiled the first chink in the Party's armour, and this was a second. While the Collerton votes were recounted, Hamble Hill fell to the LibDems and Mick Greyve-Traine romped home in Fairfields. His ex crashed to a humiliating defeat in Monkton and immediately left the building with most of her colourful supporters in tow. Jamal Ashoor scrambled back in Mitcheldean East by a handful of votes, Mel Coates and Bob Phelps went down to Lib Dems, and the Tories' Robin Smythe-Banks eased back in Rokeby-on-Bass where the Independents had deliberately not put up a candidate. Most sensational of all was Charlotte Chivers' win by thirty-seven in Milltown to become, at nineteen years and five months, the youngest ever Councillor in the Valley's history.

By noon there was all to play for. Labour led by twenty-one seats to sixteen with seven wards left to count. News was leaking of a possible sensation, and the seating set aside for the general public was beginning to fill with GROBAG supporters and fifteen gentlemen of a distinctly foreign demeanour. Labour members were put out that their collective shout of victory was no longer the loudest or throatiest in the hall. The roar and foot stamping that greeted Gwen Mackie's win for the Lib Dems in Weatherby seemed to emanate from somewhere beneath the hall's foundations. It was now worrying the Labour Party that the result could lead to No Overall Control, and that nobody would want to join a coalition with them. All the other parties now regarded a victory for anyone else but Labour as a victory for their side.

At about the same time as Hugh's Polish helpers turned up to cheer on the Independents, Tracy noticed another member of the public taking a seat in the gallery. That she was the "Woman in the Photographs" was quickly confirmed by some vigorous waving between her and Peter Wilde. He was giving her the thumbs-up followed by several other hand gestures to indicate a neck-and-neck situation. This coincided closely with Tracy encountering two emotions in quick succession. The first involved necks and their constriction, the second a feeling that she really didn't care what happened any longer. She also resolved not to look at either Peter or the female in question. It was none of her business. Though she couldn't help noticing that the woman was even taller than she expected and even younger than the photographs suggested. And, it had to be said, a little podgy, though this was quite common among the beer and crisp guzzling youth of today. She wasn't sure who ought to be more ashamed: her for thinking such thoughts, or Peter and this woman for carrying on like this. Peter had, after all, proved himself no better than her stereotypical, baby-snatching ex-husband in this regard. But it had nothing to do with her.

She got back to the business in hand by reminding herself of the score. 21-17. By now everyone assumed that she had won in Collerton, even though Ken Rudge refused to concede and demanded a second recount much against the advice of the experienced Helen Steele who doubted that her staff could have been twice mistaken.

'Then there's got to be a missing ballot box,' he argued. 'I want you to make sure all the boxes are here.'

Helen Steele glared back, speechless. The man was within his rights but couldn't see sense. She turned away and gave the order to conduct a thorough search.

In the meantime, Robin Smythe-Banks gained a Tory companion in the Council chamber for the first time in eight years when a fellow candidate squeaked home in Rosemead where she had conducted a single issue campaign based on the shortcomings of the local sewage treatment facility. Her innocent advice to residents – 'Don't swallow this' and 'Don't get caught between two stools' – had reached a receptive audience.

'No need to guess the first motion I'll try to pass in the Council chamber,' she announced to Sally Prior.

At 21-18, Labour needed just two more seats for outright victory with five results undeclared. Unchallenged for so long, Party members didn't know how to behave in a close-run race. They were indignant, resentful, incredulous. How could the people of the Valley be so blinkered, so foolish as to trust any other party but theirs? They looked on morosely at the celebrations of their opponents.

Over at the table where the Manley Central votes were being counted, Feliks was wearing a lupine grin and Hugh could hardly believe his eyes. A few of the ballots indicated a preference for the Lib Dem candidate, but paper after paper bore a cross beside his name. Alex Weaver had barely garnered two hundred votes. It was a sensational victory and a crushing defeat. The public gallery roared its approval and klaxons sounded until Helen Steele threatened to restore order by calling security.

21-19.

Wild Hill then dropped like a ripe plum into Peter Wilde's lap and he was home and dry for another four years.

21-20.

Michelle Watson's prediction that she would win Underhill West was vindicated when the postal votes were counted and she scraped home by three.

21-21.

With Collerton unofficially Tracy's, the Council was heading for NOC - No Overall Control. Labour's only hope lay in Underhill East. A win here would bring them level. Then they could begin the horse trading – a Cabinet post here, a committee chair there – and draw away one or two of those Independents who might prefer their working class brethren (plus an additional £12,000 a year) over their new, "nimby" acquaintances.

But Jim Phillips had done the work. Paul Rogers would now be able to spend as much time on the golf course as he liked without the nagging feeling that he ought to be elsewhere.

21-22.

It was now all down to the search for any absent ballot boxes.

One of which they found, placing Ken Rudge very nearly beside himself.

'I knew it!' he exclaimed, casting an accusing eye at Tracy Morgan, as if she were personally responsible for this piece of skulduggery.

Until, that is, the voting papers were poured onto the table and it became clear they were overwhelmingly in Tracy's favour. In the end, her majority was a hundred and sixty-four. It was now Peter Wilde who regarded Helen Steele with a probing gaze. Though her expression professed neutrality, Peter had known her for years and fancied he could detect a thwarted fury.

Labour 21- Other parties 23.

'What now?' asked Tracy.

'The Tories have two seats,' replied Peter. 'The Lib Dems have nine and the Independent Alliance have twelve. I'd guess the Conservatives and Lib Dems are willing to join in a coalition administration. The question is, are we? In a few minutes that lot over there,' he indicated surly Labour members, 'will start phoning us individually to see if we'd be prepared to support them. If two of us will, they get back into power. If not, we'll have to start negotiating with the others for Cabinet posts and committee chairs and generally dividing up the spoils. We'd be the biggest group and should be rewarded accordingly.'

Peter Wilde was about to demand, 'Three cheers for democracy', until forestalled by Michelle Watson.

'Well, I want to head the Planning Directorate,' she said. 'My father was a builder, so I know all about that.'

Her eleven new Council colleagues groaned inwardly but, in the interests of the fledgling Alliance, breezed discreetly through their arsenal of choice epithets without uttering a syllable.

While Tracy was accosted by every local journalist for a quote, she noticed Peter's 'woman' hanging about nearby. So she kept shifting her body position to make sure her back was forever in the woman's face. But this young biddy was determined and even pursued Tracy into the women's loo. There was no escape. An introduction was imminent. Keep your cool, thought Tracy, though she couldn't bear the enthusiastic bonhomie written all over this woman's face.

'I just wanted to say hi. I'm Kate. My dad's told me so much about you.'

'Your dad?'

'Yes. Peter. Peter Wilde. I'm his daughter.'

A few minutes later the relevant father was astonished to see a determined-looking Tracy Morgan marching towards him across the main hall of the Recreation Centre, followed by his bewildered, pregnant daughter. He broke off from giving Sally Prior his analysis of campaign and results.

'The Labour Party is facing a whinge-whinge situation...' he was saying.

'Peter!' said Tracy.

It sounded ominous.

'Yes?'

'A word? In private?'

'Sure.'

She led him through a doorway, around a corner, around another, searching for something, somewhere. Suddenly she found it. It was just a corridor with no one else in it.

'Peter...' she said.

'Yes?'

'I've been a complete fool.'

Try as he might, there was no way of replying to this beyond accepting, then returning, a heartfelt, minute-long, full-on body hug.

Part Six

Summer

38/ New Directions

Within a month of election day, the Labour Party was back in the driving seat. Michelle Watson insisted on being given a position in the new administration to reflect her role as "co-founder" of the Independent Alliance. Unwilling to risk their hard-won gains, members conceded against their better judgement. But in a very short time, reports began to emerge that Michelle Watson was not up to the job.

'Several spanners short of a toolbox.'

'Transmits but can't receive.'

'Makes a panicking chicken look like an intellectual.'

The Tory and Lib Dem members of the coalition, as well as council officers, were in barely contained revolt. She had to go, and an election for Chair of the planning committee was arranged. When it was handsomely won by Jim Phillips, Michelle Watson offered her support to the Labour Party in exchange for the job she'd just lost.

22-22.

Governing through the 'coalition' would be unsustainable. While the majority of Labour Councillors were retired or working in the public sector, most of the Alliance and Lib Dems were self-employed or worked for demanding companies. Getting time off to attend every vote was unlikely.

Michelle Watson gloated. 'That'll teach them to run me down. They're not as clever as they think.'

But twenty-fours later Tom MacDonald resigned from the Party, re-labelling himself Independent Labour.

'Being a member of the Party at the moment is like bringing ideas to a snake pit,' was the only public comment he made.

21-23.

Alex Weaver sent yet another letter to the Manley Observer protesting at the disloyalty and opportunism of this younger generation of politicians. Letter-writing was his main occupation these days. Missives to his lawyers, entreaties to parliamentarians, complaints to the police, veiled threats to former associates. At the root of them all was a firm belief that he could somehow step around the evidence of a single photograph and place his accusers in the wrong. If he couldn't dodge the facts, he'd get them on procedure.

Experience had taught Weaver that counterattack is always an option. The new Council would have to vote on the sale of Council land to Rich and Quick. If they voted against, the developer could bring a civil case against the Council for a vote that was biased or pre-determined and "against the interests" of local taxpayers. Costs would mount, and if a court found in Rich and Quick's favour, the Councillors who'd voted for the losing side would have to divvy up the costs in person.

'Costs in cases like that can rise to half a mill,' Weaver enthused in his call to Steven Rich. 'It could cost them twenty thousand each.'

'It's been tried before,' said Rich. 'Went all the way to the High Court. Not only did the judge throw the case out, he detailed the behaviour of the developer and the Council Leader in question. It cost the developer more than half a mill and a fair amount of public humiliation.'

Weaver retreated from that plan but continued to smoulder. He knew that politics is a circular game. When perceptions changed, he'd be ready.

Through it all Barbara stood resolutely by her man. She uttered not a word of reproach. When he ranted and railed, she would employ the wifely equivalent of judo.

'Yes, dear.'

But this wifely winning through the appearance of submitting was modified when Weaver learned that police had raided Reg Barton's house to discover large wads of cash hidden in packs of nappies. Nappygate. Valley residents spent many hours trying to calculate the number of twenty- and fifty-pound notes that a standard pack would hold.

Now Weaver's rages were balanced by long periods of sombre reflection.

'Somebody's out to get us all.'

'All?' enquired Barbara. 'If you're laundering money as well, you should probably tell me.'

'What do you think I am?'

'Not sure I know any longer.'

She left him to ponder that as she set off for another strenuous day doing the necessary to the best of her ability: catering to his basic needs, representing her residents in Hensley and trying to attract a new class of member to the Party.

His greatest problem was how to deal with Gerry Quick.

'It's lucky I was too drunk to remember who was drivin'. Yer could've had me in the clink an' all.'

'Nobody's going to clink.'

'Well, I aint, even if you is. I've got cops swarmin' all over me life, thanks t'you.'

But Gerry Quick was not only Alex Weaver's problem.

'We're in trouble, Stevie.'

'We are?'

'That share deal you told me about. The share price has just gone through the roof. We're gonna lose a lotta dosh.'

'You did that?'

'Well, you recommended it. Didn't you?'

'No. I was only talking theoretically. I believe it's unethical to deliberately sell shares short.'

'You … !!!'

The next ten minutes were not to be heard through a receiver close up, so Steven Rich placed his interlocutor on speaker phone and got on with more urgent work. He was tempted to repeat one of his father's favourite sayings – "Markets can remain irrational for longer than you can remain solvent" – but he thought it would be wasted on Gerald, loudly menacing but not so quick.

The threats proved as lethal as soap bubbles. Before the Indian summer was upon them, Gerry Quick was officially declared bankrupt, and bankrupts could not serve as directors of companies. His resignation was a formality. Quick and Rich would soon be dissolved then resurrected as Rich and Partners with a new plan of cautious, debt-free consolidation until uncertainty shrouding the business landscape cleared and the sun broke through once again.

Similar rationalisation was taking place at Deverill Court.

'Honey… look what I found,' said Calvin Dewum one afternoon, handing his wife a document.

'Where did you find this?'

'In a bookcase on the landing just outside your aunt's old room.'

It was a last will and testament.

'But this… this…'

'I know,' consoled Calvin. 'Looks like she made another a few days later.'

'But this gives everything to… to…'

'I know. Looks like the old bird changed her mind again at the last minute.'

'But how? And who witnessed…?' Lesley-Anne shuffled through the pages. 'But we sacked her cleaner!'

'She must have got back into the house somehow.'

'But you were supposed to…'

Calvin shrugged. 'It's a big house. Lots of ways in and out.'

Lesley-Anne considered this for several seconds. It was a poor excuse. Her aunt had been confined to one room to which there was only *one* door. But she decided to stick with essentials.

'I wonder where the cleaner is now.'

'When I told her we didn't need her services anymore, she said she'd been wanting to go back to Scotland anyway.'

'Good. We can burn this. And,' she continued, her features draining of any animation as she fixed him with a baleful stare more intense than he'd ever seen, 'never, ever, breathe a word of this to anyone.'

'We couldn't do that. That wouldn't be legal. And, anyway, I've sent images to our solicitors for advice.'

On the events of the following hour were built Calvin's justification for bringing his ill-conceived marital union to an end. No civilised man should expect to hear such language, even less when applied to him. No man with an ounce of self-esteem should be subjected to such taunts, jeers, and defamation of his intimate parts. No affection can withstand such unfounded censure, manufactured calumnies and arbitrary libel. Nor is the situation made redeemable by physical assault. The initial bare-handed onslaught might have been endured, but battery, assisted by means usually employed to control truculent creatures of the equine species, was insupportable. Calvin knew he bruised easily, but he was not aware of the brittle bone condition until Lesley-Anne carried out the empirical research.

It was fortunate that Calvin had already informed their solicitors and, for good measure, arranged for one to call at the house. It was even luckier that two of them turned up as Lesley-Anne was using her horsewhip and instep to encourage him back to a vertical position. These efforts at resuscitation were witnessed through the side windows of the grand entrance doorway. An ambulance was called, and Calvin was whisked away to a room in a private hospital that his credit card was just about good for. He had, of course, taken the precaution of sending images of the recently found will both to their own lawyers and to the firm of Bight and Maym, whose minions had been so busy about their enquiries and no doubt deserved this neat resolution of their case. Calvin was impressed by their endeavour, and doubted he'd find a better firm to pursue his own divorce proceedings if the need arose.

Lesley-Anne was banned from his room at the hospital. In fact, she had no idea where it was, and had to rely on his willingness to answer phone calls. But once he was able to speak more clearly through the facial contusions, he was magnanimous. He would not pursue charges, if she made certain statements in writing and posted them to Messrs Bight and Maym. He would send a courier to collect the few possessions and papers necessary to his existence. He would be leaving the country sharpish. He would send a forwarding address at the appropriate time.

These were trying weeks. He needed to downsize, regroup, reinvent. The world was topsy-turvy, disarranged, its head in the trashcan and rear end right out there, experiencing the full force of inclement weather. Folks would be needing some reassurance. What better than some online disaster control such as card-reading, astrology, palmistry? He hated the term fortune-telling but was prepared to give "circumstantial evaluation and expectation enhancement" a serious shot. It was a crowded market, but he knew how to carve a niche.

What he didn't need was the drag of fixed assets. He was on the road once more, footloose, fancy-free, and now with enough ponytail to tie in a band.

Lesley-Anne, by contrast, was bound to Deverill Court, at first by the effects of the three bottles of something-or-other she downed the evening she found herself abandoned. It was, in her experience, just like a man. A tap or two and down he went. Another "assist" and off he went to the sanatorium whinging to matron. It was the betrayal she hadn't expected. 'We're in this together, honey', 'We're a team' and 'If they take on one of us, they take on both' were the empty phrases, she now realised, of a man with no stamina, no puff. She would have to start again.

Reviving an old flame was, she thought, a possibility. Dimitris had been wonderfully generous, though married. Hassan could surely not have forgotten her, especially after he'd so very nearly thrown up his position, half his fortune and all his relations. Ulrich was a great-hearted admirer and a man of the world with plenty of time on his hands.

Yet all that had happened back in the eighties and nineties. People move on. If she trawled her memory for truth, she could guess that Dimitris would have found several replacements. Hassan could quite easily have repented his earlier lifestyle and become an ascetic with no interest in playthings, and Ulrich… well, Ulrich might very well be dead. But she had to be positive. There had to be a man out there with considerable means who knew the value of a well-bred Englishwoman. She could start again, she'd done it before. She believed very firmly in the institution of marriage and its considerable benefits. She just needed to work out how to protect herself from her mate.

No, there was nothing wrong with finding the right man and making it legal. It was this soggy little country she couldn't stand.

She decided that she didn't like the damp British countryside after all. Everything grew so fast and cost a fortune to keep tidy. She liked those warmer climes where the hot season kept it looking neat and you could get your riding done in the cooler hours around sunrise or sunset. Hugh could have his wretched wreck of an estate, with its recently redecorated manor house already growing mould and peeling at the corners. Keeping up such a place would leave you no time for anything else.

It needed a man of limited ambition. A mere caretaker would do. She'd gather a few choice items – that Meissen elephant was portable and so were the eighteenth-century family portrait miniatures in the glass cases – and decamp. If Hugh made a fuss, she'd pin it on Calvin. She'd always had her doubts about him. Bit shifty. Smiled at breakfast and occasionally wept during intercourse.

Of all this Hugh was blissfully ignorant. He now had an extra nine thousand a year for which he was extremely grateful and just a little guilty. Despite others' insistence to the contrary, he did not feel worthy of representing fewer than two thousand souls in the Council chamber. He was so painfully aware of his ignorance that he kept his mouth firmly shut on most occasions. Which was just as well, as in the early days he could mistake mention of a DSO as a reference to gallantry in action, or wrangles about the UDP as a conversation about Northern Ireland. On the other hand, a willingness to admit his ignorance had a winning quality, and there was no shortage of old hands happy to explain Direct Service Organisations or Unitary Development Plans.

The sadness in his life was the prospect of an empty barn. Shortly after the elections, Feliks finally rose from what seemed like a whole week in bed and announced that the Zielinskys would be gone by the end of August.

'But why? And where?'

'They've made enough money and it's time to go back and invest in their farms.'

Hugh hadn't seen their accounts for months and had no idea that they had collectively saved over four hundred thousand pounds.

'But I thought EU competition was making life difficult for Polish farmers.'

'It is. But they're going merge the farms into larger units and go organic. They're going upmarket.'

It made sense. Henryk, Kasper and Jakub – posing as Harry, Kazza and Jake – had recently been working in supermarkets. Far from just stocking shelves and working the tills, they'd been gathering intelligence on the store's buying policies for organic food. Tadeusz, Tomasz and Urban had also down-skilled to pack vegetables on an organic farm where they'd driven the farmer to distraction with all the questions they'd practised on Hugh in their English classes. There was no question: the Zielinskys were ready for a new phase in their lives, but they'd never intended to give up their birthright in order to move on. Or as Eddie would have it, 'There's no farqueue barsta make me sell land. Never! I farqueue die first.'

The ground floor of the house was now fully habitable. Hugh insisted that they build a purely functional stairway to the first floor. He could install a quality staircase when he had the cash. With easy access to the upper rooms the necessary wiring and plumbing was soon done and serviceable new floors were laid. The rest would be aestheticised in years to come as income allowed. With the job done, there was nothing to keep the Zielinskys at The Grey House.

'Will you go back to Poland?' he asked Feliks.

'Yes. I'll be doing the marketing campaigns for the farms. Might get involved in the green movement. I'll be like you and join the Polish 'Keep Them Honest' party.'

'Or start one.'

'I'll probably have to.'

Only Izzy was planning a non-farming future. The family had clubbed together to buy him a stake in a centrally located Krakow hair salon. His future would be urban and hip, introducing Silesians to 'Jekyll and Hyde' cuts by day and giving psychic readings at night.

Hugh could already feel the emptiness descending on the property. He was beginning to imagine cold grey winter nights with Bradley demanding his walks down footpaths closely monitored by Mr Paradise. He'd thought that maybe, one day, he might summon up the courage and ask if Lucy would like to come visiting. But why would she? There was an even chance she'd be away to Rio for the Olympics and, after that, who knows? Further studies on the continent? Close attentions from sleek or burly athletes? Failing any of that, a homely welcome in central Europe.

She still sent him playful texts.

'What should I call you now? Mister? Councillor? Count?'

Before he could reply to the last, Mr Bight arrived with various papers documenting his sudden change of fortune. Mr Maym, he was told, had gone directly to Deverill Court to secure the property.

Hugh spent the next few days pacing the rooms and corridors with Bradley and walking the bounds. He was delighted and thankful to be master of all he surveyed but saddened by the evidence of neglect and vandalism all around.

Mr Maym was adamant.

'Take an inventory. Anything missing, anything damaged, and we'll track those two down and make them pay.'

'Didn't you say you were Calvin Dewum's solicitor, too?'

'No, that's my partner, James Bight. Which means I'll know how to get in touch with Dewum when the time's right.'

Hugh expressed his doubts about exacting revenge to Feliks.

'Should I go after them? What would you do?'

'Me? Well, I think Maym and Bight are forces of nature. If I were you, I'd just make the list and let nature take its course.'

So he prowled the house and made his notes. Pieces of porcelain, miniatures, his grandfather's military medals. Several of the oil paintings looked disturbingly different, so he decided to call in a conservator to evaluate their condition. Treasured items of furniture were gone. Hideous sofas and chairs, priced for their exclusive design but built for obsolescence, had replaced the hand-made pieces so lovingly and expensively repaired a few years earlier. He was no advocate of the old and hand-made for its own sake but knew the third-rate when he saw it. His aunt didn't have a clue. Perhaps she imagined William Morris to have been a car designer and Rennie Mackintosh a Scottish brand of antacid.

His juices really began to boil when he finally plucked up the courage to step into his grandmother's bedroom. That the bedroom was dusty and neglected was no surprise. Several other rooms looked much the same. But the rectangle of lighter paint above the fireplace where he and his grandmother's favourite portrait had hung was insult and injury together.

He confirmed that the painting was nowhere in the house, then called Bight and Maym.

'My grandmother commissioned it from Jack Ravensclaw and it's probably the most valuable artwork we own. But it's worth more than money to me. The artist inscribed the words "All I have left" on the back. If you can retrieve nothing else, find that canvas.'

He instantly re-instated Sam, his estate manager, and they walked the grounds and farmland together, by turns fuming and grief-stricken at the neglect. In a distant field they found a handsome bay stallion abandoned and weakened by lack of food and water. There were overgrown footpaths; rickety, limb-threatening stiles; dropped, unhinged or absent gates. Hedges had gone wild, ditches had silted up and parts of the flood defences on the Bass had crumbled. A driveway from the main road to the Court had been cut but not laid. On either side of this, trees that had provided shelter for domestic animals and wildlife had been cut down, the logs left to litter the open ground. Saplings for a future avenue had been delivered but left untended. Thistle and ragwort ruled in the fields. Pools of stagnant water were breeding clouds of bloodsucking insects beside blocked drains and ditches. And everywhere were the frantic scuttlings and snakey tails of rats making themselves scarce. They were everywhere, an infestation in every dwelling, shed, garage and barn.

'You should get a film crew in here and make a record of this. Show people what happens when the ignorant rule the roost.'

'I would if I could afford it. But I haven't opened the mail yet.'

There were piles of it thrown in drawers all over the house, as if this would somehow delay the dreaded reckonings. Utility bill reminders, fines for untended footpaths, final demands from swimming pool and tennis court contractors, stonemasons and estate agents, animal feed suppliers and farriers; requests for payment from tree surgeons, gardeners, stable hands, and blistering threats from Mr Paradise the unpaid gamekeeper. Most alarming of all was a very large bill from a fine arts copying agency in London. Less surprising were the urgent letters from the US Internal Revenue Service. He passed these and all other Dewum mail to Bight and Maym.

'Oh, yes. These'll be from the debt collection agency acting for the

IRS. I should think that's why Dewum did a bunk. Any news from your aunt on her whereabouts?'

'Nothing. Looks as if she packed her Range Rover with goodies and scarpered.'

'She'll turn up.'

'And then?'

'We'll turn her over.'

It took Mr Maym less than a minute to pry more keys out of the Dewum's estate agent and, having done so, required an employee to inspect every single room of every dwelling and send a written report to Hugh. Not a single cottage on the estate was occupied, Mr Paradise being the last tenant. Putting right the chronic neglect of buildings and gardens would cost the estate tens of thousands..

On the other hand, his accountant, the normally melancholy Mr Groves, almost raised a smile.

'Masses to offset against income. It'll take years before you pay another tax bill.'

But Hugh dropped him right back in the Slough of Despond by announcing he had no intention of claiming full expenses as a Councillor but, on the contrary, would claim nothing at all.

'But you've got to think of it as a constant battle, Hugh. Every mile of travel, every phone call, every photocopy that you can claim as an expense is a skirmish won.'

'Possibly. But as a friend of mine says, "Public service ain't a private enterprise".'

Such heresy induced a cardiac flutter in Mr Groves and thoughts of retirement, if only his pension fund hadn't gone some distance down the tubes in 2008.

Hugh decided not to mention two non-deductible expenses he was planning for the Zielinsky family – the first, a party at the Court to celebrate all their successes. At first he kept it secret only because he knew Jacinta would insist on doing the catering, but he informed and invited Lucy.

'You have to tell my mum. She'll just criticise the food if someone else does it. And, yes, I'll be there.'

In the end the catering was organised by Mary and Jacinta together. Hugh busied himself getting all the rooms tidied and presentable.

Lucy arrived a day early. Compared to the rest of her overworked, pale family she looked absurdly fit and finely toned.

'How's the wrist?'

'Fine, but it won't last forever. Just don't tell my mother.'

'I've prepared a room for you, if you'd like to stay here.'

'Of course. This place is even more beautiful close up.'

'Your mum won't object?'

'Of course, she will!'

'But you don't care?'

'Yes, I care. But she wanted me to be an international volleyball player and future architect. So, I have to get used to superior accommodation. I'll just tell her the smell of 16 men's damp socks brings on my allergy.'

'You have an allergy?'

'I could have.'

They walked the grounds, and he showed her the Dewums' tennis court with its leaking roof and flooded baseline.

'But you could change it to an all-purpose court,' she suggested. 'Add a few more for different sports. You could rent out the facilities to teams for residential training.'

'That's what you'd do?'

'Of course. I love sport. I'm not one to look a horse gift in the mouth?' She noticed his smile. 'That wasn't quite right, was it?'

'Not quite. But it made perfect sense.'

She was right about her mother. Jacinta huffed and puffed as she sourced vast amounts of food, then set about peeling, dicing, slicing, baking, roasting, frying...

'She thinks I shouldn't be staying here till you've proposed to me,' Lucy announced in her mother's presence.

This prompted a long tirade in Polish that only caused Lucy to smile. It did not occur to Hugh that both of them might be serious.

The party was a huge success. The long table in the dining hall was decked for its biggest banquet since 1912, its main attraction a complete spit-roast wild boar brought in especially by one of the Zielinsky's contacts in the international haulage industry. Every placement sported four glasses: a tumbler for water, a flute for beer, a goblet for wine, and an all-important glass for schnapps. Sir James filled all of his with different coloured fruit juices.

'The old ticker won't cope, I'm afraid. But na zdrowie to you all,' he said, raising a glass. Back came a volley of 'Na zdrowie!' and 'Vivat!'

Encouraged by this social success, Sir James called upon his broad command of foreign languages about every fifth minute.

'Prosit!'

'Skål!'

'Proost!'

'A votre santé!'

'L'chaim!'

''Yia mas!'

And so forth.

When he'd exhausted the foreign variants, he challenged Hugh to match him toast for toast in the native language, with Feliks translating when needed.

'Cheers!'

'Your health'

'Bottoms up!'

'Down the hatch!'

'Hair on your chest!'

'Here's mud in your eye!'

'A full belly, a heavy purse, and a light heart!'

'Eat, drink and be merry, for tomorrow you diet!'

'To the lands we love and the love we land!'

'May love draw the curtains and friendship the cork!'

'A toast to absent friends – the recent possessors of Deverill Court. Here's to love and unity, dark corners and opportunity!'

'The love you give away is the only love you keep!'

'Here's looking at you, Hugh!'

By this point, the majority drinking grape and grain were losing control of speech and limb, so Hugh decided to make an announcement before it was beyond all comprehension. He began by waving a set of keys.

'Theezhe,' he declared, 'are the keys to zhe Grey Houze and zhe bar… I mean zhe barnnnh. An' zheezhe keezh now belong to the Zheelinshky fam'ly, to uzhe as you wishh, when you wishh, for as long azhue wishh… ish all in a leash'old 'greement. Never mind the de'ails, Feliksh'll tell you t'morrow or whenever 'e wakeshup…'

39 / The Morning After

Hugh stirred, anticipating his morning shower, its power jets massaging away whatever aches and pains remained from the previous evening's exertions. But when Bradley leaned downwards and forwards to apply a complete arsenal of skilful and alarmingly sensuous kissing gear to his mouth, he jolted awake to discover that this was not Bradley at all, but Lucy the Polish architect and volleyball player.

'Whoah!'

'Something wrong?'

'No…but, erm, won't your mother have something to say about this?'

In fact, he was wondering what Eddie, standing behind Lucy's mother, might have to say.

'She won't… *erm*… say anything.'

'Are you sure? I thought I was supposed to propose to you first.'

'But you did.'

'I did?'

'You did.'

'Did you say yes?'

'I did.'

'You'd think I'd remember that.'

'Doesn't matter. I remember. It's lucky I was sober. And you promised to come for a run with Bradley and me this morning.'

'I promised you that?'

'No, you promised Bradley. I'm his witness.'

Hearing his name, Bradley jumped up for some long overdue attention, placing one of his charmingly leonine paws in Hugh's crotch.

'Ferchrissakesbradley!'

But he realised, even as the beast pushed off, using his tender parts as a launching pad, that a woman prepared to share her bedroom with a man's second-best friend was a perfect partner for life. There was also a good chance he'd manage to tolerate her remarkably extended family.

Part Seven

Lifelines

40/ The Dust Settles… And Stirs

After pleading innocent to all who'd listen, Alex Weaver meekly accepted his three-month sentence, suspended for twelve months, with a fine of three thousand pounds and his driving licence revoked for two years. It could have been so much worse. As the judge pointed out, he'd been saved by his many years of "previous good character".

The three-month sentence put the kibosh on his standing as a candidate in a local election for at least five years. He sensed Barbara's relief that, for him, local politics were off the table, probably for the rest of his life.

He kept quiet about the anomaly in UK law that a criminal conviction of one year or less would not prevent him from standing for Parliament. As people's memories faded, he could always argue that his car accident had been contrived by shady actors for commercial or political gain. A parliamentary seat was not yet beyond his grasp. It was a case of watching and waiting for the political narratives, like tectonic plates, to shift. But, of this, he uttered not one word to Barbara.

He kept quiet too about his precarious finances and pitiful pension. Luckily, their household income was shored up by his wife's election to the chairmanship of a Council scrutiny committee, increasing their income to very nearly twenty thousand pounds a year. The replacement Jag had been repossessed when the insurance company learned of the court judgement and he now relied for transport on Barbara's third-hand Peugeot. In the same week, his fourth application for a zero per cent credit card deal was rejected. But they were able to stay in their barn conversion for the time being and could just about manage the mortgage and credit card payments.

Gerry Quick's wife filed for divorce as soon as there were no more reliable assets to be placed in her name before he filed for bankruptcy. It didn't help that the sole vehicle used by his new scaffolding enterprise was stopped and searched by police, who found some of the poles stuffed with packages of cocaine. Gerry pleaded innocence, blaming the driver and crew, but took the precaution of relocating.

This was not as easy as he imagined with his three grown-up children taking their mother's side in all disputes, and Gerry would have found himself sleeping in his car had he not kept in touch with Janine.

Rather than risk imprisonment for perjury, she had dyed her hair, changed her name and moved to Spain. If she had to run for it, Morocco was just across the Med. Gerry went to work for her, providing protection, vetting clients and doing a little debt collection on the side. There was a steep learning curve. Apart from anything else, a baseball bat was a less convincing argument than the machetes employed by rivals, and arthritic knees hampered his reactions. But Janine had to accept that he was a quick learner and, anyway, knew far too much about her to allow a faulty slashing technique to mar their long history of mutual profit. He was also good at fixing the faulty plumbing and dodgy balcony rails at her first, crummy premises.

For all their precautions, rumour carried as far as Manley Town, where Alex Weaver snorted his contempt.

'Him and that little tart.'

'Really?' said Barbara. 'There was a time, I believe, when you were quite partial to a slice of tart.'

Which silenced Alex on the subject forever. Nor did Barbara allow him more than the most perfunctory sneer about the marriage of Peter Wilde and Tracy Morgan.

'She'll regret it!'

'You think so? She seems very happy. And he's not so bad. A pleasure to do business with, even if we are opponents.'

Having Alex always at home was a trial, especially as he used most of his time while Barbara was out to amass charges of conspiracy against old enemies and ingratitude against old friends, then strew these at her feet like a dog's well-chewed toys as soon as she returned in the evenings.

Relief came when he started a political consultancy – electability not a requirement – even though he would only ever have the one client, Rich and Partners.

His first task was to line up and square all the "stakeholders" in a deal that Steven Rich was striking with Rollo Campbell-Stewart for a new housing estate in the borough to the north of the Malvoir Valley.

'Two hundred houses is not a lot,' observed Weaver in condescending mode.

'It isn't, is it?' said Rich, apparently resigned to this modest achievement. 'But we must do what we can in the current climate.'

In fact, Rich had kept his options open throughout the Rokeby saga and had been in regular touch with Campbell-Stewart, dropping subtle hints that the Council might, after all, favour his land over the Dewums'.

As this lure was dangled before Campbell-Stewart then snatched away, then proffered again, the owner of Fontby Magna offered more land for building, until the acreage was almost twice the original, none of it within Malvoir Council territory and therefore free of militant nimbys honed and emboldened by their Rokeby campaign. Rich guessed that Campbell-Stewart, like the Dewum's, needed the money. His wife was known to be a big spending socialite with a tribe of aristocratic Danes to service on their visits to London and the nearly-Cotswolds.

With carefully managed "optics", this doubled acreage could eventually support an estate of two thousand new dwellings. No need for risky sporting venues and retail parks. Just straightforward brick boxes held together with greenwash and the gratitude of a local Council hitting its building targets.

Alex Weaver, Steven Rich's political fixer, knew most of the politicians in the local authority to the north of the Malvoir Valley. He did not need to know the tactics and strategy that would eventually achieve thousands of new-build, with some built on a flood plain and others within fifty yards of electricity pylons at the edge of the estate. His job was to perform each feat of persuasion set in front of him without asking too many questions. In that respect, the fewer the questions he asked, the longer he would remain an employee of Rich and Partners.

Tracy Morgan moved to Wild Hill but kept her cottage in Rokeby as a weekend escape from the constant casework in the Collerton ward. Peter had put on weight during the election campaign and she tried to introduce him to tennis. It couldn't be said that he had a closed mind on the subject, and he willingly attended the revival meeting of the Rokeby Women's Tennis Club. Tracy hoped he might form the nucleus of a men's team, but he failed to demonstrate a basic level of co-ordination by cracking a shin with a racket while attempting to serve like Roger Federer.

'Too much follow-through,' his coach reported to Tracy as she summoned an ambulance. 'Not a good sign.'

But she did not give up on the exercise regime. As soon as Peter could walk again, she saved a shaggy-haired, happily disposed and mostly white mongrel from the town's rescue kennels. 'Sugar' was a sweetly obedient dog and was soon recognised all over town as her master walked everywhere, not exactly shedding pounds, but nicely counteracting his normal diet. This usually consisted of Manley Mild, with bangers and mash on the side, consumed by man and dog when socialising as a twosome in local pubs. That Tracy's healthy cooking with lots of tofu and fresh vegetables had little effect on Peter's body mass index was an abiding mystery. She, on the other hand, was soon down to her fighting weight and leading the women's tennis team into a new season in the regional league, but with hopes to introduce, in a few years, a new player, a natural athlete who would take them nearer to the top division.

In the meantime, she would have to get used to having a stepdaughter and grandchild in her life. Kate Wilde finally concluded that the father of her unborn baby was a loser they could all do without. As her alcoholic mother had moved from Italy to Spain to live with a dubious character, Kate decided that her future and that of her child lay in Manley.

Tracy found herself on shopping trips, helping the mother-to-be choose baby clothes, a buggy and a cot. She was getting in carpenters and electricians to secure cupboard doors and electricity sockets from tiny prying hands. Her usual reading was replaced by tomes on babies' health and child-rearing. She was not, it seemed, to be spared the patter of tiny feet after all. Which was not unwelcome news.

More of the same arrived when the police casually informed Peter that the case against him for acquiring and publicising confidential information from Council files had been dropped months earlier.

'They might have told you and spared us all that worry,' seethed Tracy.

'But that may have defeated their object,' was Peter's dry

observation.

News that Hugh had somehow recovered his inheritance reached London, and he was soon receiving invitations to prestigious London addresses. One such came from Isabella and, after a little thought, he accepted, having made sure that Lucy could join him.

The event turned out to be an informal tennis party in the private gardens adjacent to Isabella's Kensington flat. They lounged on the grass while foursomes engaged in competitive shanking on court. Hugh's acquaintances ribbed him mercilessly about being a local Councillor.

'Short step to leading the nation, Hugh.'

'Our first Independent Prime Minister.'

Isabella, meanwhile, tried hard to suppress the odd jealous glance in Lucy's direction, especially as some of the other men were clearly enchanted. But she showed her hand within the hour by challenging her foreign rival to a game of tennis.

'Fancy a knock? Singles?'

Hugh recalled that Isabella was a decent tennis player at the social level but was far from being a natural athlete. He watched as Lucy processed all the impressions she'd been receiving since their arrival: the easy affluence and powerful connections, the thrusting bankerdom, their covetous yet dismissive regard for Hugh, their suspicion that the daughter of Hugh's Polish domestic was likely to be a gold-digger.

Lucy smiled, disarmingly. 'OK. Just a few minutes.'

'Few minutes? Don't be a wimp. Let's play.'

Another pause.

'OK,' said Lucy.

A few days later, after Lucy was called up for Poland's pre-Olympic training camp, Isabella may have felt less stunned by the thrashing she received that balmy evening in Kensington. Lucy played well within herself but unleashed a few cannonades to ensure a six-love scoreline. There was no invitation to supper.

'She had no idea what you do,' said Hugh.

'She does now.'

On the drive home to Deverill Court that night, Hugh was bonce over ankles in something he'd never experienced before. So much so that he decided to pop the question again over a late-night glass of champagne.

'You expect a different answer?'

'No, just one I'll remember. Last time was a bit of a blur.'

'Yes.'

'Does that refer to the blur or my original question?'

'Which do you think?'

'Well, as the blur is the thing I do remember, even though it was, by definition, and lack of it, a bit hazy, I would expect a 'yes' to refer to that. On the other hand...'

'Apart from my mother, you're the only person I know who doesn't take yes for an answer. But I gave you my yes, even if you were – what's your word? – laddered...?'

'Bladdered.'

'Horrible word. Please don't use it again.'

'Right.'

'So you've had my yes and you're stuck with it.'

'Right. I won't forget.'

'You also promised to massage my neck, shoulders, back and legs whenever I asked.'

'Well, strangely enough, I do have a dim memory of that...'

One long massage later, they curled up together on a sofa, eating strawberries and cream, tossing strips of cold chicken in Bradley's direction. Hugh had found the ripening strawberries growing in a dilapidated greenhouse alongside some tall plants with leaves that looked suspiciously like something you could pick, dry and smoke if so inclined.

As for Calvin Dewum, he bucked the traditional advice for fortune hunters and went east, until he reached a town that had changed names and national associations several times in the space of just one century. There he changed name himself, to Khalvin, and managed an alliance with a woman of astounding business acumen, consisting mostly of what she called "focus"– pronounced fockus – and he called "the killer instinct". Within a very short time, this combination of his understanding for human suggestibility, and her firmness in getting said humans to cough up, was reaping rewards for them, and various degrees of customer dissatisfaction – without redress – for everybody else.

Meanwhile, his erstwhile companion of the heart was moving westwards. She surrendered her married name of Dewum and adopted, not her maiden name of de Broche, but the similar 'de Broke', carelessly laying claim to association with a distinguished baronial family. Heading for California once more, she was detained in Nevada by an elderly, multi-millionaire widower whose memory was no longer quite what it was. His family foolishly left him alone for half an hour one evening in a Country Club bar, which gave Lesley-Anne time enough to remind him of certain salient facts about their recently begun, intimate friendship.

She quickly, for very good tactical reasons, shortened her first name to Ann, and this proved helpful to her new friend, whose own flesh and blood had names of more than one syllable that he was inclined to confuse. For the time being, "Ann" was sitting pretty, if not entirely at ease. She had no idea, yet, that her nephew was using Bight and Maym to recover, among other precious artefacts, £3.2 million pounds worth of oil paintings missing from Deverill Court and replaced by Chinese manufactured reproductions that cost less than twenty thousand pounds to commission.

"Ann" did have occasional twinges of what others call "conscience" but which she interpreted as "bad luck" or "betrayal". As her once bright prospects continued to fade, she grew bitter about being balked by a pack of East European migrants. She was convinced her nephew wouldn't have had the wit to stay afloat without their devious, unfair and undoubtedly criminal assistance, let alone engineer a change of regime in the Malvoir Valley's local government.

By August, the advance party of these demonised Zielinskys, in the form of Ambrozy, Josef, Tadeusz and Tomasz, had returned home. They very quickly encountered a homecoming party in the form of a would-be Silesian mafia, who demanded a slice of the family's hard-earned foreign cash in return for leaving them in peace. While Feliks conducted delicate negotiations by mobile phone as a delaying tactic, Eddie and four of his more robust relatives flew home. History relates that Eddie resolved the matter entirely in the Zielinskys' favour in the time it takes to break eggs prior to making an omelette. As Feliks put it, 'It's all in the fist.'

By autumn The Grey House and barn stood empty and quiet, but by no means abandoned. Every now and then Hugh would arrive with a van-load of furniture and household goods, preparing the house for the regular visits of his new family.

Not everything was going to plan. Mr Goater of the local Planning Department had refused to allow The Grey House to be officially renamed "Zielinsky House".

'The name has nothing to do with local history.'

'On the contrary, there is every connection.'

Hugh went ahead anyway after Mary pointed out that The Grey House always had a number and road name as the second line of its address. The house name was therefore beyond Mr Goater's remit.

For the rest, Hugh's daily routine at Deverill Court was back to what it had been before his unaccountable loss of inheritance and its equally mysterious restoration. But all his earlier work had been undone and more. Now he faced the steady, gruelling and costly business of renovation. New tenants, and some of the old, revitalised the cottages. Small businesses reoccupied the stable block and the place began to hum with enterprise. When Lucy was away on tour, the place felt empty and they were both looking forward to the wedding planned for the following spring in Silesia. Mary and Jacinta were working on the arrangements, and they copied the 'happy couple' into their daily emails sent from Silesia and wherever Mary and Sir James happened to be.

'Well, as James doesn't have to stump up millions for land he doesn't really want, I thought he might like to take us both on a grand tour by railway. Thank goodness for laptops and broadband.'

41/ The Wheel Turns

'It's all Cameron's fault,' Barbara Weaver fumed at the television screen. 'He just won't stand up to the headbangers.'

It was February 20th, 2016 and Prime Minister David Cameron had just announced the date of the UK's referendum on continued membership of the European Union… or not.

Far from being exercised by the outrage, Alex Weaver was smiling at his own thought process.

'Doesn't it bother you?' demanded his wife.

'Bother? No. Every crisis is an opportunity, especially for you.'

'Why me?'

'A grenade is being thrown into the status quo. People are being asked for a straight "yes" or "no". No more sitting on the fence.' He leaned towards her to add some faux drama. 'A lot of politicians are going to be flushed out of their comfort zones.'

'Why are you enjoying this?'

'Because an awful lot of people are going to be caught on the wrong side of history.'

'But what about the country?'

'What about it?'

'If a majority votes to leave, it'll be a disaster.'

'A majority won't. Too many are doing too well to let that happen. It'll be like last time. The extreme right and left will peel off and leave a majority in the middle doing the safe and sensible thing. 60-40 for staying.' He gave it a little more thought. 'Maybe 55-45. At worst.'

'You're that sure?'

'Most people don't like change. Besides, people are better off than they've ever been. Why change it?'

'You sound like a complacent Tory.'

'On the contrary. I look forward to the chaos. And so should you. Just watch the politics of the Valley get turned upside down. First off, the Independents will be at each other's throats in no time. They'll split right down the middle. Play your cards right and you could soon be leading the Council yourself.'

'I doubt that. Gary Higgs has got that sewn up.'

Alex generated a sarcastic chuckle. 'I've known Higgsy for decades. Scratch him hard enough and you'll find a little Englander.' He switched to helpful advice. 'You should test his waters. Find out which side he supports. If he leans towards Leave he'll be on thin ice.'

'What about the ice under me.'

'Time to get your skates on. You support Remain because you think the EU is a noble force for peace and good and apple pie. Nobody will blame you for being an optimist. But Higgsy hates the EU for all the crap they get up to.'

'What crap?'

He grinned. 'That's why you could be our local leader. Because you *believe*.'

She was beginning to feel patronised. 'But what do you believe?'

'I believe in the wheel. It turns and there's going to be an almighty shakeout. I will watch and wait and choose my moment. All those people who thought I'd gone away will see me coming round again.'

This conjured an image of her husband as a miniature figure on a Swiss clock announcing the changing times with monotonous regularity, but she kept it to herself. What, she wondered, of all those constituents appealing to her for help? The lost jobs, homes, benefits, health, life prospects? What would his shakeout mean for them, and did he even care?

Barbara had long wondered what her husband actually believed. The longer he'd been in the Labour Party the more he'd behaved like a Tory, and not a pleasant Tory at that. Her daughter had asked her recently why she didn't divorce him, and she'd said something about vows. This elicited a gasping laugh of disbelief.

But he was not a bad man, just deluded. She wouldn't leave her husband for the same reason she wouldn't abandon the Party. She'd made promises. She'd meant them then and she meant them now. It was hopelessly old-fashioned, but this way seemed better than the endless shapeshifting for the sake of a few more votes right now but no real change in the years to come.

As for Alex, she still believed that he could change for the better once his battered self-esteem began to heal. "No child left behind" was not just a mantra to Barbara.

Hugh couldn't fail to notice the Independent Alliance fraying at the edges as its members declared their allegiance to Leave or Remain.

'How will you vote?' demanded Gwen Mackie in canvassing mode. Hugh guessed she was already trying to tempt Independents like him into her Lib Dem camp of uncritical Remainers.

'I'll listen to the arguments on both sides,' he replied. 'Then I'll decide.'

'But you're a landowner and farmer, sort of. Leaving would destroy the farming industry in this country.'

Hugh wondered where Gwen had acquired her sudden expertise in matters agricultural, while slyly questioning his, but he maintained a diplomatic stance.

Peter Wilde noticed Hugh's ability to calm rising tensions.

'I'm going to put your name forward as vice-chairman of the Alliance.'

'Why?'

'So that Tracy can shift some of her load. She's overworked and we need your diplomacy. The longer the Alliance keeps a lid on its differences, the longer we'll have to undo the damage done by Weaver.'

'Specifically?'

'We need to ease the Chief Exec out of this Council. But we have to be clever. We can't accuse him of wrongdoing because we might not prove it in a court or tribunal. But we know Roger Mason supported Weaver all the way through. The Council will have to pony up with a payoff and give him time to find another post somewhere else. But it'll be quicker and cheaper than going to law.'

'You mean, foist him on some other Council?'

'He may fit like a glove in another authority. We just don't want him here. But there's another person we can get rid of in short order. We can get Goater for bullying in his department. He's a goner.'

'All right, both good aims. But if you want me to be the Alliance's internal diplomat, you'll have to tell me your views. How will you vote?'

'Me? Leave, obviously. The EU is a protectionist racket.'

'And Tracy?'

'She's a romantic. She thinks the EU has preserved peace in Europe since World War Two.'

'Am I going to have to keep you two apart in meetings?'

'No. She has no idea what I think on that topic and I'm not going to breathe a word. Behind closed doors, I'm the diplomat. Whatever she says on the subject, I say "Quite right." Luckily, we have the privacy of the voting booth in this country. And I know you won't tell a soul, either. Will you?'

'I won't.' And he wouldn't, though he was already beginning to feel the burden of the diplomat's *omerta*.

From Silesia he received contradictory advice.

'On balance I hope the UK stays in,' emailed Feliks. 'The French and Germans are making such a mess of things, Poles like me will want the UK inside for security and defence.'

Eddie, on the other hand, was blunt.

'Why you want to stay? Thems farqueue barstas. They call it single market. It's no single market. It's no free trade. UK wastes billions to be in EU.'

Lucy warned him to steer clear. 'The family is having raging arguments about Brexit. Don't get involved.'

'But they'll ask my opinion at some point.'

'Do what I do. Just tell them you're in favour of Remain and Reform,' she advised.

'But that's sitting on the fence. The EU doesn't want to reform.'

'I know that! But it creates a different argument. Instead of shouting they have to think about it, and I slip away to think about something else.'

'But you can tell me. What do you think?'

'I'm for you and me remaining together. I'm for leaving the games to the politicians.'

That was the moment Hugh decided a career in politics was definitely not for him. He'd see out his tenure and never again stand for public office.

In the meantime, he worked in the council chamber and on the estate. He pushed a scheme to stop Manley teenagers in care being left homeless as soon as they reached eighteen, and another to provide computers and tech support for the vulnerable elderly who lived alone.

A group of teenagers who responded to a questionnaire about new youth facilities in their area sought his help. They'd voted by a large majority for a skateboard park in Gwen Mackie's ward. But a small group of hostile pensioners turned up at a community council meeting and refused to have "yobs" creating noise and causing trouble. Although the planned facility was a hundred yards from the nearest house and skateboarders were self-policing anti-yobs, Mackie feared the brouhaha and potential loss of votes at the next election.

With the idea dead and youths in Manley declaring that they would never vote for anything ever again, Hugh started on plans for a skateboard park on his land at Briery Hill. It would have to be accessed from a layby on the main road and he'd have to persuade the local bus company to add stops to their service. He revived his plans for an eco-village – a properly zero emissions community – and began to think about building more sports facilities that could develop into an academy serving residential guests, youth clubs and local families. Lesley-Anne's half-built avenue might serve a purpose after all.

Peter Wilde was impressed. 'It'll give more to local people than a fantasy stadium.'

But his accountant, Mr Groves, was scandalised. 'A private landowner only gives up land for private profit. Giving up territory for the so-called public good is the thin end of the wedge.'

Hugh ignored the criticism. He set himself to work and plan and work some more, until there was no need to log on to internet banking on a daily basis to keep track of income and expenses. But sometimes, if life was becoming a bit too comfortable, he'd visit an ATM and withdraw a wad of notes that he could stash in a trouser pocket. It was unnecessary, but strangely comforting. As additional entertainment, it catered to Bradley's fixation with all things paper as he often tried to pick his master's pocket.

One morning in December, Bradley pulled a sheet of paper from between two floorboards in one of the empty bedrooms and chewed it to the verge of illegibility before dropping it on the landing outside a bathroom. About to toss the creased, notebook size sheet into a rubbish basket, Hugh recognised his grandmother's handwriting.

> *H lp!*
> *That Amer an k ps brin g me tea with*
> *stra ge bisc ts wh n Les y- nn go s r ding.*
> *F l drowsy. M kes me sig pa ers.*
> *Tell Hu h*
> *Ele n r d Br che.*

42/ The Valley

Peter Wilde, Councillor and Cabinet Member for Education in the Malvoir Valley, crested Briery Hill at the mid-point of a ten-mile walk, satisfied that he'd managed the feat once more without keeling over from fatigue or heart failure. He attributed this less to a new diet and more to the competitive temperament of Tracy Morgan, his new wife. She didn't object to sitting down at various points for a rest but throwing in the towel by calling for a taxi would be filed under "disappointing" and a cause for concern.

Peter was uxorious – he rolled the word around his internal audio system – and would do anything to spare his soulmate worry or regret, so "one foot in front of the other" was the order of this unusual Saturday morning.

They kissed as they passed through the new kissing-gate – a private tradition that required no apology – and, after some scooping and brushing with gloved hands, took their places on the new bench commanding the panorama. This was the view they'd been determined to see since breakfast, a once-in-a-lifetime vista of the Malvoir Valley draped in the purest, softest layer of powdery snow in mid-April. The drop in temperature had surprised everybody and turned the world upside down for a single, glorious weekend. The opening day of the tennis season was postponed. Daffodils bowed under bonnets of frozen glitter. Children tobogganed down hillsides in near-delirious joy and a bevy of pensioners came sliding sedately by on cross-country skis.

To Tracy, this was more than a change in the weather. Some say that politicians campaign in poetry and govern in prose, but her experience in both modes had been mind-numbingly prosaic. This scene under a clear blue sky was a welcome poetic interlude. The landscape was reduced to essentials, the less aesthetic details hidden beneath a white carpet seen through the blue filter of the northern hemisphere. Trees, bushes, rocks and fences were sketched in a rare medium, their dimensions enlarged, their weights increased in fact, but lightened in appearance. Much was concealed while much was outlined, clarified and augmented in unexpected ways.

This scene lightened her mood and made the remote seem possible. She would change her life again, given time. Politics was not for her. She would get past this stupid and unnecessary Brexit referendum in June, serve the rest of her four-year "sentence", and hand the baton to someone more committed or ambitious. As Peter liked to muse in private, 'The key ingredients in politics are conviction and commitment. Most politicians worthy of the name deserve to be convicted or, at the very least, committed.' She aspired to be neither, realising that it took a special kind of courageous self-effacement to make a real difference when polarising politics contaminated the mix. But she still took pride in what they'd achieved in a battle they'd ultimately won.

Peter couldn't help but scan the view for detail. Down below and away to his right were the rooftops of the Deverill estate cottages. They were white under several inches of snow, their interior heat kept in by proper insulation. Across the valley lay an estate built in the early noughties by a construction company with national name-recognition. The rooftiles were bare, introducing a rare patch of brown into the landscape, as somebody's hard-earned cash was being spent to thaw the snow and warm the crows.

Higher up the hill were the treetops surrounding and obscuring a sight of Reg Barton's mansion. It had been built by Rich and Quick in light-brown brick and dark-brown tiles and looked more like an institution than a private residence. Peter had never been invited inside, but he'd heard of the indoor swimming pool, the nightclub-style bar with raised stage, dancing poles and enough dining tables for a hundred guests. Neighbouring rooms were rumoured to house pool tables, dart boards and a private cinema.

Reg would not be home to see the dancers dance or the garden grow this spring. He and his wife had spent all of New Year's and through the Easter holidays as guests of the National Health Service and then Her Majesty's Prisons. It's what happens when police raid your home and discover hundreds of thousands of pounds in cash. This can lead to questions about origins, and some scepticism about the accuracy of your replies. They would have been granted bail if Mrs Barton had not taken offence at some of her husband's statements that exonerated himself and implicated her. She had sharply underlined her objections by means of a large kitchen knife.

Meanwhile, Reg's beloved Manley Town Football Club was suspended from its league while the authorities investigated allegations of criminal funding, accounting fraud, match-fixing and illegal betting. A half-mile beyond the floodlights of the club's ground lay a housing estate where Barton and a couple of the bigger drug dealers had used the ownership of terraced houses as a medium of exchange for doing deals and settling debts. Local detectives had months or even years of work ahead as they tried to join the dots between local, national and international criminal activities and the people involved.

On the same side of the Valley but away to the north, the Chief Executive of Malvoir Valley Council, Roger Mason, was no doubt contemplating his future and the size of payoff he'd be prepared to accept in exchange for leaving his position swiftly and quietly. Peter and Jim Phillips were already working on a carefully crafted press release.

Just beyond the horizon to the north-west lay the barn conversion belonging to the former Leader of the Council. Peter imagined the scene from the Weavers' picture window as Alex aimed salvos of recrimination towards the town that lay well out of sight below the escarpment edge. Like a Manley Town version of Lear, but with less self-knowledge, the recently deposed "King" Weaver howled across the heath about ingratitude and betrayal.

The lonely exile did not yet know that the coalition governing Malvoir Valley Council was exploring the possibility of seeing a large housing estate of mostly "affordable" homes built across that very heath. If it came to pass, Weaver would find himself and his converted barn at the heart of a new community.

Some miles away to Peter's left, where the Valley levelled into the Malvoir Flats, Philip Goater was home on sick leave, with time to contemplate the beginning of an enquiry into allegations of bullying within the planning department that he'd supervised for over a decade.

Tracy took pride in these turns of events. She regarded them collectively as a victory. But while politics is fast, even frenetic, the process and progress of democracy can be glacial. Her first experience of its inner workings was rare, exciting, even exhilarating. In the scheme of things, it was also very short. Peter knew the daily grind across thirty years or more, mostly on the defensive, resisting costly, futile and misguided initiatives, or vainly pushing schemes that would make a difference. Many good officials and decent politicians knew the score. Local service needed to be on a local scale. Free of ego, focused on the people it served, and unglamorous to the point of tedium. Government as service, not self-service.

Tracy was right that local democracy had taken down the local bosses when their hubris outgrew their function. Four cheers for democracy. The extra cheer was for the sheer, hard slog against the odds. But Peter knew it could prove short-lived, even illusory. Fending off the ambitions of big egos combining with big business was like fighting a clatter of tanks with asparagus spears, as residents near Fontby Magna were about to discover.

The next big battle would be the referendum on the EU in June, one that Peter was sure he would lose but was determined to win. No matter what he said, he would lose because the status quo with its spray-on pieties would triumph. The country would vote to Remain as it had in 1975. But he would win by keeping his mouth shut and so preserve the love and peace in his new family. If Tracy could tolerate his paunch, and his daughter show patience with his descriptions of a cricket ball doing reverse swing, he could accept in silence their belief in the EU's "moral imperative". He might have said that it reminded him of the British Empire's "civilising mission", but that would be provocative, and he was determined to keep shtum.

As Tracy's right hand searched for his left, they noticed some figures scurrying back and forth across the snowbound drive of Deverill Court. To the left of the snow-coped turrets were the open spaces between the oaks and beeches where Peter would again help to organise Manley's summer camps for local teens. Beyond the kissing gate, halfway down the slope, were the outlines of a half-completed skateboard park buried in snowdrifts. Away to the right, beyond the River Bass, lay the fallow fields of contention that Steven Rich claimed to have purchased in good faith from a woman now on the run from Interpol. The village of Rokeby-on-Bass would likely be spared the sight of brown-brick development as lawyers on both sides argued the case for years to come. Hugh Brooke had made a verbal promise to Peter that if he got his fields back, he'd donate enough land for a community sports complex. If the Council donated some river-front land, they could add a water sports centre.

'Sounds good. Offer accepted. But be prepared. If the likes of Mel Coates and Gary Higgs get back into power, they'll turn it down out of spite. Your best bet is Barbara Weaver. So, fingers crossed, she becomes their leader.'

In the distance, the number of cars pulling into Deverill Court's driveway multiplied. Figures carrying items of various sizes hurried back and forth with short, uncertain steps, trying to keep their footing in the snow. They were members of the Malvoir Music Union setting up for their afternoon Spring Concert. Free entry for the young and elderly, reinstated as an annual event.

In the foreground, just the other side of the fence, a cock pheasant began a slow and courtly strut across the snow. His purple-bronze breastplate with the chainmail markings swept back into gold-winged plumage with its black diamond rivets. A shiny black, onyx eye set in a marble-white cornea floated in a pool of crimson. The broad white collar of a reverend bird contrasted with the electric-blue of his liberty bonnet.

Tracy and Peter exchanged a smile, certain they were thinking the same thought.

'One that got away.'

Oscar Fovarge has had the privilege of living in four European countries and observing four distinct styles of doing politics and conducting democracy.

Cover design: **Adam Evans**

Lightning Source UK Ltd.
Milton Keynes UK
UKHW011953290322
400790UK00002B/69